ARROWHEAD

A THRILLER OF CORRUPTION, LOVE, AND TRAGEDY

LEONARD FINZ

ISBN: 1-4137-4159-2
PUBLISHED BY PUBLISHAMERICA, LLLP
www.publishamerica.com
Baltimore

Printed in the United States of America

Inspiration is the energy that drives most authors. Mine has been, is, and will always be, my wife Pearl—my love, my best friend, my partner in life.

CHAPTER ONE

"This is 911," a female voice answered. According to the clock on the wall of Central Control, the time was 9:33 p.m. "What's the emergency?"

"A man near the east entrance of Carlyle Park. He's dead," a deep, raspy voice replied.

"Okay, what's your name and where are you calling from?" the 911 operator asked. There was a click...and then a dial tone....

"What have you got there?" an overweight uniformed sergeant in charge of the 4:00 p.m. to midnight shift sounded out.

"Some guy just reported a dead male in Carlyle Park. He hung up without giving me any more info. I'm dispatching the call to Central."

Within ten minutes, Patrolmen George Fowler and Ismael Ruiz of the Syracuse police department received the radio call while on a meal break at a near-by diner. They drove immediately toward the park, Fowler at the wheel.

Moments later, they reached Carlyle Park. Ruiz, a young rookie cop felt anxious. He had been on the force for only five weeks.

What's there? he wondered. *What are we gonna find?* he asked himself.

Fowler turned to Ruiz.

"Iz, get your gun ready. This could be a set-up or it could be a legit call. Anyway, be careful. Y'hear?"

The patrol car moved slowly into the park, then turned right. It was October, and there was no moon. The night was dark. The entire area was desolate. There was a time many years before, when people could go there at all hours, but that had changed. Although it was only nine forty-five in the evening, the place was overtaken with an uneasy silence.

The car, with its bright lights on, started to inch slowly along the blacktop road. The grooved rubber tires crept slowly on top of loose chunks of hard, broken road tar, sending crackling sounds off into the night, adding to its already mysterious and eerie atmosphere. Weathered and chipped concrete benches with their cracked and missing wooden slats lined the roadway every hundred feet.

Two hundred yards into the deserted road, the patrol car's headlights suddenly flashed upon something on the ground.

"I'm gettin' a little closer. I just can't make out what it is," Fowler said. His tone was anxious.

And there it was, sprawled on its side: the body of a man in a dark blue suit, white shirt, and maroon tie.

"Iz, stay put, but cover me. I'm goin' out. I'm not sure what the hell's going on here," Fowler barked out to his partner.

Fowler exited the car, his back to Ruiz, gun drawn, as he walked cautiously toward the man on the ground. Patrolman Ruiz was already holding his 9 mm semi-automatic weapon in his right hand as he radioed simultaneously to central headquarters, reporting in a hyper-ventilated voice what was happening.

As Fowler approached the man on the ground, he looked nervously around to make sure Ruiz was covering him. The car lights with their high-powered full brights continued a steady focus on the man in the blue suit.

Slowly, still looking cautiously in all directions, Fowler walked toward the sprawled figure.

He could now see more clearly. The man was on his back, his head pressed hard against the dirty pavement. His right arm was extended over his shoulder, left arm bent at the elbow, palm facing up.

The man's neck was cold to Fowler's touch.

"Dead," Fowler whispered to himself.

"What have we got?" Ruiz shouted from the car ten feet away.

"This guy's been shot. Looks like he took a bullet in the head," Fowler yelled back.

Hearing what Fowler just reported, Ruiz got out of the car. With the gun in his right hand and a flashlight in his left, he started to walk anxiously toward the motionless body.

"Any idea who he is?" Ruiz shouted out. His voice shaky, fear shrouding it.

"Don't know," Fowler shot back. "A guy dressed like him ain't out for a pleasure walk at night in this fuckin' place..." He hesitated, then continued, "unless maybe he was out ta kill himself."

Stark quiet continued to blanket the scene; one cop crouched over a dead man, another standing nervously next to the patrol car.

Fowler, a heavy-set, fifteen-year veteran of the force, and Ruiz, a young rookie cop, were in a deserted park on a dark night with a body on the ground. The older cop had been in some similar situations before, but this was a first for Ruiz. He had no special training for this kind of scene. He had strange feeling, not exactly sure what was happening. *Maybe it's because I'm a rookie and this is my first scary situation. I'm sure it's a normal reaction*, he kept reassuring himself.

Suddenly, as if struck by lightening, the figure on the ground moved. He sat straight up. His face was deathly ashen... his eyes frozen by the penetrating high beams of the patrol car that focused on him like two giant stage lights.

"This fuckin' guy's alive," Fowler shrieked excitedly as he bolted up from his crouched position and sprung back five feet.

Without hesitation, Ruiz moved in quickly. His gaze fixed on the man sitting on the ground. The weapon already in his hand was aimed steadily at the figure who remained in a spacey trance, staring at the car's full lights ten feet in front of him.

Within an instant, Fowler screamed, "Watch out, Iz! He's got a gun."

Reacting without thought, Ruiz pulled the trigger three times in rapid succession. Three 9 mm bullets ripped through the man's chest. He fell back with a thud, again sprawled out on the dirty pavement. This time, he was really dead.

"Jesus Christ! What the hell happened here?" Ruiz cried out as he stared at the body that lay still in a pool of blood spilling out and mixing with the dark gravel around the lifeless form.

Fowler and Ruiz remained frozen as they stood over the motionless figure. After a few seconds, the silence was broken.

"Where the hell's the gun?" Ruiz screamed out in panic. "There's no goddamned gun. You said he had a gun. You said he had a gun."

"I thought I saw a gun in his hand," Fowler shot back. "For Chrissakes, Iz, I thought I saw a gun."

"Shit. There's no fucking gun. Shit. Shit!" Ruiz shouted back. He had now lost all control.

"What do we do?" Ruiz cried out. "How do I explain it? I just killed an unarmed guy."

"We just tell it like it went down," Fowler said, trying to calm his sobbing partner. "Look, Iz, in a few minutes this place will be crawling with guys from the precinct. We just gotta stay cool." Trying to soothe the rookie, Fowler continued. " Go sit in the car, Ruiz. You gotta stay cool, man. You just gotta stay cool."

"What the hell have I done? How could I have fucked up this way?" Agony penetrated his voice.

Ruiz slunk into the passenger seat. He held his bowed head in both hands, eyes staring blankly at his lap. "Holy shit. Goddamn shit. Holy shit. Goddamn shit," he kept repeating as he rocked back and forth.

The sound of a police siren shattered the silence, becoming louder as a patrol car approached Fowler's vehicle. Stopping behind it, Sergeant Timothy Ryan and Patrolman John Mattis approached Fowler standing in the roadway in front of the vehicle that just entered the park.

"What the hell do we have here?"growled Sergeant Ryan.

All Ryan knew at this point was what dispatch had reported after it received the "911" call: "There's a man on the ground in Carlyle Park and he's dead."

"Sarg., we have a problem. A real bad situation. Real bad," Fowler snapped. The creases around his mouth began to tighten.

In measured tone, Fowler started to explain what happened, but was quickly interrupted.

"What the fuck are you tellin' me? Are you sayin' that Ruiz took out an unarmed guy? Is that the shit you're handin' me? Are you guys crazy, or what!"

Sergeant Ryan and Patrolman Mattis walked in rapid lockstep toward the body.

There he lay. A man in a dark blue suit, wearing a white shirt saturated with blood, and a maroon tie.

Dead.

Ryan made an abrupt move toward Fowler's car. The young rookie was in the passenger seat mumbling incoherently to himself.

"Ruiz. Ruiz," Ryan shouted, poking the distraught cop's shoulder with his index finger as if he were trying to awaken someone fast asleep.

"For Chrissakes, what the fuck happened here?" Ryan screeched. His tone was high-pitched, excited.

Ruiz gripped his face as tears welled up in his eyes."Fowler told me he had a gun. He said he had a gun. I shot three rounds. It happened so fast. It was instinct. Oh, my God. What have I done?" He began to sob uncontrollably.

"Get a goddamned grip on yourself, Ruiz. Come on, you're a cop. Act like one. Okay, you thought he had a gun." This time, Ryan's voice was softer, with a consoling quality. "Look Iz, you and Fowler will have to give a full statement to internal affairs and probably the D.A. It was an accident. That's it. Full story," Ryan said flatly as he rubbed his hand gently around Ruiz' neck massaging it lightly. "You'll be okay. Listen to me. You'll be okay."

Ryan turned to Mattis.

"Call headquarters. Report what went down. Tell 'em to send the lieutenant right away. He's gotta get here before the press finds out what's happened. Those asshole pimps will be on us like leeches."

Mattis returned to his car. He called it in as Ryan directed.

"Who is this guy?" Ryan asked Fowler.

"I don't know, Sarg. I didn't want to move him until the M.E. and forensics got here. I still haven't gone through his pockets for I.D."

"Good. The crime boys should be here soon..." Ryan paused. "...Then maybe we'll get some answers."

Within five minutes three more patrol cars arrived. The lead car carried Deputy Inspector Roy Brown and Lieutenant Brian Goody. Two other cars brought members of the crime scene unit with their cameras, chalk, and tape.

By this time, everyone at the scene knew that Ruiz had killed an unarmed man.

The area was roped off and cops were posted to secure the scene while the crime unit went into action. Camera flashes continued to pierce the darkness as photographers took shots from every angle. In the end, a white chalk silhouette was drawn on the ground around the body lying spread-eagle on the roadway.

Sergeant Ryan searched the pockets of the dead man for any identification. Looking up at Brown, he threw a surprised shrug. "There's no wallet here, Inspector. Nothing in his pockets at all. He must have been robbed first, then shot in the head." Scratching his right temple, still perplexed, Ryan continued. "What the hell was he doing in the park in the first place?" he rang out.

With eyebrows raised, Brown chimed in,"This whole thing is very bizarre."

Inspector Brown knew he would be the target of cynical questions fed by the media's hunger once it was learned that an unarmed man was gunned down by one of his cops. No way did he look forward to *this* kind of barrage. *Christ, one of my guys just shot an unarmed guy,* he repeated to himself. The press would chew up a department already under heavy mortar fire for past screw-ups.

News people began to arrive. A reporter from WXRL-TV, another from *The Syracuse Gazette*, and a third from radio station WSYR were the first on the scene.

"Keep those fuckin' guys behind the goddamned tape," snapped Inspector Brown as reporters tried to swarm the crime area.

Within minutes, another patrol car arrived. Chief of the Department Jack Thomas exited the passenger side. He approached Brown.

"Do we know who the victim is?"

"Chief, there's no wallet and no I.D.," Brown responded blankly.

Chief Thomas walked toward the dead man. He saw a body dressed in a dark blue suit, white shirt, maroon tie, and surrounded by a pool of blood. As he knelt over him, Inspector Brown, Lieutenant Goody, Sergeant Ryan, and Patrolman Fowler crowded around.

"Throw a flashlight on his face," commanded the chief as he bent down to get a closer look at the victim.

After seeing the dead man in the light, Chief Thomas got up slowly, rising to a full standing height. There was a foreboding silence. Breaking it, he shook his head from side to side, pursed his lips tightly, and winced. He started to speak in a deliberate, tremulous voice.

"Who's the bright cop that shot him?"He grimaced, a deeply pained look spreading over his face.

"It's Ruiz. He's sitting in the first car," Brown fired back, unsure of what was coming next.

"Well, that's great! Just great! You can tell him the guy he just killed—" the Chief hesitated. His voice suddenly dropped.

"Sweet mother of God..." Chief Thomas moaned, his delivery, trembling, filled with emotion. "One of our cops..." he paused, biting down hard on his lower lip as he continued slowly. "One of our cops just killed the attorney general of the United States."

CHAPTER TWO

The telephone ringing in the quiet bedroom gave off a startling sound at 1:05 a.m., causing him to jump up from a deep slumber. Instinctively, he looked at the clock sitting on top of the end table. He knew that a telephone call at such an hour meant the news had to be pressing and probably bad, since the standing order was: the president of the United States is not to be disturbed unless it is urgent.

The voice at the other end was that of Ron Blakeman, the White House chief of staff.

"Mr. President, I'm sorry to call you at this hour, but we've just received terrible news. Chuck Bradford is dead."

"What?" President John Harrington's voice was high-pitched, unsure of whether what he just heard was part of a bad dream.

"Chuck was shot in Syracuse. We're still trying to sort it out," Blakeman said softly.

"What happened, Ron? What the hell happened?" Harrington now realized that the news being reported to him was very real indeed.

"Details are sketchy at this time, Mr. President."

"I can't believe it" The president was in shock. "What happened?" he asked again as tears began to well up in his eyes. Charles Llewellyn Bradford was not only the attorney general of the United States, whom Harrington had appointed to that office, but one of his closest friends as well.

"We have very little information other than he was shot in some park in Syracuse," Blakeman answered.

"My God, this is terrible." Harrington paused, struggling to keep his emotions in check. He continued, his tone somber. "Call the vice president, Marcia Coleman, Clark Johansen, and Sam Jennings. I want them in the oval office in an hour."

"Yes, Mr. President."

By the time they all arrived at the oval office, the news was on every network and cable program; *"Attorney General Charles Bradford Murdered in New York."*

Bob Schieffer, Brian Williams, and Peter Jennings were already at the anchor desks of their television networks, as were CNN, CNBC, MSNBC, FOX, and all local cable news outlets that had pre-empted their regular programming to announce the breaking story.

Merged with the news reports were biographical clips showing Charles Bradford at different stages of his life, as correspondents took the viewers through many events in a dramatic background depicting his rise to attorney general of the United States. The feed was already in place that carried live reports from Carlyle Park in Syracuse to the rest of the country.

In an oval office containing the nation's most powerful leaders, genuine sadness filled the room, a tear coming from the most stoic of them.

And in that jungle called the Beltway, where politicians are driven by unlimited ambition and unbridled jealously, where everyone is fair game for criticism and attack, Charles Llewellyn Bradford had earned universal respect. Even in the ugly world of politics, there were not many who could find too many negative things to say about the man who most people admired, and who was being considered a logical candidate for the presidency when Harrington's term ended.

There was heavy sadness in the oval office when the meeting began. It started with a moment of silent prayer as President Harrington spoke somberly:

"Last night a great attorney general and a very dear friend, was murdered in New York." The President paused, took a sip of water, reached for a handkerchief tucked in an outside pocket of his jacket. He wiped small droplets of perspiration that began to accumulate on his forehead. He spoke again. "This is a terrible blow to our nation and extremely hard on all of us personally."

Those present in the room remained motionless as the president spoke, fighting to maintain his composure, difficult as it was.

"I have called you here to pass along what has happened in Syracuse and to try to develop a plan of action we should put into place. Although I know how terribly upsetting this is for all of us, we just can't allow events to get out of hand while we're sitting by grieving. So I'm open to any suggestions you might have. Alright then, how do we proceed from here?"

Clark Johansen, the national security advisor, started it off. "I think the first thing we must find out is whether Chuck's death was a planned assassination."

"The last thing we want to even remotely suggest to the press is that we suspect something of that kind. Until we get some hard evidence, even raising the question of assassination could create an unpredictable anxiety with the public,"Marcia Coleman, the deputy attorney general, said.

"I am not suggesting that at all, Marcia. But the public will be frightened and anxious in light of what has already happened. News stories will come out that will be filled with speculation and guesswork. Damn it, the last thing we need at this time is for some half-baked opportunistic reporter to press a rumor that Chuck was gunned down by a terrorist, or some other wild story that could start a national panic," Johansen said. He nervously twirled a ballpoint pen in his hand.

"Aren't we gettin' ahead of ourselves?" Vice President Jarrett Lee Hastings retorted in his deep Mississippi drawl. "First of all, what's the information outta New York that's bein' reported by the FBI?"

"Very little, Mr. Vice President," the White House chief of staff answered."The latest word is Chuck was shot in the head, and that some time later, he was shot again by a local Syracuse cop. Right now there's a lot of confusion and uncertainty as to exactly what happened. In fact, we weren't even given official notification until hours after Chuck had already been shot."

"Are you saying that Chuck was shot in the head first and shot again later by a Syracuse cop? Is that was you're telling us?" Sam Jennings, the speaker of the House asked.

"At this point it's not exactly clear," the chief of staff answered.

"In that case, let me ask you about that first shot. Who are the likely suspects?" Jennings asked.

"Depends who you ask. The local cops suspect Chuck may have attempted a suicide in that park, but no gun was found on or near his body. The latest report I now have is that the New York state police are investigating a possible mob hit with the theory that Chuck's body might have been dumped in the park afterwards," the chief of staff said.

Deputy Attorney General Coleman broke in. "A single bullet to the head is not the MO of a mob hit. Three shots would be closer to it. To me, it sounds more like a suicide attempt and then a foul-up by local cops who came to the scene later."

"That can't be true. Chuck had no reason to take his own life. I can vouch for that," Harrington said.

"Or maybe someone just wanted it to look like a suicide. Travis Jones who heads our FBI Syracuse office told me he's getting conflicting accounts from the Syracuse PD. They're going to protect their asses any way they can,"the chief of staff said.

"My God," the president broke in. "This gets worse as it goes along. Quite frankly, I don't know if we can trust the local cops. And I know there's no love lost between the FBI and the locals."

"But what was Chuck doing in Syracuse in the first place? And why in heaven' s name was he alone? Can anybody here explain what the attorney general was doing out of Washington without a security detail?"the bewildered speaker of the House asked.

"Sam," the president said, choosing his words carefully, "Chuck was on a special assignment that I wanted to keep under wraps. It seems he came upon important information he was going to report to me this morning. Tragically somebody got to him before he got to me. It was something Chuck had to do on his own. It was by his own choice and it was top secret. And for personal reasons he wanted to handle it *his* way."

"Personal reasons? Why all the secrecy? What's going on?" the speaker asked. He searched out the other quizzical looks in the room sensing that everyone there was sharing his concern.

"In deference to Chuck's widow, and this is very sensitive, I must beg off at this time, Sam. But I promise, you will all know very soon. And you'll hear it straight from me. Okay?"

Everybody nodded their assent.

"Good. But who could ever have dreamt that Chuck would be gone? And in this way—I still can't believe it." Harrington held his forehead. "I just can't believe it," he repeated in a whisper, as he looked up, staring blankly at the ceiling. "But this is not getting us closer to what happened to Chuck." This time his voice was stronger.

President Harrington got up from his chair, walking slowly around his desk.

"Look, I don't think we can trust the local PD. As for the FBI, they'll do what they have to. While I don't want to interfere directly with their probe, we're not going to sit by idly just waiting for their findings. Although Travis Jones is known to run a good office in Syracuse, he's not a guy who moves at top speed. He's slow, methodical, and deliberate—attributes good in your garden variety investigation. But we just don't have the luxury of time on this one. The public will demand answers, and they're entitled to them. But neither they nor we can wait while Jones goes through his usual 'by the numbers' routine. Christ, all panic could break loose if we don't get to the bottom of this and get to it quickly. We just can't allow this to turn into another Dallas."

"But Mr. President, if we're not going to leave it to the locals or FBI, where do we go?" the chief of staff asked.

"As I see it, we must pick a special investigator. And it's got to be the right guy to take it on. And what's more… he has to be prepared to act pretty much in the shadows. Okay then, level with me. Does anybody here disagree with that approach? Don't hold back on me if you do."

The speaker of the House spoke first. "Are you suggesting, Mr. President, that we find someone out of government for this assignment?"

"No. Not necessarily. But I'm totally open-minded on the subject. The first thing I would like to get is a consensus as to whether we go with a special investigator. Can we at least agree on that?"Everyone looked around the room at each other. They nodded approvingly at the president's suggestion.

"Can I take it then that you're all okay with this approach? Good. Now, let's kick a few names around. It can be anyone in or out of government service."

"How about Ralph Ormsby from CIA? He's highly regarded and well-organized," Sam Jennings rang out. "He cracked that school bombing in Atlanta last year and did a first class job."

"He also stepped on a lot of toes in the process," the chief of staff retorted.

"Ron, he's with the CIA, not the State Department. So long as he gets the job done, that's the key," Jennings said defensively.

"I agree with Ron," Marcia Coleman chimed in. "Ormsby is much too abrasive. I think we need someone far more diplomatic for this one."

"Floyd Douglas is someone you probably never heard of, but he's been in charge of law enforcement in my home state for fifteen years. He's smart and he knows his business. I would personally stand up for the guy, and I'm sure he'd accept the job with a short leave of absence," the vice president said.

"He may be okay in Mississippi, Jarrett, but I think we need someone who has a broad, federal background," Harrington said, vetoing the vice president's choice.

"I have a name I'd like to put on the table," the president continued. It came out of him as if he had withheld it deliberately until the others had been rejected.

"Marcia, what's your take on Matt Connors from Justice?"

"You know, I really didn't think of him, but you may have something there, Mr. President. Matt Connors is chief of the Civil Rights Division. He's been a career lawyer with the department for years. His credentials are impeccable."

"What do you think, Sam?" the president asked, glancing at the speaker of the House.

"I was very impressed by Connors when he testified before our Committee on Law Enforcement last year. He was thorough, analytical, and as I recall, had a real professional manner. In fact, I remember the committee members on both sides of the aisle complimenting him when he finished his report. Yep, the more I think about it, the more I like him as a viable choice. Matt Connors. Hmm…sounds good to me."

"Ron?" the president asked as he eyed his chief of staff.

"Connors is a 'no-nonsense' guy with lots of experience and smarts. Another point—he and Chuck were very close. If he can handle the assignment despite the personal relationship he had with Chuck, he has my vote."

"I disagree with you on that, Ron. I think he can handle it not *despite*, but *because of* his personal relationship with Chuck. Matt is bright, a straight shooter, and loyal to the core. I would trust him with the most sensitive assignment and feel confident that he could carry out the job and do it right. Besides, Connors has talent, skill, and survival power—one of the few in his department who can navigate through a heat shield with fiery flashes all around him and still come out without so much as a blister."

There was momentary silence as President Harrington examined the faces in the room.

"Then, it's agreed. Matt Connors it is," Harrington said. "I thank you for your help at this very difficult time."

The president shook hands with everyone as each stepped out of the oval office.

After they had gone, President John Harrington sat down in his high-backed chair. He felt a sense of relief that the first component of his plan had been accomplished—the selection of the right person for an extremely crucial and sensitive assignment. But with danger written all over it.

CHAPTER THREE

At 8:00 a.m., President Harrington lifted the telephone, dialed a number, and heard two rings before it was picked up at th other end.

"Hello."

"Hello, Matt, this is John Harrington. I hope I'm not calling you too early."

"No sir. I've been up for hours," Matt Connors answered, surprised that the caller was the president of the United States himself.

"Then you know about Chuck?"

"I just heard it on *The Today Show*."There was a slight pause. "Are you alright Mr. President?" Connors asked.

"I'm okay, Matt. No, I'm not okay. We're all sick over what's happened. It's very tragic. We're all in shock."

"I feel the same, Mr. President. Chuck was my closest friend."

"I know. And that's one of the reasons for my call. Matt, could you drop by the White House as soon as possible?"

"Of course. I'm on my way, Mr. President."

Thirty minutes later, after gaining clearance at the White House security gate, Matt Connors was escorted by a radio car that led him to a designated parking spot within the White House grounds. There, Connors was met by a Secret Service agent. Together, they walked the two hundred feet to the front entrance of the White House where they were greeted by another Secret Service agent and two spit-and-polish Marines standing at ram-rod attention. In a crisp maneuver of the rifle, right shoulder arms was snapped into port arms, the traditional military gun salute, as Matt approached them. Upon entering the White House, he was led into a large reception area by a third Secret Service agent who approached him from indoors.

Although Matt Connors had been to the White House a number of times, he had visited the oval office only once before. It was at the time President Harrington invited Connors to congratulate him personally for his handling of a sensitive high-profile civil rights case.

Matt thought about that first visit as he waited to be called into the president's office. *It was a happier time then,* he thought to himself. He remembered how gracious President Harrington had been in giving Matt a tour of the oval office. *It was like it happened yesterday,* flashed through his mind, with each word then spoken being permanently etched in his memory. He could almost hear the president asking :

"How would you like a mini tour of the oval office?"

And his own response at the time,"I would like that very much."

Matt could almost repeat *verbatim* what was said after that.......

"Good, Matt, a tour it is. Okay then, let me take a few minutes to point out some of the highlights of this wonderfully historic place. I'll start with this rug you're standing on… Every president who has been privileged to occupy this office has had the right to a floor covering designed just for him. As you can see, what we selected features colors of federal blue and gold—my favorites"

"It's most attractive, Mr. President. By the way, is that presidential seal one of your designs as well?"

"Not quite. The seal has remained the same for all administrations. The exact image of the eagle, its talons, the other fine detail together with the presidential inscription, have not been changed. It's part of the overall tradition of the White House."

"It's truly fascinating, Sir."

"See this desk here… It originally came form the British frigate, The *H.M.S. Resolute.*

I like the sound of that name—*Resolute.* And it's been in the oval office dating back to the early days of Teddy Roosevelt."

"I seem to recall that the desk is famous for other reasons as well. Am I correct about that, Mr. President?"

"In fact you are, Matt. And you're probably referring to that simply wonderful photo of President Kennedy's son John John, who was three at the time. A White House photographer took the picture of him as he was peeking out of the center well of that old desk. Little did he realize that the photo he shot of young John John would one day turn out to be an historic treasure and would find a permanent home in the Smithsonian."

"I could almost see the image of JFK sitting behind that desk with John John there at his feet. It gives me chills just to think about it."

19

"And I can appreciate why it does...but I suppose what I really love about this wonderful office is its total beauty. That's especially evident in the early morning when the sun shines so brightly through these tall windows. And from my chair, I can swing around and enjoy a perfect view of the south lawn of this great house. It's really peaceful and very serene."

"I can see it clearly from here. It's also very beautiful, Mr. President."

"Oh yes. And look at that tall fireplace over there...When I think that men like FDR, Truman, Eisenhower, John Kennedy, Reagan—they all sat next to it with so many of the great leaders of the world... I tell you Matt, it's all very humbling."

"And awe-inspiring."

"You bet it is! Original oil paintings of Washington and Jefferson on that wall...You want to know something, Matt? In all humility, it makes me feel so insignificant."

Matt was still reminiscing as he gazed with wonderment at the marble busts of George Washington, Abraham Lincoln, James Monroe, Woodrow Wilson, Franklin Roosevelt, John Kennedy, George H.W. Bush, Bill Clinton, and the other presidents who filled out the perimeter of the reception room gallery.

A few minutes later, with thoughts taking him on a journey through history, he was brought back to the present when a huge oak door opened and an attractive, neatly-dressed young woman appeared. "Mr. Connors, the president will see you now." She escorted Matt to the oval office.

"Come on in, Matt. Thank you for coming. And a sad welcome to the oval office." Harrington looked pale as he got up from his chair, walked around the large desk, and extended a warm greeting. "Last time you were here, I recall things were a whole lot brighter."

"I was thinking that just a few moments ago outside waiting to be called in. The fact is I still can recall almost every minute detail of that wonderful visit."

"I was happy to show you the office at that time, and although the situation is unfortunately much different now, it's always a great pleasure to see you, Matt."

"Thank you, sir."

"Well...."Harrington hesitated as he cleared his throat. He continued somberly. "We're all devastated over Chuck's death. It' s so damned tragic." The president appeared visibly distraught, shaken.

"I still can't come to grips with his being gone. It seems so unreal, Mr. President."

"I know, Matt. It's a sadness we all share. And no matter how much we want it to be a bad dream, it's all too real."

"Yes, sir." Matt's response was whispered. His grief was apparent as well.

"This morning I met with some members of my cabinet. They're all in deep shock. And already there's a heavy pall over Washington.

"I know, Mr. President."

"Now then, Matt, please sit down. Right here would be fine."

Matt sat in one of the chairs that flanked the old desk. President Harrington sat down as well. They faced each other in deep silence for a moment. The president spoke.

"We all know how close you were to Chuck and his family, Matt. We're also intimately aware of your loyalty to our nation, and the outstanding record you have with the Justice Department."

"I thank you for such praise, Mr. President. But I've always tried to do my job as best I could." Matt 's reply was a mix of humility, poise.

"It's not intended to flatter you, Matt. All here agree that it is an accurate appraisal of who you are."

"I appreciate that, Mr. President. I sincerely do!"

"But it's true! And that's why I'm going to ask that you undertake the investigation of the death of our friend, Chuck Bradford. You have the ability, the skill, and above all, you have the strongest of reasons to get to the heart of this tragic event."

"Sir?"

"Of course, you do. So, will you accept the assignment, Matt? I will not be offended if for any reason you feel you could not undertake it. And if your answer is 'no,' I promise there will be no recriminations at this end. You understand what I'm saying, Matt?"

"Yes I do, Mr. President."

"And your answer?"

"I am here to serve in any way I can. If that's what you want of me, my answer of course is 'yes.'"

"I knew I could count on you. Thanks, Matt. On another issue, I know that you're in the middle of the Davis civil rights case at the present time, but I'm told that it can be transferred over to a top-level assistant with the assurance that it won't miss a beat in the transition. Is it okay with you, Matt?"

"I'm sure it will be fine."

"Good. Well then, I want you to get started on this immediately. Whatever back-up you need, you have. And with the deputy attorney general's consent, you will be reporting directly to me."

Harrington inched closer to Matt as his voice took on a more somber tone.

"Matt, you are about to embark on an extremely important and sensitive mission. But before you get started, I must tell you what I know about the investigation Chuck was on when he died. The sad irony is that what he discovered cost him his life. And now I'm asking his best friend to retrace the same steps that ultimately resulted in *his* death. That's really a tough call."

"I'll do whatever I can. Anything."

"I'm sure of that. But there are some things you have to know."Harrington pulled his chair closer to Matt. He started to speak again, this time in a whispered voice.

"What I am about to tell you must remain in this room… You see Matt, Chuck was on a very special assignment."

Speaking like he was letting Matt in on a guarded secret, Harrington continued."Matt, are you familiar with Indian casino gambling?"

"In what context, Mr. President?"

"What I mean is, has your department ever been involved with issues covering the licensing of casinos on Indian reservations?"

"No, I don't believe so. Not to my knowledge anyway."

"Let me ask another question." Harrington stood up, walked around to the front of *The H.M.S. Resolute* desk, opened its top right drawer, and pulled out an 8 " x 11" sheet of paper. He remained standing next to his high-backed chair. Looking down at what he was holding in his hand, and then up again, he asked, "Does the name Vincent Scarpizzi mean anything to you?"

"I recognize the name. Could you be referring to a reputed mob boss in New York City? Is that the same fellow?" Matt asked, unsure of where the president's question was heading.

"Yes Matt, one and the same. How about Hector Santiago? Does that name sound familiar to you?"

"H-e-c-t-o-r S-a-n-t-I-a-g-o." Matt stretched the name out as he tried to run it by his memory. "I'm not sure," Matt replied, as he released a puzzled look. And then it came to him. "Is he the same Santiago who's been linked with drug trafficking in New York? Is that the one?"

"Yes. He's the guy." Glancing down at the paper again, Harrington asked, "Have you ever heard of the Pecontic tribe in Syracuse?"

"Pecontic... Pecontic." Matt repeated it slowly as he began to process the name in his brain. "Pecontic... in... Syracuse." He paused, then started up again." I'm not sure of that, except I do know that Jenny is a member of a Native American tribe in Syracuse. But I couldn't say for certain if that's the one."

Breaking an uneasy silence, the president was next to speak. "Matt, the mission you are about to undertake is extremely sensitive. Therefore, for security reasons the investigation will be called *Arrowhead*. It's the code name that only you and I will have—and it's top secret."

"Just out of curiosity, sir, how did you happen to pick *that* name?"

"In college, I took a course in archery. A short while ago, and only by chance, I happened to come upon an old handbook I had kept through the years with all of my other college texts. Leafing through it, I came upon the page describing 'arrow.' Here, Matt, let me read this one line to you: *'The arrow's shaft, with its strength and integrity, is an instrument of flight, who's accuracy relies upon the skill of the archer in attempting to penetrate the center of the target, depending upon the sharpness of its arrowhead.'*"

Harrington placed the book on his desk. "I thought about it and how relevant it is to what we are now involved in. And then it struck me. Metaphorically, the 'center of the target' of this investigation, could be the heart of mob influence and pay-offs. The 'arrow's shaft' is the strength and integrity needed for its steady 'flight.' But while its feathers guide the path, its accuracy relies upon the skill of the archer. And when sprung into action, its success is dependent upon the 'penetrating' force of its 'arrowhead.'"

"I must admit, that is a very interesting analysis, Mr. President."

"The analogy makes perfect sense. You, Matt, are my archer and arrow, all in one. And it's the head of the arrow that must penetrate the target of corruption. It makes even more sense as I think about it. *'Arrowhead'* fits. Really does! Okay with you?"

"Of course. But I must admit sir, I was absolutely fascinated with your explanation."

"Alright, it's settled then. *Arrowhead* it is. And I want you to know that you have the thanks of a grateful president who places absolute trust in you."

Harrington rose from his chair.

"And I will never betray that trust."

They shook hands.

"Check with me Matt just as soon as you have some information to report. I know that with you on it we'll get an accurate handle on this horrible mess."

"I'll do my best, Mr. President. I promise."

With the oval office behind him, Matt could now remove the stoic mask he had worn in front of Harrington. In its place emerged an emotional Matt Connors struggling to restrain the tears that were beginning to form.

He removed his pocket handkerchief and wiped his eyes and face. Matt did not want the guards at the gate to see him in such visible grief.

As his vehicle passed the striped bar raised by the security detail, Matt's sorrow became even more intense. He knew he would soon have to face Jenny, his best friend's widow, and her seven year-old-son, Little Joe. That Jenny would be the first person he would have to interview in the investigation of her husband's death.

During the thirty minute drive to the Bradford home, Matt thought about the heavy assignment just received from President Harrington, never suspecting that what awaited him would be the most devastating experience of his life.

Chapter Four

As he sat behind the wheel of his moving car, Matt thought about his own course that had brought him from childhood to a high post in the civil rights division of the United States Department of Justice. He began to reflect upon his past as the government vehicle headed toward Jenny Roundtree Bradford, the widow of his late friend:

Born in the Pelham Bay section of the Bronx, Matthew John Connors was the youngest of four children of Mary and John Patrick Connors. In those days, the Bronx was divided into three basic ethnic groups: Irish, Italian and Jewish. From the twenties to the fifties, the Irish were the predominant influence in the politics of New York City. With a powerful Democratic base in the Bronx, it was there, together with Brooklyn and Manhattan, where the political machine handed out its patronage to the loyalists of the party.

The jobs ranged from getting blue collar workers into the Sanitation Department to the appointment of city and state judges. One of those judgeships was given to Matt's father, a graduate of the evening division of Fordham Law School, as a reward for his long service to the local Democratic club.

Although he attended Sacred Heart Parochial Elementary School, Matt chose a public high school instead of the traditional catholic one that his older brothers had attended before him. Athletic, Matt played forward on Bronx High School's varsity basketball team. Six feet tall, with a solid physique and natural agility, he often scored more points in a game than others much bigger. A handsome face, enhanced by a subtle cleft on his well-defined chin, added the overall appearance of strength and character to his striking physical persona. His thick, sand- colored hair complimented light blue eyes which would register a sparkle with each smile, giving off a shy and boyish quality.

When the option was presented upon his graduation from high school—an athletic scholarship to a small college, or an academic pursuit—he elected the latter, having been exposed to a political household, and desiring a career in government service. In pursuit of that goal, Matt attended Fordham Law School (as did his father before him), graduating with honors.

It was at Fordham where he met Kathy Burns who also was an honor law student at the school. They fell in love and married on the day of their graduation.

Although both were high on the Wall Street law firms' recruitment list, it was Kathy who accepted an associate position with a large corporate firm. In contrast, Matt rejected a number of lucrative job offers and accepted an appointment as an assistant district attorney that had been arranged through his father's political connections.

Kathy disapproved of Matt's job choice, which was a constant source of irritation and friction within their marriage.

Matt recalled their first bitter encounter as if it all happened only an hour before:

"I can't understand what you're doing," Kathy snapped when Matt accepted an entry level position with the district attorney's office. In an intended put-down, she continued stiffly, "You're blowing the career that in a few years will land you a partnership in one of the most prestigious firms in the country."

"I know what I want to do with my life and it has nothing to do with getting callouses on my ass for seven years while I plod along on some boring corporate merger just so I can make partner one day. I have to do something far more meaningful than that!"

Even years after they had parted, one of her frequent criticisms of Matt was still as fresh in his mind as if made that morning:

"You make it sound like getting into a top Wall Street firm is something to be ashamed of. Any law graduate in the country would give his right arm to get the opportunity that you're pissing away. I just can't understand how you can say 'no' to a big league career and 'yes' to a nickel-and-dime political shit appointment."

The sharp denigration was intended and still remained seared in Matt's memory.

Driving along, he recalled almost every word of the angry response he fired back at the time:

"That's the difference between you and me, Kathy. You're impressed with all the big bucks and phony status of a white-shoe law firm. Well to me, that's the real bullshit! What you have difficulty understanding is that I've got to do what drives me, *not what drives you!* That means that I'm not going to waste my life shmoozing with a bunch of WASPY, button-down, nerd-heads, whose biggest rise comes from kissing the senior partner's ass while they're working seventy hours a week just to bill out more phony time."

Matt could not forget Kathy's caustic response and how she snarled back at him:

"Go ahead, Matt. Work in the D.A.'s office and pal around with those no-talent losers. If that's what you want, that's what you deserve!" Kathy said, her voice dripping with venom.

As Matt drove his car toward the airport, he remembered Kathy's stridence and the repeated insults she flung that were getting dangerously close to his flash point:

"Damn it, Kathy. God damn it! I'm talking 'zig' and you're hearing 'zag.' We can't even get our 'zigs' and 'zags' on the same page. Christ, you haven't started your job yet and already you sound like one of those pompous, striped-tied elitists. And you keep on talking down to me like I'm lower than dog shit wedged on the bottom of your shoe."

Matt recoiled in the driver's seat as he remembered how angry and frustrated he would feel after such ugly encounters with Kathy.

In the months that followed, the bitter arguments and open hostility escalated with both eventually traveling in separate circles. Within a little more than a year of their original vows, Kathy and Matt concluded that their marriage was a colossal mistake. They decided to end it, and did.

Matt remained with the D.A.'s office until he received a call one day from the U.S. attorney in Manhattan who had been on a search for a deputy chief in the Civil Rights Division:

"Matt, this is Bob Giles with the U.S. attorney's office," Giles said at the time.

A bit surprised, Matt answered, "I'm real honored to be called by the United States attorney for the southern district, *himself.*"

"I've been looking for a deputy chief of the Civil Rights Division. I spoke to your law school's head guy. Yeah, Dean Wagner. He must be on your payroll. You're the best, he says. Interested?"

"I'm really flattered, but with all due respect, he must be *on* something." Matt recalled how he jokingly answered, hoping that his attempt at self-deprecation would not come off as too transparent.

"No, I don't think so. I also did some checking around and all the reports come back solid…I think you would find the slot challenging. I would like you to interview with us A.S.A.P. How does that sound to you, counselor?"

The interview went as expected. Matt was sworn in as an assistant U.S. attorney.

Eight years later, Matt Connors was appointed chief of the Civil Rights Division of the U.S. attorney's office for the southern district of New York.

Gaining the reputation of a bright, level-headed, hard-hitting, but fair lawyer, he drew the attention of the Washington in-crowd; and when a vacancy developed, Matt's career took a giant leap when he was appointed chief of the Civil Rights Division of the U.S. Department of Justice. The joy of his vaulted position was dampened only by the sadness he felt that his parents were not alive to share in the pride of his success.

And with the promotion, Matt moved from his Manhattan apartment, relocating to a townhouse outside the nation's capital.

It was shortly after assuming his new role that Matt met Charles Llewelyn Bradford, the junior senator from Oklahoma, more commonly known as Senator "Chuck" Bradford.

Bradford had asked for a meeting to discuss a troubling issue. A group of major oil companies had made claim to certain Indian reservation lands in Oklahoma for drilling-site exploration. The Shinetuck tribe living on the land had sought the assistance of their senator, who wanted advice and possible action from the Justice Department in order to block the proposed drilling:

"Please come in, Senator," Matt said as he extended a cordial handshake to his guest. Pointing to a burgundy leather chair, Matt continued, "Please."

"Thank you, Mr. Connors." Matt pulled up a side chair and sat facing the Senator several feet from him. The leather chair behind Matt's mahogany desk sat empty as Matt chose instead to conduct the conference in front of his desk and not behind it.

After introductory pleasantries were concluded, Matt swung into the purpose of the meeting. "Now then, Senator, how can I be of help?"

Chuck's impression of his host matched what he had heard about him and he felt comfortable and relaxed as the conversation continued.

"Are you familiar with oil exploration on tribal lands in my state, Mr. Connors?"

"Before our meeting I tried to get up to speed on the issue, senator. I have read all of the transcripts of the oil execs who testified before the Commerce Committee. And I've been thoroughly briefed by my staff," Matt replied, as he leafed through several documents in his hand.

Chuck was impressed by what he was witnessing having attended far too many meetings where the other side was unprepared and seemed to be winging it. That was not the case here, and Chuck had a good feeling about it all.

"Quite frankly, Mr. Connors, what the oil companies are attempting to do has upset many of my constituents. And it's also of deep concern to me since it would be unjust for these or any other oil companies to dig burr holes several hundred feet into sacred tribal land and then desecrate them with rigs and derricks all over the terrain. You see, Mr. Connors, those lands have always been part of the Shinetuck reservation. They were obtained through treaties that the United States government entered into with the tribe more than a century ago. These agreements must be honored and the lands that rightfully belong to the Shinetucks must be protected."

Matt sensed Chuck's passion and conviction. He listened without interruption as his respect for the young Senator was rapidly rising.

Here, sitting opposite Matt Connors was Charles Llewelyn Bradford who was speaking passionately on behalf of Native Americans and against the giant oil companies. And all of this despite his being the progeny of one of the largest oil dynasties in Oklahoma—the powerful Bradford oil empire itself!

What kind of man is this Charles Bradford? What kind of person is it who is born of privilege and pleads a cause not on behalf of the oil interests so akin to his own background, but does so on behalf of those who have always been treated as second-class citizens? Matt thought.

Fully versed on the subject and buttressed by Bradford's persuasive arguments, Matt looked directly at Chuck as he said without hesitation, "It is my firm belief that the attempt by a powerfully connected oil consortium to systematically drive American citizens from their ancestral homes is fundamentally unjust. Quite frankly, I see this as a civil rights issue."

Matt paused as he flashed a determined look, then continued.

"I will therefore instruct my staff to file suit in the Federal District Court. We will seek to enjoin the oil companies from proceeding any further until a full judicial hearing is held on the entire issue."

Having made his pronouncement, Matt rose slowly from his chair, cast off a soft smile, extending his hand to Chuck.

The senator also stood up as he looked warmly at Matt. "Mr. Connors—" he started out as he accepted Matt's hand. But before Bradford could continue, he was interrupted.

"—The name is 'Matt.' "

"And mine is 'Chuck.' "

The two men held the handshake as each looked deeply into the other's eyes. They broke out into warm smiles, both sharing the intuitive feeling that a strong friendship was in its incipient stage of development.

The law suit brought by Matt Connors was filed in the Federal District Court in Tulsa, Oklahoma. It set forth the United States of America as the plaintiff and represented by the U.S. Department of Justice . The companies that made up the oil consortium were named as defendants and represented by five of the largest corporate law firms in the nation.

The court was to decide the case on the legal briefs submitted by all the parties to the action.

One month later, the Federal District Judge rendered a decision in favor of the oil consortium and against the government. With this determination, the Shinetuck tribe had lost round one in its battle to preserve the integrity of the lands it owned.

Matt took it next to the United States Circuit Court of Appeals, seeking a reversal of the lower court's ruling.

The Circuit Court affirmed the original finding of the District Court. The tribe had now lost round two.

It was time for round three as Matt took the case all the way to the United States Supreme Court, despite the strong advice of his senior staff assistants who were convinced they were on the losing side of the dispute.

Because of his deep belief in the merits of the case, Matt decided to argue the appeal himself— a departure from the usual protocol of the department.

Matt, accompanied by a staff member from his bureau, arrived at the majestic building, the Supreme Court of the United States. Its white facade, flanked by imposing Grecian columns that surrounded the many steps leading from the street level to a huge landing, presented the picture of strength and beauty combined.

The Supreme Court building was a brilliant architectural gem. Its mammoth size, strength of character, and its imposing aura were true representations of the nation's highest judicial branch of government.

Appearing in the historic chamber of the high court of the land, Matt and his assistant took seats in the first row traditionally reserved for the lawyers who are scheduled to argue a case before the nine justices.

At precisely 10:00 a.m., the voice of the chief clerk of the Supreme Court bellowed, "All rise. The justices of the Supreme Court of the United States."

As if choreographed for a stage performance, the black-robed justices emerged simultaneously, each from a specially draped door (nine doors in all) behind huge high-backed leather chairs. The ceremony was performed with military precision, and as if directed by a maestro, each justice sat down in unison, and with exact timing. The Supreme Court of the United States of America, was now in session.

After the first case was heard, the court proceeded without delay to the next one on its scheduled docket. This signaled Matt to move quickly to a seat behind a large table in front of all the justices of the court.

The green light that flashed on in a small rectangular electronic box perched on top of the counsel table in front of Matt's chair was his cue to approach the lectern and to begin his argument to the court.

"Good morning, Your Honors," Matt opened up. Before he could utter another word, he was interrupted by one of the justices. Diverted from his prepared outline, he was suddenly fielding a barrage of sharp and pointed questions fired at him as if triggered from a rocket propelled launcher. But despite the steady onslaught coming from the bench, Matt stood firm as he cited case law precedents to support the many legal points he was attempting to make.

It was the chief justice who interrupted Matt in the middle of a sentence.

"Mr. Connors, the treaty you rely upon was drawn at a time when we ceased all hostile action against the Indians who lived on the land. That was the end of the nineteenth century and long before the industrial revolution came about with its demands for totally new sources of energy."

"Mr. Chief Justice, we can no more repudiate our commitments made at that time than we can turn our backs on the Bill of Rights drawn one hundred years even before that, and thereafter argue that it does not deserve our adherence simply because society has changed. We are a nation of law that gives full meaning to our democracy and not of change, however expedient or convenient it may appear at the time." Matt argued in his attempt to display an understanding of deeply rooted constitutional principles, and not to show brashness or disrespect to the court.

Piqued by what he viewed as preaching and not sound legal argument, the chief justice reacted impatiently.

"I fail to see the analogy, Mr. Connors. And I do not believe we need a lesson on the meaning of the Bill of Rights either, counselor. But returning to the issue of the treaty—times have changed and our needs have grown to constitutionally justify another approach to the overall issue. Our court has stated many times that the law must respond to the needs of society, and if it fails to do so, our law becomes an anachronism."

"Your Honor, whether we are judging the merits of a treaty, or the meaning of the Bill of Rights, the distinction remains one of degree and not one of substance. Our nation's entering into a treaty in 1880 was the product of neither whim, nor fancy. It was the constitution that empowered the action taken and the adherence to it that it always demanded," Matt argued.

Moving forward in his chair while steadily pointing his index finger at Matt Connors, the chief justice interrupted condescendingly.

"You miss a very significant point, Mr. Connors. Our law is not stagnant nor does it live in a vacuum. It is a breathing and living institution growing out of a constitution where the framers considered the moral and lawful ends it was ratified to protect. Here, progress means the ability to employ a balance that can satisfy the larger public need, while at the same time, paying a fair price to those who would be asked to give up what is no longer relevant to a larger society. What I am saying, Mr. Connors, is that the rights to the land could be legally settled with fair and reasonable payment, thereby permitting the exploration of oil that on balance, would benefit a greater population. Such a formula would neither weaken nor compromise the constitution designed to protect the rights of all people."

Having recovered from his initial anxiety and forced departure from his prepared outline that was to have served as his blueprint, Matt was now in full command of his argument. Not about to be pushed aside, he responded boldly.

"These lands have never been challenged in more than a century. They are vested and belong to the Shinetucks. No group—and that includes a powerful oil consortium—has the right to make claim to property that belongs to our citizens acquired through time-honored treaties. It is their rightful heritage and no act of man should break the link of the past with their entitlement and security for the future."

A sudden quiet overtook the courtroom as Matt continued in a low and moving voice.

"You speak of balance, Your Honor, but I say most respectfully that a *fair* balance must fall on the side of fundamental justice. The Shinetucks have lived on this land for generations. Their children and their children's children have developed and nurtured it for more than one hundred years without interruption. True justice not only requires that their reservations remain protected from commercial invasion, but demands it as well. For anything that falls short of full justice is injustice—and that, Your Honor, is a result that neither our law nor the highest court of our land should permit. Reaching any other conclusion would make folly of a long-standing treaty and would undermine the 'due process clause' of our constitution that has made this nation the great democracy it is."

Matt was in full stride as he moved flawlessly, 'whipping and driving past the eight pole' down the stretch.

Within three months, the Supreme Court reached its final decision. It rejected the oil consortium's position and embraced Matt's arguments protecting the rights of Native American Indians. It was a landmark ruling, bringing Chuck Bradford and Matt Connors even closer together, creating a bond of friendship that would continue to grow.

Several years later, when John Harrington was elected president of the United States, he appointed his friend and Harvard Law School classmate Charles Llewelyn Bradford, attorney general of the United States.

With the appointment, Chuck Bradford and Matt Connors became closer, with Matt even serving as 'best man' when Chuck Bradford married a strikingly beautiful Native American Indian, Jenny Roundtree.

Matt's affection for Chuck was later enlarged to include Jenny and her young son, "Little Joe," in the continuing friendship that grew in close communion with each passing year. Unfortunately, it was cut short by a horrifying event in Syracuse.

It was now Matt's job to find the killers of his best friend, and to uncover the reason why so admired a figure as the attorney general of the United States was murdered in a remote and desolate park somewhere in upstate New York.

CHAPTER FIVE

"Syracuse Medical Center," Matt instructed the taxi driver after the U.S. Air Boeing 737 touched down at the Syracuse Airport.

Thirty minutes later, Matt was at the main entrance of an eight-story, institutional-looking building where he was directed to the medical examiner's office. Dr. Peter Carlucci was already waiting in the reception room, ready to greet his official visitor from Washington.

"It's a pleasure to meet you, Mr. Connors," Carlucci said, extending his hand. Matt flashed his badge as he accepted Carlucci's warm greeting.

" And I thank you for your courtesy in seeing me with such short notice, Dr. Carlucci."

"Glad to be of help," Carlucci said as he guided Matt toward the morgue. It also contained the room where the medical examiner's autopsies were performed.

"Have you completed the autopsy?" Matt asked in a somber tone.

"Just about," replied Carlucci as he escorted Matt into a room with the unmistakable smell of formaldehyde.

The area was 30 x 40 feet with a table in the center under a large light fixture that followed the dimensions of the table below. There were two large tub sinks along one wall. Two six-foot-wide wooden closets stood next to each tub. The open doors of the closets disclosed deep shelves that housed many containers and jars of different heights and widths. A smaller table next to the large one, held many trays, several of which displayed surgical instruments and tools lined neatly on top of a green cloth.

Ceiling fluorescent lights shined down upon a metal table covered with a dark green sheet. Standing next to it was Dr. Charles Woo, the assistant medical examiner.

Under the sheet was the body of Charles Llewelyn Bradford, the late attorney general of the United States.

Matt stared at the green covering. He felt a sudden chill as he fought to keep his emotions in check, knowing that his closest friend lay lifeless under that foreboding shroud.

I've got to get hold of myself, he thought firmly. *Christ, how am I going to get through this?* Matt was struggling to maintain a steady keel, hoping that Carlucci would not detect any weakness once he saw Chuck on the table. It was a daunting challenge.

Chuck's body was just a shell now since all vital organs had been surgically removed for pathological analysis. A wrenching reality awaited Matt as he bit down hard on his lower lip, trying desperately to draw a protective curtain in order to separate his official role as federal investigator from that of best friend to the dead man on the table.

As the three men stood next to Chuck's body, Matt asked, "What are your preliminary conclusions at this time, Dr. Carlucci?"

"It is quite clear that one bullet entered the skull at the top of the cerebellum," Carlucci said as he placed the fingers of his right hand on the back of his head slightly above the collar line. "That bullet, however, did not kill the attorney general," Carlucci concluded.

"One moment please, Dr. Carlucci. I have investigated many homicides in my career, but I am completely puzzled by one of the observations reported by a witness at the scene. According to one of the cops who was there, the victim appeared dead, and then suddenly sat up. It's absolutely baffling to me. How can that be explained, sir?"

"While it would appear to be a medical aberration, there is a sound scientific basis for the victim's action. Here, let me show you." Carlucci rolled back the sheet that covered Chuck Bradford, exposing his head and shoulders.

Matt was jolted when he saw Chuck's ashen color. He took several deep breaths.

Don't lose it, he repeated to himself as he turned his eyes away from his fallen friend, trying desperately to insulate himself from the razor-sharp emotions he was fighting hard to keep under control.

Oh Chuck. My God. Poor Chuck, he kept moaning over and over in his head, unable to look again directly at the face of his dead friend lying on the table. And yet, Matt had to wear the mask of objective stoicism in the presence of such a horror. He had to continue his charade of portraying a facade of professional and uninvolved detachment.

Carlucci continued as he used a pointer to identify the anatomy he was describing :

"Do you see this entry wound that is left of center of his skull right here in the lower quadrant of his head? The gun was fired at close range. As proof of that you can see the distinct powder burns on his skin. The bullet pierced the skull which protects the brain, the cerebrum, or the large hemispheric lobes, and the cerebellum that is located at the base of the skull. Would you like me to be more detailed in my explanation of the brain's centers of function, Mr. Connors?"

"I would, Dr. Carlucci. But I'm not sure I'll be able to follow you."

"I'll try to keep it as simple as possible. Of course please feel free to stop me if you have any questions as I go along."

"Thank you, doctor. I appreciate that."

"Alright then. Let me begin this way: It is the cerebellum that controls the specific motor and nerve functions of the body. In fact, all motor, respiration, heart impulses, and neuro responses are centered within the brain. I will describe it metaphorically as the central station of the spinal cord that directs all of the nerve action of the body. Are you with me so far, Mr. Connors?"

"Yes sir."

"Good. Now then, what happened in this situation, although extremely rare, is nonetheless scientifically and medically explainable."

"How so, doctor?"

"In the following way. You see Mr. Connors, the bullet, having struck the hard shell that makes up the skull, became lodged within the cerebellum, right here, in the lower part of the brain. Its penetrating impact produced a sudden and violent shock to the central nervous system causing an almost complete shutdown of the brain's total activity. As a result of the trauma, the victim was left in a moribund state except that his respiratory function, although present, was operating at the barest minimum to sustain life. Still with me, Mr. Connors?"

"I believe so."

"Very well. Therefore, with such acute and gross physiological compromise, that is, as close to death as a human being can get, the victim's body temperature fell drastically. Consequently, he would feel cold to the touch. And with vital signs of blood pressure, respiration, and pulse almost non-existent, he would appear to be dead. Except however, that he was in a deep state of brain and central nervous system shock which in any event would have ultimately led to his death."

"His coldness and absence of vital signs could account for the cop on the scene believing he was dead. Right?"

"Precisely."

"But how do you explain his sudden sitting up despite what you described as his 'moribund state'?" Matt asked as he was beginning to feel queasy, sick, and dangerously close to throwing up.

Forgetting for the moment that he had told Matt he would describe things in simple terms, Carlucci nodded his head. "The cerebellum is one of the brain's regulatory components of the extra pyramidal system. Part of its natural function is to exercise control over motor activity, or what is anatomically described as the motor cortex, via pathways that are transmitted through another part of the brain—the thalamus. It is the thalamus where all sensory impulses are relayed. Therefore, if the cerebellum is grossly damaged, as in Bradford's case, there is a resulting loss of motor control. What can then occur, as what happened here, is an aimless involuntary and rapid sudden movement. It's as if the circuit breaker stopped working. Bradford's 'sudden sitting up' as you describe, was one of those involuntary responses caused by a severely damaged and discordant cerebellum."

Carlucci paused, noting the puzzled look on Matt's face.

"Forgive me, Mr. Connors, but sometimes I forget that I am not presenting a seminar on the anatomy of the brain to a group of forensic pathologists. I hope my description was not too complicated or clinical."

"I'm trying to follow all the medical terms and the description you gave but it's not exactly easy." Matt knew that the scribbled notes he had taken in his hurried short-hand just trying to keep pace with the medical examiner's explanation, were useless.

"You look a bit confused, Mr. Connors."

"More than a bit. Could you run that by me again, Dr. Carlucci?"

"Of course. I will explain it to you in its most simplistic way: The attorney general was morbidly wounded and had all the signs of death on his face. Although he was extremely close to his demise, he was still alive. His sudden movement was directly caused by an outside stimulus that precipitated an uncontrollable reflex action of his central nervous system. It could have been triggered by the cop who touched him, or the headlights of the patrol car. Either may have energized his optic nerve. The fact is, Mr. Connors, that the body was barely alive—and I repeat, *barely* alive—when it reacted involuntarily and spontaneously to an environmental stimulus. If he had not been shot again, it is my opinion, with a reasonable degree of medical certainty, that he would have died from the first bullet that entered his brain at almost any time thereafter."

"My god," Matt whispered, shaking his head from side to side. "That's one of the most amazing things I've ever heard. But I must thank you for the further explanation. This time, I had no difficulty understanding what you said. But I do have a question: Do you have any doubt about what you have just described?"

"None at all, Mr. Connors. In fact, Dr. Woo and I have gone over every detail of this most fascinating case very carefully, and he is in full accord with everything I have reported to you. Right, Charles?" Carlucci asked, turning to his assistant.

"As strange as it sounds, there is a scientifically sound medical basis for the reflex action exhibited by the attorney general," Woo responded, endorsing the conclusions reached by Carlucci.

"As to the actual cause of death—that resulted from the bullets fired by the cop's gun into the victim's chest. The first one completely shattered the left ventricle of his heart which is the main pumping chamber. The second entered the left atrium. The third shattered the clavicle known also as the collarbone. When the left lower chamber lost its ability to pump blood and oxygen into the arteries that feed the brain, the attorney general died instantly."

"What was the time difference between the first shot to the head and the later shots to the chest?" Matt asked.

"Here, let me show you something." Pointing to the back of Bradford's skull, Carlucci continued, "You see the dried coagulated blood around the entry wound? It has a deep bluish color, almost purple. The entry wounds of the chest are of a different blood texture. I estimate that the earlier wound to the head was made approximately two hours before the victim was shot in the chest. But I wish to add something further."

"Yes?"

" I have seen many head wounds and I have testified in countless cases involving the death of a victim by gunshot to the head. Accept it, Mr. Connors, for what it's worth. This man was shot in the head by a professional killer."

"One second, doctor, please," Matt interrupted, trying to visualize his friend's movements before he was killed. Instinctively, Matt openly voiced some questions that were a reflection of his own thoughts:

"If the attorney general was shot by a hit man, what was Chuck doing in Syracuse in the first place? What the hell was his real connection with this part of New York at that time?" Matt's open-aired queries caught Carlucci by surprise.

"I'm only a medical examiner, Mr. Connors. I can explain how it happened, but I can't tell you who did it, or why. That's your job. I'm a medical detective, not a criminal investigator."

"Forgive me, doctor. I was just thinking out loud."

A few minutes later, Carlucci escorted Matt back to the reception area. Along the way, Matt admonished Carlucci, "Doctor, what you have reported to me must not be told to anyone else. The president of the United States has made this investigation a top secret priority and the confidentiality of your findings must be protected until you receive further notice from me."

Matt paused.

"Have you discussed this with anyone else?"

"No, Mr. Connors. I have not and will not, pending your further instructions."

"Good. One of my deputies will contact you this afternoon. He is Agent Frank Sanford who will make all the arrangement for the removal of the attorney general's body, all organs, tissue slides, and x-rays. Do not reduce your autopsy findings to a formal writing until I advise otherwise." Matt was concerned that copies of a written report could be leaked to the press or to others who could seriously compromise his investigation.

"I understand fully, Mr. Connors, and you can be assured that I will follow every one of your instructions to the letter."

Once outside the building, Matt took in deep breaths of fresh air. He felt relieved that he had been able to control his emotions during the visit with Dr. Carlucci. But he knew that he would have to remain in full command of those same emotions when in just a few days he would be attending Chuck's burial service in Oklahoma.

During his flight back to Washington, a question kept gnawing within Matt's brain. *Did Chuck have a special reason for looking into Indian casino gambling in Syracuse?*

As Matt's plane began its approach to Reagan Washington National Airport, he also thought about the last private meeting he had with President Harrington in the oval office.

Again Matt could not escape a nagging uneasiness as he recalled one of the questions President Harrington asked: *"Does the name Vincent Scarpizzi mean anything to you?"*

CHAPTER SIX

A military honor guard carried the flag-draped casket down the steps of the First Baptist Church of Oklahoma City, Oklahoma. Hundreds of mourners flanked the side rails as Jenny Roundtree Bradford, holding the hand of Little Joe and escorted by two soldiers in ceremonial military dress, walked slowly behind.

President Harrington held the arm of Elizabeth Llewelyn Bradford, the late attorney general's mother, who was followed by two members of the Justice Department. Walking behind Mrs. Bradford were many of Chuck Bradford's colleagues who had worked with him in the attorney general's office and in the United States Senate.

The coffin was then placed into a hearse as Jenny, Little Joe, and Mrs. Bradford entered a black Cadillac sedan directly behind it.

After all the cars were lined up, two police vehicles, lights flashing, started to move in front of the hearse, signaling the driver to follow. The cortege started to move out, heading toward Crestview Cemetery fifteen miles away, with escort vehicles in the front and rear, flanked by police motorcycles on each side of the long procession of cars.

Sitting in the right rear passenger seat, Jenny placed her arm gently around Little Joe, seated in the middle between Jenny and Mrs. Bradford. Within minutes, Little Joe fell asleep, cradled tightly against Jenny, assisted by the car's motion and steady drone of its engine.

Jenny too closed her eyes as she tried to move her thoughts away from her sadness. As she rested her head against the back of the black leather seat, a soft smile emerged as she silently reminisced how they met, fell in love, and married.

She could still see the unforgettable face of her late husband. Jenny let out a gentle sigh at seeing his image in her mind. What she saw was not the solemn flesh without life which she knew the medical examiner had viewed, but a vivid and beautiful memory of the night, too short a time ago, when she first met Chuck at the National Press Club. She knew in the moment of remarkable clarity that they were meant to be together. That their meeting was the ultimate validation of her past struggles to rise above her beginnings.

Looking back at her life with Chuck in a time frame that drifted without beginning or end, Jenny tried to draw the curtain over her grief, even if only for a brief period of time as she forced herself to think of other things that could take her away from the tragedy of her husband's death. It was Jenny's psychological circuit breaker, put in place in order to maintain her emotional stamina already at its lowest threshold of tolerance.

With great effort, Jenny moved her thoughts from Chuck and guided them toward her family, but mostly toward Joe Roundtree, whose deep love for his daughter Jenny, had helped lift her from the anguish she was suffering. As she sat in the moving car with her eyes closed, Jenny dwelled upon those events that stood out in her background—events that she had closely shared with her father.

Slowly Jenny's mind began to swirl as it recaptured her early days filled with the culture and heritage that had shaped her life…

Joe Roundtree had lived on the lands originally owned by the government, then granted over to the Pecontic tribe under a treaty signed more than one-hundred years before. His father had lived there as did his grandfather before him. It was the Pecontic Indian Reservation, and home to the Roundtree family for almost four generations.

Joe and Mary Roundtree had five children. One girl died at six months of age. Another died of pneumonia when she was one year old. Jenny was the sole surviving daughter, together with her two older brothers, Charlie and Harry. In Jenny, Joe was certain that fate had provided a destined place for her on earth.

The family was extremely poor and would often receive used children's clothing from Indian social welfare agencies. But whenever Joe could put aside any money, it would always be to buy something special for his daughter.

As Jenny began to mature, her jet-black hair, big brown eyes, and high cheek bones gave her a strikingly classic look. Her skin, showing the pigment of her heritage, was silky and smooth with a perpetual glow that was the envy of her Caucasian friends. Added to her natural beauty was an intelligence that brought her close to the genius level.

She was already reading fifth grade material in her second year of school. People who knew Jenny well would often say that she inherited her intelligence from her father whose formal education stopped when he dropped out of school in the eleventh grade; and who continued to rely more upon what he had learned in the "streets" than what he had gained from the classroom.

Although Joe Roundtree never held a steady job, he possessed the skills of a snake-oil hustler who could get almost anything accomplished for a price. He was a penny-ante wheeler-dealer, whose reputation within the Pecontic community was that of a shifty, fast-talking con-man who had neither shame nor conscience concerning his deeds. Those were his talents, or lack of them. But what Joe Roundtree did have in great abundance was an enormous pride in his daughter Jenny.

Jenny was unlike her two brothers, who resembled their father physically and in character as well. After Charlie and Harry barely squeezed through high school, Charlie worked as a helper in a gas station while Harry joined his father in whatever schemes Joe might have been involved in at the time.

"You're very special," Joe would always say to Jenny with great pride. "You're not like me or your dumb brothers. You're gonna go to college and amount to somethin' important. I'm gonna see to that."

Joe's words, "I'm gonna see to that," always remained with Jenny, whose allegiance to her father was unyielding. An inbred Native American heritage that was a strong cultural part of that tie.

When Jenny was in her last year of high school, her mother had developed a sudden high fever. Jenny was in class at the time when the principal summoned her into his office.

"Jenny, your father just called. Your mother is very sick and he wants you home right away."

"What's wrong?"

"That's all I know, Jenny. I think you'd better go home now."

When Jenny arrived at the house, she ran into the bedroom of the small wooden bungalow that was home to the Roundtree family. Her mother was burning with fever. Joe Roundtree and his son Harry were at her side.

Ten days later, Jenny's mother died of pneumonia. Although it was a heavy blow to the family, Native Americans possessed a fatalistic approach toward life and death. While dealing with her mother's passing was difficult, it was an episode in the life of a Native American that could be rationalized and accepted. And with Mary Roundtree no longer there to act as the maternal anchor, Joe's dedication to Jenny became even more extreme.

"When I finish high school, I want to stay here and take care of you and my brothers," Jenny remembered telling her father when she still had one year left to graduate. As the car continued its journey toward the cemetery, Jenny could almost hear her father's adamant response at the time, barked with a voice that left no doubt as to its authority:

"No. Absolutely no! I always said that you're special. Jenny, you're Joe Roundtree's daughter, and you'll make us all very proud one day. You're goin' to college and you're gonna amount to somethin' very important. You ain't gonna wind up like your old man or your brothers. And that's final! Ya hear what I'm sayin', Jenny?"

Jenny's S.A.T. college entrance scores placed her in the ninetieth percentile. That ranking, combined with an "A" average, should have been enough to gain her admission to almost any premier university. And when her college test scores and high school grade point average were added to her gender and her Native American heritage, Jenny received a full academic scholarship to Yale.

There, Jenny majored in political science with the thought that one day she would either seek public office or some other important position in government. Her focus and commitment to achievement remained with her throughout her four years at the Yale campus. While some of the other students found some leisure time for occasional frivolity, Jenny was always studious as she cranked out her assignments and spent every spare moment in the university library.

Four years seemed to pass quickly as Jenny's self-imposed discipline, together with her scholastic achievement, resulted in her being awarded the highest academic honors—Summa Cum Laude—for having scored a cumulative average of 3.9.

During her college years, Jenny kept close ties to her father, who was beginning to emerge as a more respected member of the Pecontic community. It was during her third year at Yale that Joe Roundtree broke the news to Jenny.

Jenny let out a soft smile as she recalled how her father had told her in a matter-of-fact way about the new direction his life was then taking. She always had a deep respect for him even with all of his short-comings. But hearing what he had to say to Jenny at the time, filled her with a very different kind of pride:

"Jenny, your pop is goin' legit after all these years. I've been asked to join the Council. Can ya believe it? Of course, it means I have to give up some of the things I've been doin' all this time. I guess ya know what I mean. Anyway, I've decided that since my own daughter will soon be graduatin' from this big ritzy college, I'm gonna put all a' my hustlin' days behind me. Yep, little girl, I'm gonna accept the Council job. Not bad, huh?"

Jenny chuckled quietly to herself as she remembered how he had stretched up to his full standing height and protruded his chin as a sign of his new accomplishment. Jenny's surprised but approving response was still fresh in her mind.

"You wanted me to be the first one in politics but I think you're beating me to it. I'm really proud of you, pop. Really proud!"

"Hey, It's just the tribal council, but I guess you could say I'm entering politics. How does that sound to you, Jenny? Pretty good, yeah?"

"Very good, *yes!* Really pop, I think it's great. 'Joe Roundtree, tribal council member.' I love the sound of it. Wow, I'm very proud of you, Pop!"

When graduation day arrived, it was "Joe Roundtree, tribal council vice chairman"—elected to that position by the other members of the tribal council. Traditionally, the one who held that title would one day become the chief of the Pecontic tribe. And one day, that role would belong to *her* father, Joe Roundtree.

But be it blessing or curse, "chief of the Pecontic tribe" was something that Jenny never dreamed could ever happen.

Long before her graduation, Jenny and her father agreed that getting a law degree would complete a resume that would be an asset toward a political career. As a Yale Native American honor graduate, combined with her high L.S.A.T. scores placing her in the ninety-fifth percentile, Jenny had a wide choice of many of the premier law schools in the country.

Although Jenny was accepted into Yale and Columbia, ranked second and fourth in the nation, she chose Syracuse Law School instead. While it did not rank in the first tier, she selected Syracuse in order to remain close to her father and her two brothers.

It was during her freshman year at Syracuse that Jenny entered into a romantic relationship with another law student. She had shared a weekend vacation with him during a school break and later found that she was pregnant. Although those close to Jenny advised her to terminate the pregnancy, she refused to have an abortion. It was a time of deep emotional trauma, made even more difficult when the romance dissolved shortly after the biological father was unsuccessful in his vigorous attempt to persuade Jenny to abort.

Jenny recalled that emotionally intense period she was now re-living in her thoughts:

"This is my baby in my womb. How dare you tell me to give it up. I shall never do it no matter what!"

Jenny remembered that her decision not to have an abortion signaled the quick exit of the biological father who she never saw or heard from again after they both graduated from law school.

Receiving moral and financial support from her father, Jenny gave birth to a boy she named "Little Joe Roundtree" in honor of her own father. He was soon called "Little Joe," the name that would remain with him always.

As she looked at Little Joe sleeping in the car, cuddled tightly next to her, Jenny felt so blessed that she was his mother. And although it was difficult for Jenny to raise Little Joe while attending law school at the same time, she still achieved an academic average that placed her in the top ten percent of her class.

One year later, Jenny received her juris doctor degree, passed the New York State bar examination with little challenge and was the first in the long history of the Pecontic tribe to become a lawyer.

Jenny's interest in politics transcended her desire to practice law, and when a vacancy developed through the death of the incumbent legislator in her district, she entered the party's primary election.

Jenny was an unknown insurgent and the only candidate to oppose the hand-picked nominee of the solidly entrenched political machine. Her opponent, who had the full support of the powerful and long-established political organization in the district, seemed unbeatable. Except for Jenny, his candidacy would have gone unchallenged. But without a significant campaign fund, it would have been impossible for Jenny to make the slightest dent in a voting district that covered such a large geographical area.

All political pundits were cruel in mocking Jenny's entry as a candidate, declaring that she had no possible chance of winning. Proof of the futility of her candidacy was in the poll results, leaving little doubt that she had no chance of coming close to her well-backed opponent.

Eight weeks before the primary, and lacking the funds necessary for even a small or respectable run, a discouraged Jenny sat in the sparsely furnished living room of their bungalow. While she was able to muster the necessary signatures on the nominating petitions sufficient to get her name on the ballot, her chances of overtaking the regular party candidate were literally zero. The few supporters Jenny had were political amateurs—members of the Pecontic tribe—joined by a naive scattering of energized but inexperienced college students looking for a special cause to rally around. In all, Jenny's well-meaning and spirited supporters were overwhelmingly outnumbered by their highly organized and solidly-financed counterparts.

Joe Roundtree was flushed with excitement as he rushed into the small room of the bungalow that served as Jenny's campaign headquarters. Sparked with enthusiasm, he pulled up a chair next to his daughter. "I know that we only have six weeks to go. But I've hired Bill Sprawn to put a first class campaign together. He'll be here in an hour. We're gonna have heavy T.V. commercials, radio, newspaper ads, and a full staff. It's gonna be terrific."

"Come on, Pop. You're dreaming."

"Maybe you're right. And maybe not. But let me tell ya somethin' Jenny, this dream is for real. Like I said before, we're gonna have a full-time staff of professionals—at least thirty of 'em. Not only that, but on primary day we're gonna have three hundred paid workers manning every election district just to make sure that the people come out and vote for Jenny Roundtree. Bill Strawn will be here soon. He'll explain the whole plan to ya.' "

Jenny had learned that a primary election was totally unlike the general election held in November. The organization candidates had always been the winners in a primary, since those who voted were usually the hard core members of the party. Most received paid jobs through a patronage system that perpetuated the political power of the regulars. But the turn-out for a primary election would be generally less than ten percent of an overall apathetic electorate— exactly what would continue to keep an entrenched political organization in power. And with the average citizen having neither interest nor incentive to vote in a primary, even that small percentage was sufficient, historically, to guarantee victory for those in control.

"Jenny, we're gonna have an army out there, and we're gonna win. I'm tellin' ya that." Joe's statement had a confident resonance.

"And what are we going to use for money? Tribal beads? Or maybe you just won the lottery."

"Well, maybe I just did."

"I know you didn't, so stop playing this game with me . I'm depressed enough as it is."

"Number one, you're right . I didn't win the lottery. Number two, I'm not playin' a game with ya.' And number three, everything I told ya is for real."

"Is that so? Well maybe you just don't know it, but what you're talking about will cost hundreds of thousands of dollars. Did you hear what I just said? Hundreds of thousands. Get with it, Pop."

"You just let me handle everything. I can do it. I'm tellin' ya Jenny, just leave it to me. Joe Roundtree will never let his daughter down. You hear what I'm sayin', daughter?"

As the cortege made its way slowly to Crestview Cemetery, Jenny focused her thoughts upon herself, remembering how she stood on the landing of the executive mansion in the state capitol, placing her left hand upon the Bible while raising her right. She recalled how proudly she felt as she looked into the eyes of Niles B. Martin, the governor of New York who administered the oath of office:

I, Jenny Roundtree do solemnly swear that I shall uphold the Constitution of the United States of America and that I shall faithfully discharge the duties as member of the House of Representatives of the Congress of the United States of America to the best of my ability so help me God.

Having taken the oath, Jenny Roundtree, a member of the Pecontic tribe and the daughter of Mary and Joe Roundtree, became the first Native American Indian Congresswoman in the nation's history.

Soon, Jenny would be in the nation's capital, where by serendipity she would meet, fall in love, and marry Charles Llewelyn Bradford, the favorite son of The Sooner State—Oklahoma.

How could I ever forget how Chuck and I met? Jenny reminisced tearfully as the cortege continued. She wiped her eyes gently as she began to re-live a most special evening in Washington that would remain in her memory for the rest of her life:

It was at one of the major annual events sponsored by the National Press Club where Congresswoman Jenny Roundtree first met Charles Llewelyn Bradford, the attorney general of the United States.

The dinner dance that was held traditionally in the regal grand ballroom of the Dorian Essex Hotel in downtown Washington had always been an event that for one evening at least, evaporated many of the partisan differences wedged between members of the House and Senate. It ranked as a special occasion: important to be seen, to meet other office holders, members of the cabinet, judges of the District, Circuit and even the Supreme Court of the United States. Historically, the two honored guests were the president and the first lady of the land.

On the huge stage was the cream of the music industry's society orchestras—Scott Forrest.

The Forrest sound was unmistakably reminiscent of the World War II era. It was a big band: five saxophones, three trumpets, three trombones, a string bass, piano, guitar, xylophone, drums with a half dozen cymbals, a separate set of timbales, a conga drum, and the extra feature of four singers billed as "The Skylighters." Fronting the large ensemble and playing the clarinet with an artistry that was a cross between the revered jazz artists, Benny Goodman and Artie Shaw, was the incomparable Scott Forrest himself.

The sounds that filled the ballroom were nostalgically lyrical as the music flowed in the palatial room known for its finely engineered acoustical balance amidst its famous high-vaulted ceiling, old world charm, and exquisite surroundings.

To those in the grand ballroom, what emerged from the stage were musical standards that drew the guests to dance to the great songs and sounds of an earlier time. It was a journey through a musical capsule that was magical in its sentimentality and nostalgic in its reminiscence.

Almost all guests were on the Washington "A" list—the nucleus and protoplasm of political power. Included within the elite of congressional persuaders, was anyone with a reputation of influence within the national scene, including the entire Washington press corps and television network moguls.

Although Jenny was not in the same power league with the others in that ballroom, she was the first and only female Native American woman who had ever been elected to Congress. That alone would have been sufficient to have justified her invitation to this specially selected group. But in addition to her unique background, were her physical features that were an amalgam of rare beauty. With strikingly dark eyes, long, shiny black hair, a sensuous and curvaceous figure—and dressed in a tight, black, strapless, sequined long gown—Jenny Roundtree presented the classical look of a Native American Aphrodite.

The Scott Forrest Orchestra was playing the old standard, "I'll Be Seeing You," when Jenny, seated at a dinner table with other guests, was tapped gently on her shoulder from behind. As she looked up, she saw a tall handsome man dressed in a finely- tailored, double-breasted tuxedo.

"I do not believe that we have been formally introduced, Congresswoman Roundtree. I'm Chuck Bradford."

Jenny rose from her chair as she extended her hand, responding with a coy smile. "We have never met but I do know of you by reputation."

"Well in that case I certainly hope I passed the test," Bradford replied, continuing to hold Jenny's extended hand.

"We will just have to see about that."

"Are you a fair grader?"

"Being fair, is one of my greatest attributes." Jenny knew it was a silly answer but somehow it was easy to respond that way.

"Alright then, please lay aside what you might have seen on CNN or 'Meet the Press,' and grade me *solely* from this point on. Deal?"

The light and frivolous banter seemed to flow effortlessly as the music from the orchestra joined the steady din of noise from the large crowd in the ballroom securing the privacy of their relaxed exchange. Jenny and Chuck were fully aware how juvenile their introductory conversation sounded but it didn't seem to matter. It was a mutual glow they shared and felt at the same time.

"But enough of me. I have observed you and in the process I do know something about *your* career. So can I grade *you* as well, Congresswoman Roundtree?"

"Only upon condition that you call me Jenny." Its sheer innocence overpowered Bradford.

"And you must call me 'Chuck.' "

"Okay then… now that we've been formally introduced, by each other that is, I do have a serious question to ask." Chuck paused. Jenny waited expectantly. "May I have this dance?"

"A serious question, calls for a serious response." Placing her right index finger to her chin she looked up with a bashful innocence, as if pondering the question. A smile gently formed at the corners of her mouth. She felt silly. School-girlish. She answered, "Yes."

Scott Forrest was at the end of the immortal, "As Time Goes By," when Jenny and Chuck walked onto the dance floor. They waited for the next song, each wishing silently that it would be a slow and familiar ballad, one that would continue the mellow mood that was beginning to envelope them. The orchestra started to play, "You'll Never Know," another memorable song of World War II. The male vocalist, backed by "The Skylighters," even sounded much like the popular Dick Haymes who had immortalized it sixty years earlier. When it was over, Jenny and Chuck remained on the dance floor as Scott Forrest announced, "And now one of the all-time greats, Glenn Miller's 'Moonlight Serenade.' "

The unmistakable Miller sound that featured Scott's clarinet as he led the five sax men who stood up on the stage with a full brass section standing behind them, brought older listeners to very personal memories of the New York Paramount Theater and the big bands it featured daily.

But in the grand ballroom of the Dorian Essex Hotel, with its lights dimmed and a large revolving circular crystal ball attached to the ceiling, throwing off tiny specs of reflected light like thousands of soft snowflakes, two people, almost unaware of the others around them, were holding each other closely, dancing to the intoxicating sounds of the Glenn Miller classic, "Moonlight Serenade."

Something very special was happening and would continue to happen for the months ahead, except for one significant factor: Charles Llewelyn Bradford was already engaged to Grace Tyler Alexander, an Oklahoma City socialite.

Reflecting on the name "Grace Tyler Alexander" brought Jenny back to her early memories of Chuck's mother, Elizabeth Llewelyn Bradford, and of Mrs. Bradford's immediate reaction when Chuck first told his mother about her. Jenny had remembered Chuck's vivid description he had given of the encounter soon after they were married, and how angry and hurt they both felt at the time...

It was on a Saturday morning at Bradford Manor. Chuck had arrived the night before having planned to return to Washington early on Monday. Elizabeth and Chuck had just finished breakfast served in the large dining area next to the kitchen. A middle-aged domestic assistant, who had been with the family for seventeen years had cleared the dishes and had poured a second cup of coffee, when Elizabeth Bradford spoke.

"What time did you arrive last night, Charles? I did not hear you come in." Mrs. Bradford never called her son "Chuck," as she thought that it was undignified to address him other than by his baptismal name, "Charles."

"Actually Mother, my plane was delayed leaving Reagan Washington National. At first it was announced as a thirty minute delay but they kept on announcing the departure time forward. In fact, we didn't take off until almost an hour and a half after schedule. Some minor repair or something of the sort. In any event, by the time I arrived here at Bradford Manor, it was well after nine-thirty and I did not want to disturb you at such an hour."

"Nonsense, Charles. I was up. In fact I was reading, and then fell asleep. But it is good to have you here whether you awakened me or not."

"And I confess mother, its good to be here."

"But why must you always rely on commercial airlines? They seem to be so undependable lately."

"Most of the time they're just fine."

"But why do you not use a government plane? I'm certain that as the attorney general of the United States you have any number of military planes at your disposal. And I'm sure that you can use them at any time. Isn't that right, Charles?"

"Of course I can do that, Mother, but I prefer not to."

"Why not, Charles? Aren't they there to be used by you when you require it?"

"Yes. Government transportation is always available to me for whatever use I wish to put it to. You could call it one of the perks of the job. But quite frankly, the last thing I need is to have some overly ambitious reporter making it appear as if by using a military plane for personal use I was guilty of a major scandal...like I just raided Fort Knox or the United States Treasury or something like that. Besides, I am far more comfortable doing it this way and I really don't mind it that much at all."

"As you wish. I just thought that it would be more direct and easier for you when you visit Bradford Manor... your home. Remember? And speaking of home... how long will you be staying this time, Charles?"

"Since I have to be back in Washington Monday afternoon, I will be leaving here that morning."

"Why so soon, Charles? In the past few months I have noticed that your visits have become shorter and shorter. It seems that the only way I can spend time with you is if *I* visit Washington instead of *you* coming here to Bradford Manor."

"That would be just fine with me, Mother. You know that you're always welcome," Chuck said, with a slight wink of his eye.

"Oh, I know that. But frankly, if I drew up a list of places I would rather not visit, Washington would be very close to the top. I suppose that is what makes me a 'Llewelyn' and you a 'Bradford.' As you know, I never had much of an affinity for politics, and that includes the kind that takes place in Washington. But obviously you are unlike me when it comes to such matters. There, you and I are clearly different, Charles. I would say that you have inherited your political genes from the 'Bradford' side of the family. But enough of politics and Darwin. Let me go to a more pleasant subject. When will you be seeing Grace?"

"This evening. I have arranged for an early dinner, then, the Philharmonic. I would have asked you to join us but I know that your passions would rather lie with a good book, not with a some contemporary Russian composer."

"You are right again. But as they say, I do thank you for *not* inviting me. You know that I do not particularly enjoy dinners out, and I am certainly no enthusiast of unfamiliar music. Beethoven, Mozart, even Shostakovitch is acceptable, but please spare me an evening with a musical ingenue, and a foreign one at that."

"My dear Mrs. Bradford, you are something else. Delicious and frank to the core as always," Chuck responded, his smile, easy.

"That obviously comes from the Llewelyn side."

"Wherever its roots, I wouldn't trade it for all the oil in the fields."

"Thank you for that, Charles. That was indeed very complimentary. You have redeemed yourself fully and are now free to run off with your Grace Alexander."

"Since you have mentioned Grace, there is something I wish to discuss with you, Mother."

Chuck switched to a serious tone.

"Perhaps we should go into the study."

The frivolous mood nursed by light banter between mother and son, suddenly took on a foreboding contrast.

Mrs. Bradford and Chuck rose from the breakfast table, walking into a large room twenty feet down the hall. At one time it had been the living room of the Manor. Expansion and change thirty years earlier had made it into a study.

Mrs. Bradford sat in the chair usually reserved for her. It was large and plushy, upholstered in a brown batik fabric with a matching ottoman, host to a tasseled square pillow used as the chair's back support. Chuck sat in a smaller chair next to a round, burgundy leather-topped table, home to a large, authentic, 19th century Tiffany lamp.

Its two walls were filled with rows of book shelves; Dickens, Shakespeare, Voltaire, and biographies of Jefferson and Lincoln stood alongside titles of fiction and non-fiction. A number of the hundreds of volumes were first editions.

A large marble fireplace with its imposing ornate sconces on either side of the tall mantle, provided character, beauty and warmth.

Oval- and square-shaped framed photographs of many generations of "Llewelyns" and "Bradfords" were displayed prominently on one large wall. They were each positioned symmetrically, sending a message of continuity, generational history and family nostalgia while exuding a museum-like aura of timelessness and antiquity.

Mrs. Bradford showed subtle signs of anxiety as Chuck began to speak.

"Mother, I know that this will come as a shock to you, but it must be said, and I must say it now."

Not wishing to add further to the concern now becoming apparent on his mother's face, Chuck continued. "I cannot marry Grace, Mother. I have fallen deeply in love with someone else."

"What are you saying, Charles? I do not believe what I am hearing," she responded rapidly.

"Mother, its true. I just didn't know how to tell you."

"This is a joke. Am I right, Charles?"

"No, Mother. You are unquestionably wrong. This is no joke!"

"Alright then, if you are serious, when did all this happen? And who is she?" Her tone became accusatory.

"I met her six months ago. Her name is Jenny Roundtree, and she is a congresswoman from New York."

"There you go again with politics! Well, I do not care if she is the Duchess of Windsor. Charles, you are engaged to Grace Tyler Alexander. The wedding date has already been set. Everyone has been notified of your coming marriage. Are you aware of that?"

"Yes, Mother, I am. Very aware of it indeed!"

"So how could you do this?" she asked indignantly.

"Mother, I did not look for it. It just happened. The plain fact is that I feel something for Jenny I never felt for Grace. Yes, Grace is a fine and lovely person, but I have come to the full realization that I cannot spend the rest of my life with her. I never really knew the true meaning of love until I met Jenny. She opened up a world for me I never dreamed existed. I could never have the feelings for Grace that I have for Jenny." Chuck spoke openly, as if he were at a confessional.

"You must be insane. You are a betrothed man. You have made a promise to marry Grace. Do you understand that?"

"Yes I do, Mother. Sadly, I do."

"In that case how in good conscience can you withdraw from that promise? Can you answer *that* for me? You must *really* be insane!"

"First, I am not insane. I have never been more sound in my entire life. And second, I would rather withdraw from a promise, as difficult as it is for me to do—and Lord knows it is—than to spend my life regretting a decision I should have made but failed to. What you do not understand, Mother, is that I could never marry Grace knowing that I let someone like Jenny walk out of my life."

"Who is this girl? What hold does she have on you to have robbed you of your senses?" Her voice was pitched with anger.

"She is a congresswoman. Just as I said. She also happens to be a Native American."

"An Indian? That is what she is? Am I hearing you correctly?"

"I just said it!"

"And I heard what you said. An Indian? Is that what you are telling me?"

"I am telling you that she is a Native American. You make it sound so damned ugly. I am telling you that she is a Native American," Chuck repeated adamantly .

"Call her by any name you choose. It still translates 'Indian' to me, and will to everyone else."

"My god, I feel like I'm talking to a complete stranger. It's as if I don't even know you."

"You just refuse to face the truth!"

"I will not listen to this. I cannot believe what I am hearing."

"What you are hearing *is* the truth, and something called *reality*. How could you, a Bradford, have fallen in love with someone not of our station?"

Chuck was offended by his mother's elitist question. He bellowed in a raised and uncommon voice, "How do you know what her station is? You know nothing about her. You never even met her. And you have no basis for what you just said. None whatsoever."

"I do not have to meet her to know that she is what she is. Period. These are people who are our servants, and now you expect me to rejoice with the expectation that I will have an Indian as my daughter-in-law?"

"I am absolutely flabbergasted. You sound just like the bigots I've been fighting all my life." Chuck felt shame at his mother's bias.

"No, Charles, I am not a bigot, but a realist. The Bradfords have always been at a different level than the others. Can't you understand that?"

"No, I cannot. But suddenly what I do understand is that my own mother—yes, my own mother—shows a prejudice that I never knew existed. I am in complete and total shock."

"Now Charles, please do not turn it around by putting me on the defensive in an attempt to make *me* the offender. It is *you* who have shocked *me* and not the other way around. Above all, let's be honest with each other. Your lady-friend, whatever her name, is what she is. No more, no less. I just wonder whether this is a temporary aberration or perhaps a bad dream I'm having," she said, attempting to brush her son aside.

"Please, Mother, this is difficult enough for me. Please don't make it worse."

"Think about it slowly, Charles. Do not act out of impulse. Give it time."

"I've given it all the time it requires. I have thought about it over and over again until there is nothing left to think about. My mind is made up, Mother. And I want to be as frank as I can… so here it is. I'll put it all in front of you…I do not love Grace. I cannot see spending the rest of my life with her. I love Jenny and I will marry her. And *that's that*." Chuck's tone was ringed with determination.

The room became silent.

Mrs. Bradford was next to speak. "When will you tell Grace?"

"Tonight after dinner, and it will not be easy for me. I obviously feel some guilt but I cannot delay it any longer."

There was momentary quiet. Mrs. Bradford spoke again.

"Charles, stop and think. Are you absolutely certain that this is what you want for your future?" This time her tone was gentler.

"I have never been more certain of anything in my life."

Mrs. Bradford sat in her chair, struggling to restrain the impulse to deliver a stern ultimatum to her son. Although devastated by the news delivered by him, she decided not to risk inflicting irreparable harm upon their relationship by throwing out a challenge that could not later be withdrawn even after tempers would have cooled down. She was also wise enough to know that nothing could be gained by such a risky confrontation. That much could be lost. A true patrician, Elizabeth Llewelyn Bradford also possessed the practicality and insight to accept what she had to, as painful as it was.

"Well, so be it," she said in a flat and expressionless tone. As she rose from her chair and stepped toward the door, she continued dryly, "We will just have to deal with it. We will just have to deal with it," she repeated.

"Mother...there is one more thing you should know." Chuck rang out.

"And what could possibly be added to what you have already said?" She continued her stiff stride toward the door, not looking back at Chuck.

"Jenny has a six-year-old son," Chuck fired.

Mrs. Bradford stopped abruptly in her tracks, spun around quickly and stared frozenly at him."What did you say? Did I hear you correctly?"Her voice was smoking with hostility.

Standing up and facing his mother squarely, Chuck repeated in a deliberate tone, "What I said, Mother, is that *Jenny has a six-year-old son.*"

"I cannot believe this," Mrs. Bradford said as she shook her head from side to side. Her feet remained grounded, as if she were anchored to the floor. "I cannot believe what I just heard."

"Believe it, Mother," Chuck said defiantly. *"And I plan to adopt him as my son!"*

...The funeral Cortege continued through the entrance gates of Crestview Cemetery as Jenny was brought back to the present... to her grief...to the ache in her heart...and to the promise she had made to help Matt Connors find the killer or killers who took her husband's life.

CHAPTER SEVEN

The sign on the front of the two-story, red brick building in College Point, New York, read *Arista Construction Company.*

To ordinary passers-by, the time-weathered structure blended unremarkably with the other two- and three-story, sixty-year-old facades that lined many of the streets in this unattractive, commercial part of Queens County, located within the shadows of La Guardia Airport. But those select few who were involved with the real business of the Arista Construction Company knew that it was a "front" for the head of New York's DiPienza crime family...And Vincent Scarpizzi, who reigned as its king, was no ordinary man. Cunning, ruthless, scarred by mob wars, and hardened with street smarts, he was feared by his enemies, admired by his detractors, and fawned over by his tight-knit circle of loyal subjects.

Harold "Heshy" Gordon, a Long Island city lawyer, was one of those closest to Scarpizzi, having proven his fealty to one of the country's most powerful and corrupt crime bosses. Gordon was a chunky, fifty-two-year-old of medium height, with a round "five o'clock shadow" face, dark eyes, and black, curly hair with streaks of gray at the side burns and above his ears.

He had graduated from Brooklyn Law School twenty-six years earlier.

Scarpizzi recalled the details of the first meeting he had with Gordon many years before:

"I appreciate ya comin' to see me, counselor," Scarpizzi said at the time as he was seated behind his desk at the Arista Construction Company. Although Vincent Scarpizzi had a home improvement business on the surface, it served as a questionable calling card for the many illicit enterprises he was in. "Sit down, Mr. Gordon. Can I get ya somethin'?" Scarpizzi asked graciously.

"No thanks, Mr. Scarpizzi, I'm fine."

"I really do appreciate ya comin' down. Can I call ya 'Harold'?"

"Nah," Gordon said, jocularly. "But you can call me 'Heshy.' " When I was a young boy, my mother would call me home for supper. I'd be playing Ring-a-Leevio, Johnny-on-the-Pony or some other kid game in those days, and she would always yell, 'Heshy, come on in. Your supper's getting cold.' The name kind of stuck with all the guys in the neighborhood, so it's been 'Heshy' ever since," Gordon said, throwing off a half crescent smile.

"Sounds good to me. Heshy. It has a nice ring to it. You can call me Vincent. Okay?" He paused, then continued. "First, I been askin' around and I like what I hear about ya.'"

Scarpizzi paused again, drawing up closer to Gordon.

"I'll tell ya why I called. Two weeks ago, I went to get a paper. I do that sometimes. So I get in my car and I drive six blocks to a 7-Eleven to get it. I'm just a block away from the store when some cop pulls me over. He says I ran a red light. I tell him it changed on me in the middle, but he ain't hearin' nothin' I'm sayin.' Then the big goon says, 'Pop the trunk.' I say, 'Hey, what for?' This big jerk says, 'Just do it.' I say, 'No way. You stopped me for a light; you give me a fuckin' ticket. You ain't gettin' near my trunk without a warrant. Before I know it, this gorilla throws me up against my car and tells me not to fuckin' move. Well I see another police car comin' down just a half-block away so I ain't goin' nowhere. The car's there in a minute. Next thing I know, the second *buvan* is holdin' me while the first guy pops my trunk. He comes out with a bag. He says it's coke. They throw the cuffs on me and haul my ass off to the station house. I'm tossed in the tank with some loud-mouth drunks and then I'm taken downtown in front of some judge. They let me make a call to my lawyer when I'm at the precinct, so when I get to the court, my lawyer, he's already there. I plead 'not guilty' to drug possession and this jackass of a judge puts a hundred grand bail on me. I gotta go back to court next week. Can you believe that shit?"

"You have a lawyer. So what's the problem, Vincent?" Gordon asked.

"No problem, Heshy, except my lawyer's a big *putz*. He never shoulda' let it go this far. I'm now facin' a goddam felony rap for no reason. Is this guy for real, or what?"

"Who's the judge?"

"Some guy named Moran."

There was a pause.

"So what's the plan, counselor?"

"The first thing you do is get rid of your lawyer."

"That's the easy part." Scarpizzi was waiting to hear Gordon's plan to get him out of his mess.

"The second thing…I make a motion to the judge to suppress the coke."

"I know what that means but lay it on me like I'm a five-year-old."

" I convince Judge Moran that without a warrant the cops had no legal right to search your trunk. You see, Vincent, a traffic infraction alone is not sufficient probable cause for them to search the car. It was an illegal search in the first place. That being the case, any contraband, like the coke that was seized through an illegal search, cannot be used in court as evidence. And without it, which the D.A. must have in order to establish possession, the charges against you have to be tossed. And you walk out the front door. That simple."

"Yeah, but it seems like we're gonna need some special juice to make sure that this Judge Moran does the right thing by me. *You read me, counselor?"* Scarpizzi asked, casting a sly wink.

"Vincent, you just leave the details to me. I'll handle it. I promise you, this whole thing will soon be history. And you can make book on it!"

And just as Gordon had predicted, it *was* history. Scarpizzi never knew how Gordon was able to get all charges dismissed, nor did he have to ask. But what he did quickly find out, was that his lawyer had shown the smarts in reaching the right people to get things done. And to Vincent Scarpizzi, that was the only end game that counted.

Following the successful result, Scarpizzi and Gordon grew closer as Scarpizzi's activities skirted the legal boundaries, sometimes going beyond, but always calling upon Harold "Heshy" Gordon, Esquire, to maneuver him through the justice system, unscathed. Over time a tight bond developed between the two as Gordon continued to prove his loyalty and value to Scarpizzi. In turn, Scarpizzi called upon him repeatedly for advice and direction in walking the sometimes grey line between lawful and criminal conduct.

Harold "Heshy" Gordon had served Scarpizzi well all those years. It was now time to call upon his loyal counselor once again.

When Gordon entered the back office of Arista, he wore an anxious expression on his face as he greeted Scarpizzi, who was expecting his arrival. Instinctively, Scarpizzi raised the volume of his CD player as Luciano Pavarotti's rich tenor voice was emoting lyrically over his tortured love of Mimi in Puccini's immortal *La Boheme*.

"What's up, Heshy?" Scarpizzi asked, as he led Gordon to a back wall of his office that had been screened for bugging devices before his lawyer arrived.

"Vincent," Gordon began in a whisper, "I don't like it. My source tells me that a special agent in the justice department has been appointed to investigate Bradford's death."

"Are you sure about that?"

"That's what I'm told."

"Is he reliable?"

"Yeah."

"Shit, " Scarpizzi fumed. "The last thing we need is to have a bunch a' goddamned feds crawling all over the joint." He hesitated, then picked up again. "Who's pushing this fuckin' thing?"

"It's the president himself. From what I hear, Bradford was a very close friend of his. Vincent, this time I'm concerned," Gordon confessed.

"Everythin' was goin so friggin' good until those goons screwed up. Ya' know who I'm talkin' about. So tell me Hesh, how is this shit now gonna play with the Indian casinos we're tryin' ta put together? And who is this fed guy they got on it anyway?"

"An agent named Connors... Matt Connors. He's been with the department for a lotta years. In fact my guy tells me he was pretty tight with Bradford also."

"Okay, but what about the casino deal? Are we in any trouble there?"

"I don't think so, Vincent. We just have to see how this Connors guy plays out."

"Damn it. He pokes his big fed nose into this business and maybe he'll be able to sniff out a lotta stuff that's goin' down. I don't like it no way. Ya' know what I mean? I'm tellin' ya Hesh, I don't like it no way," he repeated.

Scarpizzi was visibly upset. The only sound in the room was Pavarotti's lyrical tenor voice.

Suddenly struck with an idea, Scarpizzi picked up the lead again. His mood began to take on a bright face.

"Heshy, where's the guy's funeral bein' held?" Scarpizzi asked slowly, squinting his eyes as he spoke . By the sly tone of his question, Gordon sensed that Scarpizzi was hatching some kind of a plan.

"He's being buried in Oklahoma City. The funeral's today. Why do you ask?"

"Uh uh. Yeah...Yeah... That's good. Where's his house?" Scarpizzi seemed to continue in deep thought.

"Outside DC. Georgetown."

"Ya' know exactly where?"

"No, but it shouldn't be hard to find out. Where are we going with this, Vincent?"

Gordon's forehead creased as he tried to read Scarpizzi's thoughts. He listened intently while Scarpizzi demonstrated the typical quickness of the crime boss's mind, spelling out his plan to meet the new challenge now facing him.

Gordon watched Scarpizzi take out his cell phone from the inside pocket of his jacket. He saw his client punch in some numbers and give instructions to someone at the other end.

Three hours later, two loyal soldiers of the DiPienza crime family disconnected a burglar alarm and broke into the empty Bradford house in Georgetown. Their specific orders were simple and precisely followed: ransack and remove all legal documents, notes, audio tapes, records, and anything suspicious in Bradford's study.

The men assigned to the job were experienced pros who knew how to remove evidence and mess-up the house in such a way that overworked police would write up the break-in as a job pulled off by nervous amateurs.

As instructed, Bradford's study was carefully ripped apart. Hundreds of documents were removed. Although most had no relationship to the casino investigation, enough did.

After the delicate mission was completed, a phone call was made. "Vincent, the sheet rock order was delivered on time. The truck didn't break down."

Following the call, Scarpizzi's lawyer learned through a police contact that a burglary of the Bradford residence had been reported.

After he heard the results of his plan, Scarpizzi reached for a Cohiba cigar from the humidor on top of his desk. A slow smile accompanied his meticulous lighting of a 7" Havana as he sat back comfortably in his black leather chair, swivelled it in a 180 degree arc, and with quiet satisfaction, watched as rings of smoke billowed in circles above him.

Scarpizzi's plan had been justified when Gordon examined the stolen documents after they were delivered to him. He had assured the crime boss that they were dynamite. If the new investigator had gotten his hands on them it would have spelled trouble with a capital "T."

The outcome of the episode put the boss of the New York crime family in a happy mood. Once again his instincts had served him well by having removed any evidence that could possibly link him with Indian casino gambling.

With his accomplishment behind him, he began to ruminate his past triumphs. As the products of his intuitive grasp of human nature and its frailties, Scarpizzi had the uncanny ability to anticipate the most serious of problems, to act quickly even with arrows flying around him, and to come out without so much as a scratch. Such remarkable talent underpinned many of his successes. And reviewing his successes over the past forty years was a journey fueled by an ego unequaled by his peers...

Born and raised in the Red Hook section of Brooklyn, he was, sixty-two years later, the undeniable head of the DiPienza crime family. Although suspected of no less than fourteen mob murders during his rise in the family from a low level hitman to ultimately, its leader, a few minor cop-outs to misdemeanors were his only convictions. He never served any prison time, and his minor record was worn as a badge of honor of his having survived all mob struggles, and achieving power through his ruthless yet cunning ability to remove all opposition to his life's goal—to one day become boss of the DiPienza crime family!

It all started when Vincent Scarpizzi was growing up. Even while in grade school, he was a constant truant with no expectation of any long-term academic future. Although he was left back in his grade twice, it was not as a result of an inferior intellect. His I.Q. was above normal. Failing resulted from his total lack of interest in school as he used every opportunity to "cut class" and hang out with the other drop-out kids who had been involved with shoplifting, petty thievery, drinking beer, and smoking pot.

Although illiterate, his parents were hard-working immigrants, having come to the United States from a region of southern Italy. They had long given up on their uncontrollable son and consistently prayed that the Virgin Mary would one day salvage him from a life of crime and the disaster that would inevitably follow.

It was early one evening when a truant officer, whose job was to visit the parents of kids who had unexplained absences from school, rang the bell at the Scarpizzi third floor walk-up apartment in Red Hook, Brooklyn. After identifying himself, he was invited into the small kitchen of the spartan Scarpizzi apartment.

"Sit down please," Angelina Scarpizzi, Vincent's mother, said, as she pointed to a yellow wooden chair. There were five similar ones surrounding a rectangular table covered with an inexpensive oil cloth-type fabric. Showing signs of wear, it had red and blue daisies in a background of pastel yellow, obvious crack lines and a faded discoloration. Two small plastic bowls filled with wax fruit stood in the center of the table.

Seated was Vincent's father, Anthony Scarpizzi. Angelina sat in the chair next to her husband.

Truant Officer O'Malley began the conversation.

"I've tried to reach someone during the day, but I got no answer."

"We go to work," Anthony Scarpizzi answered. "So, what's the problem?"

"I'll get right to it. Your son Vincent hasn't come to school in a month. That's a violation of law. He's only fourteen and if you don't get him back right away, he's gonna be in big, big trouble. You understand what I'm saying?" O'Malley warned.

"I ask him all the time, and he tells me. He goes to school he says. How do I know if he ain't goin'? I don't know. I'm workin' all day."

"Well, where is he now? I wanna talk to him."

"He ain't here, mister. He went out. I don't know where he is. I don't know where he goes. He hangs out with a bunch a' guys. They're no good. They always get him in trouble."

"Mr. and Mrs. Scarpizzi, if your son doesn't report back to school in two days, he's gonna be transferred to another school. Let me tell you what it's like. It's a school that deals only with bad kids. You get what I mean? Look here, this is serious stuff I'm talking about."

"Yeah, mister. I know what ya mean. I try talkin' ta him but he just don't listen. I don't know what ta do widdim no more."

Finally transferred to a special school for incorrigible children where by law he would have to remain until he reached sixteen, Vincent broke loose when he was only fifteen years old. By that time, even the Board of Education had given up on him. And after the first few routine attempts to bring him back into the system were unsuccessful, he fell through the bureaucratic cracks and became a full product of the streets.

It did not take long for the low-level soldiers of the DiPienza crime family—the mob that controlled the rackets in New York City—to realize that young Vinny was a solid, street-wise prospect who they could enlist and mold for their illegal purposes.

At sixteen, Vincent was already involved in organized crime, working as a runner for the mob's book-makers. He was soon promoted to fencing goods stolen from the loading docks, graduating into the role of "enforcer." In this new job description, his capo bosses quickly became impressed with his "no mercy" approach to breaking the legs of defaulting losers who had the misfortune of borrowing money from the "family's" loan sharks at a five-for-three payback.

The vigorous, or "vig" as it was known in street parlance, was so high that every dollar paid would go only toward interest, with little or nothing remaining to reduce the principal sum of the loan. The shattering of bones with a baseball bat was usually the first and only warning shot to the borrower, leaving him with the clear message : "If you don't pay what ya owe within the agreed time, the next greetin' will be with a silencer pressed hard against the back a' ya head, followed by a twenty-two caliber shell that will splatter your friggin' brain. *Capiche?*"

Through brute muscle, young Vincent soon became an expert in the art of re-arranging the loser's anatomy—another step bringing him closer to his ultimate career goal.

Vincent's assignments went beyond mere loan enforcement: In the
1960s, his capo boss Louie "Frenchy" Franchizzi was the mob delegate
assigned to shake down a number of small manufacturers in the
garment center of Manhattan. Most "clients" paid the demanded
"protection fees" to avoid having their plants torched, since they were
usually poor risks and unable to buy a fire insurance policy. As a result,
the burning of a plant would be tantamount to a financial wipe-out.

There were those few however who refused to be blackmailed into
paying big extortion money to the low-lifes who threatened them.
Murray Goldstein, the president of Goldie Togs—a ladies coat
manufacturer in Manhattan—was one of those 'refusenicks.' Scarpizzi
remembered his first introduction to Goldstein. He would chuckle
every time he reflected upon his meeting with the hood who called
upon Scarpizzi's services...

"Hey, Vinny," Louie Francizzi called out as he summoned him to
his table tucked in a corner of the Red Hook Social Club, a private
meeting place for local wiseguys. "Come over here. I wanna talk ta
ya.'"

"Sure, Mr. Francizzi."

" Sit down, my young friend. So, how ya doin'?"

"I'm doin' okay, I guess. Could use a little more work though."

"Good. Glad ta hear it. Like to make some extra bread?"

"Sure. Whatcha got?"

I got a little job for ya," Francizzi said, taking a swallow of his
dark, bitter tasting espresso.

"Great, Mr. Francizzi. Whadiya want me ta do?"

"Listen, there's this guy, Murray Goldstein. He runs a factory in
the city. *Goldie Togs*. This son-of-a-bitch is givin' me a hard time. We
can't collect shit from the guy. Frankly, Vinny, I think it's time to
teach this prick a lesson in good manners. Know what I mean, my
boy?" Francizzi spoke through a nervous twitch.

"I got it real good." He printed the name "Mory Goldsten" on a
paper napkin.

"Now look,Vinny. All I want ya ta do is convince him nice like.
No more fa' now. You understand what I'm sayin'? Eh?"

"I got it covered. This guy ain't no problem after we have a friendly talk," he reassured Francizzi with a wave of his hand, thumb up.

Fearful that his factory on the eighth floor of the 39th Street loft building might be a target for mob arson, Goldstein installed large metal gates across the entrance. He even had a twenty-four-hour guard posted inside—a rarity in those days.

The idea was a good one. It worked for a while. But what Goldstein was not prepared for was someone like Vinny Scarpizzi who had his own special way of taking care of those who refused to meet the mob's "protection" demands.

Surveying the area, young Scarpizzi noticed that the supply of coats manufactured in Goldstein's plant during the week were usually placed on a large rack, sent down the freight elevator from the eighth floor to the street level and wheeled across the sidewalk onto a truck for delivery to a warehouse in Astoria, Queens.

On a Friday, Scarpizzi, with Tony Dee, an apprentice hood, waited in a parked car. A rack loaded with over one hundred coats was wheeled from the freight elevator side of the building, outside, and onto the street. Scarpizzi got out of his car quickly. He had a two-gallon can of gasoline in his hand. Within seconds, the shipping clerk pushing the cart was clubbed with a small bat, knocked violently to the ground. In an instant, Scarpizzi poured the flammable fluid over the coats, lit a match, and gloated all the way to the waiting car that zoomed off. Looking into the rear view mirror, he could see the ball of fire, black smoke billowing up toward the sky.

Several days later, Scarpizzi confronted Goldstein, who was standing in front of his loft.

"Hey, Murray baby, how ya doin'?" Scarpizzi asked, as Goldstein tried to quickly walk away.

"Wait up, Murray," Scarpizzi called out, catching up with him. "I wanna' ask ya a question. How did ya like the Goldie torch?" he asked breaking out into a shrill and revolting laugh.

The once macho, but now terrified Murray Goldstein was fully aware that he himself would be the next incendiary target—not the coats—if he failed to pay his full dues to the "family."

It came as no surprise to Louie Francizzi that through Vincent's good work, Murray Goldstein became a "client" in good standing, knowing that extortion money paid to the mob was far less costly than losing his plant, his business, and…his life!

Scarpizzi's role as enforcer grew after assigned to "persuade" a supplier at the Fulton Fish Market in lower Manhattan to buy a membership in the mob's extortion club.

At 4:00 a.m. one morning, Scarpizzi watched in the shadows as a truck load of fresh flounder was delivered to Alfie's Wholesale Fish Market. Alfie's helpers unpacked the cartons, laying out the fish neatly out on beds of ice to be later selected by restaurant and store buyers. When finished, Scarpizzi opened the trunk of his car, carried out two large cans and placed them on the ground. He then called out to Alfie. Believing him to be one of his customers, Alfie walked over to Scarpizzi.

Tony the "Jackel" Jackalino remained behind the wheel of the car, its engine running.

"What do ya need today?" Alfie asked.

"It's not what I need, it's what you need, you motherfucker."

Scarpizzi whipped out a Louisville Slugger hidden under his jacket, landing it squarely on Alfie's head.

After Alfie struck the ground in a bloody and unconscious state, Scarpizzi opened the cans, pouring its dark contents of car-grease all over the full display of fish. Not a gill was spared.

Upon returning from his long hospital convalescence, Alfie too became a "member of the club," realizing that a cracked skull and greased fish was just an introductory calling card, that being a *live* victim of the mob's extortion was far better than being a *dead one!*

His special talents recognized, Jimmy the "Saint" Santora, a high-level captain, or "capo" within the "family," summoned Scarpizzi to straighten out Tim Rafferty, a local tavern owner who had made a pass at Jimmy's girlfriend in Tim's bar. Despite being warned by the "Saint" to stay away, Tim had made another move on her when she returned later that evening.

A few nights after that, Scarpizzi and another goon, Benny Ferraro, hid in the bushes next to the driveway leading to Tim's private house in Woodside, Queens. As Rafferty pulled his car into the driveway, he was viciously attacked with a two-by-four and hit repeatedly until he lay bleeding and unconscious on the ground.

Without so much as a "May I?" Scarpizzi pulled off Rafferty's trousers and undershorts. Together with his partner, they carried the unconscious, naked-below-the-waist Tim Rafferty to the landing in front of the house entrance, and laid him on his back, face-up in front of the door. Scarpizzi attached the mouth of a large metal-spring clasp to the head of Rafferty's penis. He then snapped it shut. Ringing the doorbell several times, Scarpizzi was out of there before Rafferty's wife came out to see what was there to greet her.

Scarpizzi could not wait to brag to his boss about the "gift" package he had left for Mrs. Rafferty, chuckling all the way home that he felt like "Jaws" in the Steven Spielberg classic.

Tim "Loverboy" Rafferty got the message, big time. He got rid of the bar, sold his house, moved out of the city, and was never seen nor heard from again. And the good news for Rafferty: the anatomy below his belt-line was no longer in jeopardy—not from Vincent Scarpizzi's creative warnings, anyway.

What sky-rocketed Scarpizzi to a high position on the "family" ladder, was the time he lured the opposition candidate for president of the Longshoreman's Union to a bowling alley. Bobby Johnson, a candidate for president of the union, was a bowler, and a good one at that, having averaged two hundred points a game.

One evening, Bobby Johnson picked up the telephone that rang in his Glendale, Queens, house. Scarpizzi's voice was at the other end.

"Hey Bobby, Vinny Scarpizzi. What's happenin' big guy?"

"Everything's goin' good, Vinny. How're the boys?" Johnson asked, hoping that Scarpizzi's call was in response to Johnson's solicitation for a big cash contribution to his campaign.

"That's what I'm callin' ya about."

"So ya got the message I left ya?"

"Yeah. I got the message."

"So what's the story, Vinny?"

"The story is, I got a package you're really gonna like."

"That's terrific. Really great. When can I expect it?"

"Right away."

"Right away?"

"You got it. And I'm gonna deliver it personal."

"Perfect. Is it what we spoke about the other night, Vinny?"

"Yeah, Bobby. It's all there. How about I call ya 'Mr. Union President' now, or should I wait till I see ya?"

"I like the sound of it. Yeah, real nice. So how do ya wanna handle it, Vinny?"

"Look Bobby, I gotta leave town for a few days. Ya' know, on some business. And I really don't wanna' leave the stuff around. Ya' know what I mean, my friend? So whadiya say ya meet me at the bowlin' alley in College Point in half an hour. Okay?"

"Hey Vinny, for what you got for me, I can make it in twenty minutes."

"Good, Bobby. Another thing—the guys don't want nobody to know about this. They wanna' keep it private like. Ya' know what I'm sayin'?"

"Sure, Vinny. No sweat."

"So come alone. Okay?"

"Gotcha, Vinny. See ya soon."

What Johnson did not know was that Scarpizzi had already made a special deal with Bobby's opponent.

As Bobby drove into the College Point parking lot, he got out of his car to greet Scarpizzi already there, waiting for him.

"Hey Vinny, good ta see ya," Bobby said, extending his hand to greet him. You got somethin' for me?"

"Right here, Bobby."

Scarpizzi reached into his pocket. He quickly withdrew a 22 caliber pistol, silencer attached. In less time than it takes to say "oops," he shot Johnson three times in the face. Johnson went down. Scarpizzi then shot him twice more in the head to insure that Bobby's political career was really over.

After the shooting, Scarpizzi and the "Jackel" placed Bobby's body in the trunk of the car and drove to a nearby pier where a small boat was standing by. Scarpizzi, assisted by the"Jackel," then carried Bobby into the hull of the craft, pulled it away from the dock, and headed out into the Atlantic Ocean.

On board, Scarpizzi placed Bobby's body into a wooden crate. He added the special Scarpizzi touch by throwing five bowling balls on top of Bobby's limp form inside the box. After nailing it down and tying heavy nautical rope around it, the box was tossed overboard, into the Atlantic, five miles out.

None of his union cronies could figure out why Bobby Johnson failed to show up to vote at his own election. But in any case, he was no longer an opposition candidate for the presidency of the Longshoreman's Union. Bobby Johnson had gone down at least one hundred fathoms, together with his precious bowling balls. As for Vincent Scarpizzi—he had once again successfully carried out another "family" assignment.

"What a beautiful scene…ya should a' seen it. Just like a viking buried at sea," Scarpizzi mused afterward to his boss.

From an enforcer, also known as "button man," Scarpizzi was later sworn in as a "capo" and "made-man" in the DiPienza crime family. And when Joey DiBella was gunned down outside his social club in Ridgewood, Queens, Vinny Scarpizzi became the underboss to Richie Brunelli, the heir to the DiPienza throne.

Brunelli, however, made some serious mistakes, one being that he had taken up with a young Hollywood starlet. The two would be constantly photographed by the paparazzi, with their pictures and notoriety being fully exploited by the tabloids—a "no-no" within the world of the *mafiosi*.

Brunelli's response to his mob associates who frowned upon such notorious media attention was always the same: "Fuck 'em. I'm the boss. I do what I want."

The love-fest did not last too long. The starlet had found another stud and Brunelli's romance was over.

Brunelli was now faced with two options: He could either take her out—whack her, that is—or, try to win her back.

While deciding which option to pursue, Brunelli became extremely depressed, even started taking Prozac, the anti-depressant.

To bring him out of his low mood, a cheer-up party was arranged in a large penthouse suite of the fashionable Crawford Towers overlooking Central Park South. The blowout was attended by all the top family echelon, beautiful women, and Scarpizzi, the planner of it all.

With the crowd in full swing, Scarpizzi approached his boss.

"Hey, Richie. Can I talk to ya for a minute?" he asked, motioning Brunelli to step outside to the terrace.

"Sure, what's up?"

Brunelli walked toward Scarpizzi who was leaning against the terrace rail. Tony Jackalino and Al Pucci, two of Scarpizzi's thugs, hiding behind a wall, then grabbed Brunelli and in a flash, hurled him over the top.

What was found on the sidewalk thirty-two floors below was not very pretty, but it was the final exit of Richie Brunelli, whose death was officially reported as a suicide brought about by his deep depression, caused by the breakup of his Hollywood romance.

It was a beautiful funeral... and Scarpizzi cried like a baby.

Brunelli's "suicide" had been approved by the family's "board" who decreed that whether it was his heart, or his "hard-on" that brought the media spotlight to the "family," he had breached the cardinal rule of "anonymity," and would have to pay the ultimate price for his rank stupidity.

With Richie Brunelli's demise, Vinny Scarpizzi—who now demanded that he be called "Vincent"—became the undisputed boss of the DiPienza crime family—a title that he had earned through intimidation, brutality...and murder.

CHAPTER EIGHT

John Scanlon was no stranger to Medical Examiner Peter Carlucci. The six-foot, grey-haired, robust, 60-year-old district attorney of Onandagua County seldom conferred with Syracuse's chief forensic pathologist when a victim of a homicide was brought to the city morgue. The initial investigation would usually be assigned to a field agent. It was a routine drill, whether the corpse was a respected member of the community, or just a stray drifter.

But when the victim was the attorney general of the United States, there would be only one man who could handle that top level assignment- the D.A., John Scanlon himself.

Storming into the M.E.'s reception room, a livid Scanlon barked at a diminutive receptionist. "Tell Carlucci I'm here."

"Yes, Mr. Scanlon." Pressing her index finger on a buzzer, she announced, "Mr. Scanlon is here."

She turned toward him. "Doctor Carlucci is waiting for you in his office. You know where it is, Mr. Scanlon?"

"Yes, I do. Thank you," Scanlon answered brusquely as he took a quick stride out of the reception area, through a narrow corridor, and up to a door with a small sign reading,"Peter Carlucci, M.D., Medical Examiner, Onandagua County, New York."

Pushing the door open without knocking, Scanlon stormed into a 15' x 18' office. Behind a six-foot desk, the top littered with documents, x-rays, and scattered medical articles, sat Dr Peter Carlucci, the medical examiner of Onandagua County, whose jurisdiction included all of the city of Syracuse.

In his late 50's, the M.E. was wearing dark-rimmed glasses framing a cherubic face, covered with a short, stubby, greying beard and untrimmed mustache. He portrayed the stereotypical look of a university professor. A white lab coat and baggy tan chinos provided a loose contour to his five-foot, nine-inch portly frame. Unattractive blue sneakers shaped like orthopedic shoes provided the support Carlucci needed while standing on his feet at the autopsy table, typically for several hours.

Although Carlucci did not cut a sharp image, he had an intellect that was all medicine, science and forensics. No social magnet, he had gained a solid reputation as a straight arrow during the ten years he had performed the job of medical examiner. In that role, he would often be called to testify as an expert in homicide cases where the issue surrounding the "cause of death" would be in dispute.

Even before Carlucci could greet his visitor, D.A. Scanlon screamed, "Where do you come off, Peter, telling me that you're not going to fill me in on the autopsy?" His face was tight with rage.

"Calm down, John. Settle down. As I told you on the phone, I have specific orders from this agent in the Justice Department not to disclose any of my findings until he authorizes me to do it." Carlucci's response was courteous, a sharp contrast to the mercurial barrage that just hit him.

"I don't give a rat's ass who gave you orders. I'm the D.A. in this town. This is my goddamned jurisdiction. That means you take your orders from me. I don't care whether he's from the Justice Department or the ladies' garden club." Scanlon's retort was burning hot, targeted at Carlucci's cool rebuff.

"Look, John," Carlucci said, trying to maintain a calming tone, "I'm in the middle here."

"I don't care where you are. This is my show. And I call the shots. I don't give a crap about some fed investigator who thinks he can order you around and take over my job. This is Onandagua County, not D.C. You hear what I'm saying, Peter?" Scanlon shouted agressively.

"Hold on. Take it down a few notches. I received a phone call and fax from a Federal Agent Matt Connors who tells me he's acting under the full authority of the president of the United States. I really have no choice in the matter, John."

"The hell you don't. I'm sitting on top of the biggest story this county—shit, the biggest story this *state*—has ever seen. I'm telling you, Peter, no fed or anybody else is coming into my own backyard and slamming the fucking door in my face. Not with what could be the break-out case of my career."

Scanlon paused as he grappled for another thought. His rage was building.

"Look, Peter, I'm the goddamned D.A., not some two-bit courthouse flunkie. Do you get my drift? There's been a murder here. This is my goddamned jurisdiction. And nobody's going to freeze me out."

With chin jutting out, eyes icy and bulging with anger, Scanlon screeched, "I'm ordering you to give me your findings on Bradford's autopsy. Do you read me, mister? Or do I have to spell it out more for you!" Scanlon's index-finger pointed threateningly, inches from Carlucci's face.

Scanlon's demeaning attack had gone beyond Carlucci's flash point.

"I don't care who the devil you think you are. You can't order me to do anything. I don't work for you and you have absolutely no authority *over me*. Furthermore, I don't appreciate your insulting tone and your gutter manners," Carlucci said, his voice dripping with defiance.

"Peter, you and I have been friends a long time. Yeah, you heard me right. A long time. I don't want this to get out of hand, and we can't let this shit come between us." Scanlon managed a softer response. His swallowed restraint was short-lived. He fired back menacingly, "Now listen, Peter, and listen good. I'm not letting this thing get away from me. Ya' hear? This fucking train isn't leaving the station without me!"

"I don't want this to get out of hand either. Look, you're the politician. I'm not. My only agenda here is to do my job, and do it right. That means I follow the orders of a federal agent who speaks for the president himself. It's that simple."

"Frankly, I don't give a crap if his orders come from the pope. Dammit, Peter, I'm telling you for the last time. As district attorney of this county and the highest legal authority, I'm making an official demand that you release your autopsy findings to me, *and that you do it now!* Do you hear what I'm saying, loud and clear?"

"Yes I do. But, as the medical examiner of this county and under the direct orders I have from Washington, I officially refuse your demand."

Having painted himself in a corner, Scanlon totally lost it, his eyes popping with anger as he began to sputter..

"Damn—what—ach—uh—the hell—ah—shit...In that case, you're under arrest for obstructing justice and withholding information in a homicide investigation." He was ranting, completely out of control, spitting flecks of saliva with each word.

Steam coming out of his ears, Carlucci shot back."You have no such authority and I'll fight you all the way on this!"

"We'll just see about that," Scanlon screamed threateningly, as he stormed out, slamming the door shut behind him.

Even as John Scanlon was retreating in furor from the medical examiner's office, President Harrington was delivering a moving eulogy almost fifteen hundred miles from Syracuse, as the Bradford family stood silently, surrounded by a small group of mourners.

It was a private burial. As the president concluded and stepped away, the Reverend Dwight Hughes began to speak:

"It is so difficult for mortals to accept the passing of one who was taken from us so abruptly. So vibrant, so full of hope, so full of giving. The frailties of mortal life become even more apparent when such unthinkable tragedy strikes—and yet, we must live on. That is the way Chuck would have wanted it. For the legacy he leaves is the full measure of love: love of his cherished country; love of his wife Jenny, whom he adored; and his precious son, Little Joe; love of his dear mother, Elizabeth; love of his patriotic duty. And those who loved him in return will be forever enriched by his friendship. Charles Llewelyn Bradford was the consummate crusader for a better world, fighting always to replace bigotry and hatred with understanding and respect, fighting always to replace violence and vengeance with peace and reconciliation. These were the true hopes and expectations of your fine servant, Charles Llewelyn Bradford, who we now, Lord, commit to your everlasting and eternal embrace."

With the final words spoken, the oak casket containing the remains of the late attorney general were slowly lowered into the ground.

It was a private service held 1200 miles from the nation's capital in a small cemetery on a peaceful knoll overlooking the quiet village of Morganville, 35 miles east of Oklahoma City.

Jenny Roundtree Bradford, a widow at thirty-two years of age, stood in silence as she held the hand of her seven-year-old son, Little Joe. At her side was Elizabeth Ann Bradford, who at 68, stood stoically, as she watched her only son being interred in the Bradford family plot. It was the wish of this matriarch that her only offspring be buried, not at Arlington National Cemetery, but side-by-side with the other members of the Bradford dynasty whose historic roots dated back more than one hundred years earlier to the governor of Oklahoma.

As the casket gently came to rest, an honor guard fired three blank rounds into the sky. After a brief pause, the silence was pierced by the mournful tones of a bugle as it sounded "Taps," with each soulful note fading away slowly into the air above, as the gentle wind made its presence to the sadness below.

Two members of the elite honor guard gathered the American flag that had draped the coffin before its descent into the ground. Methodically, they proceeded to fold the flag with a series of military sequences until it was shaped finally into a triangulated form. It was then presented to the officer of the guard, a Marine major, who carried it with both palms up as he walked with ramrod posture and slow pace to the deceased's widow. Halting in front of Jenny Roundtree Bradford, he gently handed the flag over to her as he kneeled on one knee. The crisp command of "port arms" by the military officer in charge brought the sound of rifles as they were maneuvered into a brisk miliary salute. With the traditional ritual complete, Charles Llewelyn Bradford was put to his final rest.

President Harrington stood quietly with the others. At the end of the service, he spoke briefly with Mrs. Bradford, then to Jenny as he gave her a warm embrace and a kiss on the cheek. Bending down, he gently stroked Little Joe's head, whispering words of affection to him.

The president walked over to Matt. "Can I give you a ride back to Washington?"

"That's very kind of you, Mr. President, but there are some things I do have to take up with Jenny. And this might be a good opportunity to do just that."

"As you wish, Matt. In any case, please keep me advised of your progress in the investigation."

"I certainly will. And once again, I thank you for your invitation."

The president left in the motorcade and headed for the airbase where *Air Force One* was there to fly him back to Washington.

After most of the mourners left, Jenny stood at the foot of the grave. She held Little Joe's hand and closed her eyes. A moment later, Matt walked over, stopping at her side. This time he was there, not as the chief investigator of Chuck's death, but as his closest friend.

Matt touched Jenny's shoulder gently. Her large, dark eyes showed the puffiness produced by tears and strain as she looked mournfully at Matt.

"Jenny, there are no words that are ever right at a time like this. I just want you to know how truly sorry I am—and how very deeply I feel for you and Little Joe."

"I know that, Matt." Jenny's soft voice was barely heard through her sad smile. "Chuck was so close to you…and I know how much he valued your friendship."

The silence that followed was proof that no further words had to be said as sadness washed over them.

A few moments passed. They walked towards the car that had brought Jenny to the Bradford family plot. Chuck's mother was already seated inside.

"What are your plans, Jenny?" Matt asked. "Are you returning to Washington, or will you be staying here for a while?"

"President Harrington was kind enough to offer me a flight back to Washington on *Air Force One*, but I have decided to stay with Chuck's mom tonight. I'll be taking the 9:10 out of Oklahoma City in the morning."

"Will it be alright if I call tomorrow after you're settled in?" Matt asked. "There are some matters I must discuss with you." Seeing through Jenny's sadness, Matt knew that this was not the right time to raise questions surrounding Chuck's death—questions that could painfully compound the distress that Jenny was already suffering.

"That will be fine, Matt."

"Are you sure, Jenny? It can wait if you're not up to it."

There was no response.

"Please forgive me, Jenny. I know this is the worst possible time for you. But I've got to know what Chuck was doing his last few days. And you could be of such great help. But it can wait until tomorrow." Matt's tone was contrite, apologetic.

Jenny trembled with emotion. "I understand completely, Matt. I've got to know what happened also."

"We'll talk then tomorrow…in Washington. Try to get some rest tonight."

Matt kissed Jenny on the cheek. He kneeled low, holding Little Joe in his arms for a moment. He gave a soft smile as he kissed him gently on the forehead.

Matt opened the door of the limousine as he watched Jenny and Little Joe enter the rear compartment. Stretching his head inside the vehicle, Matt took Mrs. Bradford's hand, expressing his condolences to her.

Tracking the car as it drove away from the cemetery until it was out of view, Matt returned to the grave site. Once there, he stared silently at the fresh mound that bore the temporary marker of his late friend, *CHARLES LLEWELYN BRADFORD*.

Looking pensively at the grave, Matt raised the collar of his black rain coat to protect him from the sudden chill he felt. He vowed to himself, *I swear to the Almighty that I will find those responsible. I give you my word, Chuck…so help me God.*

Matt Returned to his car as he entered it and started up the engine. He moved out as the vehicle inched slowly toward the cemetery's exit. In the stillness, he could hear the distinctive crunching sounds made by the tires of his car as they rolled over the loose gravel that was scattered throughout the cemetery's narrow road.

Gazing to his left and right, and looking back at Chuck's grave site for the last time, Matt could see the tall, polished headstones around him. To Matt, they seemed to stand at respectful and quiet attention. A thought suddenly entered his mind…

Those buried here, so still and peaceful, share in my sadness as they welcome Charles Llewelyn Bradford, who now joins them in his eternal rest.

Driving through the cemetery's stone arch at the end of the narrow road, Matt repeated his vow openly: "I will find those responsible, Chuck. I give you my word; I will find them…so help me God."

CHAPTER NINE

Vincent Scarpizzi was satisfied that he had effectively crippled the investigation into Chuck Bradford's death. Once again, he had taken pride in how he was able to deal with anyone who got in the way of his money-grabbing schemes.

Scarpizzi now reflected back to the grandiose plan he had so cunningly devised more than six months earlier...

As he looked at himself in the long mirror attached to the door of his bedroom in Astoria, Queens, Scarpizzi remembered exactly how he had felt back in March. He remembered heading for an appointment that would justify the self-congratulatory good mood he had been in as he continued to view himself admiringly in the mirror. Scarpizzi really liked what he saw.

Look at me, he thought. *I'm wearin' a three-thousand-dollar, hand-tailored suit. I got two dozen more in the closet. I'm not bad lookin' for an ole' guy in this here three-hundred-fifty-dollar silk shirt. And the fucker is made in France just for me. With my name on the back of the collar. That's class. And how about the twenty-eight more in the drawer! Not bad, eh? I'm also walkin' in eight-hundred-dollar Bellini shoes made in the ole' country.*

Scarpizzi's self-adulation was the end product of his daily "I look terrific" ritual.

Hey, I'm the boss. I'm a big, big man. I made it to the top, he would chuckle to himself.

I can have any friggin' thing I want, he would repeat in his mind, patting down the sides of his dyed black hair that would always be perfectly styled—,a tribute to his personal barber who would attend to him five days a week.

As Scarpizzi would continue to gaze approvingly at his reflection he would see a perfectly groomed figure of a man with power, money, and the highest respect from his peers.

His suits, fitting as if they had been sculptured first and then later hand pressed on him, would be the essence of sartorial perfection. *What guy wouldn't wanna' be like me?* he would often boast to himself.

His bodyguard, Vito Bootsie, would knock on the door as he had done hundreds of times before. He would advise his boss that it was time to go. Together they would walk downstairs to the living room, where, as always, they would be greeted by two burly men sipping espresso. Tony "The Jackel" Jackalino, his driver, and an enforcer for many of the years Scarpizzi moved up the ranks, would wave dutifully to him. Also, Al "Fatso" Pucci, a "capo" who remained loyal throughout the many family wars that ultimately made Vincent Scarpizzi its undisputed leader, would stand up and bow his head deferentially. He would show true respect to his boss. It would be a daily tribute.

And the conversation would always be the same:

"You ready to go, Vincent?" the "Jackel" would ask.

"Yeah, let's make tracks."

Constantly on guard against unexpected treachery on each trip by automobile, Scarpizzi would expect the "Jackel's" same question, "Where you sittin' today, boss?"

"Hey, you gotta look out for security. You never know who's watching ya." Scarpizzi would say. And with survival as his ultimate guide, he would alternate his seating habits in the car. One day he would sit in the right rear passenger seat, the next, in the front. Sometimes, he would even drive the car himself.

"You can't take no chances,"Scarpizzi would always warn. He would switch from the left rear passenger seat, to the right, with Tony next to him while his other two loyalists would sit up front.

This time, their destination would be *Luigi's Ristorante* on Queens Boulevard in Forest Hills. Scarpizzi remembered it well and could describe everything that happened that day, recalling every detail...

They had arrived at *Luigi's* in twenty minutes and proceeded directly up the stairs to a small room used for private parties. Once it was checked out for bugging devices, three bottles of Chiante were placed on a table that could seat eight. Antipasto soon followed with baskets of fresh baked Italian bread, escorted by two tall bottles of extra virgin olive oil.

Within minutes Joey "Sailor" Salise, Angie "Moose" Mooslia, and Tommy "Goodie" Guardino, all captains in Scarpizzi's family, showed up. They paid their usual respects to Scarpizzi, taking their assigned seats at the table. Their drivers and bodyguards remained downstairs in the restaurant, joined by Scarpizzi's driver, Tony "the Jackel." Their table was always positioned to give them a clear view of the front door. And today, as always, there would be no surprises.

Upstairs in the private room, Scarpizzi disposed of family business quickly as he counted the cash payoffs taken in from loan sharking, prostitution, and shakedowns. The tally completed, Scarpizzi left *Luigi's* to keep an appointment with his lawyer.

A half hour later, Scarpizzi arrived in his car, ready to pick up Harold"Heshy" Gordon, already waiting in front of his office building.

Gordon, who three months later would warn Scarpizzi about Matt Connors, the new federal investigator appointed by the president, was carrying a brown leather briefcase. It showed all the signs of wear, including the scars from the many litigation wars he fought in the explosive battlefield trenches of the courtroom.

As the Benz came to a stop in front of the building, Al Pucci quickly exited the car and walked over to Gordon. He escorted him to the right rear passenger door, opened it, and shut it firmly after he was seated inside. Without hesitation, Pucci returned to the front passenger seat, switching the electronic door button to a locked position. This signaled the "Jackel" to rev the engine and head toward the 59th Street Queens Borough Bridge.

"Thanks for meetin' me with such short notice," Scarpizzi said. He embraced Gordon, each exchanging their customary kisses on the cheek.

"Hey, Vincent, you call, I'm here."

"I appreciate it, Hesh."

"What's goin' on, Vincent?"

"Let me tell ya what's on my mind. Last night I was thinkin' about a bunch a' things. Ya' know, I ain't been too happy with my business. A lotta things have been fallin' off and I been thinkin' maybe I gotta look at a few other places."

Gordon sat next to Scarpizzi, looking at him quizzically. He was unsure of what the meeting was about.

"Ya' know," Scarpizzi continued, "green has been dryin' up. A lotta things I got goin' ain't as good as it used to be. To be honest with ya, I ain't too happy with that. So I thought, when we had all the action goin' in Vegas and Atlantic City, we were really doin' terrific. Casino green was beautiful. But those fuckin' casino commissions screwed us up. So we're out. But who's in? Different kind a' guys. But the same shit is happenin.' Except it's now MGM, Hilton, Venetian, Mirage, Bellagio, Mandalay, and a bunch a' others. But I ain't got no goddamned part a' it. I'm askin' myself, what the fuck is goin' on?"

"The world has changed, Vincent. It's now the big corporate giants who run the casinos. The take is still tremendous but the guys who really score big are not the ones you grew up with. Sure, the action is all the same. It's just the bosses who now run things who are different."

"That's the point I wanna make, Heshy. The action is all the same, but it's in the hands a' guys we can't do no business with. We're out in fuckin' left field with this bunch a' hard-ons and it's not gonna change. Y'agree, Hesh?"

"Yeah. I do. And I think you're absolutely right, Vincent"

"But let me tell you somethin' else, Hesh." Scarpizzi's brow creased, thinking how he should convey his new idea to Gordon.

"You can talk about your General Motors, IBM, Microsoft, now Kmart and Sears, even all them bank deals. No question, big operations—all of 'em. But ya know what? The bread that flows from gamblin' in this country makes 'em all look like small potatas."

"I hear what you're saying, Vincent."

" You can buy computers and cars, and even all that Martha Stewart shit at Kmart, but ya don't buy 'em every friggin day. Maybe that's why the market goes down and down in the toilet. And now I been takin' a real heavy bath. They keep on sayin' the economy is gettin' better. Ya' know what I say? Bullshit! The whole economy sucks. And all we hear is us havin' to get even with a bunch a' dickhead A-rabs."

"That's all we really see on the news."

"And we're gonna' teach these bum's democracy. Or some shit?"

"Yeah, right. One of the problems is that it is always about 'my religion is better than yours,' or some story like that."

"Sure, Hesh, and what they don't tell us is we're in a mess up to our eyeballs."

"Better believe it."

"C'mon. We blew this bum Sadam out of Iraq, but still can't win this goddamned war. New stuff is breakin' out every day, all over the country. And it's bad. They're now talkin' Iran and North Korea. Maybe even another war. And our GIs are gettin' shot up and diein' like dogs in the street. We got wounded soldiers comin' home without arms and legs, and their brains like oatmeal. I tell ya Hesh, it's a real goddamned shame. What if it was your kid, or mine? It's enough to make ya sick. And those suicide bombers every other day, and all that crazy stuff. It's not good. We're in a real jam, and it don't look like it's gonna get much better."

"Tell me about it. My sister's kid's in Iraq. I got another nephew who volunteered in the Marines and just finished basic training in Paris Island. My family's worried sick about them."

"I can understand why. And all this crap about homeland security from those shitheads runnin' Washington. They couldn't find their ass with both hands. But even with the whole world comin' to an end, 'Joe Schmuck' still has ta gamble. Ya' know why, Hesh? I'll tell ya… when it comes to gamblin', people got it in their blood. Give 'em a casino and they part with their bread because everybody's lookin' for a big score the way things are today. And while they're at it, their dollars are goin' down 'el draino' in slot machines, Blackjack, and crap tables. When the economy stinks, and people are scared, the suckers spend their last buck tryin' to hit it big. It's an escape. Like breakin' outta the joint. That's the only thing that keeps 'em goin', war or no war. Listen ta me, Hesh, I know what I'm talkin' about. I ain't no college professor, never got outta high school, but I know what I am sayin.' Ya' know what I mean?"

Gordon *was* listening intently. When Scarpizzi completed his thought, he broke in."Vincent, you're absolutely right. That's how Vegas and A.C. always made a killing."

"That's the point I wanna make," Scarpizzi said, pulling out a piece of paper from his inside pocket. It had scribbles all over it. "I've been doin' a little research on my own, Heshy, and this is what I come up with. You can forget about Atlantic City. Even with the new forty-story, gold front hotel they put up near the Marina. It's called the

Borgata. And as far as Vegas, it's all changed. They got palaces like the Bellagio. They put in a big lake right in the friggin' desert. Fountains that go up fifty feet, and all that shit. Do ya know they spent over a billion and a half? The Hilton people put up a joint called the Paris and laid out over a billion for something that looks like the Eiffel Tower and the Arch of Trump or somethin' like that. Two other big joints are already up a couple years. The Venetian with gondolas and all that lake runnin' in the lobby. And some joint called the Mandalay which cost more than three billion big ones. Are ya followin' what I'm sayin', Heshy?"

"I'm listening. Go ahead, Vincent. It makes sense."

"Look, in the next two years alone, Vegas will be buildin' over eighteen more hotels and casinos. Even this guy Steve Wynn, who made a fortune sellin' his casinos to MGM, is buildin' a joint that'll cost over three billion where the old Desert Inn used to be. And this guy's even puttin' his own mountain just to block the view from the strip. But with all the big stuff goin' on there, the gamblin' business is really changin' in Vegas."

"What do you mean? What's changing?" Gordon asked.

"I'll tell ya.' Vegas is no longer the big Disneyland in the desert, where Mr. and Mrs. Joe Schmuck and their five screamin' kids check in with dirty laundry, bags a' Doritos, and a case a' Mountain Dew, where they get four-dollar buffets and thirty-nine-dollar rooms, play the slots 'til they blow their big hundred dollar gamblin' money, and then hang around for three more days aroun' in the pool. And the twenty-five-dollar bettor ain't much better off. Those guys sign a bunch a' markers and maybe get comped for their room with a breakfast buffet tossed in. Big deal."

"And not always."

"That's right, Hesh, not always. But today, even *that's* history. It don't happen no more. You wanna buffet? Twenty-five bucks a head and don't expect no freebie for junior. You wanna room? Two hundred bananas, maybe more. Vegas ain't for the average putz and his whole family no more. I'll let ya in on a secret, Hesh. In the old days Vegas was run just by a few wiseguy families from New York, Chicago, New Jersey, and the coast. That's all changed. But ya know what, my friend? Today, instead a' callin 'em ' families', they call 'em 'casino operators.' And only four of 'em own the whole ball a' wax.

That's it, just four of 'em!" Scarpizzi counted out the number starting with his left pinkie, ending with his index finger. He held up his left hand in front of Gordon, fingers pointing upward, a gesture to further emphasize the point he just made.

"Let me tell ya what I mean… MGM owns the Bellagio, Mirage, Treasure Island, Golden Nuggett, Balleys, and of course, the MGM. And they just paid more than eight billion on the line for the Mandalay and a couple other hotels in Vegas, like the Monte Carlo, tossed in on top a' all a' that. So the MGM is like one of the wiseguy families of the old days. But listen to this—Harrahs is buyin' Caesars, already owns the Rio, and a couple other joints in Vegas. That's like a second wiseguy family. Now between the two families alone, they got eighty percent of Vegas in the pocket. Toss in Wynn and the big Venetian operation, and you got all of Vegas really owned by only *four fuckin' families*…just like the old days. In fact, they're even goin' back to callin' it 'Sin City,' which it always was when our guys first started it, remember? Now they come up with some PR bullshit about 'what happens in Vegas, stays in Vegas.' It's a joke! I'm tellin' ya, Hesh, it's like the old families are all back in business again, only with different names. And my piece a' the action? Zero! Goose eggs! Double zero! So far as I'm concerned, Las Vegas sucks! So what about it, Hesh, you agree?

"Yeah, I certainly do. But go on, Vincent." Gordon was fascinated, impressed by the homework Scarpizzi had done.

"So where do the everyday suckers go to gamble their paycheck and rent money without all the bullshit glitz and five-star hotels, volcanoes, gondolas, twenty-four-hour strip joints and art museums they spent over three hundred mill for alone? They're out in fuckin' left field unless they got casino action close by. And it's got only one purpose. They wanna gamble and pray to Jesus they win while they're pissin' away' the whole family farm."

"You're getting me excited, Vincent." Gordon inched closer to Scarpizzi. "But you have something special in mind. Right?"

"You got it. You wanna hear?"

Scarpizzi laid out how he had become intrigued with the new kind of gambling popping up around the country on Indian tribal lands. It was the perfect counterpart to today's Las Vegas and other casino venues. The creation of a network of gambling palaces scattered throughout America on Indian tribal lands was a natural. It could be the ultimate oasis to the scores of millions of average workers and the retired who might visit Las Vegas once every ten years for that fantasy "lost weekend" but who would be the everyday patsies and steady losers at an Indian casino located just a few miles from where they lived.

Indian casino gambling was the perfect alternative for the player who could be lured by the irrepressible desire to "hit the high note" — a dream that would almost never be reached. But while dumping the mortgage money in such a pursuit, the cash-intake around the country would be many times greater than the combined handle of Las Vegas, Atlantic City, and the "Mickey Mouse" river boats scattered around some of the shorelines of the Mississippi waterfronts of the midwest and Gulf of Mexico.

According to Scarpizzi, this was like virgin territory, with gushing cash-wells just waiting to be tapped. But before he could hope to develop a plan to move in on the big green, he had to know more about the origin of Indian casino gambling. Who's in charge? How do you get a license? Who are the political players you have to connect with? These were some of the questions Scarpizzi had. And that's where his lawyer would come in.

Scarpizzi had called Gordon the night before and asked that he set up a meet to find out how an Indian gambling casino gets started....

"Heshy. This is Vincent."

"Vincent, good to hear from you. What's up, my friend?"

"Heshy, there's somethin' I want ya to check out for me. And I gotta have some word by tonight." Scarpizzi sounded excited.

"Whatever I can do, Vincent. Anything."

"Here's the ticket. I gotta know how an Indian gamblin' casino gets goin.' D' ya know somethin' about that?" Scarpizzi asked.

"Indian casinos? No, Vincent. I never had that situation before. But let me do some checking around. I'd say... give me about an hour, more or less. I'll get back to you as soon as I can."

"Okay, Hesh. Now listen, it's real important. I'll be waitin' for your call."

"I'll get on it right away, Vincent, and I'll call you as soon as I have something."

Although a big order with such short notice, Gordon was always up to the task. That was what Scarpizzi admired in his counselor. Give him the job. It's done. No questions asked.

It was already after eight in the evening when Scarpizzi called. Gordon went right into his computer index, remembering that he once had a professional dealing with Jonathan Carswell, a law partner with Rollins, Cadberry, Byers, and Jones, the white-shoe Wall Street firm. Gordon had come to the rescue of Carswell when a member of his family got all jammed up with the Queens district attorney's office in a D.U.I., "driving under the influence." Gordon worked out the drunk driving charge to everyone's satisfaction. When it was over, he refused to take a fee. His "I was glad to be of help," fell upon very grateful ears.

Carswell was most appreciative of the favor, with Gordon filing away the I.O.U. for potential future use. It was now pay-back time, since, according to the information on the internet that flashed on Gordon's computer screen, Carswell had been the lead attorney for an Indian tribe seeking a license to permit full casino gambling in Connecticut. He agreed to meet with Gordon the following morning at his law firm located in downtown Manhattan.

"Vincent," Gordon said, calling Scarpizzi back in less than forty minutes, "I arranged an appointment with a lawyer friend of mine. He owes me a favor, *big time*. And he's really up to speed on this Indian gambling stuff. In fact, I've arranged to meet him at his office at eleven tomorrow morning."

"Where's his office?" Scarpizzi asked.

"It's in the Wall Street area."

"Good. I'll pick ya up in front of your buildin' at 9:30. We'll talk in the car."

"Sounds fine with me. See you then. Good night, Vincent."

"Good night, my friend. See ya at 9:30," Scarpizzi said, his voice thick with excitement.

As the black Mercedes passed City Hall, heading south on Broadway toward Wall Street and Carswell's Building, the next morning, Scarpizzi turned to Gordon and asked, "How much time do ya think ya need with this guy?"

"I'm not sure, Vincent. He canceled something heavy so he could meet me. But I don't think I'll need more than an hour."

"Perfect." Scarpizzi's voice reflected the high he was feeling by being on track with what he envisioned could be an unbelievably lucrative venture.

Gordon was let out on Wall Street in front of a forty-eight-story, gleaming glass building. "It's now a couple a' minutes before eleven. I'll meet ya here at twelve-fifteen."

Scarpizzi felt secure that his lawyer had the smarts to get information quickly without leaving any hint as to the real reason for the visit, or the identity of the client he was representing.

An hour and twenty minutes later, Scarpizzi's car pulled up to the glass tower. Gordon was already waiting for him. The right rear passenger door was opened for Gordon as he entered the car, taking a seat next to Scarpizzi.

"How'd it go?" Scarpizzi asked.

"Here's the scoop...."

In the next twenty minutes, Gordon reported in detail how a casino license was issued, as the car made its way north on the East River Drive heading toward the 59th Street Bridge and Long Island City.

Hanging on every word, the boss of the DiPienza crime family heard how a federal law, entitled, "The 1988 Federal Indian Gaming Regulatory Act," gave the right to Indian tribes to establish gambling on their lands. Gambling was limited to bingo, but in order to receive a full license for slot machines, craps, Blackjack, and roulette, a compact with the governor of the state was a prerequisite.

"Wait'll you hear what else I've got to tell you, Vincent. You won't believe it... it's almost too good to be true." Gordon's eyes sparkled as he saw riveting interest flame in his client's face.

"Vincent, Indian casino gambling is like an open invitation for you to walk in and load your pockets with gold nuggets! No limit! And there are no real laws or regulations to stop you! Here's how it works...."

In the next half hour, Scarpizzi learned how gambling was first proposed as a tool for Indian economic development. The plan was to build casinos on rural reservations where Indians had subsisted lethargically, living in poverty with the highest unemployment rate in the country. The gambling sites were envisioned to be installed on those lands where tribes had lived for generations.

But the idea proved faulty. Reservations located in rural or inaccessible areas *could not produce enough would-be gamblers.* The remote ones, not surprisingly, failed. The solution: a mad scramble by tribes and their non-Indian financial partners to find prime real estate they could claim as "reservation" land, and on it, build mega gambling spas—small cities with every kind of amenity to make gamblers welcome and eager to come back.

The choicest spots were near big cities and along major highways. It did not matter if the tribes had ever lived there since a fictional device, a "trust," would be created in order to move undesirable reservation land to a more profitable location. And all of this maneuvering was legal!

"The tribes have jumped at this once- in-a- lifetime opportunity to have big cash machines—you got it, casinos—on their land. It's a real sweet deal for everybody," Gordon beamed. "In most cases, the tribes are paid up-front with green that covers all expenses and even pays salaries to tribe officials. And this is before a single shovel full of dirt is ever turned. But there's more. If the feds don't recognize a tribe, which means, it's pissing against the wind before it could ever get a license, there's another sweet gimmick that's used. The outside investors with all the start-up money will actually bankroll genealogists. These are the guys who trace ancestors and try to find even that one drop of Indian blood in your background. They call it creating a family tree. They then hire big-time lawyers and some of the most influential people in Washington—lobbyists who know what it takes to get to the right people. Bottom line: they do whatever it takes, and nobody gives a rat's ass how much payola it costs, or what politician to pay off no matter how high he is on the pecking order, so long as the tribe is officially recognized. I repeat: whatever...it...takes—*Capiche?*"Gordon nodded as he rubbed his index finger and thumb together several times—a familiar gesture Scarpizzi had no difficulty recognizing.

Gordon concluded his description of the Indian casino gambling business by pointing out to Scarpizzi that government oversight of the financial backers was almost nonexistent. With under-staffing, limited funds, minimal supervision, and lacking any effective policing powers, the National Indian Gaming Commission had little insight or knowledge about who the investors were, the sums invested, the source of the money raised, or the return they were to receive.

And while by law, all contracts entered into between the tribes and the management companies had to be approved by the gaming commission, there was a gaping loophole big enough to drive a tractor trailer through that could be a *legal* escape hatch for any onerous approval requirements. Either by intentional omission, or by sharp lawyering, all that the street-wise Indian leaders, steered by the Washington insiders, had to do to avoid commission review of its contracts entered into with non-Indian management companies (the conglomerate Las Vegas and international casino operating moguls), was to hire *outside consultants* (who could be the very *same* Las Vegas and international casino operating giants).

Not being controlled by any regulations, such "consulting companies" would be free to conduct their slick business with the tribes as if they were, in fact, "management companies," but without any approval by the commission, or supervision as required by law. The result: investors and consulting firms, not being subject to the commission's review (without any agency official looking closely at the cozy and cuddly deals secretly worked out between them), could operate with almost absolute impunity. It was pretty much a free ride for the big-time profiteering non-Indian, who was *not* the needy person congress had originally intended to benefit when it passed the law permitting gambling casinos to be operated on Indian reservations!

"There are two king-pins in this whole business," Gordon continued. "First is the commissioner of Indian affairs in Washington, a fed put there by the president himself. The second is the governor of New York. He's got to give his okay to the deal in order to get casino gambling. Get those two wrapped up and you hit the lotto."

Gordon stopped for an instant and took several deep breaths. After getting his hyperventilation under control, he picked up again.

"But now, here's the real eye-opener in this whole Indian gambling business. The talk is maybe the government doesn't want to regulate the Indians too closely because they'd look like they're running the whole show for them. And that's bad PR for the politicians in Washington. Or maybe they just don't have enough staff to do it. Who knows? But whatever the reason, what I 'm saying, Vincent, is that it's like hundreds of millions, and maybe billions in cash — that's right, *green cashiola* — that's getting a free ride from Uncle Sam."

Scarpizzi could not believe what he was hearing.

"Hold on, Heshy. Are you tellin' me that the feds who hand out the license to the Indians keep their sticky fingers off the operation? Is that what you're sayin'? Lemme hear. Lay it on me again."

"That's what I just said, Vincent. But there's more. A whole lot more. According to my source — and listen to this one — there is absolutely *no*, what is called "oversight." Do you know what I'm saying? That means, Indian casino deals are made, and *nobody* — I repeat, *nobody* — knows *what* they are, *what* they say, or *who's* behind it, because there's no fed agency looking into them. That's what "oversight" is all about. *Nobody knows who gets what, how, or when.* It's a perfect set up for a billion-dollar, all-cash business."

"Holy shit," Scarpizzi blurted. His wide-opened eyes assumed the voracious look of the pouncing cat that just cornered the canary.

"The point Vincent is that everything is secret. Nobody on the outside knows what's really going on inside."

"This is fuckin' unbelievable. It's the perfect set-up for me. What have I been doin' screwin' around with small time shit when this gold mine is close enough for me to shack up with? Jesus H. Christ. It's just like Vegas in the old days. Only better. It's even got a kicker! All that *bellisimo* cash pourin' in and floatin' around and no fed is lookin' at it? And nobody really knows where all the green is goin' or who's gettin' how much of the take? Is that what you're tellin' me, Hesh?"

"You got it right, Vincent."

"Jeez, today in Vegas and Atlantic City you got more government casino control guys climbin' up your ass than you got hairs on your head. Ya' skim off the top, the next thing ya know you're rakin' leaves along some dirt road, wearin' an orange jump suit, with some six-foot-four mother-fucker guardin' ya who's got a badge, big cowboy hat, dark glasses, and a double-barrel shotgun pointin' right at your balls. What I'm hearin', Hesh, in this Indian set up, is that the government boys are like those three dumb monkeys. They see nothin', They hear nothin', and they say nothin', right?" Scarpizzi's raspy voice was filled with amazement.

"You bet, Vincent."

"I'm tellin' ya, Heshy, this Indian casino business is tailor-made for a guy like me."

He paused, flashed a broad smile, and nodded his head approvingly.

"Counselor, you did good. Real good. So we gotta get the fed commissioner in Washington and the governor in New York. Eh?That's what you're tellin' me?"

"Yeah, Vincent. But there's also a third guy."

"Like who?"

"Like the guy who can deliver the Indian contract."

"Ya' mean like a chief? Or some guy like that?"

"Yeah,"Gordon said.

"We get all three..."

Scarpizzi paused, moving his head up and down like it was attached to a spring wire. "We get all three,"he repeated, "and we got the fuckin' moon."

Gordon could feel the electrical current lighting Scarpizzi as if a three-hundred-watt bulb had been screwed into his head. The incandescent rush spread over Scarpizzi's face was a reaction Gordon had rarely seen him display before.

In a slow, cautious tone, carefully designed to place some restraint upon Scarpizzi's uncontrolled excitement, Gordon said, "Vincent, you have to understand that we're talking here about a fed commissioner appointed by the president of the United States, the governor of New York, and the chief of an Indian tribe. That's a pretty big order."

There was a brief silence.

In response, Scarpizzi bit down hard on his lower lip until a sly sneaky smile began to emerge. His exhilaration yielded to a calm demeanor as he reached into the inside pocket of his jacket and removed a monogrammed sterling silver case containing three cigars. From it, he took out one of the seven and one-quarter inch Havanas it housed. It was not the usual seven-dollar Prince Philip, but instead, a thirty-five-dollar Cuban Cohiba.

Scarpizzi rolled the cigar gingerly with his fingers and felt its fine, firm texture as he passed its length slowly under his nostrils and admired it caressingly. Retrieving a small 18-karat-gold cutting instrument from his outside jacket pocket, he carefully snipped a small hole in the head of it.

The delicate surgery completed, he placed the tip end gently into his mouth, rolled it between his lips and smoothed out the surface incised by the cutter. Satisfied that he had a good draw, Scarpizzi struck the flint of the gold gas lighter, and lit it. He twirled it around gingerly to ensure every surface was exposed evenly to the flame as he exhaled a puffy cloud of white Havana smoke. It rose, swirling up almost in slow motion as it made its way to the sun roof above.

"A governor, a fed commissioner, a chief... *do I know what that means?*" he asked rhetorically.

Scarpizzi broke out into a wide, megawatt smile, answering his own question with a drawn-out *voce andante...*"No problems, my friend."

CHAPTER TEN

Only three days had passed since the murder of Jenny's husband when American Airlines Flight 238 touched down on runway 5 at the Reagan National Airport in Washington.

It was 1:30 p.m. as the DC10 taxied over to gate B7. Two chimes sounded, signaling that its passengers could now leave their seats. Sitting in the first row, Jenny Roundtree Bradford slid over to the aisle, reached up to the overhead bin, and removed her carry-on bag. She remained in the aisle until the door opened. First in line, she exited the airplane quickly.

As Jenny entered the terminal, lights began to flash while cameras kept clicking and television reporters charged all around her. Microphones and shoulder-held television devices blocked her escape as she became the target of questions shouted at her.

"Is it true that the attorney general was investigating casino gambling on the Indian reservation in Syracuse?"a reporter yelled out, shoving a microphone within inches of Jenny's face.

ABC, CBS, NBC, CNN, Fox News, and an army of other cable, radio, and wire service people encircled Jenny as she tried desperately to run away from their crush.

The media was out for a story. The press would not relent until it received one.

With neither control nor direction, countless rumors surrounding Chuck Bradford's death began to circulate. The last reported rumor: the attorney general had been depressed and shot himself in a failed suicide attempt.

Other unverified stories swirling around alleged that Bradford was in the middle of a federal investigation and that his life had been taken by those he was about to expose.

There was even talk that the attorney general was the victim of terrorists on a mission to strike back at the United States as part of a global anti-American plot.

The television and cable channels were full of "news leaks." Dozens of theories floated around, many based on information received from "confidential sources."

As she fought to free herself from the crowd of reporters, Jenny realized that she was the focal point of a growing national hysteria. With all the ingredients of a high-impact news story, the killing of a high public official would always feed the insatiable appetite of a starved media that comes alive with shocking sensationalism whenever a sudden crisis occurs. This time it was the untimely death of Attorney General Chuck Bradford—an event that zoomed like a space rocket as it captured the public's attention with all of its alarming uncertainties and unanswered questions. This was front-page stuff for the print media and sure-fire pay-dirt for a television and cable industry bent upon pursuing the Bradford story with such unrelenting and voracious intensity.

"Is it true that you and the attorney general were having matrimonial problems?" one of the reporters shouted, thrusting a microphone almost into Jenny's mouth.

"Was there any connection between the attorney general and the Indian gambling license?" another rang out.

"Please let me through," Jenny pleaded, her passage having been closed off by the hordes of reporters and sound people who gave her no way out.

"Were you and your husband going through a divorce?" a cable reporter shrieked at Jenny as the sound-man stuck out a long pipe with a microphone attached to its end.

"Please…. Please…. Let me through," Jenny cried out. Her voice had the ring of desperation that fell upon the deaf ears of reporters hungry for any sound bite that could headline the evening news.

"What was the attorney general doing in Syracuse when he was shot?" another shouted.

The carnivores were out for red meat and were not about to retreat from their mission.

Jenny tried pushing her way through the media barrage, but even as she struggled to maintain some semblance of dignity, she was seized with an uncontrollable panic, trying without success to free herself from the net that had entrapped her.

Suddenly, a bellowing firm voice was heard above the noises of the crowd.

"Back off, you guys. Dammit. I said back off! Show some respect and decency to Congresswoman Roundtree." It was Matt Connors who had forcibly elbowed his way through the television cameras and throngs of reporters, finally reaching Jenny.

"We're getting out of here, Jenny."

Matt grabbed Jenny's right arm and like an NFL fullback, forcefully charged through the line of reporters and cameras. Holding her tightly, he ran Jenny toward a staircase leading to the sidewalk outside the terminal. There, they made their way to Matt's car that he had parked earlier alongside the curb. An airport security officer was standing guard as Matt rushed Jenny into the passenger seat of his government vehicle.

"Thanks, Bill. I owe you one," Matt shouted out to the guard, quickly opening the driver's door and leaping behind the steering wheel.

As the gallery of reporters and their camera people rushed to catch up with them, Matt started up the engine, pressing down hard on the gas pedal. He gunned off quickly, causing the four tires to screech and sending off piercing squeals from the car's sudden acceleration.

Once out of the airport, Jenny sat back in the passenger seat. She breathed deeply between heavy sighs."I didn't know what to do, Matt. They came at me so suddenly."

"I would have been there sooner if I had known about all the press."

"But the important thing is that you did come, and that you're here now."

"Damn. I wish I could have gotten there before you. They acted like hungry animals!"

"They were just trying to do their job. I can't be angry with them for that."

"Well, I'm just glad I was there."

"And so am I, Matt...and I feel so grateful to you..." There was a pause. Jenny continued in a whisper, "and so vulnerable."

"That's only natural, Jenny. This is a very difficult time and I know what you're going through. I intended to call you this afternoon once you were settled in. But when I got word that the sharks were out to nab you at the airport, I got there as soon as I could."

There was a long silence.

"Are you okay, Jenny?" Matt asked.

"I'm fine now, just fine." Instinctively, Jenny placed her left palm on Matt's hand...then withdrew it. The warm touch lasted a moment.

"The news hounds will be all over your house, Jenny. They'll try to grind you up like a buzz saw."

"I'll just have to deal with them. That's all."

"But not tonight, or tomorrow morning either. You've been through enough for one day. Look Jenny, I've already ordered a couple of federal agents to keep them at bay. They'll be there shortly. And you're not staying there tonight with all that's happened."

"I'll be alright, Matt. Believe me, I'll be alright."

"Of course you will. But you must give yourself a little air space even for a short time. You know how damn pushy the media can be, and I don't want those paparatzzi types doing their ambush routine on you when I'm not there to provide cover."

"I think I can handle it. I can't continue to run away from them forever, Matt."

"I'm not talking about forever. I'm talking about *now*. Tonight, you're staying at my place, and that's final!"

"But Matt—"

"—No *but*'s, and that's a direct order from Agent Matt Conners!"

"Alright, I guess you're right, Matt. I do feel so totally numb. And I suppose the last thing I want is to face those awful cameras and reporters again."

"It's settled then. Believe me, Jenny, it's the best thing to do."

Having made the decision, Jenny rested her head against the headrest of the seat. She closed her eyes as the car headed toward the Bradford home.

Thirty minutes later, Matt turned into the driveway. They exited the car.

Jenny inserted her house key into the outside lock. She was startled to see deep scratch marks on the brass plate around the metal fixture and small gouge marks on the edge of the front door. A sudden fear that someone had broken into her home was confirmed as she entered the hallway. A cut wire hung loosely from the ceiling of the foyer where a siren alarm had been concealed.

Jenny walked quickly into her dead husband's study off the hall. Matt was at her side as she saw with horror, couch pillows spilled on the floor, drawers of a large cabinet open and rifled, and papers and documents strewn all over the carpet. There was disorder in every corner of the room.

"Wait outside until I get you, Jenny. I want to make sure there's nobody in the house."

Matt removed his sidearm from its shoulder holster. He proceeded cautiously up the stairs to the bedroom area. Checking out each room and closet, he returned quickly to the ground floor. After searching every area on that level, he opened the kitchen door leading to the basement, flipped on a light switch, and with gun in hand, descended cautiously down the steps. Satisfied that there were no intruders in the house, he returned to the main level, speaking quickly into his cell phone.

Opening the front door, he told Jenny that it was safe to come inside. "Jenny, there's no question about it, there's been a burglary."

He followed Jenny as she ran up the stairs into the master bedroom. Every cabinet, bureau, and night-stand drawer was open. Clothing was in total disarray. Empty jewelry boxes were on top of Jenny's and Chuck's clothes, all piled helter-skelter on the bed. Dresses, blouses, suits, shirts, even shoes were scattered about. The room was in shambles, the obvious work of burglars looking for jewelry, cash, and other valuables.

"I can't believe what I'm seeing." Jenny began to cry bitterly. A break-in, on top of everything that happened during the past week was beyond her emotional endurance.

Reaching for Jenny's hand, Matt said softly, "Come downstairs with me to Chuck's study."

When Matt and Jenny surveyed the room, they were in disbelief when they saw the thoroughness of the vandalism before their eyes. The savagery of destruction took their breath away: Cabinet doors were ripped from their hinges. Loose papers were strewn all over the large mahogany desk and on the floor. The desk itself had deep gauge marks made by a sharp instrument. Manila file folders were torn, scattered everywhere.

The wreckage of the study had been systematic, ruthless. Dozens of porcelain figurines, citations and testimonials in glass frames, and paintings that could have hidden a wall safe, all were broken, smashed.

"I can't believe what I'm seeing. It's a nightmare!"Jenny covered her eyes with both hands. She began to sob quietly.

"Jenny, this too will pass. It will." Matt placed his arm around Jenny, trying to console her. "It will be alright, Jenny. It will be alright," he kept repeating.

Jenny looked around the room, bewildered, as tears continued down her cheeks. "We never kept much jewelry or cash in the house. Chuck kept most of the valuables in a bank vault. Aside from this horrible mess, I'm really not too concerned about what was taken. We have insurance for that. But to have strangers rummaging through my things and destroying for no reason, just makes me sick. On top of everything else, I feel so violated." She began to sob again.

"The people who broke into your house Jenny, were not here for valuables or jewelry."

"What are you saying, Matt?"

"What I'm saying is that they broke in to remove documents and papers Chuck kept in his file cabinets which I'm sure had something to do with his murder in Syracuse."

"What?"

" Jenny, this has the fingerprint of professionals all over it. They cover up their real purpose by leaving a lot of destruction and confusion in their tracks. I'm certain the motive surrounding the break-in was to grab any records Chuck may have left behind that could point to Syracuse."

The word "Syracuse," the city where Chuck was murdered, sent involuntary shivers through Jenny.

"There's not much we can do here, Jenny. While you were outside, I notified the local police as well as my own department. They'll be here very soon."

Matt opened the front door ten minutes later as Detective Bill Crawford, together with a uniformed cop and another with a camera, entered. Shortly after that, two Justice Department break-in specialists arrived.

"Tom," Matt said, addressing one of the federal agents, "We're not staying. I want you to remain here with Hank and conduct a thorough search of the house. It probably won't do any good, but we may catch a break. Take pictures of everything and call me on my cell if anything comes up. I'll contact you later tonight for a full report. And under no circumstances do you let any of the press in the house, ya hear? Your answer to them-and they'll be swarming around very soon-you don't know where Congresswoman Bradford is! Got it?"

"Loud and clear, sir."

"Good,"Matt said.

Matt held Jenny gently by the arm, walking her to the passenger side of his car he had parked earlier in the driveway.

First, Chuck's tragic death. Then his funeral. Next, all the questions his visit to Syracuse raised. Now, the break-in. When will it end? Matt thought.

There was little doubt in Matt's mind that documents Chuck left behind which could incriminate key people involved in his murder, were stolen. It was an effective method to shut the doors on his investigation. He had to find an alternate means of prying them open again.

Jenny has some of the answers and she may not even be aware of what she knows, Matt acknowledged to himself. It was now his job to get Jenny to remember what Chuck may have told her about the suspicions he had harbored just before he left for Syracuse.

After walking out of her wrecked house with Matt, Jenny knew she would be unable to cope with all the details she would soon have to muddle through in the next few days.

Jenny drifted into silence as she sat next to Matt, hoping that another terrible day in her life would soon come to an end. At the same time, Matt headed the car toward his small, attached, red brick townhouse located in the west end of Washington.

Stirring in her seat when Matt pulled into a short driveway, Jenny asked through eyes almost shut tight by fatigue," Are we here, Matt?"

"Yes Jenny, this is it."

Matt opened the one-car garage with a remote, driving his vehicle gingerly into the parking spot inside. Again using the remote, he brought down the overhanging door, the mechanical parts squealing as the garage mechanism brought the door down to the ground with a solid thud.

Matt exited the driver's seat, walked briskly around to the passenger side, opened the door, and assisted Jenny out of the car.

Jenny looked tired, the shadows under her eyes showing the strains of the last three days. But even with sadness and little sleep as her recent companions, Matt could see the underlying beauty of

Jenny's Native American features. Somehow the slightly darker areas now appearing under her eyes created a natural contrast, making them appear even more striking.

"They won't get to you here," Matt said, as he took Jenny gently by the arm, leading her to a door in the garage that opened into a short set of stairs and into the kitchen of the house.

Inside, Matt escorted Jenny to a small livingroom neatly furnished with a brown leather couch, two side chairs, and a glass-topped table. Several lamps, a small oriental rug, a wall unit housing a twenty-seven inch Sony, Panasonic VCR, compact disc player, and bookshelf with a wide assortment of law books, completed the decor.

As Jenny tried to settle into one of the side chairs, her strain continued to show.

At the same time, Matt walked into the kitchen and opened a cabinet above the sink. He withdrew a bottle of Hennessy, gathering two large brandy glasses from another cabinet, poured some of its contents into each glass, and carried them back to where Jenny was sitting.

"Here, take a few sips of this. It will take the edge off things and help settle you down." Matt handed Jenny one of the glasses. It contained an inch of the rich dark nectar. Holding the other glass in his hand, he pulled up a chair and sat down facing Jenny.

Nothing was said.

They sipped the brandy slowly.

Matt finished his drink, walked into the kitchen and poured himself another drink.

He returned to Jenny.

To Matt, the taste of Hennessy the second time around seemed less biting.

They both sat still. Silent. Looking at each other and then looking away.

After a while, the quiet was broken.

"Are you feeling any better, Jenny?" Matt's voice was soft, sensitive.

"Yes," Jenny whispered.

"Good."

Again, they fell silent. At times their eyes met, remaining fixed upon each other for a brief moment. As quickly, they would move to other objects in the room.

A strange, disquieting feeling began to overtake Matt. Here he was, a federal agent on a presidential mission to uncover the murderer of his closest friend. Yet, he could sense the warm, soft feminine presence of Jenny—his best friend's widow. While it made him feel protective, he was angry at himself for permitting even the slightest compromising thought that could float shamefully in his mind.

And there was Jenny, so sad-eyed, fragile.

Matt cupped Jenny's hand gently into his. "I know this is probably the worst time to bring this up, but I must begin the job of finding out what happened and who is responsible for Chuck's death. Would it be alright if we talked about it now, Jenny? Just say no, and we'll do it another time."

"Things won't be any different tomorrow, or the next day, or next week. Chuck is dead. Nothing can ever change that."

"I know. But perhaps there'll be a better time…when you've had some rest."

"No, Matt. There will never be a good time or a bad one for me. I am so desperate to find out what happened. And we just cannot wait until I feel better. If we did…." Jenny began to cry softly, unable to complete her thought.

"Jenny…It can wait!"

"I know that you're out to protect my feelings as much as you can, but I've lost Chuck, and I must begin the process of finding out what happened. I 'll have no rest until I do…. Can you understand that, Matt?"

"Of course I can."

"Then, please…I ask you to do what you have to. And if that means asking me questions that may give you some helpful answers, then do it. And do it now. Please, Matt…"

"I'll do what you ask, as difficult as it might be for both of us."

"Thank you, Matt."

"Alright Jenny, is there anything you can tell me about what Chuck was involved in before his death? Who he saw? Where he went?" Matt hesitated and then asked,"What do you think really happened, Jenny?"

Jenny sat pensively without response. Her eyes welled up with tears as she reached for a tissue out of a black leather purse. She began to sob openly. Matt tried comforting her, seeing her tremble, but was unable to halt the stream of tears that kept flowing down Jenny's cheeks.

The sudden sound of ringing was startling. Matt picked up the telephone.

"Hello. Yes. I'll be meeting with the two police officers tomorrow. I hope to have a report for you by evening. Shall I call you then?" After a short pause, Matt said, "I'll do my best. Goodnight, Mr. President."

Matt returned to Jenny.

"We'll talk tomorrow. Believe me, it will be best, Jenny."

"Uh, uh,"Jenny said, patting her eyes with a tissue.

"And you're sleeping in my room tonight. I'll use the couch."

"No, I can't put you out this way. I can sleep on the couch."

"You're taking my room tonight... period."

"If that's the way you want it, Matt."

"Yes, it is. Oh yes, Jenny, I'm taking the 7:50 morning flight to Syracuse. I'll be out early. I think it will be best if you stayed in my apartment tomorrow as well, where you'll be out of the reach of reporters. There's enough food in the fridge so you won't have to go out. I'll call you from Syracuse. I should be back here by seven."

"Why are you going there?"

"The two cops in the park were the last to see Chuck alive. I want to get some answers from this fellow Ruiz who said he shot Chuck accidentally." Matt tried to choose his words carefully, seeing that Jenny was at the edge of an emotional slope.

"How could he have done that, Matt? How? Chuck was alive. And he shot him. What possible explanation can there ever be for such a terrible act?"Tears began to flow freely again down her cheeks.

"Jenny, please. I don't want to upset you further. I said we can talk about this tomorrow," Matt said, attempting to soothe Jenny's torment.

Standing up with renewed strength, Jenny looked defiantly into Matt's eyes.

"No, Matt. I have decided. I want to discuss it *now*. Please.... I'm sure you want to protect me. I know that. But I will have no peace until I learn what went wrong, and it just cannot wait for another time. It cannot wait."

"But I will know more tomorrow, Jenny....after I interview the two Syracuse cops. Sure, this young cop did a terrible thing, but it doesn't start or end there. We know that Chuck had already been shot before the two cops entered the park. Who did it? And why? That's what I have to find out." Matt's tone was now quieter, measured, still concerned that what he might innocently say, could have an even greater impact upon Jenny's already fragile state.

"But that's enough for now. We'll talk again tomorrow."

"Please, Matt. Please do not try to protect my feelings. I know that this is as difficult for you as it is for me. But I must be able to handle it in my way. And I will not be able to do that if you continue to shield me as much as you do."

"Jenny, I promise I will tell you everything I know. But this is not the time to discuss it. You must trust me."

"And I do, Matt, more than anything in the world."

"Look, Jenny," Matt continued as he held her hands in his, "I am going to Syracuse in the morning. I will be back tomorrow night. I promise I will tell you everything I've discovered. Nothing will be hidden from you. I promise."

Matt squeezed Jenny's hands reassuringly.

"After I interview this Ruiz fellow, I will speak to Fowler, the other cop who was in the park with him. I am confident I will obtain information I don't have now. And Jenny, I will share it all with you."

Matt put his arms around Jenny. He held her tenderly.

"I give you my word, Jenny. I will find out what happened to Chuck, and who is responsible." Matt kissed her gently on her cheek.

"I know you will, Matt. I know you will."

They remained in an embrace as Matt could taste the sweet moisture of Jenny's cheeks while holding her close to him.

With Matt leading the way, they walked together into his bedroom. He removed a cotton blanket and small pillow from his closet, and placed them on his bed. Returning to the closet, he lifted a wooden hanger that held a navy blue pinstriped suit. There, he reached for a blue and maroon striped tie from a rack, moved over to a chest of drawers where he took out an undershirt, a pair of briefs, and a light blue dress shirt. He then gathered the clothes in one hand and approached Jenny who was still standing in the bedroom.

"Goodnight, Jenny. Maybe things will look a little better in the morning. But for now, you must try to get some sleep."

As he was leaving, Matt took Jenny's hand, held it for a moment, and kissed her tenderly on the cheek. Closing the bedroom door, he walked downstairs to the small livingroom where he carefully spread the blanket onto the couch. He undressed quickly as he stretched out on his make-shift bed, pulling the thin cover up to his shoulders. Reaching up to the lamp on a small table, he switched it off and lay there in total darkness.

The image of Chuck Bradford was present even in the blackness of the room. In the stillness, a reflective smile slowly came upon Matt's lips as he recalled some of the memorable moments that he had shared with Chuck just before his marriage to Jenny....

The two men had been standing in a temporary room set-up for the bridegroom located in the rear of the main sanctuary of the First Baptist Church. Outside the door, there were many rows of seats occupied by guests who were waiting for the ceremony to begin:

"You're looking mighty handsome in that cutaway jacket and striped pants, Chuck," Matt said, flashing a smile of approval.

"And so do you, my dear friend," Chuck responded as he straightened the pin on Matt's four-in-hand tie.

"You're a lucky guy, Chuck. Jenny is not only beautiful on the outside, but inside as well," Matt said, punching Chuck's left shoulder lightly with his right fist.

"Lucky is not a strong enough word to describe it. To have Jenny as my wife.... I feel like I just won the lottery."

"Well, Chuck, you *have* won the top prize. But then again, so has Jenny. The fact is, I can't think of any other two people who are so perfect for each other," Matt said as he threw his arms around Chuck in a manly embrace.

"And what makes it even more perfect, Matt, is that my *best friend* is my *best man*. How often does such lightning strike in one's life? I am doubly blessed."

"Oh, come on, Mister Attorney General. No need for all the accolades. I just happen to be the guy who was available. And besides, I work real cheap and you don't have to go out-sourcing for help either!"

"And why else do you think I hired you for the job? Certainly not for your looks."

"Okay, wise guy, you keep this talk up and I'll take the wedding rings I have in my pocket and hock 'em. But knowing the big spender you are, they probably wouldn't get me more than a tank of gas, given today's prices—and low octane at that! So behave yourself, fella.' Ya' hear?"

The two men stopped the light banter and faced each other in silence. A warm smile broke out between the two of them. Instinctively they reached out to each other, once again becoming locked in an embrace.

A knock on the door interrupted their act of friendship as a young voice announced, "The wedding ceremony will begin in five minutes."

Chuck and Matt walked out of the church office, joining the other members of the wedding party.

The sound of the church organ could be heard playing selections from Bach and Handel. It announced the procession of the bridal party as they walked slowly down the aisle. A familiar passage from a Brahms piano concerto served as the cue for Matt, as best man, to approach the altar.

Following Matt and the maid of honor, and with the sound of Mendelssohn's traditional music signaling the entrance of the bridegroom, Chuck was escorted by his mother, Elizabeth Llewelyn Bradford.

When the organ trumpeted the entrance of the bride, all eyes became focused upon Jenny with her exquisite beauty, wearing a white lace gown with a long, ornate and delicate train.

As Matt lay on the couch, he chuckled as he recalled being asked by the minister to produce the gold wedding bands that almost slipped out of his hand in his nervousness, as he attempted to retrieve them from his vest pocket where they had been tucked away.

"Do you, Charles Llewelyn Bradford, take Jenny Roundtree to be your lawfully wedded wife, to love, honor, and cherish, so long as the two of you may live?" Pastor Boland asked.

"I do," Chuck said, placing the wedding band on Jenny's third finger of her left hand.

"And do you, Jenny Roundtree, take Charles Llewelyn Bradford to be your lawfully wedded husband, to love, honor, and cherish, so long as the two of you may live?"

"I do," Jenny said, as she placed the wedding band on Chuck's third finger of *his* left hand.

"With the power vested in me under the law of the Almighty, and the law of Washington, District of Columbia, United States of America, I now pronounce you husband and wife, and may God forever bless your happy union. You may kiss the bride."

Exuberant applause broke out spontaneously from the audience.

Matt remembered throwing his arms around Jenny and Chuck as they were about to leave the altar. He had never forgotten the blissful glow reflected in their faces, and his own joy in being a part of such happiness.

But all of that had changed, so abruptly, so tragically.

Reality now returned to Matt, and with it, the presence of Jenny being very much alone in his bedroom, and in deep sadness over the loss of her husband.

There she was—a young, frightened and bereaved widow in Matt's bed. He wanted desperately to console her, to comfort her. To bring solace and support to her. But Matt knew he was far too vulnerable at this very sensitive time, as was Jenny in her fragile and emotional state. He was ashamed at the treachery of his thoughts... Jenny, there, alone... He was afraid to admit to himself that he wanted her in his arms. It would be a deception he could not stand to live with. He would have to dismiss the image of her lying in his bed, as he fought to remove such thoughts from his head.

At last, Matt was able to switch his focus to the Syracuse mission he would face in the morning: He had planned to speak to the last two people who had seen Chuck Bradford alive—Ismael Ruiz, a rookie cop who shot him, and George Fowler, a veteran of the department who witnessed it all.

But as Matt's eyes remained tightly closed in the stillness of the room, his mind once again returned to Jenny, wondering if she thought of him at all beyond the tears she was shedding for her dead husband...as he finally drifted off into an anxious and restless sleep.

CHAPTER ELEVEN

Four days after meeting with Heshy Gordon, Scarpizzi arranged another meet with someone he saw as indispensable to the success of his plan—Hector "El Lobo" Santiago.

The loud raps on the door sealing the upstairs private room at *Luigi's Ristorante* was a signal that Scarpizzi's guests had arrived.

"Santiago and Mendoza are coming up," Tony "the Jackel" barked as the door opened.

"Who's with him?" Scarpizzi asked, casually brushing off his lapel.

"Two other guys. I've seen 'em but I don't know their names," "the Jackal" answered.

Soon, Hector Santiago, the boss of the New York Latino crime family, walked into the room with his under-boss, Willy Mendoza. Knowing the protocol, Santiago, a tan-skinned, handsome man in his middle forties, walked directly to Scarpizi.

"Good to see ya, Vincent," he said, exchanging a warm handshake. "You know Willy Mendoza."

Mendoza gave a nod. He was a balding, portly figure— a sharp contrast to Santiago's good looks.

"Sure, thanks for coming. You know Joey Salise, Angie Mooslia, and Tommy Guardino," Scarpizzi responded.

The introductions complete, Santiago and Mendoza were directed to seats opposite Scarpizzi.

"Good friends should have a drink together," Scarpizzi said, as "the Moose" poured wine for everyone in the room.

It was a curious assemblage. Vincent Scarpizzi had met Hector Santiago at political functions and social gatherings, but never sat in the same room for the purpose of talking business. Although each had a natural suspicion of the other, there was an unwritten law they each obeyed: "I don't fuck with your business; you don't fuck with mine."

The DiPienza crime family, with Scarpizzi on the throne, represented the last remnants of organized crime in New York. While labor racketeering, kickbacks and loan-sharking still provided it with a steady cash flow, the gold-filled halcyon days were over. The U.S. attorney's office had taken care of that. And while the family always had a small piece of action that came out of Las Vegas, Atlantic City, and Puerto Rico, the mob influence in gambling operations was already becoming an anachronism.

Scarpizzi was not alone in the drought that was engulfing the big crime families of America: the once all-powerful Curaci family that had Chicago under its thumb for years, was all but extinct. In its place, little splinters of black hoods, Hispanics, and a mixed assortment of dregs, fought over what had been an impregnable crime organization. Los Angeles, long the headquarters of the Tortelli dynasty, had given way to the new breed of Mexican thugs and young Asian toughs vying to carve out their own private territory. Once the hub of big time *mafiosi*, Miami was scattered in its organized crime operations. No longer was it under one family rule as in the days of the Gerace family. Now the mix of miscreants from Cuba, Haiti, and the Dominican Republic ran the massage parlors, prostitution rings, book-making, and drug operations. Even the new racketeering phenomenon, the Russian mafia, had now infiltrated the Miami mob scene.

The dissipation of the powerful crime families of the 70s and 80s however, did not seem to have affected the power wielded by Hector Santiago and his supporters…

Having emigrated to the United States from Bogota, Colombia, twenty years earlier, he moved to Jackson Heights in Queens, New York, a community that during the post-war period of the 50s and 60s was almost exclusively Jewish. It was one of the strongest Democratic strongholds in the country, returning its party representatives to office repeatedly with more than an 80% plurality. Most of that changed when immigrants from Central and South America started to arrive. As they moved in, others moved out. Local kosher delicatessens and retail shops that used to thrive, and were mainstays in the neighborhood for generations, disappeared completely, giving way to *bodegas* and Latino social clubs.

When Santiago left Bogota, he moved in with relatives whose apartment was in a four-story walk-up located between Roosevelt Avenue and Northern Boulevard in Jackson Heights. He discovered quickly that he could be a big man in the street only if he was feared, and if he had the blessing of *Los Gauchos*, a local fraternity of hoods and gang members who met regularly in the neighborhood social club.

Hector Santiago, the thin, dark-haired, six-foot Hispanic with rugged handsome features and dark eyes, soon let it be known he had strong ties to the Colombian cartel, that he was not to be taken lightly. Although a number of drug related murders were linked to Santiago, the Queens County D.A. was never able to muster sufficient evidence to present to a grand jury.

It was no surprise that Santiago, a low level thug, was emerging as a strong-arm hood whose *bravado* and *machissimo* would one day catch the approving eye of the Colombian *padrones*.

With enormous pride, Santiago would acknowledge his present success. He would throw out his chest, flex his muscular pectorals, admire the large tatoos below both strong shoulders, and enjoy reliving in his mind how it all started twenty years earlier. It was in a Latino social club called *La Vida*...

One evening, while sitting at a table, Santiago was signaled by Pablo Calderone, a local punk who always carried a fat roll of big bills in his pocket.

"Hector," Calderone called out. "Come over here, man. I wanna talk to you for a minute."

"Sure," Santiago answered, as he left his table, swaggering over to where Calderone was sitting.

"Sit down, *Amigo. Como estas*?" Calderone asked in Spanish.

"*Muy bien, gracias. Y' usted*?" Hector Santiago answered in their native tongue.

"Hey, *muchacho*, we'll keep it in English. Okay?"

"Sure. Whatever you say, my man."

"So, how ya been, Hector?"

"Now you didn't ask me over to find out about my health, didja?"

"That's what I like about ya. Ya don't waste no time with a lotta bullshit! Right, *amigo?*"

"I don't like to waste time like the ole men at the coffee house. Ya' know what I mean, *compadre?*"

"Yeah, Hector. I know. I'm the same fuckin' way, man!"

"Bueno! So watchya got, Pablo?"

"Okay, I'll get right to it…Hector, a couple guys have been watchin' ya.. They like how ya operate."

"What guys. Do I know 'em?"

"I don't think so."

"Gaw 'head. Lemme hear."

"Now, I'm talkin' about some real big honchos. No small shit. Know what I mean?"

"I'm listenin.'."Santiago took two big swallows from a bottle of *Corona* beer he brought from the other table.

"Look my friend, I know ya been dealin' in hot car radios, also air bags and some chop-shop shit. Whadya make? Fifty? A hundred? Two hundred a night?"

"Hey, man, I do okay," Santiago snapped, displaying hot-tempered annoyance at Calderone's attempt to belittle him.

"Relax, Hector… Relax…. Don't get so up tight…. I'm here to talk some serious business about some serious *dinero*. You got an interest in *serious dinero, amigo?*" Calderone asked, raising an eyebrow while flashing a teasing smile.

"Go ahead, Pablo. I'm listenin.'."

"Okay, here it is. The guys I told ya about, they got real good stuff, and they told me to talk to ya ta find out if you're interested in, like, bein' their guy here."

"You talkin' about pot?"

"Gimme a break, man. Like I told ya, this is serious shit I'm talkin' about, not nickel-and-dime crap. Real heavy duty stuff, *amigo!* Pure white coke." Calderone paused. "There's a lotta bread ya can make here my good friend…*Mucho pan verde. Comprende?*"

"Who are these guys?"

"Let's say they ain't from aroun' here. But Hector, lemme tell ya somethin' else. These guys are big—very, very big. *Muy grande.* And they're connected. Real big time."

"Why me, Pablo?" Santiago asked, pointing to himself. "Why not you?"

"Because these guys have been watchin' you. They think you're smart. They think you're a tough *hombre*. They think you're the right guy for 'em. Anyway, I got my own thing goin.' So, Hector, what do I tell these *hombres*?"

"How much we talkin' about here?" Hector asked, his eyes squinting with curiosity.

"*Mucho, mucho dinero, amigo*. The sky's the fuckin' limit. Ya move the stuff fast; ya make a fuckin' fortune. This ain't no nothin' burger...So tell me Mr. Santiago, you ready for major league baseball, *Senor El Lobo*?"

The magic words spoken, Santiago made his deal with "the big guys," who in fact were spear-heads of the Colombian drug ring, looking to establish a solid network in New York. In Hector Santiago, they had found their point man.

Drugs had always been the lifeline of the cartel that dealt with its own kind, contrasted with seeking partners of varied ethnic backgrounds. It was only natural that Santiago, having risen to power through petty crime, brutal assaults, and street smarts, was soon regarded as the local Latino boss. Given the pseudonym *El Lobo*, "the wolf," he was feared as the one who would lead the pack in carrying out a planned mission of crime.

Running operations that ran the gamut from stolen car radios and air bags to chop-shop deals, he graduated to fencing stolen goods, and then to drug trafficking. Twenty years later, Santiago had earned the biggest prize of all—the New York state cocaine franchise direct from the infamous Colombia drug cartel. This was no small feat. The operation covered the entire state of New York, from Montauk in the southeast, north through Syracuse and Rochester, all the way northwest to Buffalo. With an organization set up for the distribution of cocaine in every major city, Hector Santiago was the headman, the chief honcho, the New York C.E.O. of that vast illicit empire.

There were two main distribution points: one in Jackson Heights that supplied New York City and the suburbs, and the other in Syracuse, serviced Albany, the State capital, and the cities to the north. All of New York state was Santiago's domain, and he knew the most influential players of all. A summer home in Syracuse, where he spent almost as much time as he did in Jackson Heights, was just part of his "corporate" obligations. Meeting with local politicians and interacting with top power brokers, was yet another aspect of his role. Being liberal with big cash contributions to local and statewide campaigns, provided almost unrestricted access to the most influential people few others enjoyed at his level. This was real power—the kind that officials in the highest echelons of government had come to respect, and fear.

But while drugs accounted for millions of dollars of revenue to the cartel, the signs of trouble were everywhere. Money laundering transacted with ease through the Bahamas, the Caymans, Puerto Rico, Atlantic City, and even Switzerland, was now under the hawking eye of federal agents. More busts were being made at JFK Airport, as *mules* carrying narcotics strapped to their bodies, were being sniffed out by trained canines and airport police. JFK, once the largest and most profitable port of entry for the major drug rings of the world, was now under a constant 'drug alert' zone in a collaborative drive by federal and state authorities. Although low echelon messengers took the rap when caught, there were continuing signs that the drug operations already under heavy attack, would finally begin to net the heavy-duty dealers at the top.

For the first time in a decade, the Colombian government was cracking down on the operatives with middle level bosses arrested and hauled off to Colombian jails, as tons of contraband were being intercepted by federal agents working closely with the Drug Enforcement Agency. What appeared just a short time ago as an uninterrupted cash flow, was now under severe pressure that was resulting in a continuing erosion of open drug trafficking.

And here were the two kings facing each other: Vincent Scarpizzi, who knew that his power base was being threatened by federal prosecutors, and Hector Santiago, whose reign would continue only so long as the cocaine money machine remained uninterrupted by government intrusion...

Small talk ended with the meal.

Each had a purpose at the meeting.

Each had a mission.

And each knew he needed the other now more than ever if their empires were to survive.

Scarpizzi took the last sip of his espresso. The biting sweetness of *sambuca* was all but gone when he sat up straight in his chair, removed the white cloth napkin covering the front of his white silk shirt, folded it neatly, and placed it on the table.

It was now time to talk business.

"Hector, I been around a long time. I seen guys come an' go. Some of my best friends ain't here no more. You know what I mean?" Scarpizzi asked. His tone reeked with melancholy.

"Sure," Santiago agreed. *What's this guy up to?* he wondered.

"Hey, you and me, we're still aroun.' Ya know why, my friend? I'll tell ya.. We're what all the fancy Dans call 'survivors.' "

"They got a TV show by the same name, right?"

"Yeah, Hector, that's right. Those fuckers probably named it after us. We're the real survivors! And you know why? Because we're smart. We know what's happenin' aroun' us, and we move in even with all the punches flyin'. Ya know what I mean, eh Hector?"

"Man, you got it so right. Middle of the target. Bulls-eye!"

Scarpizzi liked Santiago's answer, even if he knew he was being romanced.

"Okay then...you and me, we keep goin' because we're smart enough to have action in a lotta things."

It was now Santiago's turn to throw out his chest, whether he thought he was being jobbed, or not.

Scarpizzi continued. "And I give ya a lotta respect. And ya give me respect back, right?"

"Sure, Vincent. I give you respect. You give me respect. Works good both ways," Santiago answered. *What's this guy buildin' up to?* he pondered.

"We both made it pretty big because we had the smarts ta play the right action at the right time. You gotta go where the action is when it's right. You agree, Hector?"

"Man, no question about it. Right action...right time. That's the combo!"

"But, ya see, as smart as we are, sometimes we're not smart enough."

Santiago was not about to acknowledge Scarpizzi's last comment without hearing more.

After a two-second pause, Scarpizzi picked up again.

"Y' wanna hear a story, Hector?"

"Sure, why not? I'm listenin.' "

"Okay, here it is: When I was in my twenties more than forty years ago, a guy had a dream. That dream was to go to a desert in Nevada one day and build a gamblin' casino."

"Yeah, I know, Vincent. I saw the movie," Santiago said, grinning widely. The others in the room also reacted with a nodding smile.

Scarpizzi went on. "The rest is history. First, there wasn't a single gamblin' operation in Vegas that wasn't connected. Sure, in twenty years things got real heated and a lotta big money dried up. But we all got maybe twenty good years outta it before the ball- busters and the do-gooders took over what guys like us started."

Suddenly, Santiago was beginning to show signs of interest in what Scarpizzi was saying.

Scarpizzi sensed that Santiago was now becoming a listener.

"Twenty good years, Hector. How much more do a guy need outta a' single operation?" Scarpizzi pressed on, satisfied he now had a very interested Santiago at the other end of his conversation. "Vegas dried up. Atlantic City's tough now, sure, but in the first couple years it was wide open for us. Man, the bread came out like they were comin' from giant ovens. Ya' hear what I'm sayin?"

"Yeah, Vincent. Go on. I'm listenin' real good."

"But ya know what, Hector? The action was great while it lasted. But it's over now. Today you got these guys from Wall Street. These big college hard-on type a' guys, ya know. These *walios* come in from big important schools, with all their fancy degrees and all that shit. And they're runnin' the same kind a' operation. Only they make it look legit. Ya know, it's good guys like us that ain't got none of the real action goin' no more. But these yahoos make it sound like it's big corporation stuff. That's real bullshit. They're fuckin' the public and makin' it sound like their business is run different than when we ran it. That's just plain crap. That's what gamblin' is today. That's who's operatin' the casinos all over the country—big corporations all over the world. Not like the old days. Not like it used to be."

"Yeah, I know that," Santiago said, still wondering where Scarpizzi was going with all of his talk.

"Hey look, Hector. Let me stop screwin' around and get right to it. Ya see, I gotta tell ya somethin'. Last week, I'm invited by a good friend a' mine, strictly as a guest, to an Indian casino. 'Vincent,' my pal says, 'you wouldn't believe what ya see. They got a gamblin' operation that's the biggest in the world.' Okay. So we go to see it. It's about two hundred miles away, in another state. I had to prove it to myself...You ever been to an Indian casino, Hector?"

"Yeah, once. In Florida. It wasn't much. They had slots, some poker, but no craps or Blackjack tables. Nothin' like that."

"Well, the Indian joint you were at didn't have the license for that kinda gamblin.' That's why they only had slot machines and poker. But what I saw blew my fuckin' mind. You wouldn't believe it. Let me tell ya. Ya'gotta take the interstate for about a hundred forty, fifty miles, and then you get off. Not a sign nowhere. No billboard. We drive up country roads. No cars aroun'— nothin'. I think to myself, *Is this guy jerking me off, or what?* We turn here, we turn there, then I see these little signs no bigger than this menu, with just a picture of a tree and an arrow. Imagine, a tree and an arrow pointing in a direction. After a half-hour of goin' through woods, there it is. Ya' wouldn't believe it. It's like a fuckin' oasis. The biggest spread I ever saw. Brand new, with guys wearin' ya know, construction hard hats all over the joint. We drive the car in this big driveway...maybe twenty lanes. One of the jocks, he takes the car. We walk inside. This you gotta see— right in the middle of this big lobby, a statue of an Indian like about five stories tall. Yeah, a big, big Indian with feathers an' a bow an' arrow, and all that shit. The whole thing in white marble. Now, we take an escalator to the second floor. Hey, you and me Hector, we been in all the casinos in Vegas and Atlantic City—Mirage, Caesar's, Taj, Resorts, MGM, Bally's, Bellagio. But let me tell you about this one. There are three casinos. We go in the first. It's the size of four goddamned football fields with a zillion slot machines. You wouldn't believe the crowd. It was like a mob. You couldn't even walk through, it was so jammed. People, like, as far as you can see. I thought to myself, *They gotta be usin' mirrors or somethin'.* I asked the guy who brought me. I say, 'Hey, where's the Blackjack and where's the crap tables? I don't see 'em.' He tells me there's a whole big casino in the other side of the buildin' just for that. Where we were was just for slots. So we walk to the other side. This you wouldn't believe. It's like a football field, only four times bigger. Blackjack, crap tables, roulette. People lined up five deep just waitin' for a seat. I seen big action but I ain't never seen nuttin' like that. Unbelievable. Let me ask ya Hector, you know somethin' about this Indian gamblin' stuff?"

Santiago pursed his lips, shaking his head from side to side.
"Hey," Scarpizzi picked up again, "I didn't know nothin' about it
neither. So when we get home I asked a lotta questions. Now, who do
ya ask? Ya ask the guy who got the answers. The lawyer, who else? I
tell him, 'Find out about these Indian casinos. What's the deal in
getting a license? What do ya have to do to get started? Ya know,
things like that. I wanna full report. First off, how can ya open a casino
when casino gamblin' is against the law?' I say, 'Get me all the stuff on
it.' Next day he gets back to me—you followin' me so far, Hector?"

"Yeah, gaw 'head. I'm hearin' every word."

"Okay. He says somethin' like this. The government—yeah, the
U.S. government—made some kind of a' deal with the Indians a lotta
years ago. It was somethin' like, the Indians were gonna have their
own country. Yeah, like a country in a country."

"Whadya mean, 'country in a country?' "

"Real simple. The way it's explained ta me, they got their own
country right in our country. They got land that belongs to them.
They got their own schools, their own laws, even their own cops—Do
ya follow me so far, Hector?"

"Sure. You people took what belonged to them in the first place
and then you give back what you don't want. That don't sound like a
very straight deal for the Indians." Santiago's early childhood of
poverty in Colombia and the injustices of the system (ninety-five
percent of the people lived in squalor while the remaining five
percent were upperclass, living a lifestyle of baronial opulence) gave
him an empathetic identification with the Indians' plight. *But,
thought Hector, when is this guy goin' to get to what this meetin's all
about? He keeps talkin' and talkin'. Get to the fuckin' point already!*

"Well, before you run a benefit for them, here's the good news.
The government has a department. They call it somethin' like the
Indian Affairs, or the Indian Commission, or some shit like that."

"It's the Bureau of Indian Affairs," Al Pucci broke in.

"Yeah, right, the Bureau of Indian Affairs. There's some head
honcho there called a commissioner and a couple other guys. This
outfit's job is to find out what the tribes need and work it out so they
get it. It's like the social security department for Indians. A couple
years ago one of the chiefs went to the Commission and said the only
way they're gonna get enough money for their people was to get a

gamblin' license to run their own casinos. They were smart enough ta know they could make a lotta bread with a gamblin' operation."

"What about the money they were gettin' from the government?"

"Hey man, the last guys who get somethin' from the government are the Indians. They're even lower down than Latinos in this country. It seemed like a pretty good idea to give 'em gamblin' instead of a lotta money out the pockets of the people in the country. So the government gave 'em an 'okay' to go ahead."

"Let me ask ya a question," Hector broke in. "What about the place where they run their gamblin'? Like this place you saw? Don't the government have somethin' to say about that?"

"You're a smart *hombre*, Hector. Ya see, once the fed commission says 'okay', it's then up to the state to cut a deal with the chiefs. Once the deal is set, casino, here we come. And that's what happened in the joint we were in. In just a couple years it's thrown off more than a billion in green. Are ya hearin what I'm sayin', Hector? One billion in beautiful greenola cash, and goin' up."

Santiago and Mendoza were almost hypnotized by what they were hearing. The enormity of what Scarpizzi reported was just beginning to sink in.

"I want to say somethin' else." Scarpizzi knew he now had a captured audience. "Casino gamblin' is the biggest cash operation in the whole fuckin' country and it will get even bigger. And two of the smartest guys around, don't have no goddamned piece a' the action. That's you and me, *amigo, capiche*?"

There was a pause, then total silence.

Scarpizzi started up again. "Florida, New Orleans, Mississippi, riverboat gamblin', the West, the South, but nothin' yet in New York. That's where you come in, Hector. Remember, I said we need two things: the commission in Washington has to give the 'okay,' and the chief has to cut a deal with the governor."

Scarpizzi suddenly sat up in his seat, moving closer to Santiago as if letting him in on a confidence. His voice was lowered to a whisper as he started to speak in a slow, deliberate tone.

"Okay, here it is. I got the New York and Washington guys in my pocket. I take care a' that end. You, Hector, have heavy action upstate. Nobody's better connected than you in Syracuse. There's an Indian reservation there. The name of the tribe is—" Scarpizzi hesitated and reached into the inside pocket of his hand-tailored jacket, retrieving a piece of paper. Before he could report the name written on it, Santiago broke in.

"Pecontic. Is that what ya got on that paper?"

"I knew I was talkin' to the right man," Scarpizzi said, flashing a broad smile of approval. He went on.

"We gotta connect with the right guys and make our deal. Once we do that we're swimmin' in a billion-dollar cash operation over the next three years. And that's just the start. We can have a piece of every Indian gamblin' operation in the whole fuckin' country, Hector. I'm talking billions in cash money. Do ya read me, *hombre*? We don't need twenty good years for this operation. Gimme ten, even five, and I cash it in. Interested, Hector?"Scarpizzi asked in a drawn out, teasing manner. He hesitated for a second, then asked, "Whaddya say, my friend?"

Santiago glanced over at his underboss. "Willy, let me talk to ya for a minute."

The two men left the table and walked over to the far corner of the room, twenty feet away. With their backs to Scarpizzi, they could be seen having an animated discussion. A few minutes later they returned to the table.

Santiago spoke first. "Two things. Number one, I wanna a week ta think about it."

Scarpizzi knew Santiago would require clearance and approval from his Colombian bosses, that some time would be needed for that mission.

"Number two, what's my take of the action?"

Scarpizzi had no connection with the Indian tribal community in Syracuse. But he was convinced that Santiago could deliver *that* contract necessary for his plan to succeed.

While Scarpizzi knew that in the end he would have to agree to a 50-50 split, he started his negotiation by offering Santiago a lower percentage.

"Hector, I'm not gonna play games. And I'm not gonna disrespect you. The deal is, ya get a third, I get two-thirds. I could have said 25-75, but I wanna be straight with ya. When ya think about the split, you'll find it fair. After all, it's my idea and there's some heavy-duty contracts I gotta take care of at my end."

"Okay, Vincent, I'll get back to ya in a week."

Having finished their business, the two men, leaders of their own kingdoms, stood up and faced each other. They were two emperors, two rulers, two bosses, two mobsters, showing respect one to the other. Instinctively, each reached for the wine glass on the table, raising it to his lips. Santiago toasted in Spanish, *"Para tu salud, muchacho."*

Scarpizzi answered in Italian, *"Gratzie, amigo, salud."*

The two swallowed the last drops in the glass as the unprecedented meeting at *Luigi's Ristorante* came to an end.

CHAPTER TWELVE

The alarm, set for 6:00 a.m., gave Matt a jolt. He was suddenly awakened and momentarily unaware of his surroundings. Suddenly realizing he was on the couch, he quickly reached for the clock to shut off its sound, hoping its shrillness would not awaken Jenny, still asleep upstairs. The hall bathroom was sufficiently removed from the bedroom, muffling the sounds of the shower he was in and out of in less than five minutes.

By 6:40 a.m., Matt was behind the wheel of his black Ford Taurus, on the way to Reagan National Airport. Parking his car in the twenty-four-hour lot, he walked briskly into the terminal as he waited to board US Airways Flight 217 to Syracuse, with a scheduled quick stopover at New York's La Guardia.

Taking off on time, the Boeing 737 landed at the Syracuse Airport at 9:15 a.m. A deputy sheriff whose name tag read "Albert Kelly," was already waiting for Matt at the arrival gate. Kelly then drove the federal agent to the sheriff's office where arrangements had already been made for Matt to interview Ismael Ruiz and George Fowler.

Inside the building housing the Sheriff's Department, Matt was escorted into Lieutenant Brian Goody's office, one of the first officers on the scene following the report that Patrolman Ismael Ruiz had shot a man in Carlyle Park.

"Good morning, Lieutenant. Matt Connors, U.S. Justice Department." Following protocol, Matt flashed his ID and shield.

"Good morning, Connors," replied Lieutenant Goody, a heavy-framed cop whose twenty-two years with the sheriff's department showed signs of a paunchy body and protruding belly.

"Coffee?" Goody asked, trying to relieve the uneasiness both were experiencing.

"Yeah. Thanks."

"Kelly, bring me a black, no sugar. How do you take it, Connors"?
"Same."

Goody escorted Matt into a small office. It had the look of *cop* all over it. Covering a plywood wall were many plaques, each with a police shield and printed language of commendation surrounding the name, "Brian Goody."

A second wall was covered with the shoulder patches of hundreds of police departments throughout the country — insignias ranging from the smallest counties, to the big cities, like the NYPD and LAPD. It was a wall decoration only a cop could love.

Behind Goody's coffee-stained desk, crowded with police documents and scattered papers, was an oak-grained plywood wall. Attached to it was a large street map on one side, bar graphs with crime and arrest statistics on the other. Directly behind a black imitation leather, high-back chair with worn armrests, was a personnel chart. A manila strip at the top was printed in free hand with a black marker. It read, "Table of Organization — Syracuse Precinct."

The wall to the left of the entrance was clear glass, providing an unobstructed view of the desks within the precinct and the activity of the personnel assigned to them.

"Take a seat," Goody said, pointing to a straight wood chair with a slightly faded checkered cushion. "Fowler and Ruiz will be here when you want 'em."

"Thanks," Matt said. He sensed that Goody was being professionally polite, but not overly friendly — the coldness that situations of overlapping police jurisdiction sometimes create. He also knew that locals had always been suspicious of the feds, almost as if they were on the other side of the fence. That's the way it would be in Syracuse as well.

"I want to talk to the shooter first. That's Ruiz, right?" Matt asked.

"That's right," Goody answered. His tone was dry, impassioned. "Do you want him now?"

"Yeah. I'd appreciate it."

"Sure thing. I'll call him in."

"That's fine. But I want to speak to him alone. Is there a room we could use?"

"You can use my office. I'll get lost for a while," Goody volunteered.

"I appreciate that, but I'd prefer speaking to him some place without a glass wall or two-sided mirrors." Matt knew he had raised a sensitive issue, but he had to ensure total privacy, full confidentiality. Diplomacy would have to wait for another day.

"You understand, Connors, Ruiz has not been formally charged with any misconduct. And the D.A. is running his own investigation. I just want to make sure his rights are fully protected. You understand what I'm saying?" Goody asked, knowing Ruiz was scheduled to appear before a county grand jury—standard operating procedure whenever a cop was involved in a shooting.

"Let me reassure you, I'll be speaking to him informally. No notes. No recording devices. I just want to get a feel for what happened. Do you see any problem with that?" Matt was attempting to be conciliatory although he had unrestricted authority of the United States government to subpoena Ruiz and Fowler, and could question them in the Syracuse office of the FBI, if he chose that route.

Goody understood the power of the Justice Department. He was not about to challenge Matt at this time. "Nah. I see no problem with that, so long as Ruiz says it's okay with him."

"Good. Then it's settled."

Kelly entered Goody's office, two containers of coffee in his hands. He handed one over to his chief, the other to the federal agent. Matt and Goody took little sips. Small talk made up the conversation. Suddenly, there was a knock on the door.

Officer Ismael Ruiz, the rookie cop who shot and killed the attorney general of the United States, entered. He looked visibly anxious. Missing from his neatly pressed uniform was a sidearm. It had been marked earlier, bagged, and locked away in the inventory room of the precinct. It was the same 9mm Glock automatic that Ruiz fired off when he shot and killed Chuck Bradford.

"Ruiz, this is Agent Connors of the Justice Department," Goody said.

"Hello, Officer Ruiz. How are you?" Matt's tone was professional, but gentle.

"I've been better," Ruiz responded meekly.

"I'd like to talk to you. It won't take long. I've already spoken with Lieutenant Goody and he says it's okay with him. I wish to assure you what you tell me will in no way prejudice your rights. Is that agreeable?"

"I have nothing to hide," Ruiz answered nervously. "I'll tell you what I've told everybody else. It's all the truth."

"Good. Lieutenant, if you could show us the room where we can talk in private."

Goody got up from his chair, lifted the half empty Styrofoam coffee cup in his hand, and motioned Matt and Ruiz to follow him to a room down the hall.

It was a typical police department interrogation room, containing a scratched-up table and three wooden chairs, but no wall mirror. Matt was satisfied his conversation with Ruiz would be neither taped, nor recorded.

They sat down. Matt saw a cop, visibly shaken, who was no more than twenty-five years of age. He could clearly see the pain that lined his face, the darkness that accompanied the ridges below his eyes. Ruiz had not seen sleep in more than two days. It showed. Matt knew the young cop in front of him was a frightened rookie who was experiencing a personal torment.

"Can I call you Ismael?" Matt's tone was fatherly, sensitive.

"Sure. But I prefer 'Iz.' That's what everybody calls me."

"Fine, Iz. That's what I'll call you, also." There was a pause. A faint smile came over Matt's face. "Why don't you tell me in your own words what happened?"

Ruiz looked at Matt, unsure of how to begin. There was a delay but Matt exhibited patience. Ruiz attempted to speak several times, then would abruptly stop. He was having difficulty getting the first words out to describe his nightmare. Matt waited patiently. "Take your time, Iz." Again, Matt's manner was gentle, calming. "I know it's been rough on you."

Feeling more relaxed by Matt's soft demeanor, Ruiz let out a heavy sigh. Started to open up. He spoke haltingly, but with emotion. After describing what happened in the park that night, his eyes welled up as tears began to run down his face.

Ruiz' account of what occurred made it clear to Matt that Ruiz shot Chuck Bradford when the attorney general sat up suddenly from the ground. He fired his weapon instinctively when Fowler shouted, "He's got a gun."

"It was an accident. A terrible, terrible accident." Ruiz began to sob, his shoulders shaking.

Matt believed what he was hearing from Ruiz.

As Patrolman Ruiz left the interrogation room, a troubling thought continued to plague Matt Connors. Could Ruiz have been set up to kill the attorney general of the United States? If so, by whom? And why?

Once Ruiz was out of the room, Goody, who had been eyeing the door from a distance, entered. "There's been a change of plans. Fowler's on a special assignment and won't be available until tomorrow morning." He positioned his large frame in the opening between the room Ruiz just left, and the connecting hallway.

Matt was not to be intimidated by Goody's attempt to challenge his authority. Staring coldly into the lieutenant's eyes, he said firmly, "You will have Patrolman Fowler in this office at two o'clock, or I'll have federal marshals pick him up, throw on the cuffs, and take him to our FBI office in Albany. Do I make myself clear?"

Goody's face turned pink. He started to protest but thought better of it as he swallowed hard, answering in a disgruntled tone, "Yes...SIR."

"Fine, I'll be back at two."

It was exactly 2 p.m. on the round clock on the wall behind the duty sergeant's desk when Matt walked into the precinct. He made his way to the same examining room he had used when he questioned Ruiz. The cop waiting for him this time was the fifteen-year veteran, Patrolman George Fowler.

"I'm Matt Connors, Department of Justice," Matt said, as Fowler sat in the chair used by Ruiz a few hours earlier.

"Nice to meet you, Mr. Connors," Fowler answered formally.

"I take it you know why I'm here. Right?" Matt's tone was dry.

"Yeah. I've been briefed by Lieutenant Goody. So, Connors, what can I do for you?"

Matt did not take too kindly to his last name being used without a "Mr." in front of it.

"As you can see, this is an informal session. No recording devices. No stenographers. Alright then...Tell me everything that happened after you got the radio call that night. Tell me exactly as you remember it."

"As I've already told everybody a bunch a' times, my partner Ruiz and me, we were in the diner on a meal break. It's just a few blocks from Carlyle Park. Sometime around 9:30 that night, we get a dispatch that a 9-1-1 caller reported a body in the park. We're assigned to check it out. So we take off right away."

"Who was driving the patrol car?"

"I was."

"What about your flashers and siren? Were they on?"

"No. As I said before, we were just a couple a' minutes from the park. Anyway, I certainly didn't want to telegraph our coming, just in case somebody else was there."

"What happened next?"

"Well, when we got to the entrance of the park, we moved in slowly."

"Did you have your lights on?"

"Yeah. The brights were on."

"Were there any lights in the park?"

"Except for a few street lamps, it was pretty dark."

"Did you see any people there?"

"Nah. It was totally deserted inside."

"Go on. What happened next?"

"Suddenly, the car lights flashed on a body sprawled on the road. I stopped the car about ten feet away."

"Where was your partner Ruiz at this time?"

"Ruiz, he was in the right passenger seat."

"Did you give him any instructions?"

"Yeah. I told him to report what was there."

"What did you do after that?"

"I then got out of the car and told Ruiz to stay put."

"Tell him any thing else?"

"I said, 'Cover me.' "

"Then what?"

"As I got closer to the guy on the ground, I could make out it was a male in a suit."

"Was he moving at all?"

"Nah. He looked pretty dead to me."

"Go on."

"So I approached him, and was about to check him out, when all of a sudden he sits up. I'm startled as hell and jump back, ya know...like a reflex action."

"What happened then?"

"Well, I think I see a gun in his hand and I yell to Ruiz, 'Iz, look out! He's got a gun,' or something like that. Iz lets go three rounds. And the guy falls back. That's about it."

"That's all of it?"

"Yep. That's it."

"Nothing else?"

"Like I said, that's it."

Matt would now ask some tougher questions:

"Okay...Did you ever find a gun?" Matt began to show a sudden change of tone.

"No. He didn't have a gun," Fowler answered, his eyes glaring guardedly into Matt's face.

"So what was it that you saw when you yelled out to Ruiz he had a gun?" Matt's voice was firm, slightly raised.

"I'm telling you, I thought I saw a gun. Maybe it was the way the car lights flashed on his hand. I don't know. It happened so fast," Fowler shot back defensively.

"You're a seasoned cop. Are you telling me you couldn't tell the difference between car lights flashing on a human hand, and an actual gun you say you *thought* you saw? Is *that* your answer?" Matt's disbelief was beginning to approach full display.

Fowler started to shift nervously in his chair. Tiny beads of sweat were beginning to form on his forehead. "I told you what I told you. I said what I thought I saw. That's it," Fowler barked back at Matt's hostile question, his temper starting to rise.

"I heard your answer, patrolman. But what exactly did you expect Ruiz to do when you shouted out to him that the man on the ground had a gun?" Matt asked, this time elevating his tone sharply.

Fowler was visibly annoyed."Like I said, I just wanted to warn him. I wanted to alert him to be careful, that's all. Christ, I never expected him to shoot the guy... Look, Connors, I've been with the goddamned force for fifteen years. Ruiz, he's a rookie. Green. No experience. He just let go. I guess he didn't realize what he was doing." With each pointed question, Fowler felt more like a hostile witness being mercilessly attacked on cross-examination. He didn't like it one bit.

"Where were you when Ruiz fired his weapon?" Matt pressed, continuing to hammer away at the veteran cop.

"I already told ya. Maybe ya didn't hear me the first time. Like I said before, I jumped back. It was like instinct—an instant reaction when I suddenly saw the guy on the ground sit up. It happened so fast."

"How much time passed from the time you were next to him on the ground, and when you saw him sit up?"

"Hold on. I didn't have a stop watch with me. What kind of bullshit question is that?" Fowler was getting visibly upset with the direction of the interview.

"You were there, Fowler. I wasn't. Was it a minute? Thirty seconds? Two seconds?" Matt demanded, attempting to pin him down.

"Now look here, Connors, I'm not here as your patsy. And don't treat me like I'm a two-bit drug dealer on some fuckin' buy that went sour." Fowler suddenly sat up rigidly in his chair, eyeing his examiner scornfully. "Hey, I don't like what's happening here. I told ya how it went down. That's it," Fowler shot back as he crossed his arms over his chest in a stance of defiance.

Undeterred, Matt pursued the hunt. "At any time, did you see a wound on the victim's head, or any blood, or a bullet hole?"

"No," Fowler recoiled, anger flooding his face.

"You were inches from him. The car lights were on, you said. He sat up in full view and you still didn't see a wound or blood on his head? Is that what you're telling me?" Matt bellowed.

"Maybe your problem is you just don't listen," Fowler shouted back, acid spilling from his tongue. "What I said is what I said. That's it. End case."

"I don't think so, mister. That's not it. You've been on the force for fifteen years and you want me to believe you acted more like a rookie than Ruiz? You knew there was no gun. And you were close enough to the victim to have seen the bullet wound and blood on his head," Matt snapped, grimacing with contempt.

"Just hold it there, Connors. We're not in court and I'm not here so you can beat up on me," Fowler flared, slamming down the palm of his right hand on top of the table. "I don't know what the hell you're thinking."

Matt charged in for the kill."What I'm thinking, Mr. Fowler…is that you're lying! That there was no gun. That maybe you deliberately panicked your rookie partner into firing his gun." Matt expected Fowler's reaction to the incendiary accusation as he assessed his body language closely.

"Are you on automatic pilot, or somethin'?" Fowler fired back, his puffy cheeks becoming flushed and crimson. And borrowing the line of a Southern politician, he shouted, "Get outta my face!" He ranted on, "You keep on this way, I don't talk no more without a lawyer." Fowler sat back and stiffened. A nervous tic in his right facial muscle began to pop in and out.

"Threatening me with a lawyer speaks volumes." Matt's tone was flat and expressionless. Throwing an icy stare, and with disgust in his voice, Matt continued, "This interview is officially over. If I were you, I'd think seriously about where I was going to spend the next twenty years." Matt's earlier suspicion that Fowler had already been briefed by a lawyer continued to feed that speculation.

The fear he saw in Fowler's eyes, together with his shifty demeanor, fed Matt's visceral suspicion that the veteran cop was not being truthful, that in some way he was involved in Chuck Bradford's death.

"I'll leave you with a simple warning: Don't leave this jurisdiction. Don't even think about it. That's an official order from the United States government. Do you read me, Mr. Fowler?"

Matt rose to his feet.

Sneering and tight-lipped, anger and hate dripping from every word, Fowler let go in a drawn out, raspy, and radioactive whisper, "I say nothin' else without my lawyer."

CHAPTER THIRTEEN

After his first meeting with Vincent Scarpizzi, Hector Santiago wasted no time meeting with his boss, Louis Varga, at an arranged location in Puerto Rico, in order to get his okay for the casino partnership.

It was a typically hot, sunny afternoon in San Juan, Puerto Rico, when Hector Santiago and Willy Mendoza stepped from the airlines terminal building onto the sidewalk.

Santiago always enjoyed that part of the world. It reminded him of home, with its climate, vegetation, and language. Oftentimes, he and Mendoza would take a special charter flight out of La Guardia in New York and spend three or four nights in one of the four-star casino hotels in San Juan. The casino hosts couldn't do enough for him, "comping" his party to the best suites, matched with the finest aged wines and beautiful, sexy women.

They were big action players capable of winning or losing $200,000, sometimes even more on any given night. This level of casino action alone would have been enough to grant Hector Santiago the usual high-rollers' amenities and compliments of the house. But in addition, Santiago was a very connected man whose high position with the Colombia cartel, although never mentioned by the casino hosts, was reason enough to treat him with great deference and respect.

Santiago was quite pleased when his immediate boss, Louis Varga, one of the top kingpins of the Colombia connection, directed Santiago to meet him at The La Ultima Hotel and Casino in San Juan, Puerto Rico, to talk over the deal Santiago had discussed briefly with Varga one week earlier.

A new black Lincoln was parked outside the terminal building, a driver behind the wheel. Santiago spotted an old friend standing in front of the sedan as both men approached each other, arms extended.

"Rodriguez, *amigo, cómo estás?*" Hector Santiago asked in a friendly tone as he and his *compadre* shared a macho embrace.

"*Muy bien, Senor Santiago. Vamanos por favor.*"

Santiago and Mendoza entered the car as it sped off toward The La Ultima Hotel, a forty-five-minute drive from the airport which took them through small villages and the poorest sections of San Juan.

Out of the view of poverty, *The La Ultima Hotel and Casino* was a magnificent complex consisting of a palatial main building, surrounded by charming European villas, waterfalls, and floral gardens, all perched high on a mountain overlooking the Atlantic Ocean to the east and the blue Caribbean to the west. The views were breath-taking.

The storybook setting had been constructed many years before. In its early years, it prospered with the influx of big dollars from the high-rollers throughout the world who left millions behind in casino losses. Known as "whales," they came from Arab countries, Hong Kong, Korea, and Japan, having amassed hundreds of millions of dollars from family fortunes and questionable enterprises. They were financially capable of losing a million dollars in a single night of gambling without leaving the slightest dent in their obscene net worth.

But that was the period of the 70s. The 80s were not as kind to the operators of *The La Ultima Hotel and Casino,* who had suffered from the overall economic drought following the market crash of '87. After several seasons of heavy red ink, the hotel was forced to close its doors, remaining dark for five years.

Winds, rain, and sun took a heavy toll on the buildings, which were neglected, no longer maintained. The depressing signs of deterioration were everywhere, until a consortium, headed by wealthy Asian investors, purchased the hotel at an upset price in the mid-nineties, pouring millions of dollars into the renovation of the interior and exterior buildings. When completed, it was restored to its pristine splendor, and beyond.

With suites designed and furnished to make the most princely of potentates feel at home, and with the backdrop of stunning architectural structures, beautifully landscaped gardens, Romanesque pools, and high water fountains, *The La Ultima Hotel and Casino* had returned once again as the jewel of the Caribbean.

Within its spectacular main structure was its casino where the most lyrical sound to the table gambler would always be, *"pagando Blackjack,"* the traditional message delivered in Spanish by the dealer in a voice loud enough to alert the pit boss that an ace and face card, or ace and ten, had been dealt to the player—*Blackjack*—thus calling for a three-for-two pay out. This was the practice of the house to ensure the dealer was not paying out more than he should to a potential clandestine partner masquerading as a legitimate player.

Santiago, Mendoza, and Rodriguez exited the car as it came to a stop in the huge arched driveway in front of *The La Ultima's* main entrance. Shortly, they were escorted to a huge suite with floor-to-ceiling windows looking out to the ocean below, and the mountains to the south. A large, round, thick glass table, was in the sitting room. Dividing the two bedrooms on either side, was a huge basket filled with exotic fruits, Swiss chocolates, macadamia nuts, and a bottle of Dom Perignon standing in a bucket of ice on a tray, surrounded by etched champagne glasses. Leaning against the one-hundred-fifty-dollar bottle of vintage champagne, a handwritten message from the management welcomed Hector Santiago to the hotel.

Within minutes of their entering the suite, the telephone rang. Willy Mendoza picked it up.

"Okay," Willy said, placing the telephone back in its cradle. "Varga wants to see you right away, Hector. Two of his guys are coming up. They'll be here any minute."

Shortly after Mendoza hung up the telephone, there was a knock on the door. Two of Varga's men had been sent to escort Santiago to Varga's suite located on the penthouse floor of the main building.

As they exited the elevator, Santiago walked with his escorts until he reached a double-door. It had a large brass plate attached to the center of it, inscribed, *"Cambio del Rey"* —"Chamber of the King."

Santiago had been in extravagant suites before but this was beyond opulence. The gold leafing and paintings on the ceiling were so ornate, reminiscent of the Cistine Chapel and the Palace of

Versailles, combined. Authentic renaissance tapestries draped the walls, flanked by massive hand-blown sconces leafed with solid gold.

The furniture was a combination of original Louis XIV and Louis XV with plush hand-woven carpets and deep red drapes all laced throughout with Florentine gold. The furnishings and surrounding art was of distinct museum quality. And although it's rate for a single night was $15,000.00 a night, it was complementary to those "whales" who had a one-million dollar line of credit. It was also complimentary if one just happened to be a powerful drug lord from Colombia!

There, in the middle of the palatial surroundings, stood Senor Louis Varga, a 60-year-old, tall, robust man with a commanding presence. A full head of white wavy hair framed a tanned, craggy face showing off strong and striking features. Looking at Varga, one could sense the power and machismo of this South American.

Varga was dressed in a white silk shirt, his cuffs rolled, showing the heavy gold jewelry he wore on both wrists. A white alligator belt with a large sterling-silver buckle was secured through the loops of his white jeans. White alligator slip-ons, and no socks, completed his overall look of true casual elegance.

Both men embraced.

"How was your trip, Hector?" Varga asked.

"Fine, Louis, and yours?"

"It was very nice. Relaxing. I enjoyed it." Varga went on. "I wanted to greet you as soon as you got here. But we can talk business later. How about you coming by at seven-thirty? We will have dinner in my suite. Okay?"

"I'll be there," Santiago said, respectfully giving a deferential nod to his boss.

Santiago said goodbye as his gut messaged he was in the middle of something very big.

Back in his own suite, Santiago was pouring himself a Vodka on the rocks when the door chime sounded.

"Willy." Santiago rang out. "Get the door."

Mendoza walked to the double doors, opening the one not bolted to the floor.

"Hector," Mendoza called out, after seeing who was at the other end of the entrance. "Varga sent us a couple a' presents."

Moving away from the bar located next to the entry salon, Santiago positioned himself for a clearer view. Seeing who was at the door, Santiago broke out into a broad smile. "Hello, *senoritas*. Come right in."

Two strikingly attractive young women entered. They looked like models. One was a platinum blond in her twenties with the face of a starlet and figure to match. A low-cut white dress showed the round fullness of two beautifully contoured breasts which stuck out firmly over a tight waist and perfectly round bottom. The dress clung tightly to her well-tanned skin, highlighting the outline of her thigh-high panties—the kind usually worn by go-go dancers. Long, curvy bare legs that narrowed in perfect symmetry to her ankles, were supported by white satin shoes with three-inch spike heels. She was dazzling, voluptuously sexy, and invitingly sensuous.

Her companion, although not quite as pretty, was equally endowed. Dark long hair that fell to her shoulders in straight and perfectly styled strands, contrasted her light, clear skin. A pink, sheer, button-down blouse, with four of them unbuttoned, showed curves of firm breasts. They needed no artificial support. A white silk skirt with a side slit almost to the waist, displayed a figure obviously worked on and pampered. Her pink pumps matched the color of her blouse, throwing off a look of youthful innocence.

Speaking to the young blond, Santiago asked, "What's your name?"

"Beverly. And you must be Mr. Santiago."

"Yeah, that's right, Beverly. Who's your friend?" Santiago asked as he signaled to the young women to join him in the living room section of the suite.

"My name is Annette. And if you are Mr. Santiago, then you must be Mr. Mendoza, right?" .

"Well, you got the names right," Mendoza replied.

After an uncomfortable pause, Beverly asked, "Well then, gentlemen, what is your pleasure?" Beverly and Annette were no amateurs. They had been through many of these situations before.

Realizing that Varga intended that Beverly be paired with Santiago—she was the better looking of the two—Santiago nodded to his under-boss. "Willy, take Annette with you. Beverly and me, we're gonna have a drink in my suite."

While the young ladies were available for any kind of sport—group, individual, or otherwise—Santiago was in San Juan for a very special business purpose—to meet with his boss, Louis Varga, and to nail down the Indian gambling deal, if possible. However, since Varga was generous enough to provide such attractive diversion, he would accept the offering, but without making a full day of its erotic menu.

With his right arm around Annette's waist, Mendoza and his guest walked out of the suite toward his own room several paces down the hall. Before closing the door, Santiago sounded out, "Willy, call me in a couple a hours. And don't forget."

Alone in the suite with the young blond-haired girl, Santiago spoke first. "So, how about a drink, Beverly? Whattle ya have?" Santiago asked politely. "I have champagne. Or anything else you want."

"Vodka on rocks would be just fine, thank you."

Santiago filled two short-barrel glasses with ice, and poured the vodka, filling them to the top. He handed one of the glasses to Beverly. *"Salud"* Santiago toasted as they clinked glasses. Both took little swallows.

"Look, Beverly, what do ya say we go down to the casino. When I'm in a gamblin' joint I first gotta play a little Blackjack. It's a thing I have. I'll give them action for maybe twenty minutes, a half hour, no more. And then we can come back here. Okay?"

"Sure," an agreeable Beverly replied. "I'll bring you luck. You'll see."

Santiago picked up the telephone and asked the operator to connect him with the casino manager. Speaking to him, Santiago told him he would be playing Blackjack. That he wanted a special table reserved only for his play.

After completing the call, Santiago turned to his young guest. "You play Blackjack, Beverly?"

"No. I play the slots now and then. But I'm really no gambler. It's too easy to lose. And I don't like that very much."

"Well, you'll sit next to me. I'll teach ya how to play Blackjack. Okay. Lets go."

He placed his unfinished drink on the bar counter. Beverly did the same. They exited the suite, arm in arm.

Having been to *The La Ultima Hotel and Casino* many times before, Hector Santiago walked directly into the large casino. The distinctive sounds of slot machines with their different musical chimes and tones, were familiar ones. People around craps tables, screaming with excitement as players rolled the dice, were part of the noisy ambiance and high energy that was to be found everywhere. Casino noises—shrieks of hysteria from a delirious winner, the whole maddening and crazy action of the place—made Santiago's adrenaline rise sharply.

Marveling at the casino's remarkable ability to detect cheating through its intricate security system, Santiago gazed up at the ceiling. He could see the globe-like fixtures he knew contained hidden cameras over each gambling area. They provided an overview of the floor action to special screen watchers holed up in a large room above the casino. Equipped with a wall of television monitors, its state-of-the-art technology was capable of zeroing in on a suspected cheater with such magnification as to fill an entire fifty inch screen with as small an object as the ring on a player's finger, if necessary. Santiago knew that everything viewed by the camera lens would routinely be filmed so that big brother upstairs could play back any portion shot by the camera one frame at a time if either an employee, or gambler, was suspected of cheating.

There were even hidden cameras focused upon the upstairs watchers to ensure that their job was being performed honestly, and that they were not conspiring with any cheaters on the casino floor.

The chain of security in the casino was designed as to have each person who handled money or chips, watched closely by another, who in turn, would be tracked by yet another. Santiago was aware that this was standard procedure, employed by all casinos to protect against cheating, or skimming from the cash and chips passing through so many hands.

How could I use some of those ideas in my own business? Santiago wondered. There were huge sums of cash and hundreds of pounds of cocaine that flowed daily from original sources in Colombia to the entire New York market. Security was always a top priority. And improving it was a continuing challenge to Santiago.

As he passed through aisles, the surrounding roulettes, Blackjack tables, slot machines, and players tipping scantily-clad cocktail waitresses who served complimentary drinks, were all part of Santiago's mood elevators.

Santiago held Beverly's hand as he headed directly to the "pit," a private and separately roped-off section of the casino. It had three Blackjack tables, a Baccarat table and a private lounge. It was an area reserved exclusively for high-rollers.

"It is always a pleasure to see you, Hector," Albert Diaz, the pit boss, said, extending his hand warmly.

Last names would never be used in such a gambling setting, in order to protect the confidentiality of the player should someone be close enough to overhear the name used. And big-action players had many reasons why they would not want their identity broadcast in public.

"What can I get for you?" Diaz asked. His manner, as always, was gracious.

"Fifty thousand," Hector replied. This meant he requested a marker, or IOU he would have to sign in exchange for fifty thousand dollars in chips.

Diaz removed the "reserved" sign that stood on top of the Blackjack table. The betting limit was shown by a printed card inserted into a small stand resting on the left hand corner of the table. It read, "Minimum bet $1,000. Maximum bet $10,000." The minimum of $1,000 was the amount that Santiago requested.

"Can I order something for you, or the young lady? Drink? Coffee? A cigar, Hector? Anything?" Diaz asked.

"No thanks, Albert. We're fine."

Santiago sat on the left corner stool and Beverly was seated to his right. He was the only player at the table.

Diaz instructed the dealer, whose name tag pinned to his shirt, read, "Danny Cole/Reno, Nevada," to give Santiago fifty thousand dollars in chips. Reaching into a large tray which was in front of him, and lined up in precise systematic order with different chip denominations, Danny counted out, stacking chips in different piles on the table. There were four purple chips, each with a value of five thousand dollars; twenty orange chips, valued at one thousand dollars each; sixteen brown chips, a value of five hundred dollars each; and twenty black chips, each valued at one hundred dollars. The chips totaled fifty thousand dollars.

"Good luck," Danny said politely, once Diaz verified the chip count. The dealer pushed the stacks gently over to Santiago along the green felt that covered the table.

"I'll start off slowly," Hector said. He placed two one thousand dollar chips on the betting circle in front of him.

Beverly blew a kiss. "For good luck."

Santiago liked that.

Danny dealt from a "shoe" that housed six decks of cards already shuffled. The first card delivered to Hector was a 5. Danny dealt himself a 9. The second card to Santiago was a Queen. It had a value of 10, giving him a total of 15. The second card Danny dealt himself was buried face-down under the 9—the hole card.

Turning to Beverly to his right, Santiago said, "The Queen is a 10, and the 5, gives me 15. The dealer shows a 9 on top. I don't know what his hole card is, but I must play my hand like he has a 10, or a picture card under his 9."

"Why is that?" Beverly asked.

"Because the odds are that he has a picture—it's called a face card—or a 10. With six decks, I gotta play the odds. That means, I'm gonna hit my 15. I don't like my hand. But that's why they call it gambling. If I get anything over a 6, it's a busted hand. It means I'm over. And I lose."

Tapping the cards dealt to him lightly with the index finger of his right hand, it was a signal to the dealer to give him a card. With a 15, the odds did not favor Santiago.

Danny drew a card from the shoe, passing it face-up to Santiago. It was a 5, giving him a total of 20. Waving his right hand to the side, palm down, and stopping abruptly in the air, was the sign given to the dealer that he was sticking with the cards he had.

Danny turned up his hole card. It was a Jack, giving him 19. Santiago's 20 won the hand. Danny paid him with two one-thousand-dollar chips taken from his tray.

A big smile broke out on Santiago's face. "We got real lucky that hand. Good way to start."

Santiago placed the two one-thousand-dollar chips on top of the original two chips. His bet was now four thousand dollars. Beverly nestled closer to him. She kissed him on the cheek. "This is for luck." Santiago liked that too.

On the next round, Santiago's first card was an Ace. The dealer's card, a King. The second card to Santiago, another Ace. The dealer dealt himself a hole card, face-down.

"Now it gets interesting, Beverly. I got two Aces. Means I can split 'em. It's like playing two hands. But I have to put up another bet in the same amount I started with. And I can only take one card on each Ace. That's it."

"You have to put up four thousand dollars more?"

"That's right. Now I have eight grand on the table," as he placed four orange one-thousand-dollar chips, stacking them behind his first Ace.

"Gimme luck, Beverly." In response, the voluptuous young blond threw her left arm around Santiago, kissing him again on the cheek. It left an imprint of lipstick on the right side of his face.

"Okay, let it come," Hector sang out to Danny.

The card dealt on the first Ace, was a 7. "The Ace is a 1 or 11. The 7 on my Ace, gives me 18 on that hand. Not great. But not too bad either."

Danny dealt Santiago a 10.

"Yes!" Santiago shouted, his right fist going straight up in a victory gesture.

"You have Blackjack," Beverly screamed, excitedly.

"It's not Blackjack when you split Aces. Only when you get it on the first two cards. But this is the best hand I can get. If I win, I'm paid the same amount I bet. Not the three to two if I had a Blackjack. Understand, Beverly?"

"I think so," she answered, shrugging her shoulders slightly.

"If the dealer has an Ace in the hole, that gives him a 21. We push on the hand. I don't win. I don't lose. Got it?" Santiago asked.

"Yep. That, I understand," Beverly replied.

Danny turned up his hole card. It was a 3, giving him a total of 13. Under the rules, anything under 17 required he take another card. If he had 17 or over, he would have to stick with what he had.

"Break. C'mon break," Hector shouted enthusiastically, hoping the card Danny would deal himself was either a 9, 10, or a face card. If that happened it would take him over 21, "breaking," or busting his hand—and Santiago would win.

Danny dealt the next card. It was a 2, giving him 15.

"Break. Break." Beverly joined in.

The next card was a 7, giving the dealer 22. Danny busted. Santiago won the hand.

Filled with the rush of victory, Santiago slapped the palm of his right hand on the felt table hard several times. "Yes. Yes." Danny removed eight orange, one-thousand-dollar chips from his tray, paying off the bets Santiago had placed.

"Two in a row. Wow! Keep it up. Don't stop now."

In two hands he had won five thousand dollars. He placed five orange chips on each slot. His total bet was ten thousand dollars, now playing two hands.

"C'mon baby. Give me a kiss for good luck." Beverly responded willingly. The dealer started the next round.

Danny dealt Santiago a 6 on the first hand a 4 on the second. Danny dealt himself an 8. The next card on Santiago's first hand a 4, giving him a 10. The card dealt to Santiago on his second hand a 5, giving him a 9.

"This is gettin' interestin.' I have two double-downs."

"What's that?" Beverly asked.

"Since I have a 10 on the first hand, and a 9 on this hand, I can double-down. That means, I get one card after I put up enough chips to match the bet I already got on the table."

"So you have to put up an additional five thousand dollars on each hand?" Beverly asked.

"You got it right, baby."

"You'll be betting twenty thousand dollars?" Beverly asked, crinkling her face in shocked reaction to the high stakes of the game.

"Like I said before, Beverly. That's why they call it gamblin.' Ya win. Or ya lose. But we're gonna win, right?"

"Yes." Beverly made a hard fist, sharply pulling her elbow back in a victory gesture.

"Double-down," Santiago sang out, placing a five thousand dollar chip along side each original bet of the same amount.

Danny dealt the next card to Santiago. It was a 9, giving him, 19. The card on Santiago's second hand, an 8, giving him, 17.

"Watch out." Hector knew his 17 would be a loser if the dealer had a 10, or a face card in the hole, giving him an 18.

"C'mon Danny. Turn up an 8. No pictures. C'mon, do it right. Do it right."

Danny turned up his hole card. It was a 2, giving him a total of 10.

"Christ. Damn. Don't come up with a face card." A 10, or a face card, would give the house a 20— and wipe out Santiago's twenty thousand dollars he had spread on his two bets. An Ace to the dealer would also result in a loss to Santiago, since it would add up to 21.

Santiago grabbed Beverly's hand, squeezed it hard as he waited anxiously for the dealer's next card.

Danny dealt himself a 6, for a total of 16. Being under 17, and according to the rules of Blackjack, he would have to deal himself another card.

"Now a face card. Now,"Santiago belted out, squeezing Beverly's hand even harder.

Diaz, the pit boss, watched the action closely, as Danny drew the next card from the shoe. It was a 6, giving him a total of 22. An over, or busted hand.

"We did it. We did it. Yes. Yes," Santiago shouted euphorically.

"Wow. Wow. I'm drained,"Beverly joined in.

Danny removed four five-thousand-dollar chips from his tray, placing two alongside each ten-thousand-dollar bet Santiago had made.

Santiago continued playing for the next fifteen minutes, winning some hands, losing others.

"This is my last hand," he said, playing one slot, as he placed two five-thousand-dollar chips in the betting circle for a total bet of ten thousand dollars.

Danny dealt Santiago an Ace. He dealt himself a King.

"Be there. Be there. Show me a picture, Danny. C'mon, Beverly. Gimme luck."

Beverly took Santiago's hand, held it locked together in his, raising both hands high above their heads as if they had just been elected to a high political office.

Danny dealt another card to Santiago. A Queen—Blackjack! Beverly went wild with excitement.

"Not yet, Beverly. If his hole card is an Ace, I don't win Blackjack. It's a push. So c'mon, Danny. Do the right thing. No Ace, ya hear?"

Danny turned over his hole card. It was a Jack. Santiago's Blackjack was a winner—fifteen thousand dollars for repayment of his ten thousand dollars. A three for two pay-out.

"Yes!... Yes!" Santiago shouted out. He took Beverly's hand, held it locked with his, and kissed the back of her hand. With a broad smile, he said, "Beverly, you are my good luck charm." He followed it by kissing her on the lips.

"Albert," Santiago called out to the pit boss standing next to the dealer, "I'm cashin' in." With both hands on the felt table, he pushed all the chips stacked in front of him toward Danny. "I'm also gonna pay off my marker."

Danny Cole counted the chips. The pit boss watched closely. Total count:$88,600. Setting aside $50,000 for the marker Santiago had signed earlier, Danny gently pushed $38,600 in chips toward Santiago, the amount he had won in less than twenty-five minutes of big-action play.

Santiago tossed a brown and black chip to Cole. "Danny, that's for you. You did real good for me."

"I thank you very much, Sir," Danny replied appreciatively. A $600 tip, for less then a half-hour's work equaled an entire week's salary.

"Albert, please put $36,000 in the cage for me. Okay?" Santiago held back two orange $1,000 chips. He held them in his hand.

"It is my pleasure. I will have your 'paid' marker and cage receipt for $36,000 in just a moment," Diaz said, walking to a computer screen several feet away.

Returning with the $50,000 marker stamped "paid," and a credit receipt from the cage for $36,000, Diaz said, "Here you are, Hector." Hector tore up the marker, folded the cage receipt, and stuck it in his wallet.

"It's always a pleasure to see you, Hector. And we thank you for your action." All pit bosses knew from experience that the casino might in any single session lose, but the odds were so heavily stacked in its favor, that at the end of the day, it would always come out the winner.

"Thank you, Albert. I'll be back later."

He and Beverly rose from the table.

As they started back through the noisy and crowded casino, Santiago stopped before they reached the hotel elevator. Facing Beverly, he took her hand, and placed the two orange $1,000 chips in her palm. Closing one finger at a time around them, Santiago raised Beverly's hand to his lips, kissing her fingers, gently. "This is for you.

You were my good luck charm. Get yourself somethin' real nice."
Santiago smiled broadly.

"Oh, that is so sweet of you. Thank you so very, very much."

The two returned to Santiago's suite. Once inside, he pulled her up against him, kissing her, firmly. Beverly's response was warm. Together they walked into his bedroom, Santiago's right hand gliding slowly down her smooth neckline to the tender softness of her curved bottom.

Walking over to the bar, Santiago retrieved the champagne he had earlier stuck into the ice-filled bucket. He returned to the bedroom with two fluted crystal glasses in his left hand, the vintage bottle of chilled *Dom Perignon* in his right.

Having stripped down to a low-cut, sexy brasier and black silk, string bikini panties, Beverly lay coyly on the king-size bed, sensuously massaging her shapely breasts. She invitingly awaited Santiago's return.

Two hours later, after Beverly had dressed and quietly left his suite, Santiago lay in a soporific daze, thinking how much he was valued by Louis Varga. He felt the relaxed tiredness that always follows uninhibited and high-energy sex. Winning over $35,000 at Blackjack was an additional bonus-component of his overall mood of euphoric contentment.

But the main event was yet to come: the private dinner he would soon share with his Colombian boss, Louis Varga, and the plans for their entry into the exciting world of Indian casino gambling. It had all the glitz and pizzaz that would fill most fantasies. But most of all, it had the unbelievable cash prize waiting there to be grabbed!

CHAPTER FOURTEEN

During his return flight from Syracuse to Washington, Matt had a nagging thought. Although the mist covering Chuck's murder was beginning to lift, there was no doubt in his mind, that Fowler was in some way involved. He was also convinced there was far more to be uncovered in Syracuse.

Leaving Reagan National Airport in Washington, he went to his car parked in the twenty-four-hour lot, and proceeded directly to the Justice Department building. Once inside, he headed straight for Chuck Bradford's office, hoping to find Alice Lacy, Chuck's secretary. Making his way through the many layers of security protecting the office of the attorney general, Matt greeted Alice, who was seated in the reception area of the suite.

"Alice," Matt said softly, gently embracing the young woman who had served Chuck Bradford with such loyalty.

"I have to talk with Frank Stanford, but when I'm finished, I must speak to you. You'll be here?"

"Oh, yes sir," she said, moist-eyed. "I still can't believe that he's gone. It's all such a horror. Why would anybody want to hurt Mr. Bradford? "

Matt left the reception area, entering an office Alice had set aside for him. Matt could have used Chuck's office, but decided not to. His death was too recent, too raw, and too shocking for those who had been close to him in the department. The office remained empty. Everything there was just as Chuck had left it before he went to Syracuse.

Frank Stanford arrived shortly after receiving Matt's telephone call. As Stanford rushed into the office to report to Matt, he was bubbling over with information he couldn't wait to share with his superior.

"I think I may have found something important, sir."he said excitedly. " I may have uncovered the reason the attorney general went to Syracuse. At least, I believe I know why Mr. Bradford was interested in Syracuse."

"Don't stop now, Frank. Let me hear."

"Yes sir. Well, I came upon a cover story that appeared in the December 2002 issue of *Time* magazine. It was a real eye-opener—all about Indian casino gambling. Did you happen to see it, Mr. Connors?"

"No, Frank, I didn't. What was it about?"

"It reported the background of Indian casino gambling in the United States, and how certain questionable investors have taken advantage of some loopholes in the law, making it an easy mark for big profiteering. But even beyond that—possible corruption."

"That's very interesting. Go ahead."

"Well, the article gave me an idea. So I checked with a clerk I know who's with the Bureau of Indian Affairs. And here's the cliff-hanger, Mr. Connors."

"Go on."

"I discovered that an application had been approved, granting a permit to the Pecontic tribe to operate full casino gambling on its reservation land in Syracuse."

"Hold on a second, Frank. That sounds harmless enough to me, without knowing more. But my question is, why would the attorney general have been interested in that?"

"I have no absolute proof that he was, sir. But after going over the *Time* article carefully, it occurred to me that Mr. Bradford's interest level might have been raised since, according to that story, there's been a lot of abuse in the whole system of Indian casinos in the country. It's a very sensitive issue and I don't know exactly how it fits. That is, if at all."

"How what fits? Exactly what are you saying?"

"It's a delicate matter. How can I put it....?"

"Just come out and say it. That's always a good start."

"Alright sir...Well, Congresswoman Bradford, Mr. Bradford's widow, is a member of that same Pecontic tribe, the very same tribe that just had its licence approved for full casino gambling on its reservation."

"Therefore...what?"

"Therefore…Well with your permission, sir, may I read a few excerpts I clipped from that *Time* article?"

"Sure, Frank. Go ahead. I'm still a little in the dark."

"This may clear things up a bit. This article gives a quick insight about what's been happening since Congress passed the act that gave the right to Indian tribes to operate gambling casinos on their reservations. As you know, the purpose of the act was to improve the economic conditions on reservations, but it hasn't worked out that way."

"How do you mean, it hasn't?"

"Well, according to the *Time* magazine report, and I quote: '*Instead of regulating Indian gambling, the act has created chaos and a system tailor-made for abuse. It set up a powerless and under-funded watchdog and dispersed oversight responsibilities among a hopelessly conflicting hierarchy of local, state, and federal agencies. It created a system so skewed that only a few small tribes and their backers are getting rich; it has changed the face of Indian country. Some long-dispersed tribes, aided by new, non-Indian financial godfathers, are regrouping to benefit from the gaming windfall. Others are seeking new reservations—some in areas where they never lived, occasionally even in other states, solely to build a casino. And leaders of small, newly wealthy tribes now have so much unregulated cash and political clout that they can ride roughshod over neighboring communities, poorer tribes, and even their own members.'* "

Matt listened. His interest continued to peak.

"In fact, Mr. Connors," his young assistant continued, "the take last year from Indian casino gambling was enormous—almost $13 billion. And according to *Time*, the casinos held back $5 billion or more of the total revenue received."

Shocked by what he just heard, Matt leaned forward across his desk. "From what you just read to me, I can understand why Chuck might have been interested in Indian casino gambling in Syracuse—particularly the connection with the tribe both his wife and father-in-law were members of. Okay Frank, do you have anything else?"

"Another concern that Mr. Bradford may have had… May I read you a further portion of the *Time* article, Mr. Connors?"

"Sure. Please."

"This is quite interesting."

"Let me hear."

"Yes, sir. 'While most Indians continue to live in poverty, many non-Indian investors are extracting hundreds of millions of dollars sometimes in violation of legal limits from casinos they helped establish, either by taking advantage of regulatory loopholes or cutting backroom deals. More than 90 percent of the contracts between tribes and outside gaming-management companies operate with no oversight. That means investors' identities are often sacred, as are their financial arrangements and their share of the revenue. Whatever else Congress had in mind when it passed the regulatory act, presumably the idea was not to line the pockets of a Malaysian gambling magnate, a South African millionaire, or a Minnesota leather apparel king.

" 'The tribes' secrecy about financial affairs and the complicity of government oversight agencies has guaranteed that abuses in Indian country, growing out of the surge in gaming riches, go undetected, unreported, and unprosecuted. The tribal leaders sometimes rule with an iron fist. Dissent is crushed. Cronyism flourishes. Those who question how much the casinos really make, where the money goes, or even tribal operations in general may be banished. Indians who challenge the system are often intimidated, harassed, and threatened with reprisals or physical harm. They risk the loss of their jobs, homes, and income.' "

After his assistant completed the report, Matt's face lit up with excitement. "You may have hit on what Chuck was looking into, Frank. At the moment, I'm not quite sure how it all comes together, but you can bet your government pension we're going to find out. I'll go through my copy of the file you've made for me and get back to you tomorrow."

When Stanford left, Matt made his way to Alice Lacy's desk.

Smiling cordially at her, he said, "Thank you for waiting, Alice. I hope I haven't delayed you from what you were working on."

"Not at all, Mr. Connors."

"Good. Now, if you don't mind, I'd like to ask you some questions."

"Of course, Mr. Connors."

"And the answers I hope to get from you, is one of the reasons I'm here. With the funeral and everything, I've been unable to meet with you until now."

"I understand."

"You could be of great help me to me in the investigation President Harrington has commissioned me to conduct."

"Anything. Anything at all I can do. You know that. Just name it, Mr. Connors."

"For starters, Chuck must have had some record of what he was working on just before his death. The burglary in his house left us empty-handed. Whatever Chuck may have had in his study relating to Syracuse was removed. So, my first question, did he give you any memos that mentioned Syracuse, or the Pecontic tribe, or anything at all like that?"

"No, sir."

"Let me try it this way...before he left for Syracuse, did he leave anything with you, or in his office that was less than routine in nature? Anything?" Matt was hoping there might be some trail that would lead to Syracuse, no matter how oblique.

"I'm really not aware of any," Alice answered apologetically.

"Okay, but I'm going to ask you to think hard, Alice. Try to remember," Matt urged. "Do you recall anything out of the ordinary? Was Chuck working on something special, or different? Something he might have said? Something you overhead?"

"No, Mr. Connors. You know how Mr. Bradford was. He never carried what he was thinking or doing on his sleeve. He was very private that way."

"What about conversations he had with you?"

"Mr. Bradford kept things pretty much to himself for the most part."

"Uh, huh. Okay...let me try something else. Were there any unexpected or unscheduled visitors a few days before he went to Syracuse?"

"None, sir. None at all."

"What about any e-mails he might have received or was responding to that might have crossed your desk? Any like that?"

"A negative on that also. I'm sorry."

"Any unusual faxes that he might have mentioned to you at the time?"

"None that were out of the ordinary." Alice was upset at her inability to be of more help to Matt in his search.

"Perhaps there was an odd letter that came in. A phone call he received?"

"Nothing odd or strange, Mr. Connors. Routine correspondence, that's about it."

"Try, Alice. Try. Was there anything at all, as remote as it may seem to you now, anything different just before Chuck left for Syracuse?"

"No. No. There's nothing I can recall. In fact, Mr. Bradford didn't even tell me that he was going to Syracuse. All that he said was that he would not be in the office. That he would call in."

"Well, did you ask him where he would be?"

"No sir. I didn't think it was my place to ask. If he wanted me to know, I'm sure he would have told me."

"Well, didn't you think his absence from the office was strange, or unusual?"

"Not at all. Mr. Bradford had done that from time to time."

"What about Chuck's activities in the office the day before he went to Syracuse? Was there anything that sticks out in your mind at this time? Anything at all?"

"I'm sorry, Mr. Connors. I just do not recall anything unusual happening." Alice paused. Her face crunched up. A sudden quizzical expression took over.

"What, Alice? What?" Matt broke in.

"There was something...but it was probably nothing." Matt slouched closer to Alice, his eyes fixed on her face. She continued. "Mr. Bradford did close the door to his office, which he usually kept open. I do remember that he asked not to be disturbed. He said he had to get something out and that he didn't want any distractions. I asked if I could help him with what he was working on, but he said he would do it himself. I have no idea what it was. But he was typing something on the computer."

"Didn't that surprise you, Alice?"

"No, Mr. Conners. Mr. Bradford had done that many times before. It certainly was not unusual."

Matt let out a heavy sigh. His eyes took on a curious sparkle.

"I see, but you remember that he did close the door."

"Yes sir, I have a clear memory of that."

"That's good, Alice. Very good! Now tell me, how long was his door closed?"

"I'd say... at least an hour."

"Well, didn't you consider that strange?"

"No, I didn't. Not at the time."

"Well, how do you figure it was about an hour?"

"I maintain a log of every telephone call that comes in." She bent over her desk, lifting a large volume, imprinted, 'Daily Calendar.' Here it is for that day, October 16. The first call I logged in after Mr. Bradford told me he was not to be disturbed, was at 2:10. The next call he actually took, was at 3:15. After that, he opened the door to his office, came into the reception room, and told me he was leaving for the day."

"We could be on to something. May I see that log, please?" Matt asked, trying to hold back the rush he was beginning to feel.

Scanning the page, Matt's eyes focused upon the entries for October 16 just read by Alice. He examined them carefully, noting the last telephone call Chuck received before the 2:10 entry, was logged in at 1:45. According to the log, he remained with the same call until 2:05. The other phone calls logged between those two time periods, were recorded under the "message received" column.

"Alice, I see here that Chuck took a telephone call at 1:45, and was on the phone until 2:05. Would there be any way of knowing who he was talking to during that twenty minute segment?" Matt's pulse was beginning to race more rapidly.

"No, Mr. Connors. The caller would not give his name, other than to say something like, 'Tell the attorney general it has something to do with an Indian license.' Those two words, 'Indian license' are what I posted in the log under the 'message received' heading, as you can see."

My god. This could be the first real break in the case. Matt was beginning to hyperventilate.

"Well, didn't that in and of itself raise some questions in your mind at the time?"

"No, not at all. Mr. Bradford was always receiving telephone calls from many people about dozens of different things. I always tried to screen them as much as possible. But Mr. Bradford was always open to telephone calls he would get from a lot of sources. He wanted everyone to have access to the office of the attorney general. That was the way Mr. Bradford was. Always open, and available to the public. It was a standing rule of his."

"Yes, I think we were all aware of that. But please take me back to the message about the 'Indian license' log entry."

"The message sounded rather routine to me at the time, and probably accounts for the reason it did not come to my mind right away when you asked me to remember that day's events."

"Let's zero-in on that for the moment. Is there anything else about that message that you remember?"

"No. Nothing else other than what I have already told you ."

"What about Chuck's computer? Could you open it and find out what he was working on?" Matt asked anxiously.

"Mr. Bradford 'password-protected' some of his documents. For security reasons of course. The document, if there is one, would be under a special file name. We could do a file search by date, but once again, if its password-protected it won't come up."

"Why not?"

"Without typing in the password, any document protected by it will remain hidden. And if I do not know the password Mr. Bradford used, I will be unable to open it up."

"I see...then, let's try this. Please locate all the documents for that day. Maybe there's an outside chance that he didn't use a password. Perhaps he just forgot to put a password in or maybe he was distracted just when he was about to do it.... In any case, could you go through everything that's entered for the 16th, Alice?"

"That, I can do. I'll search for all documents that were created on October 16."

Matt let out his breath slowly, mentally crossing his fingers. He sat next to Alice positioned in front of Chuck's computer screen, as her right hand guided the mouse in her search for all of the document file names created on that day.

Minutes passed. Suddenly, Alice cried out excitedly, "Here's a document that was created at 2:07. It was last modified at 3:11 p.m. on October 16."

"What's the name of that document?" Matt jumped in.

"Indian Casino License—Syracuse."

"That's got to be it. Open it, Alice."

"I'm trying to get it on the screen. No, it won't come up. It's asking for a password."

"How about the password he always used. You would have it, wouldn't you?"

"I do have a password to get into Mr. Bradford's computer, but if there's a document he specifically password-protected, I will not be able to get into it, unless I created it myself."

"Type it in. It may work."

"It doesn't, Mr. Connors. This is a document that Mr. Bradford assigned his own special password to...and I do not have it."

"Where does that leave us, Alice? There's got to be another way." Open frustration was showing itself throughout the room.

" At this point, Mr. Connors, I'm stuck. Real stuck" Alice looked crushed.

"One minute, Alice. Let me take a crack at it." Matt spoke out loud, asking himself, *What code word would Chuck have used to get into a report about a license issued to an Indian tribe?* "Alice, plug in 'gaming.'"

"It reads 'Access =Denied.' 'Gaming' is not the password, Mr. Connors."

"Try 'gambling.' "

"No. That's not it either."

"Casino."

"I'm sorry, Mr. Connors. Access denied."

"How about 'arrowhead'?"

"No. 'Access denied.' That's not the password." Alice let out a deep sigh.

For the next hour of frustration, Matt continued to toss almost every possible code name at Alice: birthdays, anniversarys, family names, places, slogans—whatever came to mind. Nothing worked. All came back, "access denied." Their anxiety, fueled by continuing disappointment, was shattering.

Think, Matt. Think, he kept hounding himself. *You knew Chuck. What code name would he have used for such a document? Could it have had something to do with the tribe? Tribe...* he repeated. Excitedly, Matt rang out, "Alice, perhaps it's been in front of me all this time, and I just couldn't see it."

"See what, Mr. Connors?"

"Chuck's password of course," Matt continued in a flat, deliberate tone. "Alice, I want you to type in the word 'pecontic.' " The pronounced creases that suddenly appeared on Matt's forehead evidenced his guarded anticipation.

Alice keyed in each letter: P-E-C-O-N-T-I-C. She then hit <enter>. There it was, a document with the header: PRELIMINARY REPORT OF INVESTIGATION OF GAMING LICENSE ISSUED TO PECONTIC TRIBE, SYRACUSE, NEW YORK.

It was a five-page memorandum, marked "CONFIDENTIAL." Under the word 'source', was the following: "Anonymous tip, Indian gambling license, those involved with issuance, others who will profit from its operation."

As Matt started to read the memo; he appeared visibly shaken. He became aware for the first time about an Indian casino gambling scheme in Syracuse, involving the names of very high-profile individuals: Vincent Scarpizzi, New York's crime boss; Pierre Treausance, the United States Commissioner of Indian Affairs; Niles Martin, the Governor of New York; Joe Roundtree, Chief of the Pecontic tribe; and...Jarrett Lee Hastings, the vice president of the United States

Conscious of the power behind the names, knowing that they could possibly reach into the White House itself, Matt understood immediately how such a conspiracy, if it existed at all, would have played out ruthlessly in an attempt to stop any investigation into its illegal purposes. Chuck's death could certainly have been carried out to conceal the identity of the conspirators involved. And if the memo, based upon an unsubstantiated anonymous tip, were ever to be leaked, the media would jump all over it. It would be open season on President Harrington's administration and the media would treat it like raw meat in a cage filled with hungry lions. But even without solid proof, the mountain of ugly publicity and political maneuvering that would occur behind closed doors, could severely compromise Matt's investigation into the death of the attorney general.

No matter how the story came out, President Harrington would be smeared, his administration irreparably tainted. The American people would be dealt another blow, feeding their continuing cynicism about the politicians they elect to the highest offices of the land.

Matt now understood that Chuck Bradford's trip to Syracuse was probably an exploratory one. But the questions Chuck must have asked had to have been so alarming as to produce the immediate and deadly response by his killers, Matt surmised. It was now his job to take up where his friend had left off, knowing how perilous the journey would be.

Matt turned slowly to Alice. "You are sworn to secrecy. Under no circumstances are you to disclose to anyone what you have just learned. That includes employees of this department. You are to speak to no one about this matter, unless you receive full authority from me. Do you understand, Alice?"

"Yes I do, Mr. Connors. You know that you can count on me."

"I know that, Alice. Thank you for all of your help."

Matt left the office. His first mission now was to report fully to President Harrington with his shocking discovery. Matt was angry at the duplicity of the vice president of the United States, who had been personally selected in good faith by President Harrington, whose judgment would be brutally attacked for having hand-picked such a running-mate. The news of Hastings' involvement in a gambling scheme, if true, could trigger the biggest scandal since Watergate. As a seasoned Justice Department professional, Matt was keenly aware that Chuck's memo was loaded with potential disaster, but most of all, it had the high explosive powder to bring down the entire administration, including the president of the United States, himself.

The alarming document also named Joe Roundtree, Jenny's father. But, Matt agonized, *How could I deal wisely with such a personal dilemma that could possibly destroy any meaningful relationship I ever hoped to have with Jenny in the future?*

As for now however, the meeting with President Harrington, and the riveting urgency attached to it, was his top priority. The sensitive face-off with Jenny regarding her father, whatever his true connection with the Indian casino corruption scandal, *would just have to wait for another day!*

CHAPTER FIFTEEN

In his Washington residence, dressed in a casual open-collared shirt, Vice President Jarrett Lee Hastings continued to pace from one side of the den to the other. The twenty-year-old Chivas scotch he had poured into a tall ice-filled glass, provided little relief from the high level of stress he was feeling. The rumor circulating around the beltway that the late attorney general of the United States had been looking into the casino license issued to the Pecontic tribe at the time he was gunned down in Syracuse, continued to hound him.

My God, could there be a possible connection between the Bureau of Indian Affairs that gave its okay to the license, and Bradford's death? Hastings wondered, pacing nervously about as if he were competing in a marathon walk.

Pausing only to refill his glass, he resumed his anxious, around-the-room, quick step. "Holy shit!" he sounded out with a full-throated resonance, as if the bust of one of his heroes, Lyndon Baines Johnson, sitting on top of a tall marble pedestal, could actually hear him. But not wanting to be found talking to himself, he kept the balance of his statement within his own thoughts. *Holy shit,* he repeated in his head. *Could my telling Pierre Treausance to grant the license after that horseshit meeting I had with Scarpizzi's two-bit lawyer, have had some connection with this whole attorney general business? Of course it could, stupid!* He swore at himself, angry at how he could have handled things so poorly.

Throughout his career, Hastings' slick political maneuvers had been the benchmarks of his success. But what he might have to face if he were to be dragged into the net of federal suspicion because of a tight relationship with Treausance, could be disastrous. While manipulation had always been the template of his life, this "Indian casino thing" could be the destined predictor of his ultimate Waterloo.

Goddamn, he beat down hard on himself again, beads of cold sweat beginning to form on his already creased brow. *How could I have been such a dumb-ass idiot! Everybody knows I was the guy behind the Treausance appointment. The whole thing could blow-up in my face big-time. Shit!*

Falling deeper into uncertainty over what the Treausance connection might ultimately lead to, Hastings had a sickening feeling: that he was strapped down, chained to the chair of an emotional Ferris wheel, revolving…over and around…around and over…to its place of origin, despite his frantic efforts to free himself from the danger beginning to consume him. Worse, he felt as if he were drowning….sinking, with his whole political career beginning to flash in front of him.

He stopped pacing and poured himself another drink. He sat down in the big leather recliner in front of a huge brick fireplace. Surrounded by the mess he thought he helped create, his troubled thoughts were immediately drawn to Pierre Treausance. None of this would be happening, he kept thinking, if it weren't for his close relationship with him. When did it all start?

Trying to search out hidden answers, his mind carried him to the events that led to the president's appointment of Pierre Treaussance as federal commissioner of Indian Affairs…

Having met Pierre Treausance, Hastings knew immediately that Treausance was not the typical beltway bureaucrat. With roots firmly ensconced in the parochialism of backwoods Mississippi politics, southern fried chicken and black-eyed peas were more to his taste than *pate de fois gras.* But yet, he had the killer instinct and brilliant cunning of someone who was in many ways heads and shoulders above those who fancied themselves as professional political gurus.

They first met at a regional party bash early in Hastings' political rise. It was being held at the local chapter of the Veterans of Foreign Wars the night before the party's state convention was to select a gubernatorial candidate.

Treausance had been a parish delegate to the Mississippi state political convention, one voice among hundreds in the ranks there to cast votes for their party's next candidate for governor. Hastings had been scheduled to deliver a "rah, rah" address to rank and file members at the convention.

He wore a large, three-inch, red-white-and-blue button pinned to his outside jacket pocket, visible to everyone, which read, "Hi, my name is Jarrett Lee Hastings." This flamboyant exhibition was intended to attract those at the gathering, and it did. One whose attention it caught, was Pierre Treausance, who, while having known of Jarrett Lee Hastings by reputation, had never met him personally.

The large button pinned to Hastings' jacket now served as the invitation for Treausance to approach him.

"Hello there, Jarrett. I'm Pierre Treausance," he said, holding a scotch on the rocks with his left hand, while extending his right hand in a friendly handshake.

"Pleasure to meet you, Pierre. Are you the same Treausance who is a delegate to the convention?" Hastings asked, accepting Treausance's hand firmly.

"One and the same."

"Well, it's indeed a pleasure to meet you, sir."

"The pleasure's all mine."

"So tell me, Pierre, how do you find the hoopla so far?"

"This is my seventh convention and frankly, as they say, 'the thrill is gone.' "

"You don't mean that you're tired of politics?"

"Hell no. It's just that I'm getting a bit bored with the same political bullshit and the typical players I see all the time. That's all."

"You know what, Pierre. I think it's time for me to buy you a drink," Hastings said.

"Quite the contrary, my friend. I see your glass is empty so it's time for me to buy *you* a drink."

"Sure, thanks. Frankly, I think you and I have a lot to talk about."

The two politicians strolled over to the bar.

Hastings had a very special agenda. He needed someone like Pierre Treausance, a man with the reputation of a knowledgeable political strategist, and an experienced fund raiser.

"What are you drinking, Pierre?"

"Chivas on the rocks. Twist of lemon."

"Right on. That's my drink also. I just knew there was something about you I liked right away."

"Maybe I read your mind, Jarrett."

"Spoken like a true politician! To success,"Hastings said, clinking glasses.

The two men swallowed their drinks in one gulp.

In the next hour, Hastings began to open up to Treausance. Over two more drinks, he laid out his plan to capture the governorship of Mississippi.

At the time, Hastings had already worked his way up the ladder to the top echelons of Mississippi politics. He now needed someone who had an intimate knowledge of the tricky game of politics and who could run the slippery interference necessary to win the big prize.

"Pierre, you'd be perfect for me. We'd make great team. Look, you've got the smarts, you're ambitious, you're aggressive, and you know the drill. But most of all, you can compliment my style. You'll make me look even better than I *am*. So, what do you say?"

It was the beginning of a strong and powerful alliance between them.

Hastings had held many appointive positions in government, the highest being secretary of state of Mississippi. He had been forced to surrender that office when the opposition party won the state House three years earlier. The mad scrambling to find a candidate for governor was now in progress with at least six wannabes declaring. The field narrowed down to four when two of the hopefuls failed to gain sufficient financial support to make the run.

Although Hastings had conducted himself publicly as if he were his party's choice for the office, the candidate ultimately hand-picked by the Mississippi delegates was one Jimmy Conklin, the ranking state senator in the legislature. Despite his disappointment at not being named as his party's standard-bearer, Hastings was intent on proving that the judgement of the delegates who chose Conklin as their man, was faulty. In a bold and risky political move, Hastings entered his own name as an insurgent candidate for governor in the fall primary election. By that action, he became the sole opposition candidate for governor, running against the organization-backed, and longtime state senator, Jimmy Conklin.

"What are my chances, Pierre?" Hastings asked Treausance in the small back room of his campaign headquarters located on Front

Street. "Conklin's been around the state legislature for years and he's had a long time to make a lotta friends."

"That's a positive, Jarrett, without question," Treausance said, standing with his face up to a large map of Mississippi, depicting demographics, its many counties, districts, and parishes. Examining the map closely while inserting color-coded stick pins to identify the varied political, civic, and ethnic groups, he continued. "But being in office as long as Conklin, could also be a heavy-duty negative."

"How do you figure that, Pierre?" Hastings asked, his eyes continuing to scan the map to determine where the pockets of his voter strength were likely to be found.

"A long time in office gives him just as much time to make as many enemies as friends."

"Well, I know I've got plenty of friends in Mississippi, Pierre. But we have to find a way to reach out to everyone in the state."

"You got it right, Jarrett. The only effective way to get your message across is with a focused and concentrated TV campaign."

"It seems we're doin' okay if you listen to Bud Crayton. Lord knows we're paying him enough for those polls he's been running. And the reports look pretty good. But what we need now, Pierre, is a big push and a flooding of 'Jarrett Lee Hastings' on the TV tube." Hastings popped open a can of Coke, taking big swallows.

"On that score, I spoke to Ernie Fox this morning. He told me he could put together four or five different thirty-second commercials. And he could do it all with just a few days lead time. He showed me what he's proposing, and between you and me Jarrett, it looked pretty damned good. This guy's a real pro."

"Did he cover the issues we agreed upon?" Hastings asked.

"Every one of them. I think it's top-drawer stuff. First rate."

"What's the angle he wants to go with?"

"One of the rushes he showed me has you talking to the kids at the Biloxi Junior High School. It's a great piece on the education reform bill you're sponsoring."

"Sounds good to me, Pierre. What else?"

"Remember the video shots of you with all those union factory workers clamoring for higher pay and more benefits? Well, Ernie and his people put together a whole montage with you talking to different employees at the plant. You look real good, Jarrett. And real concerned. I like it a lot. And there's no question that it shows you as one of them. It's a great image to project."

"Yeah. I remember how well-received I was by the rank and file. It could be a terrific showcase for our proposed wage and benefits bill," Hastings said approvingly. "What else did Ernie show you?"

"Well, we always have the school prayer issue and all the pro-life stuff like late term abortions and stem cell research."

"I think it would be a waste. Conklin's and my position are pretty much the same so what's the point?"

"Yeah, I guess you're right. I almost forgot. We're in Mississippi, red country, not New York blue. But all in all, I like what Crayton has put together on the other issues. He has my vote."

"Before we jump head-first into a shallow concrete pool, I first gotta know, how much will the whole TV thing cost?"

"Whatever it takes; we'll just have to raise it."

"I like your style, Pierre, but what budget did Ernie price out for the whole deal? Remember, we must get enough coverage to flood the whole market for three solid weeks before primary day." The ring in Hastings' voice spelled "urgent."

"He told me he'll have it for us by tomorrow morning. It will be a bottom line number."

"Good. In any case, I'm sure it will translate into 'very expensive.' So what's the plan, Mr. Fundmeister?"

"Just leave it to me. We'll need a lot to mount the five-star TV campaign Ernie Fox has laid out for the closing weeks. And my job is real easy—just to raise as much cash that we need. That's all."

" 'That's all,' you say? Sure, but geez, how many times can we tap the same well?"

"There are still a few holes I haven't drilled. In fact, I've been saving them for something real special like this."

"Who you talkin' about?"

"They're a small group of well-heeled investor-types who hired me a couple of years back to help them get first dibs in the New Orleans Casino Palace. I was operating out of Louisiana at the time."

"But I thought the whole deal went south when the fed investigators started to put their long noses into it."

"Yeah, that's right, Jarrett. The thing never got off the ground. But I know these guys. And I'm real sure they'd be interested in putting big cash in our campaign."

"Why would they do that? They don't even know me."

"True. But they would soon fall in love if it could open the door to a riverboat gambling operation in Biloxi. And we know that the governor of the state could be a mighty powerful friend to such a venture."

"I think I could be persuaded. On the merits, of course," he said with a sly wink. "But who are these guys? Give me some names."

"In fact, one of the guys in particular is a big-time heavy we certainly would want on our team."

"Name?"

"Vincent Scarpizzi."

"Sounds Italian."

"So what? His cash is all green."

"Hmm. Interesting. Do you really think you can pull this thing off, Pierre? Now don't hand me any bullshit."

"Never with you ,Jarrett. But yeah, you bet I could. Just leave the details to me. I'm fully confident that within a week we'll be giving Ernie Fox the green light to buy all the TV commercial time we need."

"I am leaving it with you, Pierre. But just remember, we've got to hit every note on the scale."

"Trust me on this one, Jarrett. We will! And most of those notes will have a 'C' in from of them."

Treausance promised he could deliver, and he did! Ernie Fox's budget needs were met with some to spare.

The TV campaign was a success, and Jarrett Lee Hastings Hastings went on to win the primary election, becoming the party's official candidate for Governor of the State of Mississippi. Going on to win the general election that November was not as contested as the primary since the name recognition Hastings had achieved in his successful full-blown state-wide television commercials had made him into a household name.

But the sights of Governor Hastings were already on goals far beyond the executive mansion. His big money backers saw him as a potential national figure on a springboard to higher office. In fact, they were betting Hastings would be a natural should circumstances call for a Governor from the South for the national ticket.

The party had just nominated United States Senator John Harrington of Massachusetts as its presidential standard-bearer. The search was now on to choose a vice presidential candidate who could add balance to the ticket. As the governor of a bible-belt state, Hastings was elated when informed he was on the short-list of vice presidential contenders.

It was the third day of his party's national convention held in San Diego when Hastings, in his hotel suite at the Pacific Towers Hotel, was surrounded by Pierre Treausance, Ernie Fox, and Bud Crayton.

In the tense room, each was volunteering a special reason why Hastings should be the logical choice as John Harrington's running mate.

"Harrington's from the Northeast. A vice president from Mississippi would provide just the right kind of geographical balance to the ticket," Treausance said.

"Harrington's Catholic. You're a Baptist, Jarrett. The mix is right. Besides, you would be very attractive to the voters in the country who support good Christian values. In addition, the battleground states that will carry this election will eat up your evangelical background. As everyone knows, middle-America loves candidates who talk with a Southern drawl, and speak their language.

"Even the difference in political ideology makes absolute sense. Harrington is seen as a northern, stuffy kind of guy—you know, a moderate type who leans just a wee bit left of center. You, Jarrett, are a southern, church-going, middle-of-the-roader, with a rep for strong family values, and leaning more to the right. I'm telling you, the marriage would be a natural," Bud Crayton said.

The hours passed slowly as they waited, hoping for the telephone to ring. It did.

Treausance picked up the receiver. "Jarrett, it's Senator John Harrington. He wants to speak to you," Treausance sang out, unable to contain his excitement.

"Hello, Senator Harrington? Jarrett Hastings here." Hastings was hyperventilating with anticipation.

"Governor, how would you like to join me as my vice presidential candidate?"

"It would be my personal honor, sir," Hastings answered formally, while breaking out into a wide, but silent smile, his right thumb stretching pointedly in the air for all his entourage to see.

"Then it's done. Please join me at my hotel as soon as you can. I will make the announcement publicly at that time."

"I'll be there shortly. And I thank you again, sir, for the confidence you have placed in me."

Once the telephone was secure in its cradle, the shouts of delirium rising from Hastings' suite at the Pacific Towers Hotel, could be heard all the way to San Francisco.

Later, joining John Harrington on the campaign trail, their slogan "H&H for P&P," translating to "Harrington & Hastings for Peace & Prosperity," caught on. It lead to a victory that November, after capturing fifty-six percent of the electoral votes.

Although mostly ceremonial, the new vice- president, *at his request*, was given the exclusive right to appoint the commissioner of Indian Affairs, a rather remote position when contrasted to the more significant cabinet appointments made by the president—but this was the specific job Pierre Treausance wanted for himself.

The remote ancestry stemming from the Caddo Indian tribe several generations back, was sufficient justification to quiet those critics who questioned the selection of Treausance as the new Indian Affairs commissioner.

And weeks later, when Jarrett Lee Hastings Hastings telephoned Pierre Treausance, his grateful friend was quick to take the call:

"Jarrett, good hearing from you. Everything okay?" Treausance asked.

"Things couldn't be better, Pierre. Oh, by the way, do you think you can make it over to my office? There's something real important I 'd like to talk to you about."

Slightly light-headed from all the scotch he had already consumed, Hastings knew he had no choice but to make certain that Treausance made the right decision concerning the Pecontic tribe's pending application seeking a license for full casino gambling.

Christ! How could I ever forget the persistence of that two-bit lawyer who called me just a few weeks ago? Hastings recalled painfully.

It all started with the buzzer sounding from his office intercom. He remembered, with a scowl, how irritated he had become.......

"Who's callin' me, Betty Jean?" Hastings asked his secretary.

"It's a Harold Gordon from New York, Mr. Vice President."

"I don't know a Gordon from New York," Hastings answered. His tone was impatient. He clicked off the intercom.

A moment later, Betty Jean buzzed again.

"He says he's a lawyer and it's important that he speak with you."

"Just brush him off."Hastings punched off again.

The buzzer sounded a third time.

"It's that Harold Gordon fellow again," Betty Jean reported apologetically. "He said he'll keep on calling until you talk to him."

"What in the Sam Hill does he want?"

"He said he wants to talk to you about a mutual friend of yours," she said in a typical deep southern twang.

"I don't talk to people I don't know, Betty Jean. I told you that a million times."

"I know that, sir. But this gentleman is very persistent. Perhaps I should give this call to Peter to handle. But oh dear, he's meeting with some congressmen this morning. Or maybe I should just transfer the call to Pete's voice mail. What should I do, Mr. Vice President?" Betty Jean asked meekly.

Unwilling to introduce Peter McFarland, his chief of staff to a matter that could be compromising, he pressed Betty Jean further. "Well, find out who this mutual friend is. This Gordon could be a sales guy trying to pitch me or somethin'," Hastings barked back.

"I'll do my best, sir," Betty Jean said softly.

"Just sweet talk him and find out what it's all about. Then get back to me." Hastings clicked off, writing the name "Harold Gordon, NY lawyer" on a pad.

Within minutes, Betty Jean's voice was heard again through the intercom.

"He repeated he was calling on behalf of a mutual friend and that it was personal. I tried to get more details out of him, but oh my, all he would say was he wanted to talk only to you, or to get an appointment." She sounded stressed, frazzled.

Concern began to show on the vice president's face. He started to squint. Ridge lines began to appear on his high forehead. He was experiencing an uneasy anxiety, disquietingly reminiscent of feelings he had many years earlier, when as a young man, he had faced financial difficulties; receiving hounding and threatening telephone calls from bill collectors. Somehow, what he had gone through before, was in some strange subliminal way awakening unpleasant memories of the past. Whatever it was, his instincts told him not to take the call, not to see this Harold Gordon person.

"Betty Jean, you just tell him I'm in conference and that my appointments are all filled up." Hastings switched the intercom to the "off" position.

Five minutes later, the buzzer sounded again. "What now, Betty Jean?" Hastings was abrupt, openly annoyed.

"It's that Gordon fellow again. He just won't quit. Said it's absolutely urgent."

"Goddamn, get rid of the guy."

"I told him that you could not talk to him, Mr. Vice President, but he keeps on insisting that you will. He said he has an important message from a Mister "S." And he's very persistent. Lordy be, I just don't know what to say anymore." His secretary sounded like a distressed Scarlet O'Hara.

Mister "S"? Hastings scratched his head as he thought to himself, *Who is this Mister "S"? Wait a minute…Could that be…? That's probably the guy. If so, what the hell could he want? Maybe I should just see this Gordon fellah and find out. If he's the Mister "S" I think he is, I'm sure I can handle it. No point getting all worked up. It's probably nothing, and I see no reason to get Pete McFarland involved at this time.*

Hastings gave his secretary the instructions just worked out in his head.

"Okay, Betty Jean, listen carefully. This is what I want ya to do. Get his goddamned number. Tell him I'll get back to him in half an hour."

"Yes sir."

The vice president sat back, gaining the full support of his heavily upholstered leather chair. Stretching his legs stiffly under the well of the huge walnut desk in front of him, he clasped both hands around the back of his neck and pondered, *Maybe I shouldn't even call the son-of-a-bitch back. Nah, that wouldn't be such a good idea. And if this guy is Mister S's lawyer, he sure in hell won't quit until he gets through to me. Yeah, I'll just have to call the bastard and let him know that I don't bend too easily to his bullshit tactics. After all, I am the vice president of the United States. And who is he? Some horse shit shyster message carrier? No harm in hearing what he has to say.*

Thirty-five minutes later, the telephone rang in room 507 of the Washington Arms Hotel.

"Hello," Gordon answered.

"This is Jarrett Lee Hastings. Who the hell are ya and what do ya want?"

"I have very special regards from Mister 'S', and I just want to talk to you." Gordon's tone was courteous and soft.

"Look here Groton, or whatever your name is," Hastings said impatiently…

"The name is Gordon," he interrupted politely.

"Yeah. Right. Whatever. Well, I'm pretty busy and very pressed for time. We'll just have to have our little chat some other day."

Hastings was about to hang up the telephone, when Gordon broke in.

"I don't think you quite understand what I'm saying, so I'll repeat it slowly. I have very special regards from Mister S., and I want to talk to you *now*—not some other day. Do you understand what I'm saying, Mr. Vice President?" Gordon's tone was soft, but firm, leaving little doubt he was not about to be put off another second.

Having earlier made the connection as to who Mister S. was, Hastings decided it would be best to deal with the matter at that time rather than be taken by surprise when he least expected it.

There was a short pause. "Okay, Groton, I mean, Gordon. Meet me by the entrance of Bryant Park in an hour. It's right over the Potomac Bridge about a quarter mile west of I-95. Do ya know where that is?"

"I'll find it," Gordon said. His tone was in stark contrast to Hastings' hostile manner.

"How'll I know ya?" barked Hastings.

"I'll know *you*, Mr. Vice President." Gordon hung up the telephone.

Hastings was irritated by the necessity for him to sneak out in order to elude his Secret Service detail. He wasn't too happy about the security breach either, but he felt he had little choice to do otherwise.

After his brief conversation with the vice president, Gordon walked the few steps into the bathroom of the junior suite he was checked into. Looking at himself in the mirror, he brought his face close to the reflective surface, peeling off a small, crusted scab that had formed on his chin from the razor cut received while shaving earlier that morning. After removing it, he applied a wet washcloth, flecking off specs of dried blood.

Gordon thought: *This guy may be the vice president of the United States, but he sounds like a real redneck who may just need a few basic lessons in common courtesy. My God, whatever happened to old fashioned Southern hospitality? Yeah, perhaps he needs a course in plain good old-fashioned manners taught by a humble lawyer from New York? Well, whatever. I'll soon find out.*

Gordon tossed the wet washcloth into the corner of the tub on top of other towels he had used when he showered earlier that morning. Stretching his chin up close to the mirror, he inspected it for any residual signs of his razor cut. In the process, he took on the look of quiet satisfaction, slowly braking out into an open grin, having secured a rare meeting with the vice president of the United States, soon to take place.

At eleven in the morning, Bryant Park was a quiet escape nestled in a neighborhood area. It was used mostly by the local residents to walk their pets or to babysit toddlers who used the swings and surrounding sand boxes.

One hour later, Gordon entered the park, drove his rental into one of the many empty parking spaces near the entrance, and waited. In ten minutes, a gray Lexus pulled alongside him. Jarrett Lee Hastings was behind the wheel, and alone.

Recognizing the vice president, Gordon exited his vehicle, walking quickly over to the driver's side of the Lexus. The closed window came down three quarters of the way as Gordon approached. Reaching the car, he positioned himself next to the partially opened window, crouching down to meet it. "I bring very special greetings from Vincent Scarpizzi, Mister S.," Gordon said. He eyed a nervous Jarrett Lee Hastings who remained in the driver's seat, both hands knuckle-tight on the steering wheel.

"Who the fuck are ya and what do ya want?" barked Hastings, vulgarly, pointing his right index finger menacingly at him, attempting to intimidate Gordon with an opening and aggressive thrust.

"No call to be nasty, Mr. Vice President. No call for that at all," Gordon said calmly.

"Well, what do ya want?" Hastings blurted out with impatience and bristling hostility. "I had to duck out and give my Secret Service guys the slip 'cause you said this was important. Well, it just better be."

"Vincent just wants a little favor of you, that's all." said Gordon.

Having heard Gordon's response, Hastings climbed out of his car, unwound his 6-foot-two-inch frame, and stretched himself vertically to the limit, facing-off inches from Gordon, who was considerably shorter.

"What kind of a favor?" Hastings asked through squeezed lips, gritting his teeth at the same time.

"Vincent would be very grateful if you would ask your friend Pierre Treausance from the Bureau of Indian Affairs to give his okay to a license for Indian casino gambling in New York. That's it."

"Is that what all this shit is about? For Chrissakes, I don't have anythin' to do with that. Tell Scarpizzi to try someone else." Hastings felt relieved the meeting Gordon had been pressing Betty Jean for all morning was as remote as a license for Indian casino gambling. *This is ridiculous,* he thought to himself, feeling less tense.

"Maybe you don't understand what I just said. Vincent wants *you* to handle this little favor for him, *nobody else*," Gordon said, maintaining a stern but courteous manner.

"Well, maybe ya didn't hear what I just said. I have nothing to do with that, so see somebody else, ya hear?"

Hastings reached for the door handle to his car.

"Mr. Vice President, Vincent didn't tell you to see somebody else when you asked him for help in your campaign for overnor. And he helped you. Big-time. Remember?" Gordon spoke slowly, his voice rising slightly in pitch.

"Are you trying to shake me down, you little prick?" Hastings shot back in anger, face flushed to a deep red, as his right carotid artery started to bulge and throb.

"Not at all. But when you needed quick cash you didn't hesitate to call Vincent Scarpizzi. And he delivered just what you asked for. And on time. You didn't seem to care where it came from, although you knew it was all green cash from his financial interest in the Biloxi Riverboat Casino." There was a pause. "Does... that...jog...your...memory... a little...bit, Mr Vice President?" Gordon asked, deliberately stretching and exaggerating each word to gain the maximum impact of its pointed delivery.

At his present state of power, arrogance and ego, Hastings was unaccustomed to being the direct target of such a verbal assault. Unable to restrain his anger, already hot and smoking, he lashed out instinctively.

"You tell that guinea bastard that I don't scare easily. That he can go fuck himself. I'm not about to get myself all jammed up with some Indian casino bullshit. Ya' hear what I'm sayin', boy?" Hastings' demeaning response addressed Gordon in an as undignified a manner as if he were sweating in a Mississippi cotton plantation one hundred fifty years earlier.

"Well, I'm really sorry to hear you say that, knowing how Treausance was hand-picked by you. I'm sure he would go along with the favor if you would just ask him. It would be so easy. And Vincent would be so very grateful to Treausance." He paused for effect. "And of course, Vincent would show his profound gratitude to you, as well."

"Counselor, this fuckin' meeting is over as of now. Ya hear? You can inform your client that he is screwin' around with the wrong guy. You act like you don't know that I'm a pretty powerful fella and I don't have to take shit from you, or your so-called big time boss. You tell him that I ain't buyin' what he's sellin.' You got it, mister? And fuh-ther, I don't need him to send a piece a' crap like you ta do his bidding. Oh yes, one more thing. I don't wanna hear from you, or your Mister S. again. You got what I'm sayin', Mr. Big-time Lawyer from New York?"

The vice-president hurriedly opened the car door, positioning himself back into the driver's seat of the Lexus. He abruptly turned the key of the ignition and started the engine up. But before he could shift into a driving gear, Gordon quickly leaned into the open window. In the same instant, he pulled out a tape recorder from his jacket pocket. He quickly flipped the switch to the "play" position. The operation took all of one second.

The tinny sound coming from the machine, stunned the silence:

"Jarrett, you got two hundered G's in that envelope, just like you asked."

It was Vincent Scarpizzi speaking on the tape.

The response was from a very recognizable voice:

"Vincent, you're a lifesaver, and I'll never forget ya for that."

It was the voice of Jarrett Lee Hastings, the *then* insurgent primary candidate for governor of the state of Mississippi, and *the now vice president of the United States of America.*

172

CHAPTER SIXTEEN

A White House security guard escorted Matt from the VIP parking lot, delivering him to two Secret Service agents waiting to greet him at a side entrance. In quick step, they brought Matt to the door of the oval office. Following three polite raps, the door opened as President Harrington extended his hand warmly.

"I have only a few minutes, Matt. I'm in the middle of a conference with the prime minister of Canada, but please sit down."

"Thank you, sir."

" You *did* say it was urgent, right Matt?"

"Yes, Mr. President. I would not have asked for this meeting if it wasn't," Matt replied soberly.

"This sounds serious."

Harrington pulled up a chair, faced Matt. "Now then, what's it all about?"

Withdrawing five sheets of paper from his briefcase and passing them along to Harrington, Matt said, "Mr. President, I found this memo Chuck typed out just before he left for Syracuse."

President Harrington began reading the documents just handed to him. With each page, the canyons in his forehead deepened. When finished, he stared blankly at Matt, a deeply troubled expression on his face.

"My God. I can't believe what I just read. I just cannot believe it. Hastings? My own vice-president in the middle of mob pay-offs? And bribes?"

"That's what it says, sir."

" My Indian Affairs commissioner? Governor Martin? Jesus. This is disastrous," Harrington said, bewilderment joined with a look of having been betrayed.

"I had to show you this right away, Mr. President. It's a shocking document." Matt attempted to choose his words carefully.

173

"It goes far beyond shocking, Matt. If this is true, it's a nightmare. Remember, I'm the one who picked Hastings despite misgivings from some of my closest advisors. I'm absolutely stunned beyond words," Harrington said.

"Yes, sir."

Harrington rose from his seat and walked slowly around the huge oak desk. With a troubled sigh he flopped into the high-back chair behind it. Supporting his head against its hard leather, eyes closed, he said,"This whole business can wreck the country. Tell me, Matt, does anyone know of this memo besides us?"

"Chuck's personal secretary, Alice Lacy. But I swore her to secrecy. She's one hundred percent loyal. Can be trusted fully."

"Look Matt, thirty years ago, another man who sat in this very office was forced to give up the presidency because he was accused of a cover-up. That's not me. I *do* not, *can* not and *will* not, act that way." Moving forward in his chair and switching to a formal tone, Harrington continued. "Last week, I appointed you to head an investigation into Chuck's death. Your assignment is hereby enlarged. You are now to investigate the role of *every* person named in Chuck's memo. And you are to furnish me with absolute proof of their innocence or guilt. You'll have all the resources you need; and keep the investigation under wraps until it is concluded. I'll start building fences here for the arrows that are sure to come our way once the news breaks."

"Mr. President, you must know that what you're asking me to do might uncover a scandal that could possibly shake up the whole nation. Is that what you want of me?"

"Damn it to hell, Matt, what I want is for you to get to the truth, to bring light to this whole mess. I owe it to the American people to tell them exactly what happened to Chuck, why it happened, and who was responsible for his death. But even beyond that, if we have the proof, our citizens will be told about the payoffs and bribes, and yes, even the mob connections. I don't care how high it goes. As one of my predecessors who sat in this very office once said, the buck stops here.' And I intend to see that it does. I owe at least that much to the people of our nation."

"I understand fully, Mr. President."

ARROWHEAD

"Quite frankly I think it's whistling in the dark to entertain the notion that the memo is nothing more than a series of phony accusations. Chuck's dead, murdered, and you don't go to those lengths unless you've got something very serious to cover up."

"I agree completely."

"And if there is even one scintilla of truth behind the memo, we must search it out and report it in full sunlight."

"That's exactly what I will do, sir."

"When we've gathered all the proof and are fairly certain that we are on solid ground, we show it openly to the country. *But we must have solid proof.* What the people thereafter decide, is what we call 'democracy.' I'll accept their decision, whatever it is."

"You know I'll do my best, Mr. President."

"Matt, our nation and I are depending on you, now, more than ever," Harrington said, walking around to the front of his desk.

Matt rose from his seat.

"Well, that's it. I must get back to the prime minister. Again, it's urgent that you come up with absolute proof, one way or the other."

They shook hands.

As Matt left the oval office, he was met by the same two agents who escorted him out of the White House and to the VIP lot where Matt's car was parked.

Matt opened the door, sat behind the steering wheel, and positioned his head against the upright back rest behind him. Closing his eyes, he fell deep in thought. *How can I tell Jenny that her own father is mixed up with the mob in this casino license scandal? I know how close she is to him. What do I do? If Joe Roundtree is part of a criminal conspiracy, he could be sentenced to a federal prison for years.*

He bit his lower lip as he struggled with deep troubling thoughts. *I could never hurt Jenny. But yet, what am I to do? I'm damned if I go after her father and expose him with the others. I'm damned if I don't. Damn! Damn! Damn! I'm caught in the middle of a Hobson's choice. What do I do?* he pondered. *Whatever happens Jenny, I just pray you understand.*

Both hands cupped against his temple, Matt felt the sickening pain of his wrenching dilemma as he stared hypnotically at the stars and stripes of a flag hanging on a pole in the distance. "What am I to do? What am I to do?" he repeated softly to himself, raising his head up toward the sky, as if an answer would come from that direction.

175

Matt started up the car as he moved away from the White House grounds, heading directly toward Jenny's home in Georgetown. He knew that in thirty minutes he would have to face her, reporting things that could drive a deep and irreversible wedge between them. He dreaded what he would soon have to do, but knew he had no other choice.

Matt arrived at Jenny's house. "Where's Little Joe?" Matt asked, greeting Jenny at the front door.

"Playing out back," she answered. "I'm glad I decided to stay here even with all that's happened," she added.

"Outside," represented a large grassy area in the rear of the townhouse that ran more than one hundred and fifty feet from the back door to the next property line. Surrounding the grounds measuring seventy five feet across, were huge oak and maple trees. In the spring, fall, and summer seasons, their leafy plumage provided a full screen of privacy from the adjacent houses. The 18 by 36 foot, granite, oval-shaped pool with a six-jet hot tub, was a perfect recreational and aesthetic feature of the attractive Georgetown house. With its surrounding patio of old red brick set in sand, the scene was warm and charming.

Inside, Matt loosened his collar as he stepped out onto the rear lawn. There, he saw Little Joe, small baseball bat in hand, hitting a whiffle ball. Resembling an actual baseball, it was made of hard plastic with many holes through its surface.

"Hey, big guy," Matt rang out, affectionately. "Who's winning?"

"We're beating the Yankees 3 to 2," Little Joe answered. "You wanna pitch?"

"Sure. But watch out for my curve ball." Matt feigned a serious look.

Little Joe tossed the ball to Matt who positioned himself twenty feet from a square piece of cardboard used as home plate. Another square base was already in place thirty feet away. It served as first, second, and third base, all in one.

For the next twenty minutes, Matt pitched the plastic ball to Little Joe. He swung his bat, running out everything hit on the ground or on the fly. With each swing of the bat, Matt became the infielder, outfielder, and catcher, all in one, intent on tagging Little Joe out before he could cross home plate.

After the last inning was played, Little Joe shouted out with boyish excitement, "We beat you, Matt. Orioles 10, Yankees 6."

"You beat me again, big guy," Matt said, acting out disappointment. He exchanged a high-five, lifting Little Joe high in the air, shaking him gently. Little Joe's giggles and laughter filled the yard. Matt's hug followed.

When the game was over, Matt returned to the house, wiping beads of perspiration from his face and forehead with a towel he had taken from a recliner next to the pool. Inside, Matt reached into the refrigerator, took out a large pitcher of iced tea. and poured it into a tall ice-cube-filled glass.

"Who won?" Jenny asked, a smile covering her glowing face.

"He beat me again," Matt replied, head nodding, left eye winking.

Matt took a full swallow of the cold drink he held in his right hand. With his left, he gently touched Jenny's elbow, guiding her to the living room next to Chuck's study, now under renovation following the burglary.

"There's something we have to talk about," Matt said. He closed the glass pane door of the walnut-paneled room.

"There's something we have to talk about," Matt repeated. He sat down across Jenny, who was already seated in a large chair upholstered with a fabric that depicted a European pastoral scene, circa 16th century.

"Jenny, what I'm going to tell you is confidential. It must not go beyond this room."

Jenny sat in silence. She raised her eyebrows, furrowing her forehead slightly. She was alarmed by Matt's somberness.

"I have information that the Federal Bureau of Indian Affairs issued a license to the Pecontic tribe for full casino gambling on its reservation."

"Many people in Washington already know that. So, what's the problem, Matt?"

"Nothing on the face of it. But what everybody in Washington doesn't know, is that the license may have been issued only after members of organized crime made some big payoffs to some very high government officials."

Matt paused, dropping his eyes as they remained focused on his lap. After a moment of silence, he raised his head slowly. Catching Jenny's eyes, he continued. His voice was soft.

"Jenny, I have reason to believe that your father may have some involvement with these people. According to our sources, it seems he cut a deal with the mob...and apparently carved out a good piece for himself in return."

Jenny rose abruptly, her voice filled with protest. "I can't believe that. It cannot be true." Matt felt her indignation.

"Please, Jenny, please. I don't know for sure that it *is* true. And I pray that it isn't. But it is my responsibility to either confirm it or dismiss it completely."

"What you're saying is that my father is corrupt. How dare you say that to me?" Tears began to well up in her eyes.

"Listen to me Jenny, please." Matt stood up to face her. He held both arms gently. "You have to prepare yourself, if it *is* true."

"You just do what you have to. Go ahead," she said angrily. Tears were now streaming freely down her cheeks. Breaking Matt's hold, Jenny started to walk toward the hallway. Matt followed.

"Listen to me, Jenny. Please. You know I would do anything in the world for you. But there are some things that just cannot be done."

Jenny pivoted abruptly. She confronted Matt squarely, fire in her eyes. "Does that mean you are going to prosecute my own father? Send him to prison? Is that what you're saying?"

"Please don't put me on the spot that way. Listen, Jenny, I know that Chuck told you *exactly* what I just said. Don't deny it Jenny. He told you what he suspected just before he left for Syracuse. You knew he had flown there the day he was killed, for the sole purpose of questioning your father about his possible involvement with the casino license issued to the tribe and his connection to mob payoffs." Matt hated himself for having hurt Jenny so deeply by telling her what he had learned about her father. He knew it could destroy the intimacy that had begun to develop between them.

Jenny became silent for the moment. She dropped back into her chair, head down. Neither spoke for the next few minutes, as she relived the almost identical encounter she had experienced with Chuck shortly before he left for Syracuse. Her mind raced wildly, thinking of the telephone call she had made to her father soon after Chuck shocked her with his suspicions.

Jenny flashed-back to remembering how she had punched in a familiar telephone number. She recalled its three rings, and her father's answering at the other end in his Syracuse bungalow. . . . .

"Hello."

"Pop, how are you?"

"Jenny, is everything okay?" Joe responded, surprised to hear from his daughter in the middle of the day. "Anything wrong with Little Joe?"

"Little Joe is fine. And so am I, Pop. But I have to talk to you about something."

"Sure. What's up?"

"Pop, you have to be honest with me. No tricks. No stories. Just straight talk. Do you hear?"

"Now this is getting to sound serious, Jenny. Is there a problem?"

"I hope not. That's why I'm calling."

"I'm listening."

"Chuck is going to call you later to arrange a meeting with you tomorrow in Syracuse."

"Why does he want to do that?" Joe asked, pretending he had no clue.

"Pop, this casino gambling thing. What is your connection with it?"

"I told you before. In order to get the okay from the government, the chief of our tribe had to make the first move. Well, I just happen to be the chief. Remember? And I started the ball rolling after the tribal council gave me the go-ahead sign. So what's wrong with that?" Joe asked, his voice dripping with false innocence.

"Nothing on its face, Pop. But Chuck received a tip that organized crime is involved," Jenny hesitated, then resumed, "and that you are in some way connected with them. Is that true? Now, don't lie to me, Pop. I want the real truth. None of your made-up stories." Jenny's voice was beginning to crack.

"What? That's crazy. Totally nuts. No truth to it at all. I don't know where you're gettin' that stuff from. Look, Jenny, I've done some real dumb things in my life. Real dumb. But I'm not stupid enough to do somethin' like that," Joe protested, his voice sounding convincing.

"So where does all that stuff come from? It just can't be mere rumor, and nothing else. There's got to be more to it than that."

"Look, Jenny. Ya know...there are always people who envy me, and are jealous because I'm chief of the tribe. They'd say

179

anything…do anything…just to cause me trouble. Who knows? Maybe it's their big chance to get even with me for stuff I coulda pulled a long time ago. Ya know, I did some pretty crazy things, then. But, I'm telling ya…not now!" Her father's explanation was reassuring.

"Are you really being truthful with me, Pop? If there is a problem, let's talk about it together… and see if we can work through it. Be honest with me, Pop. Is there a problem?"

"Forget it, daughter. There's nothin' goin' on. But if Chuck wants to talk to me about it, why not? Fine. I got nothin' ta hide. And nothin' ta worry about. And Jenny, the same goes for you." To Jenny's relief, Joe's manner appeared free of anxiety or the slightest trace of guilt.

"Are you sure, Pop, or is it that you just don't want me to worry? Which is it? Tell me, please."

"Am I sure? You bet I am. And after I talk to Chuck, tomorrow, he'll be sure too. I give you my word. Hey, daughter, have I ever broken my promise to you?" Joe's voice sounded jocular, exhibiting no sign of concern.

"You don't know how much better I feel," Jenny said, relief in her voice. "I love you, Pop,"she let out instinctively.

"And I love you, little girl. I'll talk to you tomorrow after Chuck comes over. Just don't worry. You'll see, everything will be fine. You'll see."

"I hope so. Goodbye, Pop. I love you."

"And I love you, Jenny. Goodbye."

Jenny could not have known that after she placed the telephone in its cradle, her father, shoulders hunched forward, lumbered slowly into the kitchen of his small-framed bungalow, opened a worn cabinet door above the sink, and retrieved a bottle of rye whiskey. She could not have known that he poured some of its contents into a glass resting on the counter and gulped it down in two quick swallows; that within minutes, he returned to his sparsely decorated bedroom, sat on the bed, lifted the telephone, and dialed a familiar number. When it was answered at the other end, her father's response was, "Hello, Vincent. There's something very important I have to tell ya…JENNY COULD NOT HAVE KNOWN ANY OF THAT."

CHAPTER SEVENTEEN

At exactly 7:30, Hector Santiago, dressed in a light blue silk shantung suit, dark blue shirt and white silk tie, pressed the lighted doorbell next to the entrance doors to Varga's royal suite. Greeting Santiago was Jose Benitez, one of Varga's lieutenants who escorted him into the spacious salon.

"Mr. Varga will be out in a minute," Benitez said. His tone was expressionless, dry. "Make yourself a drink," he said as he pointed to a huge bar with four cushioned-back stools, a wide assortment of premium liquors, soft drinks, and a bucket of ice.

Five minutes later, Louis Varga appeared from the master bedroom suite, hand extended. They greeted each other warmly. Varga was dressed in a white silk jacket with white linen slacks. He completed the ensemble with a black, shiny, silk mock-turtleneck, a red silk handkerchief folded causally in his outside jacket pocket, and white crocodile boots. His stark white hair appeared even more striking, contrasting sharply with the black shirt that hugged his strong chin line.

"I trust you had an enjoyable afternoon, Hector," Varga said, throwing off a wink and sly grin.

"Most enjoyable, Louis. Most enjoyable. And Willy and I thank you for your very gracious hospitality," Santiago answered, returning Varga's raised-eyebrow expression.

"I am delighted. And now my friend, you will join me for dinner? Yes?"

"It will be my pleasure. Thank you, *padron*."

"Good." Humberto is preparing a very special meal. It should be ready soon."

Humberto Fuentes was one of the hotel's executive chefs. His sole assignment while Varga was a guest in the Cambio del Rey suite, was to prepare whatever food specialties Varga desired, and in the manner he wanted them prepared.

Varga's suite was a true chamber of the king. Part of its seven thousand square feet of splendid ambiance was decorated with old world antiques and furnishings, including a full state-of-the-art kitchen. It was staffed by an executive chef, an assistant to the chef, and a butler, during the time the suite was occupied, by either a "whale" such as an Arab emirate, a million-dollar credit-line player, or a Colombian kingpin like Louis Varga. The amenities were story-book lavish.

A tuxedo-clad butler entered the room announcing dinner was being served. Varga escorted Santiago into the dining room. Two full elaborate dinner settings were in place on a large Spanish-style heavy oak table. The chandelier above with its many soft-lit candelabras showned down upon two tall, lighted candles standing at attention alongside a large and colorful display of fresh tropical flowers.

The menu selections could have been served at a state dinner. It started with a "Maryland crab pozole," followed by a main course of "peanut-crusted filet mignon, podaland whipped potatoes," and a "fava bean and chanterelle ragout."

Chef Humberto, specially assigned to Varga while he was a guest in the Cambio del Rey, had kept an ongoing file of menus served throughout the state houses and monarchies of the world. The food served to Louis Varga and Hector Santiago followed in that tradition, being the identical menu prepared several months earlier at a White House dinner honoring a foreign president. A choice of dessert had also been provided. It consisted of either a "mango and coconut ice cream dome atop fresh peaches with tequila saboyan," or a specially created Chef Humberto souffle. Varga and Santiago chose the latter.

There was no talk of business over dinner, both men aware that a private conversation would be difficult to have. The *piece de resistance* however, was the dessert prepared by Humberto. The souffle, made with the most delicate of ingredients, had been slow-baked in the oven for forty-five minutes. When Grand Marnier was added to its culinary poetry, it had the texture and taste of a true work of epicurean art. The separate exotic sauces that accompanied the grand finale, ranged from a rich vanilla, to a subtle cherry-flavored creme. A double espresso with a touch of anisette, was the perfect partner to the souffle.

Wearing the tall white chef's hat and white chef's jacket, the hallmarks of his craft, Humberto made his courtesy appearance at the end, taking his well-deserved bows for the excellence of preparation, taste, and presentation.

After dessert, Santiago followed Varga into another room with high-gloss wooden bookshelves stacked with assorted books. There were many paintings of horses and fox-hunts throughout. The entire chamber gave the appearance of an old English study, filled with its dark forest green walls, rich cherry woods, and works of art. This was a man's place. The two large black leather chairs flanking a high, glass coffee table supported by two lionheads carved out of ivory, completed the exceptionally warm, but masculine decor.

"Let's talk business over some brandy," Varga said. He sat in one of the stuffed chairs, signaling to Santiago to sit in the other.

"Robert," Varga summoned the butler, who was standing by to receive his after-dinner instructions, "please bring some brandy."

After Robert left the study, Varga reached into a small boxed mahogany humidor, retrieved one of the imported Havana cigars from the box, and offered it to his guest.

Santiago waved Varga off politely.

"I know guys who would kill for a box a' real Cubans. But, I could never get used to them." Santiago said.

"Neither could I," Varga said, placing the vintage box back into the humidor.

The butler appeared, holding a silver tray with a bottle of twenty-four-year-old Courvoisier—the Brandy of Napoleon—and two huge Waterford crystal brandy glasses. He uncorked the bottle, poured enough to cover a half-inch of the bottom of each brandy glass, and handed them to Varga and Santiago.

"Will there be anything else?"

"Not at the moment. Thank you, Robert," Varga replied.

The butler shut the solid mahogany doors firmly behind him, as he exited the study. The privacy of Varga and Santiago was now assured.

"To your health," Varga toasted, his brandy glass lightly touching the one held by Santiago.

"And to yours," Santiago answered, clicking Varga's glass a second time.

"Now," said Varga, " I'm ready to talk business. So, tell me. What's this thing all about?" Varga asked, cupping his hands under his chin, looking intently at Santiago.

Santiago sat up straight in his chair opposite Varga, stretched his neck upward several times, in deep thought as to how he should start off his presentation. He spoke rapidly. "Louis, I think we have a big chance to make a killing. This Indian gambling thing could be real terrific for us. I mean *real terrific.*"

Holding up both palms as if he were a traffic cop, Varga interrupted, "Slow down, Hector. You're talking too excited. And you're going too fast, my friend. We got plenty of time. So slow down to twenty miles an hour." Placing the index and middle finger of both hands on his right and left temples, he continued, " Give me details. I want to know what this business is really all about. And relax, my friend. We don't have to catch a plane."

Santiago spoke slower. "What it's about, Louis, is making lots of cash and making it quick. This can be a real easy score," Santiago said, shifting slightly in his chair.

"It always sounds easy in talk. But I learned a long time ago, easy money comes with a very high price and usually a big risk. Go ahead, convince me I'm wrong."

Santiago moved his head forward, hunching closer to Varga. He continued excitedly, "We're talking about controlling Indian gambling, not only in one place, but in all of the states in the country, Louis. We're talking about being in the biggest cash business in America. We're talking about having a piece of the action in every Indian casino that's gonna to be licensed. Hundreds of them all over. Do you understand what I'm saying, Louis?" Varga sensed Santiago's rush.

"You make it sound like all you have to do is push a button, and 'Bingo,' we got it. How are you going to pull this whole thing off? Walk me through it, *amigo. Step by step.*"

Santiago started to explain his plan. It was as if he were letting someone in on a secret he had been harboring for a long time. "Louis, we first start in New York. Syracuse is only the model. Once we got it all set up there, we move out to maybe a dozen other places in the state — Buffalo, Niagra Falls, Rochester, Albany, Lake George, the Catskills, the Rockaways, and maybe even the city itself. We got Indians lined up in all those places, and we can have a legitimate reason to get licenses for casinos in every one of those cities."

Varga crossed his legs, folded his hands around his right knee, and looked with steely eyes directly at Santiago's face. "And how do you expect to do that? Tell me."

Santiago answered reassuringly. "Like I said before, Louis, the formula is the same. We first start in Syracuse. That's where we get the chief of the tribe to give his okay."

Eyes squinting, Varga asked, "How can you be so sure, Hector, that you're going to get this, whatever you call him, this chief to give his okay?"

"Because he's part of the deal. That's how," Santiago shot back.

"What do you mean, he's part of the deal?"

"I'll tell you, Louis. He has a daughter who's running for a political job. She don't stand a prayer without big cash needed to run her campaign. We give the chief what he needs; he's in, that simple," Santiago said, certainty flooding his tone.

"Mmm...I see. How much are we talking about?"

"Whatever it takes. I can move enough of our stuff to raise plenty a' cash. I'm telling ya, Louis, whatever our investment is will be small next to the pay-out we can get."

"Last week you told me something about the New York governor. We need his okay also, don't we? Didn't you tell me that, Hector?"

"That's right, Louis."

"Well, you can arrange that?"

Santiago sat up in his chair, answering with authority, "That's Scarpizzi's end. He tells me he'll have the governor in his pocket in ten minutes. Sure, it will cost. It always does. Don't it? But he'll say 'yes' to the deal we offer him. And don't forget, Louis, he's the same guy who'll be saying 'yes' to all the other casino deals we work out in the state. No question, Louis. I know this guy. He'll get the governor to go along. Trust me on this one."

"Okay then, but are you sure that this *hombre* Scarpizzi, whatever his name, can be handled, Hector? Are you sure of that?"

"Yes, I'm sure, Louis."

"Let me ask a different question. Do you think we really need him?"

"For now, yeah. Scarpizzi's important to us because he can take care a' the governor and the feds in Washington. Let's be honest, Louis. We don't have those kind of connections. This guy Scarpizzi does."

"Sure, Hector, but can we trust him? How big a guy is he anyway?"

"He's the boss of the biggest Mafia family in New York. And maybe the biggest in the country." .

"But I'm asking you again. Can we trust the guy? You know, my friend, he's not one of us. Can we count on him to deliver his end of the bargain?" Varga uncrossed his knees, leaning forward closer to Santiago.

"Look, Louis, right now we need Scarpizzi. And he needs us. He'll keep up his end to make sure the deal goes through. That's what the guy wants. Once we get started in New York, then we can operate like we please. If this Scarpizzi fits in, okay. If he don't, we do what we have to. That's it. No problem."

"I hear you, Hector. I hear you. But tell me, how do we move the operation into the other places in the states?"

"Once we get started, we make our deal with the right people. You always taught me, Louis: big cash is like a magnet. Spread it around and a lotta things will stick to it. That's what you told me and I've never forgotten it. With this deal, we'll have the cash, the connections, and the whole formula. Louis. !his Indian gambling operation is a natural. It can't miss," Santiago said, making a fist, further emphasizing his confidence.

"Hector, I've got to be very sure about this. For now, do what you have to with this Scarpizzi *hombre*. Keep him on the hook." Varga paused. In a slower cadence, he asked, "What split is he lookin' for?"

"Scarpizzi wants sixty to him, forty to us. I told him I'd think about it and get back ta him."

"We get fifty-percent or we don't even think of going in," Varga instructed brusquely.

He looked pensive, rubbed his palms anxiously, then announced his decision."Okay Hector, here it is. We give it one shot. You know the split. If he goes for it, we're in. If not, good-bye, see ya around.'"

"If it's alright with you, Louis, I wanna call Scarpizzi right now and tell him where we stand. Is that okay with you?"

"Sure. Makes sense. Do it. We gotta know one way or the other."

Santiago removed a small notebook from his breast pocket, thumbed a few pages and lifted the telephone. He dialed. The voice at the other end, Vincent Scarpizzi.

"Vincent, it's good to talk to you. This is Hector Santiago here."

"Hey, Hector, what's up my man?"

"Let me get right to it Vincent. I been thinkin' about the deal. Fifty-fifty and it's a go."

"Forty-sixty," countered Scarpizzi. His voice sounded firm.

"Fifty-fifty. That's it, Vincent. Anything less is a deal-buster." Santiago's tone was adamant.

Following Scarpizzi's brief response, the conversation ended.

Without expression, Hector placed the telephone back in its cradle.

The momentary silence was interrupted by Varga, abruptly rising from his chair. Impatient, he blurted out, "For Chrissakes, *que pasa amigo*? What's the story? Let me hear."

In response, Hector Santiago, king of the New York latino drug family, bowed his head slowly, displaying both reverence and respect to his boss. With each word uttered, Santiago took on a greater look of confidence, finally blossoming into a broad smile of satisfaction. Speaking in a slow, deliberate tone, he let it out, "It gives me great pleasure to announce to you... " He paused after milking each syllable. Both fists raised high in a victory pose, Santiago continued excitedly, "Senor Louis Varga, we—got—ourselves—a—deal!"

CHAPTER EIGHTEEN

"How'd it go with that government man?" Agnes Fowler asked, as she anxiously greeted her husband at the front door of their small frame house in the Chelsea section of Syracuse. It was a blue collar, lower middle class neighborhood with rows of one-family housing that housed civil service, factory, and office workers.

"I need a drink," Fowler rang out almost on the run, heading straight for a wooden cabinet against the wall of a small dining room. Quickly opening the door, he removed a bottle of Seagrams 7. Pouring the rye whiskey into a short-barrel glass, he filled it almost to the brim. Half of it went down in one swallow. Its sudden sting tightened the thin muscles around his mouth.

Agnes, a 45-year-old frumpy woman who looked ten years beyond her age, watched in silence. Married to Fowler for 18 years, she knew his many moods. This time, his karma sent a clear message: *stand back, and wait for him to speak first.*

Fowler poured another Seagrams 7 into his half-empty glass, filling it almost to the top. Carrying it into the living room, he flopped into a large stuffed chair. Agnes followed, sitting silently on a worn tufted sofa next to her husband.

"The son-of-a bitch asked me a bunch a questions. I was prepared for most of them but a couple caught me by surprise," Fowler said, taking another gulp of straight whiskey. This time the sting was less.

"Didn't the lawyer prep you for the interview?" Agnes asked. She had worked as a secretary for an attorney in a small Syracuse law office and had some familiarity with the process of briefing a client for a deposition or for trial.

"Yeah," Fowler said. "We spent some time together, but that guy Connors is no hack. He's good. Big time. Real good," he snarled.

"What happened, George? Tell me." Her concern was showing.

"I think the guy suspects me. Shit, Agnes, I'm sure he does. This Connors, he's no small-time flunky. He's a top gun in the Justice Department, appointed by the president himself to investigate this goddamned mess." Fowler seemed visibly shaken.

"Look, George, who's there to say anything different from what you already told him?" Agnes asked, attempting to support her troubled husband any way she could.

"That's not the point. He started off okay and then he came down hard, asking me questions about the gun. I kept on repeating that I thought I saw a gun in Bradford's hand. I know he didn't buy my story about the headlights shining on the guy's hand, and that I *thought it was a gun.*" The repeated slugs of 86 proof Seagrams were making Fowler feel woozy and unsteady.

"Without a witness, you'll be okay, George. I think you're over-reacting to this whole business," Agnes said, trying to reassure her husband.

"For Chrissakes, Agnes, don't you get it?" Fowler lashed out. "He's a fed. He'll have a bunch of crew cut college-type investigators doing all kinds of background checks on me. These pros won't stop with the 'Cop of The Year' award I got from the Syracuse PBA. They're trained to dig deep into everything, covering all bases. They'll do full audits of every bank account we ever had, every transaction we ever made, and every check we wrote for the past 15 years. They have ways of finding out what we bought, how much we paid, how much cash we used. These bloodhounds will come up with whatever we owned, how much we spent on vacations, and even how much goddamned toilet paper we use."

Alarmed, Agnes started a question. Fowler interrupted, posing his own to her first. "How long do you think it will take those Justice Department sons-a'-bitches to find out about all the property we bought, and sold, and own, up to now? Agnes, I'm really scared. Fucking scared."

"But we bought and sold other properties all in my mother's name. The lake house we have is in my mother's name right now. They'll never be able to trace all of that," Agnes answered back.

"Oh yeah? Do you think that's going to stop them? In no time they'll find out that everything was bought for all cash and that your mother couldn't even afford her own pot. They'll put the squeeze on all of us. Those bastards don't give up easily." Fowler stopped, letting out an angry snicker. "But that could be the good news. You wanna hear the bad? Once Scarpizzi finds out that I'm the target of a federal probe, my life isn't worth shit." Fowler was near hysteria.

"You can't mean that, George! Why would he want to hurt you?" Agnes cried out.

"Where you been all these years? I can't believe you could be so dumb! It doesn't take a brain surgeon, Agnes, to figure out once Scarpizzi discovers that the heat's on me, I'm an absolute dead man...and you too."

"Stop it. Stop what you're saying, George. I don't want to hear this anymore," Agnes begged, covering her ears with her hands. Alarm and terror began to overwhelm her.

"Where do you think the dough came from that we've been spending like we're bank executives? On a cop's pay? What a joke! No way I can pay cash for a two-hundred-thousand-dollar house next to the lake, on a cop's salary. As soon as Scarpizzi finds out the feds are after me—and he will; he's got ways—he'll think I cut a deal by ratting on him and handing him over to the government. Both of us— yes, both of us-you and me-will wind up in a bag of wet cement and dumped in the foundation of some building that's goin' up. One day, we're missing. Gone. Forever. They'll never find us. They'll never find us," Fowler repeated, sobbing brokenly.

Agnes draped her arm gently around her husband's shoulder, trying desperately to comfort him. Unable to control her own emotions, she too started to sob openly. After a few minutes, Fowler stood up, walked slowly to a picture window in the middle of the living room. Looking pensively at a large maple tree that shaded the front of his house, he said quietly, "Maybe we could just take off and disappear someplace. Start a new life, maybe."

"If you think that would be best George, I'll do whatever you say." Her eyes remained fixed on her distraught husband.

Fowler turned around, staring blankly at his wife. "Ah shit, Agnes. That wouldn't work. There's no way I could raise enough cash in such a short time even if I had it. And although we could run away, I'd be a federal fugitive. Because the attorney general was involved, they'd never give up. There's no place we could hide. The feds would hunt me down. Sooner or later, they'd find me, and my life would just about be over anyway." Haltingly, Fowler continued. "Scarpizzi on one end. The feds on the other. Agnes, I'm goddamned trapped. I'm a fuckin' dead man." He walked, shoulders hunched, to his chair and slid down slowly, burying his head in his hands. "I'm a dead man," he moaned. "A fuckin' dead man."

Neither spoke for what seemed an endless time. When Fowler started to speak again, his voice had pain in it. "Agnes, there's only one real way out." He reached for the telephone after withdrawing a business card from his shirt pocket. It had been given to him earlier that day. He dialed the cell number printed in the lower left-hand corner. A voice at the other end answered.

"Hello, Matt Connors here."

In a soft, tremulous voice, Fowler spoke, "This is George Fowler. It's very important that you meet me in the coffee shop of the Marriott Hotel in Troy, New York. It's about a half hour out of Albany. Can you make it tomorrow at 5:00 pm?"

"What's going on?" Matt asked, his tone, guarded.

In a shakey delivery, reeking with distress, Fowler said, "There's something very important I have to talk to you about. Can you make it?" Fowler hated himself for screwing-up his life so badly and having now to grovel in such a demeaning manner.

Matt hesitated for a moment. Flushed with an excitement, he masked completely. His answer was cold, expressionless. "Yeah, I'll be there."

CHAPTER NINETEEN

Harold "Heshy" Gordon was already standing on the Brooklyn side at the rail separating the walkway from the East River. He examined the skyline of New York City as it appeared on the other side of the river. The Empire State Building stood tall, the Chrysler and Citicorp Buildings to its north. With the tragic collapse of the World Trade Center brought about through an evil terrorist plot on September 11, 2001, the Empire State Building once again assumed its role as the tallest structure in New York. But with the tragic demise of the Twin Towers, the world famous Manhattan skyline would never be the same.

Gordon was looking at his watch as Scarpizzi's Mercedes Benz S 600 drove up. Flanked by Al Pucci and Tony Jackelino, he approached Gordon, arms extended.

As the they greeted each other warmly, Pucci and Jackelino kept a watchful eye fifteen feet away. Scarpizzi spoke. "I thought this was the safest place to meet. You don't know who's watchin' or who's listenin'. So tell me, my good friend Heshy-boy, what do we got?" Scarpizzi asked, pulling up the knot of his silk tie to better meet the tight angle formed by the long-peaked collar of his white custom-made shirt.

"Vincent, it came down just as planned. You remember what I said to you in the car after I spoke to that Carswell lawyer. The formula worked like a charm," Gordon said.

"Talk to me, Heshy. Tell me about it. I want details."

"Vincent, it's a done deal. The governor has agreed to sign the contract with the chief. The fed commissioner, that putz Treausance, gave his okay after he got the squeeze from the V.P. Vincent, the whole deal's in place. We did it!" Gordon said excitedly.

Scarpizzi broke out into an open smile as he reached into his breast pocket and withdrew a Cohiba cigar, lighting it pleasurably. After the first cloud of smoke, he looked at Gordon. Scarpizzi could not contain his excitement. "Heshy, we really pulled it off. Godammit, you beautiful son-of-a-bitch, we really pulled it off."

Gordon smiled, accepting Scarpizzi's high praise. What he had learned from the crime boss was a deep understanding of the subtle method of buying a politician's loyalty. Throughout the years of their association, Scarpizzi had taught Gordon that bribery was an art. It had to be offered in a manner that convinced the taker that his acceptance of it was a justified payment for the power he possessed, and the favors he could grant. Certainly, greed was a factor, but for it to be exploited effectively, it had to be called something else.

Part of Scarpizzi's success was his uncanny understanding of human weaknesses, and the manipulation that usually followed. He knew people, their strengths, their frailties, their attacks, and their defenses. Rising as the leader of the most powerful crime family of New York — and surviving that role — was clear evidence that Scarpizzi could locate the weak link of any person in order to gain the advantage he sought. He was a Machiavellian maestro, skilled in the art of deception; a street hood *extraordinaire,* but one with a mastery that left his victims unaware of his evil motives and devious plans. He laughed with villainous self-gratification as he reconstructed in his own mind, how he and Heshy Gordon got Governor Niles Martin, fully on-board Scarpizzi's Indian casino gambling scheme...

Niles Martin, the fifty-six-year-old, silver-haired governor of New York, with a lanky frame, a toothy smile that seemed etched permanently to his facial landscape, and an ever effusive "How ya doin'?" was the complete portrait of a political animal. He was a clubhouse stereotype who rose through the ranks of Queens County, New York, politics. With a population of more than two million, the county was larger than most of the major cities of the nation. And in New York, it was second only to Kings County — better known as Brooklyn — out of a total number of sixty-two counties in the state.

His early years of working as a district captain out of his local political club, obtaining routine nominating petitions on behalf of club candidates at election time, and his service on mundane and perfunctory committees that most politicians shunned, finally rewarded him with a nomination to the State Assembly. Although an unknown beyond his district, he was swept into office as a result of the national landslide registered by the popular presidential incumbent.

Martin enjoyed the role of elected official. It gave him a rush of power, while attracting many special interest groups and lobbyists who were quick to hand over whatever was necessary in exchange for favored treatment. Meeting with representatives of those industries seeking his favor, was a common occurrence.

It was after Martin's first election to the New York State Assembly when he received an invitation from Glen Turner, the chief lobbyist and point-man for the tobacco industry. Turner's goals were to wine and dine those legislators whose vote could potentially be swayed against an assembly bill sponsored by the organized anti-smoking groups in the state that sought to prohibit smoking in all public areas throughout New York. The passage of the law would have had a significant financial impact upon cigarette sales and its bottom line, a proposal that Turner was commissioned to defeat.

"Assemblyman Martin, Glen Turner here," Turner said, as a call Martin expected, was dispatched directly to him.

"Hello there, Glen. One of my staff people did say you were trying to reach me the past few days. I apologize for not having gotten back to you. I've been rather tied up in committee work and was unable to return your call. But I have you right on top of my 'call back' list," Martin said.

"Well, Assemblyman Martin, I'm sure that the citizens of the state will take great comfort in knowing that at least one of their legislators is hard at work, and not out on some golf course," Turner replied, his tone whimsical.

"That's me, Glen. My constituents know that I'm working my ass off all the time," Martin answered in the same light vein. "So, what can I do for you?"

"Well, I would like very much for you to join me for dinner."

"That's kind of you, Glen. What did you have in mind?"

"I was considering the *Chateau Imperiale* Restaurant, if that meets with your approval, Assemblyman."

The Chateau Imperiale had a five-star rating, having earned its culinary award with its superb continental cuisine, impeccable white glove service, and outrageous prices to match. It had been a stone farm house constructed more than one hundred twenty-five years before it was converted into one of the posh dining establishments of New York state. Its location just several miles north of the state capital in Albany, removed it from the downtown commercial area full of its attendant crowds, noise, and traffic. With a warm and gracious ambiance throughout its dining room, and four cozy and private rooms toward the rear, it served as an ideal venue for those who appreciated award-winning food, discreet privacy, and who had the financial where-with-all to spend lavishly for a single evening's dining pleasure.

Knowing of the *Chateau Imperiale* Restaurant by reputation only, Martin was quick to accept the invitation received.

"*The Chateau* sounds great, Glen. What date do you have in mind?" Martin asked, as he thumbed through his calendar of plugged-in events.

"I don't believe in putting things off. So how does tomorrow evening sound?"

"Tomorrow evening? Uh, let me see. Oh yes, here it is. I see from my calendar that I have a number of things scheduled already."

"Well, is there any way you could fit it in? It would be great if you could."

"Let's see. I have this meeting…I could possibly rearrange that one. Here are a couple of other meetings I have scheduled with some of my constituents. They want a traffic light put up in their neighborhood, or some such crap. Yeah, Glen. I don't see anything that's really pressing. It looks like I'll be able to rearrange my schedule." Martin was anxious to meet tobacco's Mr. Big, and to get a freebee at the fabulous and expensive *Chateau Imperiale* Restaurant.

"That's great, Assemblyman, I'm delighted. A car will be at your hotel at seven tomorrow evening. I do look forward to meeting you at that time. See you then," Turner said.

"Same here."

As he hung up the telephone, Martin shouted to his secretary seated at her desk in a small reception room, next to his office. "Maggie, cancel what I have for tomorrow night. And give my usual apologies."

Being the guest of a deep-pocketed tobacco lobbyist with all the big "perks" it would throw off, held too much allure for him to pass by solely for the mundane business of anxious constituents wanting something as unimportant as, a traffic light—just to protect their kids from being hit by a car. To Martin, this was a no-brainer.

A black Cadillac sedan was waiting in the circular drive in front of Albany's Ambassador Hotel when Martin emerged from the revolving door. Standing to the right rear of the car was Glen Turner, a tall, handsome man in his forties, dressed in a well-tailored, gray herringbone suit.

"Assemblyman Martin. It's so good to meet you," Turner said, extending his hand graciously.

"Pleasure meeting you, too, Mr. Turner." Martin extended his hand, in return.

As Turner opened the rear door of the car, signaling his guest to enter, Martin was surprised to see that in addition to the driver behind the wheel, there was an extraordinarily attractive young woman seated in the left rear passenger seat. She had straight, blonde hair, cut short, high-fashion style, sparkling blue eyes, full lips, with a face showing off beautiful features. All were highlighted by subtle, and perfect make-up, giving her an appearance of just having been pampered at a Fifth Avenue beauty salon.

"Say hello to Mitzi Brown, Assemblyman. Mitzi's one of my associates, and if you have no objection, she will be joining us for dinner. Is that alright with you?" Turner asked, making the slightest sign of a raised eyebrow as he asked the question.

"If you're asking me whether I'd object to having dinner with you and a beautiful young lady, what can I say? The pleasure's all mine." Martin leaned into the rear compartment, extending his hand in a warm greeting. He sat next to Mitzi.

"Well, okay then. It's off to the *Chateau*," Turner said, shutting the car door once Martin was seated. Turner entered the right front passenger seat next to the driver who maneuvered the car out of the parking circle, and onto the roadway.

Polite introductions and casual small talk occupied the fifteen-minute drive to the *Chateau Imperiale*. When they arrived, Martin and Mitzi Brown followed Turner into the restaurant. There, they were met by a *maitre d'*, dressed in formal attire. He gave Turner a warm, friendly greeting, escorting the party to one of the private rooms in the rear.

"Antonio will be your captain, and Rafael will be your waiter. They will visit you shortly. As usual, Mr. Turner, I will be sending Jacques over to you, as well. Is there anything further at this time?" the *maitre d'* asked.

"No thank you," Turner replied.

Within minutes, two tuxedo-clad waiters approached the table, accompanied by a sommelier. Addressing him, Turner said, "Jacques, be good enough to bring a bottle of that wonderful vintage champagne you recommended the other night. Make sure you have another one of the same year on ice."

"At your service, Mr. Turner," Jacques said, the large crest and medallion of his craft, dangling from a wide red silk ribbon that hung around his neck.

Speaking to the captain who introduced himself as Antonio, Turner said, "We will first have champagne, Antonio. Then you can tell us what the chef's specials are."

"As you wish, Mr. Turner," Antonio replied courteously, leaving the dining room accompanied by Rafael and Jacques.

The first glass of champagne led to the next, then to the next, as did the first bottle of champagne. Others followed it. As the imported vintages were poured into high, crystal, fluted glasses, their contents not only complemented the extraordinary cuisine served, but induced an atmosphere that became more and more relaxed, as each empty bottle was turned upside down in the stand-up silver ice bucket, inviting an immediate replacement.

Mitzi Brown is a beautiful, sexy woman, with a gorgeous figure to match, thought Martin, as the alcoholic content of the champagne succeeded to peel away the natural inhibitions that a public dining place would normally create. The effects of the champagne, interspersed with Mitzi Brown's flirtatious talk and double entendres, were feeding Martin's sudden lust. *I must get that woman in bed,* he repeated in his head.

"You have to break away from some of your serious work, Niles. Relax a little more," Mitzi teased, placing her right hand on top of Martin's hand, keeping it there, as she was speaking.

"This kind of relaxation, I'll take every time." The bubbly vintage and Mitzi Brown's body contact, combined with the sweet scent of her exotic perfume, were beginning to guide his dialogue.

"Well, Niles, you're a pro at politics, but as the commercial says, 'leave the relaxation to us,' " Mitzi said, as she squeezed Martin's hand suggestively.

"See, Niles, you never knew that dinner at the *Chateau* could be so interesting, right?" Turner asked, pleased with how the evening was progressing. Although he had a very special purpose in having Niles Martin as his dinner guest, he did not discuss the subject of his true mission, deciding it would be more diplomatic and more productive not to do so at such a time.

"Dinner at *The Chateau*, interesting? You're so right, Glen. So very right," as he moved closer to Mitzi. He suddenly felt the outline of her bikini panties, his hand rubbing against her tight silk dress. He was feeling extremely aroused.

"Excuse me. I have to make a call. Be back soon," Turner said, getting up from his chair. He walked out of the private dining room and closed the door behind him, leaving Mitzi and Martin alone.

"Well," Mitzi said, "here we are."

Once alone, Martin grabbed Mitzi's shoulders, pulling her toward him. In the same instant, his mouth came hard against hers, as he kissed Mitzi with an uncontrollable passion.

Mitzi attempted to push Martin off. "Niles. Please, Niles, not here."

"I'm sorry, Mitzi. But, my God, you're driving me a little crazy. What say we get out of here before I lose all control and do something real stupid. Okay?" Martin knew he was at the mercy of his extremely sensuous dinner companion.

Thirty minutes later, Mitzi and Niles were on top of a king size bed in a lavish hotel suite, compliments of Glen Turner, who had earlier made a discreet departure. Sex is one thing. Wild sex is yet another. Extraordinarily crazy and wild sex, is but the fulfillment of one's erotic fantasies that many dream of, but few experience. As for Niles Martin, having spent the entire night with Mitzi Brown, qualified him to join the statistical category of the extremely "privileged" few.

Martin expected the call he received the next morning at his office.

"Well, Niles, I hope you had an enjoyable evening," Turner mused, tongue in cheek.

"Hey there, Buddy, I would say...yeah you could call it interesting." Martin still felt a throbbing, but satisfying strain in his groins, that a wild sexual encounter can sometimes produce. Turner had fulfilled his role. Mitzi Brown, also. And big tobacco had bought a new and accessible ally for its powerful team!

In addition to tobacco, banking, insurance, and power companies, other corporate giants had a strong ally in Martin as well. He came to expect tangible thanks of some value for every favor he delivered—the quid pro quo for which there were few exceptions.

The payout could take the form of a substantial cash contribution to Martin's ongoing campaign fund or first class trips to exotic parts of the world where he would be pampered with five-star hotel comforts while embarking on some fact-finding pretense, an inside stock tip, a real estate deal, or the company of other exotic Mitzi Browns.

Extravagant gifts to satisfy the insatiable appetite of this "dedicated public servant," would always be part of his prize.

After serving in the State Assembly for four years, he moved on to the State Senate, with even more gifts and more favors for his political benefactors and cronies.

The New York Herald, the pinnacle print media of good-government crusaders, blasted Martin continuously, accusing him of being a machine party hack—incompetent, demanding that he be removed, or rejected at the polls. One editorial even called for a grand jury investigation into his questionable practices, but those attacks created even more reasons for the sensational self-promotional tabloids of New York to join forces in supporting their "dedicated hard-working legislator." *The Herald* was out-of-touch with the needs of the average working person; it was a newspaper oriented toward its elitist readers, argued Martin's ardent supporters in their defense of him. Martin, they protested, was a true representative of the average worker, having sponsored programs, as if one of them.

But there are those politicians, who, devoid of true ideals, or basic principles, become political parasites who feed continuously at the trough of public largesse. Niles Martin was one of them.

He had chosen public service, not for the sacrifices he could make to further a better society, but for what society could gift over to him, to satisfy his power, greed, and influence. He was there to take, not to provide. Whatever the giving, it was a pretense, and an illusion for the consumption of his voters who were misguided by his surface pretenses, electing him each time with even greater pluralities. Credit Madison Avenue and its creative image-makers for the hand-crafted package they sold to the public in presenting Niles Martin as a fighting crusader on behalf of the underdog.

Martin's rise to governor was inevitable. Although he received less than forty-five percent of the total vote cast, three other opposition candidates divided the remaining percentage. His second term as an incumbent won him fifty-three percent of the total vote, with two other candidates dividing the balance.

The governorship comfortably in hand, Martin was able to maintain the surface appearance of accomplishment, while his questionably acquired wealth and growing power, fueled an arrogance that masked all underlying vulnerability. After all, he was the governor of the Empire State. He had appointed the chief judge of the state's highest court, together with four other of its high court judges. He knew most of the state's prosecutors on a first name basis. He controlled a private army of state police, who protected, escorted, and insulated him during his many adventures outside his marriage. He even boasted for all to hear, that the vice president of the United States was one of his closest friends, and allies.

Governor Niles Martin lived in the executive mansion paid for by twenty million residents of New York, providing him with the finest furnishings, wines, and the accouterments to serve him in the most kingly of styles. He felt totally removed from the intrusions of the do-good meddlers, and good- government puritans. As each day passed, his self perceived invulnerability, created in his mind an untouchable despot who could commit any misdeed, without ever being called to task. Such is the elixir of power, and Governor Niles Martin, was the prototypical example of such unfettered arrogance. Executive hubris at its zenith!

Vincent Scarpizzi knew the real Niles Martin, as few did. He had supported Martin's early rise in politics, recognizing that he had an ally willing to return favors in exchange for the right price. It was that knowledge that Scarpizzi would call upon to exact the gubernatorial consent required to seal the third link toward full Indian casino gambling in New York.

As Scarpizzi's emissary, "Heshy" Gordon had already met with Pat Hughes, the governor's chief of staff, and Martin's top confidante. In addition to his official duties that included placing him in charge of

Governor Martin's huge executive staff, scheduling, and overall legislative and political strategy, Pat Hughes was Martin's unofficial "collector." All major cash contributions, expensive gifts, or other sacred emblements of value given to Martin from his many grateful business and other "friends," in exchange for preferential treatment, always went through Pat Hughes.

Known in political jargon as "bagman," Pat Hughes' job was to continuously nourish and feed his boss' insatiable appetite, while at the same time protecting and insulating him from the probing and annoying eye of investigative agencies, as well. He was the trusted soldier, always prepared to take the heat, to throw himself on the sword, to take the full blow, if any of the governor's wrong-doing became a serious public issue. This was the price Hughes was expected to pay in exchange for his own political status and concomitant power. He knew he might have to take the bullet intended for the executive target. But the job, once accepted, meant that there could be no turning back.

In his role as point-man for the governor, Hughes had finalized the terms of the arrangement for the issuance of the license to the Pecontic tribe for full casino gambling on its reservation. While he did not have the final word on such a significant matter, Hughes knew that once its terms were passed along to Niles Martin, the great governor of the Empire State would be salivating.

Heshy Gordon recalled the time he had cooled his heels in the waiting room outside the governor's office. Gordon could visualize what was happening inside, almost as if he had been a witness to the actual events...

Pat Hughes opened the door that led to the governor's private office. Martin was in his shirt sleeves, collar opened, drinking a Dewars on the rocks. Martin spoke first.

"Okay, Pat. What did that Gordon fellow want?"

"You know, Niles, he's Scarpizzi's man," Hughes replied.

"Yeah, Pat, I know that. We've dealt with him before. Have you found him to be straight with us?"

"I give Gordon and Scarpizzi pretty high marks. And you and Scarpizzi go back a long time, to the early days in Queens County."

"Okay then. So what did the guy want?"

"Scarpizzi wants your consent for the Pecontics to have casino gambling in Syracuse."

"What the hell is Scarpizzi's interest in Syracuse?" Martin shot back.

"He's got some kind of a plan to bring casino gambling to New York. The voters have rejected Vegas-style casino gambling every time it came up in referendum. Scarpizzi thinks going the Indian route is the way to accomplish the same goals—even *better*. So he's looking for your okay. He's got the chief of the Pecontics under wraps, and apparently an okay from the feds in Washington. The consent, or compact with the overnor of New York is all he needs for his deal to move forward."

"That's all he wants? He, and fifty other Indian chiefs, that's all," Martin let out a cynical laugh.

"But the other chiefs aren't going to pick up two hundred fifty grand of markers you have spread out between Vegas and Atlantic City."

"Play it again, Sam," Martin said, unsure of what he had just heard.

"I said, Scarpizzi will take care of one hundred grand you have outstanding in Vegas, and the one hundred fifty you owe in Atlantic City. But there's more. You get fifty large up front on top of that."

Looking at his half-consumed glass of scotch, Martin broke into a satisfying smile. "That sounds pretty damned good to me," as he belted down the balance of the drink, in one gulp. "How will Indian casino gambling play out in the press?"

"I got it covered, Niles. You come out publicly for a percentage of the action to be set aside for education, another percent for AIDS, cancer research, and some for Alzheimer's, and other senior bullshit. You'll come off as a big hero."

Pouring himself another Dewars, Martin asked slyly, "Well how about something additional for the guy who makes it all happen? You know Pat, I'm like a one-man research and development division, and I gotta be funded."

"I thought of that too, Niles. Once the casino is in full operation, I'll be picking up an envelope each week with ten grand in green. Now, how does that grab you?"

"I like it. I like it. It grabs me pretty good. I'd like it better if it was more like twenty grand, but I guess I can't be a pig about it. Cut the deal with Scarpizzi. But I want to see those markers stamped 'paid,' and canceled, otherwise there's no deal," Martin shot back. He was referring to promissory notes he signed in exchange for chips he had gambled and lost. To protect his identity, the marker information had been redacted from the general computer memory, filed under a false name. The original markers signed by Martin were kept in a vault and confidential lock-up, segregated from the I.O.U.'s of other casino patrons.

"Just leave it to me. I'll take care of it. Tomorrow, Joe Roundtree, the chief of the Pecontic tribe will be here at three o'clock. I'm calling a press conference for four o'clock to announce a compact New York is entering into with the Pecontic tribe.

Martin broke out into a euphoric laugh. "Pat, you sweet son-of-a-bitch. You're a fucking genius— almost like me," Martin said, toasting Pat Hughes with his scotch-filled glass as he flashed a big, toothy smile.

CHAPTER TWENTY

Hector Santiago's cell phone rang fifteen minutes after Scarpizzi left Gordon. He reached into his pocket and lifted it to his ear. "It's me," Scarpizzi said at the other end.

"Hey, Vincent, what's up?" Santiago asked.

"Meet me at Luigi's at six o'clock. We're gonna do some eatin', some drinkin' and some talkin'. Okay, *compadre*?"

"What's goin' on?"

"Nothin.' I just wanna have a little talk. That's all."

"About what?"

"Like I said…We're gonna eat. We're gonna drink. And we're gonna talk. Ain't that what partners do? *Capiche*?"

"Sure, sounds okay. See ya there, *amigo*," Santiago said with a faked lift in his voice as he hung up. *Who does that wise-guy mafiosi prick think he's dealing with?* Santiago thought cynically. *He wants to talk, eat, and drink like partners do? Bullshit! He's up to somethin'., I can smell it. Well, maybe I got it wrong. I'll just wait an' hear what he has ta say. Why not? I'll give him the benefit a' the doubt. But he better not try pullin' somethin' fast on me.*

The double espresso was even more enriched with the sweet alcoholic nectar of *sambucca* and the two traditional dark brown coffee beans added to the shallow cup. Dinner for two in the upstairs dining room of *Luigi's* was now over. Vincent Scarpizzi removed a large *Cohiba* cigar from its leather case, bit off a small hole at the top, and started the ceremonial lighting at the other end. As the smoke billowed above his head, he gently removed the white napkin that was tucked into his shirt collar, neatly folded it four times and laid it on the table next to the empty espresso cup.

"Now to business," Scarpizzi said, as he gestured casually to Santiago seated opposite him. Their separate platoon of soldiers were downstairs as Vincent Scarpizzi and Hector Santiago faced each other.

Scarpizzi spoke. "Hey *compadre*, we pulled it off just as I said we would." He paused, then continued. "We did it, just like I told ya when we first met right here in this restaurant."

"Yeah Vincent, it worked like a charm. And now the real fun begins," Santiago said. He continued to ask himself, *What's this hombre up to?*

Scarpizzi moved closer to Santiago. "That's what I wanted to talk to ya 'bout, Hector."

"Yeah? Like what?" Santiago thought, *Here it comes.*

"Ya know, this whole thing was my idea. And I feel a little uncomfortable to say what I'm gonna say." The slight surface smile over Santiago's face instantly changed into a quizzical look.

"Relax, Hector. Hear me out. I think you'll like what ya hear."

"I'm listenin'," Hector answered, he too inching his face forward. *Now it's comin'. The no good bastard,* raced through his mind.

"I'll get right to it," Scarpizzi said. The earlier friendly voice, was now replaced by one that sounded strident, blunt. "Hector, I don't wanna partner. But I'm gonna offer ya a fair deal."

"What are ya sayin'?" Santiago screamed out. *I was right. The no good son-of-a bitch scumbag,* he repeated to himself.

Scarpizzi continued. "What I'm sayin' is that I'm gonna give ya mucho cash for what ya did. Look Hector, it's a fast buck for ya an' I pay ya off fair an' square. It's good business all aroun'. Ya go your way; I go mine. That simple. No sweat."

"Say again."

"I buy you out. You're outta the deal."

"Are you kiddin' me? Is this a joke, or what?"

"I ain't jokin'. Look, it ain't gonna work, you an' me. So I'm gonna give ya a fair pay-out."

"You're gonna buy me out, and I'm gonna walk. Is that what you're sayin'?" Dragon fire was beginning to pour out of Santiago's mouth. "Here's what AH-MEE-GO," stretching the word out defiantly, "I offer *you* the deal, and *you* walk. How does that grab ya?" Raw hostility now charged the air.

After a long pause, and with steely eyes fixed on each other, Scarpizzi answered through clenched teeth. "I'll think about it, and let ya know."

With those words, two kingpins—the boss of the DiPienza crime family and the lord of the Colombian drug cartel—rose abruptly from their seats. Santiago started to walk slowly toward the door. He stopped and turned around quickly, facing Vincent Scarpizzi three feet behind him. He hesitated for a moment, searching for the right response, and stretched to the full limit of his six-foot height, straightening the points of his open-collared shirt.

"You're gonna think about it, and let me know? Is that what ya said?" Santiago continued, hate-filled, dead-eyed. "Yeah. You do that. I'll be waitin' for your answer," he warned in a threatening whisper. Santiago turned sharply, offering his stolid back to Scarpizzi as he walked stiffly, and with bristling fury, out the door.

Vincent Scarpizzi stood silently at the top landing, puffing away clouds of smoke from his *Cohiba*. He watched Hector Santiago descend the narrow stairs, feeling the uneasy challenge spawned by Santiago's ominous threat.

Each knew what now had to be done...

After his encounter with Santiago, Scarpizzi wasted no time in putting into action a plan he had conceived even before his show-down meeting at *Luigi's Ristorante*. It was from a lake house near Syracuse that he arranged to meet Joe Roundtree three days later. He was the house guest of an old pal who had been operating porn shops in Syracuse's blue-line district.

Scarpizzi dialed Joe Roundtree's phone number.

"Joe, Vincent here."

"Hi, Vincent. What's doin'?"

"I'm here in Syracuse."

"What ya got in Syracuse?"

" I'm stayin' at a friend a' mine's house. He's on the lake."

"Yeah? That's a nice area. Maybe we can get together while you're here."

"Sure. That's what I'm callin' ya about. We'll have a couple a' drinks at the lake house. Okay with ya, chief?"

"Fine with me."

"Terrific! We'll pick ya up so ya don' have ta bodder drivin'. How's that sound?"

"Yeah, sounds good. Ya know how ta get here?"

"No. But lemme put Tony on. He'll pick ya up. Just tell him how ta get ta your place."

One hour later, Tony Jackelino pulled up to the garage door of the lakeside house with his passenger, Joe Roundtree. They entered the one-story building and proceeded into a large family room with a ceiling that had heavy wooden crossbeams running across it. A huge stone fireplace, highly polished wooden floors, and a stuffed moose head surrounded by an oak frame, added to the informal decor. Floor-to-ceiling windows provided a clear view of the scenic lake 200 feet away.

Seated in a large brown leather chair, Vincent Scarpizzi shifted the Cohiba cigar he was cradling in his right hand, to his left, as Joe Roundtree entered the room. Throwing his arms around the chief as a gesture of affection, Scarpizzi spoke first.

"It's so good to see ya, Joe. Thanks a lot for comin'. I appreciate it. What do ya wanna drink, chief?"

Before answering, all that Joe Roundtree could think of was that he had finally made it in the big league. Being wined by the most powerful mob boss in New York made Joe's ego rise rapidly. "Straight whiskey," Joe said. "I don't go for all the fancy stuff. With me, it's just straight whiskey."

"My kind a' guy," Scarpizzi said, as he reached for a bottle of Seagrams V.O. standing on the table next to bottles of gin, scotch, vodka, and bourbon. He poured the V.O. into two tall glasses. "To our partnership." They clinked their glasses and took big gulps.

"Tony, get lost," Scarpizzi said, instructing his bodyguard to leave the two by themselves. "The chief an' me—we don' want no company when we're drinkin'."

"You got it, boss. I'm outta here." Tony exited, closing the two solid wood doors behind him.

The two men sat in chairs opposite each other. Within minutes, they consumed their second drinks.

"Joe, I appreciate ya comin' here and I appreciate the respect ya gimme. And I give ya respect back, don' I?"

"Yeah, sure ya do, Vincent," Joe said, as he swallowed the balance of his third straight whiskey. It made him feel even more light-headed, looser.

"What I gotta say is important." Joe sat forward, anxious to hear every word.

"I know you and Hector Santiago get along pretty good." Scarpizzi hesitated before continuing. "But maybe there could be a real problem."

"Whaddya mean 'real problem'?"

"I'll tell ya straight out. Ya see Joe, Santiago's not his own man."

"Whaddya mean 'not his own man'?"

" Lemme give ya an example. You, Joe, you take orders from no one. That's good. Real good. You don' have ta answer ta nobody. You're your own man. See what I mean?"

"G'on Vincent, I'm listenin'."

"Okay. I'm like you, Joe. I don't have ta answer ta nobody neither. I'm the boss. I'm my own man. I make a deal; I keep it. You make a deal; you keep it. Right, Joe?"

"Sure. I make a deal; I keep it."

Scarpizzi nodded, then continued. "Now, I like Hector. I like him a lot. But right now we're talkin' business, and when it's business you're talkin', sometimes ya gotta put aside whether ya like a guy or not. Ya follow what I'm sayin', eh?"

"Go 'head."

"Ya gotta know everythin' about the guy ya doin' business with. That's a smart thing ta do. Agree?

"Sure."

"Okay. Now there's somethin' ya don' know 'bout Hector Santiago."

"Like what?"

"Well, he's not like you an' me. You an' me, we ain't got no bosses over us. We don' work for nobody. But Hector Santiago, he's different. He got a boss. Yeah, a big-time boss. You didn't know it, did ya?"

"No, I didn't know none a' that."

"I know ya didn't. And ya didn't even know that Hector can't make no deal with me, or you, until he gets clearance from his boss. Ya' didn't know none a' that 'bout Hector, did ya, Joe?"

"No, I didn't know that either. That true?"

"Yeah, believe me, Joe, it's true. And it's news to ya, right? Well, let me lay it out for ya plain-like. He works for a big- time guy, Louis Varga. He's the head honcho of the Colombian racket boys. Hector…he's just a middle man. Let me tell ya, he ain't no general. More like a sergeant. Takes his orders straight from the top…that's Varga. Now, he's the *real* general. The truth is, chief, Santiago can't even take a piss without gettin' an okay from Varga. Look…what I'm really tryin' to say here, Hector, is Santiago ain't his own man. No way. He makes a deal; he keeps it, but only if Louis Varga, the big boss, says it's okay to keep it. See what I mean?"

"I'm not real sure. Just what are you tryin' to tell me, Vincent? Go 'head. Say it straight out. "

"What I'm sayin' is that, sure, maybe I can trust Hector Santiago. But I don't trust this Varga guy for one fuckin' minute. Ya' see Joe, Varga's our *real* partner in this whole deal, not Hector. And I know Varga will screw us first chance he gets. That's the way he operates. He got to be top guy by bein' the slimy, double-crossin' son-of-a-bitch he really is." There was a pause. When Scarpizzi spoke again, his voice was softer. "Joe, what I'm sayin' is that Varga is not a guy we should be doin' business with. Varga is not the guy we should be partners with in the biggest gamblin' operation in the country. Joe, he'll fuck us both, and you and me, we'll both be out in left field, waggin' our dicks with zero, zipperino, my friend. Are ya hearin' what I'm sayin', chief?"

"I'm listenin', Vincent," Joe said intently. His discomfort was beginning to show.

"Joe, what I'm sayin' is that you, me, we can be fifty-fifty partners in the biggest gamblin' deal aroun'. Do ya know what that means in cash? Look, Joe, I trust ya.' You trust me. I'll never let ya down. Believe it. You can make a book on it. And I know you'll never let me down. Come on, Joe, I respect ya. You got respect for me. I can take it to the bank. But the big question, can we really trust Louis Varga?"

Joe Roundtree was becoming uneasy. "What are you really tryin' ta say, Vincent?"

"Okay, bottom line." Scarpizzi inched closer. "What I'm sayin' *is…we take Hector Santiago out, and Louis Varga is history. Finito! Kaput!*"

"Take Hector out?"

"Yeah, Joe. Then, you and me, we become equal partners. Just like that. But first we gotta take get Santiago outta the deal—permanent like. Varga and Santiago are like bags a' cement pullin' us down. I'm tellin' ya, chief, ya gotta cut the cord before it strangles ya. There's no other way. Do ya follow what I'm sayin', Joe?" Scarpizzi paused, then asked, "Whaddya say…ya with me on this?"

Joe Roundtree sat back, shifting nervously about in his stuffed leather chair. He closed his eyes for a moment. His head was spinning. Clouding his mind were images of Hector Santiago's face. How could he betray a man who provided the big dollars for Jenny's congressional campaign? *Without Santiago's help, would Jenny have won?* The question kept repeating itself in his head.

Opening his eyes slowly, the deep ridges on his forehead becoming more furrowed, Joe began to speak. His voice sounded troubled. "Vincent, Santiago was good to me when I needed a lotta money for Jenny's campaign. How do I turn bad on a guy who helped me out so much?"

"Joe, there's somethin' ya don' know. And I never told ya.' But I'm gonna tell ya now. Just listen…. I gave you as much bread as Hector Santiago did. Even more. The big difference is what you got from him, he got straight from Louis Varga. It was not Hector's own cash. But what I paid out at my end for ya came direct from my own pocket. We needed your help to get a license. So ya don't owe Hector nothin.' It's this guy Varga ya really owe. And he's a guy ya don't even know. A guy who don't give a shit about you or your daughter. With Varga in the deal, we're pissin' up stream an' against the wind. He's a guy who'll knife us the second our back is turned…. Look Joe, I learned a lotta things in my life. But there's one thing I learned and never forgot: Ya' don't wait till the bee stings ya.' Kill it and it won't bodder ya no more. I learned it the hard way I'm sorry to say. And it cost me a lot. You're my friend so I'm given' it to ya fa' free."

Joe remained silent.

Scarpizzi continued. "But there's more. A whole lot more. Ya' see Joe, Hector wasn't goin' to give ya a dime without gettin' your okay on the spot that ya could deliver on your end. No question abowddit, he had to get clearance from Louis Varga. And if you took the cash and couldn't han' over what he was payin for, you'd be in shit way over your head, Chief or no Chief. Know what I mean?"

"Pale face scalp red face! Yeah?"Joe intended no humor.

"You, got it right, my friend. But it's a whole different ball game with me. I gave ya what ya wanted. No strings attached. I did it for ya strictly like a favor. That's the way I run my business, Joe. That's the big difference between this guy Louis Varga and me. What I'm tryin' to say Joe, you owe me everythin.' You owe Santiago nothin.' It's that plain and simple." Scarpizzi paused… "I'm askin' again Chief, are ya with me in this? Do we have a deal?"

Joe maintained his silence. Slowly, words began to form on his tongue as his response to Scarpizzi's pointed question came out in a whispered somber tone.

"Yeah, Vincent ... we have a deal."

With his answer "we have a deal" delivered personally to the boss of the DiPenza crime family, Chief Joe Roundtree knew that he was now committed to a course from which he could never withdraw.

CHAPTER
TWENTY-ONE

As US Air Flight 63 flew over Manhattan having departed Washington's Reagan National Airport one hour earlier, the famous skyline was missing its landmark twin 115 foot vertical Trade Center towers. In their place, was the 17-acre vacant lots-ground zero- on which they had stood, tragic reminders of September 11, 2001.

Although the Empire State Building now stood as New York City's tallest survivor, the Chrysler Building was still a world-class art- deco architectural gem. It was now these two towers that dominated the skyline of a city that had suffered such a tragic assault.

Within minutes, the Boeing 737 zoomed low over the Grand Central Parkway as it touched down on runway three. Glancing anxiously at his watch, Matt was concerned that his jet's thirty minute late departure out of Washington due to traffic build up around LaGuardia, had left him only twenty minutes to make the commuter flight to Albany. When Flight 63 moved into the gate, Matt and his deputy Dan Sanford had already positioned themselves at the front of the cabin. As the doors opened, they moved quickly into the terminal and were seated in the thirty passenger turbo jet to Albany with ten minutes to spare.

One hour later, they were in a taxi at the Albany Airport giving instructions to the driver. Matt had asked Dan to accompany him to the interview. His assistant was bright - a Harvard Law Review honoree before he graduated and a quick read of suspects he had interviewed. A rising star within the Justice Department.

"Marriott Hotel in Troy," Matt barked, as the yellow cab moved out heading north. Twenty-five minutes later they were inside the lobby of the Troy Marriott. At ten minutes of five, they walked into the hotel's coffee shop and were seated at a booth in a quiet corner of the restaurant.

At five p.m., George Fowler, the veteran Syracuse cop, dressed in off-duty casual clothes, appeared, walked directly to Matt and sat in the booth opposite him and Dan Sanford. Clad in a brown zippered jacket, tan slacks, and slip-ons, he looked anxious. Fowler spoke first, unsure how to start the conversation. "I appreciate you coming, Mr. Connors." Matt smiled to himself, noting how the bravado displayed by the police sergeant during their first interview was visibly missing.

The coffee shop was empty except for a middle-aged couple seated seven booths away, well out of hearing range. Fowler spoke again. "I have a few things to say but I'll hold it until the waitress takes our order."

Soon, a middle-aged uniformed waitress came to the table. "What can I get you boys?"

"Coffee, black, and a toasted English muffin, butter on the side," Matt answered.

"Same," Sanford said.

Fowler ordered coffee and a sugar doughnut.

He picked up the conversation after the waitress left the table. "Look Connors, maybe we can work something out. Maybe we can't. But I wanna talk to you about something."

"I'm listening," Matt said. There was no emotion in his voice.

"Are you interested in a deal?" Fowler asked in a low voice.

"What kind of a deal?" Matt was there to listen, not to promise anything before he knew the value of what Fowler had to say.

"Suppose I told you I have information on who shot Bradford, and why."

"Exactly what kind of information?" Matt's excitement was beginning to stir.

"Two coffees and toasted English muffin, and a coffee and doughnut," the waitress interrupted, placing the food and drinks in front of Matt, Dan, and Fowler.

As soon as she was beyond ear reach, Fowler continued. "I have the information you're after. What I could tell would make you a hero," he added with a smirk. "Okay, Connors? Here it is. I can deliver the guys you want. Interested?"

"Depends on what you have," Matt answered cautiously.

"You're making this damn tough for me, Connors. I gotta know. If I hand over what you want, you hand over what I want. Can we start off on that note?" Fowler looked quizzically at Matt.

Matt wanted to cheer out loud. He felt like he was in an open car waving to crowds at a ticker-tape victory parade down Broadway. But he kept a straight, dour face. "What do you want as your end?"

"I blow this whole fuckin' thing wide open for you, and you give me full immunity. I testify for the government and I give you these guys on a silver tray, but only if my wife and me are put in the federal witness protection program. That's what I want," Fowler said firmly.

"What's your wife's role in this?"

"Nothin'. Absolutely nothin'. She's never been involved in any of this shit. But she has to be part of the deal, or there's *no* deal. If we can do business, you guys will have to arrange the sale of our house in Syracuse. The one we have on the lake that's in my wife's mother's name, stays put. After she dies we get the money wherever we are. You want me to keep talkin', or do you want me to take a hike?" Fowler asked, pointing his left thumb toward the door.

"I'm listening, Fowler. Go ahead," Matt said.

"That's not good enough. Look, I deliver the whole package to you and you pay my price. I want assurances. Otherwise, no *sale*," Fowler said flatly.

"Look, Fowler, don't come on strong with me. Maybe you don't get the full picture of your ass being surrounded by a chain link fence. I can put the cuffs on you right now and toss you in the tank in a heartbeat. Why should I go for a deal I haven't even *heard* yet?" Matt's voice was filled with cynicism.

"You bag me, Connors, and my mouth stays shut. You get nothing outta of me after that. And I'll give you odds on that. If you think I'm bluffing, go ahead, try me. Call my hand. Do it. But you're gonna lose. If we have a deal, it goes down now, or it never happens. Do you think I give a rat's ass what you can get me on? Hey, all you got is me being on the take. That's it. So I give up my badge. Pay a fine. Do some time. Big fuckin' deal. Then I'm outta there." Fowler spoke with bravado. He knew he was running a bluff, but he also needed a guarantee since the second he opened his mouth and blew the whistle he would be the target of Scarpizzi's assassins. So what if the feds could indict him for obstruction of justice or even conspiracy to commit murder? It still beat being at the butt end of a .45 pressed against his head as it shattered, satisfying Scarpizzi's vengeance. At the moment, Fowler's game was to play hard ball, knowing all the risks of such a dangerous stategy.

Matt remained silent for a moment, knowing that his assistant Dan was thinking the same thoughts he had. If Fowler had inside knowledge of the killing of Chuck Bradford, and knew the reason why he had been murdered, in all of its shades of conspiracy and crime, the government would be short-sighted not to offer this crooked cop and his wife the immunity and protection he sought. The man across the table from him probably had been dirty for years. He knew the price for ratting on the people who had been paying him off. He also knew that if he kept his mouth shut, he might go down with the men he was prepared to name. It would be foolish of Matt, he thought, not to give the cop what he wanted. The sooner the investigation could be ended, the earlier the fence mending could take place after disclosure to the public of the scheme and identification of those involved.

"Okay, Fowler, let me hear what you have to say."

"Not until I hear from you that we have a deal. Do we have it?"

"Yeah. Go ahead. I'm listening."

"Before I talk, I want to call my wife and tell her the deal is on. I don't say nothin' until I know she's safe."

"It's okay with me. In twenty minutes I'll have two FBI agents take her to the Syracuse office. She'll call you from there."

"I'm calling her now to tell her that two of your guys are coming over. Once I hear she's out of the house, and okay, I'll do my talking. Agreed?" Sweat began to form on Fowler's forehead.

Thirty minutes later, Fowler's cell phone rang. "You outta the house, Agnes? Everything okay? Fine. I'll get back to you in a little bit."

"We're going into one of the conference rooms upstairs," Matt said, getting to his feet, waiting for Fowler to move out in front of him.

Leaving the coffee shop, Matt, Dan and Fowler walked into the lobby elevator and got off at the eighth floor. Walking to his left, he stopped in front of a door with a brass plate imprinted "East Conference Room." Removing a plastic key card handed to him by the hotel manager, Matt opened the door and walked into a fourteen-by eighteen-foot room. It had an eight-foot rectangular table, six chairs around it. He motioned Fowler to sit at the far end of the table as he and Dan sat across from him. Reaching into his briefcase, Matt removed a small Sony tape recorder and placed it o n the table a foot in front of Fowler. "The tape is rolling. Start talking." Matt's eyes were fixed on Fowler. After a brief pause, Fowler cleared his throat. He started to speak:

"There's this guy Vincent Scarpizzi..."

For the next hour, except for a quick bathroom break, Fowler described in detail the plan that ultimately led to the shooting of Chuck Bradford. Matt and Dan sat quietly, fascinated with the story of the fifteen year police veteran whose incriminating words were deadly enough to convict *everyone* he identified.

Fowler admitted he was an active participant in the casino gambling scheme. He even related that he knew Chuck Bradford's trip to Syracuse had been delayed because the attorney general had been forced to take a later flight, arriving in Syracuse after 8 p.m. Continuing without hesitation, he recited how Chuck planned to confront Joe Roundtree, Jenny's father, in order to hear first-hand Joe's deceptive role in the Indian casino license scam. It was the first time Matt learned that Jenny innocently had alerted her father of Chuck's visit, and the questions he was going to ask.

Fowler slowly, meticulously laid out the sequence of events from the moment Chuck headed west on State Road 118 toward Joe Roundtree's house 22 miles away. It was a flashback with terror scrawled all over it...

Chuck had visited 310 Barrow Street just one time before. It was when Jenny brought him to meet his future father-in-law just before their marriage. The small-framed bungalow was as Chuck remembered it. The dark wood shingles covering the outside of the house still showed the signs of age and neglect. As Chuck walked up the four worn wooden steps to the porch, they squeaked loudly as he placed his weight upon them. He pressed a small buzzer in the center of a brass plate that showed signs of corrosion from weather and use. Within a minute, the front door that bore a facade of dark green paint with dried water streaks overlapping chipped areas—signs that 310 Barrow Street had not been touched by a paintbrush in many years— opened.

In painful detail, Fowler continued to narrate the events leading to Chuck's death. They unrolled and played back like a film in Matt's mind, feeling as if he were actually there at 310 Barrow Street mounting the steps of Joe Roundtree's house, standing next to Chuck ringing the doorbell. It was as if Matt himself was an actual eye-witness to everything that Chuck confronted that night in Syracuse:

"Chuck, come on in," a smiling Joe Roundtree said, offering a friendly greeting.

"Thanks, Joe," Chuck retorted, as he stepped into the foyer of the framed bungalow.

Joe led Chuck into the livingroom, pointing him to a large stuffed brown chair that from a distance looked like genuine leather, but was an imitation, close up.

The "how have you been" pretense was the preamble to the more directed inquiry behind Chuck's true objective of the visit.

"Can I get you a drink or somethin'?" Joe asked.

"No thanks," Chuck answered. Pausing momentarily, he continued. "Joe, this is very difficult for me to say. But I have strong reasons to believe that you are involved with a mobster, a Vincent Scarpizzi. And some drug lord named Hector Santiago."

"What?" Joe interrupted quizzickly. "You must be kidding me."

"Joe, you have to understand, I'm in a tough spot here. I'm the attorney general of the United States. Your daughter is a United States Congresswoman. I'm her husband and the father of my adopted son Little Joe, who just happens to be your grand son. And you're my father-in-law."

"That's a whole mouthful, Chuck."

"And it's also what puts me in a bind. Look, I didn't come here to play games.I'm leveling with you, Joe. I know all about the Treausance contract, and even the whole business with the governor of New York. Joe. If this is all true, this is very, very serious stuff."

"It sure sounds like it, Chuck." Looking over his shoulder, Joe suddenly yelled out, "You there, Harry?"

In an instant, Joe Roundtree's older son, Harry, charged into the livingroom. Chuck was startled by his sudden entrance. Instinctively, he looked quickly around the room, as if searching for escape. In a flash, Joe withdrew a small pistol hidden in his waistband and pointed it within inches of Chuck's head.

"What the hell's going on here? What's happening? Are you guys crazy? I'm out of here," Chuck shrieked in panic as he made a rushed move toward the door.

"You're goin' no place," Joe shouted.

Without uttering another word, Joe pulled the trigger at point blank range, firing off a single shot above Chuck Bradford's right ear. It crashed into his head. Blood started to escape from the hole made by the entry of the bullet. His eyes rolled back. Letting go a slight groan, Chuck fell to the floor. Lifeless.

"He's dead. We gotta work fast, Harry," Joe barked excitedly.

Together, Joe and Harry picked Chuck up from the floor, quickly carrying his limp body out to a pickup truck parked in the rear of the bungalow. They placed Chuck inside the bed of the truck and covered him with a blanket that was crumpled in a corner of the pickup's floor.

"Now listen to me, Harry, and listen good," Joe yelled, once Chuck's body was completely covered. "Drive to Carlyle Park. Dump him in the road. Take the gun." Joe had already wiped it clean of his own fingerprints. "Make sure you wear gloves. Take the gun and plant it in his hand. And get the fuck outta there fast. It's gotta look like a suicide. Just the way we planned it. Remember, it's gotta look like a suicide. Okay?" Joe barked.

"I got it covered," Harry said. "I know what ta do. Don't worry, Pop. I heard ya. It's gotta look like a suicide. It's a done deal."

When Harry arrived at Carlyle Park thirty minutes later, it was dark. The place was deserted. He drove into the park and stopped his pickup several hundred yards from the entrance, pulling over to the edge of the blacktop road. Looking around and satisfied that he was alone, Harry quickly grabbed Chuck's legs and dragged him to the rear of the truck. He picked him up, threw him over his shoulder, and carried him a few yards. He placed him face-down in the middle of the roadway.

In a rush, Harry returned to the passenger side of the pickup. He snapped the glove-box open. Harry had hidden the gun inside the compartment after he left Joe Roundtree, thirty minutes earlier.

Suddenly, he saw the headlights of a car entering the park. In a panic, Harry shut the glove-box and slid over to the driver's seat. In an instant, he gunned the pickup and headed toward the park exit.

Unbeknown to Harry, the passengers in the car entering the park had two teenagers looking for a lovers' lane. The car made a quick U-turn after the driver was frightened off by the pickup ahead, and raced it toward the entrance now used for the get away.

Carlyle Park was dark and still, as it had been on previous nights. This time it was different. Now, the body of Chuck Bradford, fully clad in a blue suit, white shirt, and maroon tie, lay lifeless on the surface of the road within the park.

Out of the silence, a homeless derelict suddenly emerged from the bushes behind a leafy tree, one of many that ran the perimeter of the road. Searching around to ensure that he was alone, he ran to the body on the ground. He groped hurriedly through Chuck's pockets, found his wallet and tossed it into a worn plastic bag he was carrying. With the speed of a sprinter, he disappeared into the woods, shielded by the black of night.

Darkness continued its course over Carlyle Park as a lamp, yellowed with the grime of its cracked glass cover, threw a weak and indistinct light upon the silhouette of a man on the ground—Charles Llewelyn Bradford, the attorney general of the United States of America.

Fowler's precise recitation seemed as flawless as a rehearsed part in a play while the silent cassette tape recorded every word. His narrated flash-back continued:

Joe Roundtree was gulping down a half glass of rye whiskey when he heard a key turn in the front door lock of his bungalow.

"That you, Harry?" Joe sounded out.

"Yeah, Pop."

"Did everything go okay in the park?" Joe asked anxiously.

"Yes, and no."

"Whadda ya mean, you moron?"

"I'm no moron, Pop. I told ya, yes, and no"

"Look, Harry, I'm not waitin' till you drop me a postcard. Tell me now. And fast. What happened?" Drops of sweat started to appear on Joe Roundtree's forehead.

"What happened is I dropped him in the park. Just like you told me. What didn't happen is, I didn't get a chance to plant the gun."

"What? What the hell are you saying? Tell me," Joe screamed out as he grabbed Harry's shoulders, shaking them forcefully.

"I told ya. I did just what ya told me ta do. I took him off the truck, and put him in the road. You told me to keep the gun in the glove box. That's what I did. Just like you told me. After I put him on the ground, I went back to the truck to get the gun. I saw lights comin' from a car.

It coulda been the cops; I don't know. I didn't know what the hell to do. So I got outta there fast." Harry was near tears. His face became flushed, the muscles of his jaw contracting with emotion and fear.

"So Bradford is on the ground in the park with a bullet hole in his head but no fucking gun? That's just great, you dumb ass." Joe grabbed Harry's shoulders, shaking them again, violently.

He finally released the grip he had on Harry, turned around, and slunk into a big upholstered chair in the room. He gulped what was left of his drink, staring vacantly at a dirty water stain in the ceiling.

Joe spoke. "I gotta handle this before they find his body. I just hope they haven't found him already. Where's the gun?" Joe 's tone was now quieter.

"It's still in the truck."

"Get it," Joe ordered, "and give me the keys to the truck."

Harry returned with the weapon. He handed it, together with the ignition keys, over to his father.

"Whaddaya gonna do, Pop?"

"What I'm *not* gonna do, is tell Scarpizzi how we fucked up. That's for sure. You stay here 'til I get back."

"Where ya goin', Pop?"

"I'll see ya later. Just stay put. And don't leave the fuckin' house."

Joe Roundtree rushed out of the bungalow and into the driver's seat of the pickup parked in front. He headed toward an all- night diner located one half mile from Carlyle Park. Arriving at the diner, he drove into the parking lot and into a spot next to a patrol car. It bore the markings of the sheriff's office of the Syracuse police department. Joe Roundtree knew that he would find a certain cop inside the diner who would be on a food break at this time.

In a hurried pace, he entered the diner. Once inside, Joe Roundtree observed two uniformed police officers seated inside a booth, chewing on sandwiches.

As chief of the Pecontic tribe, Joe Roundtree was known in the area, and recognized easily by the police officers seated in the booth. He walked over to one of them, and in a friendly greeting,

Joe said, "I got that travel brochure you asked me about. It's in the truck outside. Do you want me to bring it in?"

"No. It's okay," the officer replied. "I'll go out with you."

The uniformed policeman got up and turned to his partner seated in the booth. "I'll be back in a minute. Don't eat any of my sandwich. Ya hear?"

The uniformed officer and Joe Roundtree left the diner together.

Once outside, Joe quickly reported the shooting, the planting of Bradford's body in Carlyle Park, and the foul-up with the gun.

"Give me the gun. I'll take care of it myself. And just get out of here, pronto," the uniformed cop said.

Returning to the diner within a minute, he resumed his seat in the booth, the small gun tucked in his belt. After swallowing the balance of his coffee, he got up.

"I've got to hit the john," he said, as he headed toward a small, enclosed foyer that separated the men's and ladies' washrooms. Once inside, and satisfied he was alone, he lifted the telephone attached to the wall of the foyer, slipped a coin in the slot, heard a dial tone, and punched in three numbers. A female voice answered.

"This is 911." It was 9:33 p.m.

"What is your emergency?" the voice at the other end asked.

"There's a man near the east entrance of Carlyle Park. He's dead," was the reply in a voice that sounded raspy and deep.

"What's your name, and where are you calling from?" asked the 911 operator. There was a click, and then a dial tone.

The officer left the foyer and walked toward his partner, still seated in the booth. He sat down, when suddenly a dispatch from headquarters was received on the officer's walkie-talkie.

"Let's get moving. We gotta check out a guy who's reported dead in Carlyle Park," he blurted out.

The two police officers ran out of the diner, and quickly entered the patrol car parked outside.

Within minutes, they arrived at the entrance. The police car moved slowly into the park entrance, and then turned right. It was October, no moon. The night was dark. The park was deserted. The car, with its bright lights, inched slowly along the blacktop road. Broken park benches were scattered every forty feet, lining the roadway. Two hundred yards into the park, the patrol car's headlights suddenly flashed upon something lying on the ground, next to one of the benches.

"I'm gonna get a little closer. I can't make out what it is," the driver of the patrol car said.

And there it was. Sprawled on his side, was the body of a man, dressed in a dark blue suit, white shirt, and maroon tie.

Fowler exited the car, his back to Ruiz, gun drawn. Patrolman Ruiz already had his 9 mm semi-automatic weapon in his right hand as he was radioing excitedly into central headquarters and reporting simultaneously what was happening.

As Fowler approached the man on the ground, he looked nervously around to make sure that Ruiz was covering him. The car lights, with their high-powered full brights, continued a steady focus on the man in the blue suit. Slowly, Fowler walked toward the sprawled figure, looking cautiously in all directions as he approached.

He could now see clearly. The man was on his right side with his face pressed hard against the dirty pavement. His right arm was extended over his head. His left arm bent at the elbow, palm facing up. His neck was cold to Fowler's touch. He's dead, Fowler thought to himself.

"What have we got?" Ruiz shouted from the car ten feet away.

"This guy's been shot. It looks like he took a bullet in the head," Fowler yelled back.

Hearing that, Ruiz got out of the car, and with gun in right hand and a flashlight in his left, started to walk slowly toward the motionless body.

"Who's the guy?" Ruiz asked in a shaky voice.

"I don't know," Fowler shot back. "A guy dressed like him just doesn't take a pleasure walk in this fucking place." He hesitated, then continued, "unless maybe he planned to kill himself."

There was a stark quiet that blanketed the scene: one cop crouching over a dead man, and another standing nervously next to a police car. Fowler, a heavy-set, fifteen-year veteran of the force, and Ruiz, a young rookie cop, there on a dark night in a deserted park, with a body on the ground. Fowler had been in similar situations before, but this was a first for Ruiz. He had no special training for this kind of situation. Ruiz felt an uncomfortable strangeness. He was not quite sure what was happening. There remained with a nagging and anxious feeling. Perhaps it was the normal response of a rookie cop in a first-time, real, scary encounter. Suddenly, as if struck by a bolt of lighting, the figure on the ground moved, quickly turned, and sat straight up. His face was deathly ashen. His eyes frozen by the penetrating high beams of the patrol car that focused upon him like two giant stage lights.

"That fuckin' guy's alive," shouted Fowler in a shriek of excitement as he instinctively pushed up from his crouched position and sprang back five feet. Without hesitation Ruiz moved in, his weapon aimed pointedly at the figure that remained staring in a fixed trance at the car's full lights ten feet ahead.

As Ruiz reached the man, Fowler suddenly screamed out, "Watch out Iz! He's got a gun."

Reacting without thought, Ruiz pulled the trigger three times in rapid succession. Three 9 mm bullets ripped through the man's chest. He fell back with a thud, again sprawled out on the broken black and dirty pavement. Motionless, and dead.

"That's the whole story, Connors. All of it. Satisfied?"

"I'll let you know in a minute. What about the shooter?"

"The shooter was my partner, Ismael Ruiz. I still had the gun I took from Joe . It was the same one he used to fire a single bullet into Bradford's head, thinkin' he killed him. I was the cop who was supposed to plant the gun but everything went wrong. I did it for Joe Roundtree who got his orders from New York's top crime boss—a guy named Vincent Scarpizzi. He's been paying me off for years to do alotta things for him. Like I said, that's it. Nothin' else."

"Tell me about Treausance and the vice-president. I want everything you know about them," Matt commanded.

"Treausance was sand-bagged by vice president Hastings. He was paying back an IOU to Scarpizzi for a big cash campaign donation. They're all connected in the same Indian shit."

"Anything else?" Matt asked, looking at Dan Sanford to see if his assistant had any additional questions.

"I told you all I know," Fowler said as he sat back in his chair, letting out a sigh of relief.

"Okay, Fowler. I'm satisfied for now." Speaking to his assistant, Matt directed, "Call our Albany office. Make all the arrangements to have Fowler and his wife moved to D.C. under protective custody." Returning to Fowler, Matt said, "You are now on notice. From this point on you are under the official protection of the Department of Justice and a permanent guest of the United States of America!"

CHAPTER TWENTY-TWO

Joe Roundtree drove his late model Lincoln town car to the curb at the arrival station of New York Airlines, located at the Syracuse Airport. One of his tribal members was the assistant head of security, so it was no problem for him to leave the car parked alongside the curb in the tow-away zone.

The Boeing 737 carrying Hector Santiago and Willy Mendoza had left La Guardia Airport on time and was expected to land in Syracuse on schedule. Joe was fifteen minutes early and had enough time to walk to the arrival gate, where he greeted the two Colombians as they emerged from the chute and into the terminal.

"Hey, good to see you, Joe," Hector Santiago blurted as he extended his hand to the chief of the Pecontic tribe. Willy Mendoza joined in the social greetings as the three men walked to the escalator that took them down to the street level below.

Reaching the town car parked outside, Joe opened the right, front passenger door for Santiago. "I'm real glad you were able to make it, Hector. I know you're gonna like the land we have for our casino operation."

"Hey, chief, if it's on the reservation, it's fine with me. Right, Willy?"

"You bet, Hector. Can't wait to see it," Mendoza answered as he entered the car and sat in the seat directly behind Santiago.

Joe got behind the wheel of the car, opened the window, and waved the security guard over to him. "Thanks again." He cupped a ten dollar bill and slipped it to the guard who was dressed in a baggy uniform that looked too large for his frame. He acknowledged his largesse with a friendly nod. "Anytime, chief."

The car moved away from the curb and was driven toward the exit signs posted along the airport roads.

"Joe, how far is the reservation from here?" Santiago asked. He buckled himself into his seat.

"It's about a twenty-minute ride without traffic. At this hour, we should be okay."

"Sounds good. So, Joe, how long you guys have this land?"

"The tribe has owned it over a hundred years. We have our own schools, our own stores, our own police department. And now our own casino." Joe broke out into an open laugh.

"Maybe I oughta become a chief. But first I guess I gotta join your tribe."

"Not so easy, Hector. You don't join the tribe; you're born in it. Latino blood don't make it here." A flash of irony struck Joe as he made his statement, recalling that it was the Spanish Conquistadores of the 15th and 16th centuries who had massacred the Indians when the Spaniards first landed on the shores of the newly discovered continent. It took the passage of many centuries to reach the historical twist when an Indian was now the equal of a descendent of the original conquerors from Spain.

Joe Roundtree had estimated the travel time to the reservation accurately. Twenty-five minutes after leaving the Syracuse Airport, he exited State Highway 241, proceeding onto a two-lane, black-topped, winding road flanked by tall leafy trees on both sides of the pavement. A small, weathered sign bolted to a four-foot iron post cemented to the ground read, "NOT A THROUGH STREET. ENTERING THE PECONTIC RESERVATION."

The town car continued until it reached a large iron gate, its frame attached to a heavy steel mesh fence that separated the road inside from the one they were traveling on. The gate was shut tight, a large padlock securing its locked position.

"We're here," Joe rang out. "I just have ta get a key to the lock. We keep it over there in that barn," He said as he pointed to a wooden frame structure one hundred feet to the right of the road. "The land I wanna show you is just about a mile in. Be back in a minute."

Joe exited the car, walked to the rear and started his approach towards the barn.

Santiago squinted strangely at Mendoza. His quizzical glance had wariness written all over it. Street smarts he had gained from his many years of drug trafficking and survival needs were sending powerful messages that something was not right, and he suddenly felt as if he were a live character in a plot over which he had no control.

Santiago's mind raced crazily as he quickly reached into his jacket pocket, but the short handled pistol he always kept loaded was not there. "Shit!" he cried out loudly remembering that he had left the weapon in the drawer of a bureau in his bedroom back in Jackson Heights, Queens, knowing he would have to go through a metal detector at La Guardia airport before his flight to Syracuse. *Something is wrong. Fucking wrong*, his instincts told him.

For Crissakes, Santiago asked himself, *why didn't Joe have the fuckin' key with him? Anyway, he's takin' too goddamned long. Somethin' here just don't add up.*

An ominous feeling of danger suddenly engulfed Santiago. "Willy, get outta here quick," he screamed to Mendoza. The two Latinos grabbed the inside handles of the car doors in a desperate attempt to escape what they sensed was impending doom.

As they tried frantically to open the doors, a dark Ford parked at the side of the road twenty feet from the padlocked gate, shielded by the thick overgrown vegetation, shot out, coming to a screeching stop inches behind the town car. Instantly, four giant-size men jumped out of the Ford. Before Santiago or Mendoza could catch a breath, the doors were yanked open. They were pulled forcibly out of the car by strong and overpowering arms.

"What's happenin'? What's goin' on? What are you guys doin'?" Santiago screamed in panic.

"Shut the fuck up and walk," commanded one of the burly men who had Santiago in a headlock as he was hustling him out of the car. With guns pressed hard against their faces, Santiago and Mendoza were shuffled hurriedly into a heavily wooded area thirty feet from the road.

"Look, I got plenty a money. I"ll give ya as much as ya want. I'm Hector Santiago; I'm a big boss in the city. Whatever you want, you got. Name it..." His desperation spiked with every word.

"I told ya'. Shut the fuck up!"

Acting like robots, the four hit men methodically fired six .38 caliber bullets from four silencers into Hector Santiago and Willy Mendoza, shattering their skulls. They were dead on the ground when three more bullets were fired into their lifeless bodies.

With emotionless precision, the killers dragged their victims to a spot ten feet away where a deep pit dug just hours before lay open like a raw sore. Quickly shoveling the dirt over the dead men and filling in their deep grave, was a job they completed in less than ten minutes. Soon the area was restored to its original quiet as the professional assassins returned to the Ford. The wheel-man spun it around, dirt flying, and gunned it toward the main highway. When the vehicle was out of sight, Joe Roundtree emerged from the barn and quickly entered the town car.

Joe had told Vincent Scarpizzi they had a deal. And with Hector Santiago permanently out of the way, Joe Roundtree—the chief of the Pecontic tribe—had now fulfilled his dirty end of the deadly bargain.

CHAPTER TWENTY-THREE

Returning to the Justice Department in Washington, Matt was excited when he dialed the private number to the oval office. "Mr. President, I'm calling to bring you up to date on the investigation."

In fifteen minutes, Matt told Harrington everything he had learned since their last meeting, emphasizing Fowler's detailed statement that set out the whole Indian casino gambling scheme and leading up to Chuck's murder. Matt also reported that one of his investigators had located the derelict who had been in Carlyle Park the night Chuck's body had been dumped and who had rifled the attorney general's pockets. The vagrant was arrested in a department store while attempting to use one of the credit cards stolen from Chuck's wallet. Interrogated at the Syracuse FBI office, he described the Ford pick up and the man who unloaded the body from it. It was short work for the federal agents to identify Joe Roundtree's truck from the residue of blood stains on the floor of the pickup. DNA testing matched that of the attorney general, nailing Jenny's father Joe Roundtree and her brother Harry to Chuck's murder.

"You've done a great job, Matt, " Harrington said, "What's the next move?"

"I'm convening a grand jury within forty eight hours. George Fowler will be the government's key witness And I expect quick indictments."

"That's fine, Matt. I'll have the pleasure of informing my vice president personally that he's under arrest. I am not a vindictive man but I want to see his damned face when I tell him."

Matt hung up the phone knowing he would now have to tell Jenny the whole truth about her father's role in Chuck's death. He left his office and drove directly to Jenny's D.C. apartment. Although Georgetown became Jenny's home after marrying Chuck, she kept the apartment in Washington that they shared when staying overnight in the nation's capital.

Earlier, Matt had called Jenny's congressional office, telling her he would be at her apartment at seven and would bring her favorite Chinese food direct from the *Szechwan Palace*. Jenny looked forward to those evenings with Matt. Little Joe boarded out during the week at the special children's dormitory at the Travers Academy—an elite private school that catered almost exclusively to the children of members of the House and Senate. It was an ideal learning environment for him. In addition, security matters ranked almost as high as academic ones. All this gave Jenny a comfort level that permitted her to operate her congressional duties on a full-time basis without the concerns of having to rush home to attend to the needs of her seven-year-old son. During the school week, those requirements were fully satisfied at the Travers Academy that provided the best trained staff of teachers and counselors in the Capital district.

Weekends and holidays were different. They were high-quality times Jenny shared with Little Joe, picking him up on a Friday afternoon and taking him to their Georgetown home. Jenny would return him on Sunday in the early evening. After Chuck's death, Matt spent as much time with Jenny and Little Joe as he could. This brought Jenny and Matt even closer. He was protective. Caring. Genuine. Sensitive. He showed an affection for Jenny that spilled over and reached Little Joe, now becoming an important part of his life as well. With each week's passage, the bond between the three became stronger, and although Chuck's death was an overwhelming tragedy to Jenny and to Matt, each found a special comfort, a personal solace in their shared loss, making the bond between them even tighter and closer.

Picking Little Joe up from the Travers Academy each Friday afternoon became a joyous ritual, not only for Jenny, but for Matt, who was always included as well. Weekends were a joy for the seven year old, for Jenny and for Matt—all enjoying the unique pleasures of a shared togetherness found only in the closest of families. In much the same way, Jenny, Little Joe, and Matt were just that- the closest of families.

Matt saw himself as a surrogate father to Little Joe, full of the deep feelings of most biological parents. To Jenny, Matt was becoming more than her late husband's best friend. He was transcending those usually restricted boundaries, developing a dimensional and emotional connection with Jenny, as she was with Matt. It was a coming together of two souls, each having gone through extreme and profound loss, intrinsically drawn together by a common tragedy, yet experiencing a mutuality born of deep feeling and true affection. Events can occur in mysterious and unpredictable ways. Jenny, Matt, and Little Joe were examples of how tragedy can sometimes produce an analgesic to conquer emotional pain. It may not happen often, but it is magical when it does. And for them it was.

The table was already set for dinner. Hot water that would soon be poured over an exotic tea bag was near its boiling point in a pot on the stove.

The door chime sounded. Jenny moved quickly as she looked through the peep hole, opening the door latch.

"I bring you gifts of joy from the Asian Gods," Matt said, as he held up a large plastic bag. "And a rose to a Goddess," handing it over to Jenny with his other hand. It was more than a single rose. There were six deep red American beauty roses, each one wrapped in a delicate light green paper tied with a ribbon of white silk.

"They are beautiful, Matt."

"And so are you, Jenny." Matt placed the plastic bag and flowers on a side entry table. He embraced her gently. "And you smell so good."

"Enough of that, Matt. I'm flushed enough as it is."

"Is that all it takes, food from the Szechuan Palace and roses?" Matt continued to hold Jenny close to him.

"Well, you are forgetting the third component. You." They released each other from their embrace. "Alright. Enough of this for now. The water is about to boil over and the food is getting cold."

"I'm at your service, my dear Jenny." Matt kissed her gently on the lips.

It was a dinner of chicken in a special house sauce, exotic vegetables, and a mixture of white and brown rice. A bottle of chilled California Chardonnay was just the right addition to the Szechuan delicacies.

After dinner Jenny and Matt walked into the living room.

It was a chamber beautifully decorated with traditional chairs upholstered in a fine silk containing subtle and artistic patterns. A large sectional leather couch with many tufted and tasseled pillows, two huge oriental vases filled with silk leaves attached to bamboo shoots, and a double-tiered, glass-top table with gold leaf ornamental designs around its perimeter, added to the homey decor of the room. In addition, exquisite antiques that Chuck had gathered from Bradford Manor in Oklahoma, provided an especially warm atmosphere.

The large, museum-quality tapestry covering an entire wall of the livingroom hand-loomed in France in the 18th century, depicted an understated but charming tranquil scene of the Burgundy countryside.

The mantel of the floor-to-ceiling stone fireplace, held several long-stemmed silver candle holders that housed striated white candles. These sterling pieces were next to a large frame of burnished mahogany that surrounded a portrait of Charles Llewelyn Bradford taken at the time of his swearing in as attorney general of the United States. A smaller frame containing a photograph of Chuck, Jenny, and Little Joe—all with happy smiles—taken on the sands of Virginia Beach, completed the display.

Jenny uncorked a bottle of Remy Martin, pouring just enough to fill the bottom of two large brandy glasses. Matt twirled the rounded glass slowly, the distinctive nectar of the dark red liquid swirling against the sides of its inner surface as he sat on the couch next to Jenny. They each took a sip, allowing its warmth to gently bathe the insides of their mouths as the cognac made its way further down.

Looking pensively at his brandy glass, Matt spoke first. "Jenny, I've tried to keep you informed of my progress with the investigation. But I didn't want to report things to you until I was sure I was right." Matt paused. He was struggling to find the words to continue. "I think I now know what happened to Chuck, and why."

"What? What? Please tell me, Matt," Jenny implored softly.

In the next half hour Matt told Jenny what he had unearthed. It was a journey that took him to Vincent Scarpizzi, Hector Santiago, Patrolmen George Fowler and Ismael Ruiz, the license issued by Commissioner Pierre Treausance, the pay-offs to the governor of New York, and the bribing of the vice president of the United States.

It was a full account, except for one intentional omission—the involvement of her father, Joe, and of her brother, Harry.

Although Matt had overwhelming proof that Joe Roundtree was responsible for Chuck's death, he could not muster the courage to tell Jenny. Instead, he told her that Scarpizzi had ordered the killing of Chuck, which he did, but that Scarpizzi had acted alone. Jenny had been hurt enough. Matt was too sensitive; he would not compound her anguish by telling her the unthinkable—that her own father and brother were the real killers of her husband. Matt knew that Jenny would learn the truth soon enough, but still could not face up to hurting her so deeply at this time.

At the end, they remained holding each other tightly. Jenny's sobs of anguish joined the tears that could no longer be restrained from Matt's eyes either. They lay in an embrace for a time without measure. No words were spoken as they drifted off, surrounded by deep silence.

When dawn arrived, Jenny and Matt were still side-by-side on the couch. But when Matt awoke, he had hoped that his dream of sharing a future with Jenny had not reached its final ending.

CHAPTER
TWENTY-FOUR

"Arista Construction Company. Can I help you?" answered a receptionist, as she chewed on a powdered sugar donut. "Yeah, Margie, this is Al. Put me through to Mister S."

"Hang on, Al." There was a momentary pause and then, "Here's Mister S."

"What's doin', Al?" Scarpizzi asked in a whisper.

"Yeah, Vincent, I sent off the package today."

"Good. You sure it was wrapped okay and it had enough stamps on it?"

"I doubled-checked it myself, Vincent. The delivery's on time."

"Okay, Al. Listen carefully. This is what ya do. I want you and Tony ta stay put a couple days. Call me on my cell tonight, and I'll talk to ya then." Scarpizzi hung up the phone. A smile crossed his lips as he reached for a Cohiba cigar from a walnut humidor sitting on his desk. "Margie," he shouted across the unopened door, "tell Vito to get my car. I'm goin' home."

After reporting to Scarpizzi, Al "Fatso" Pucci stepped out of the telephone booth next to a convenience store he and Tony Jackelino had driven to, and returned to their rental car parked a few feet away. With Jackelino at the wheel, the two men headed back to the Claridge Hotel in Syracuse, where they had checked into a two-bedroom suite the night before.

Arriving at the Cherry Street entrance thirty minutes later, Tony parked the rental in the guest parking lot as the two men proceeded to their tenth floor suite.

Inside, Tony took out a bottle of Johnnie Walker Red from a small carry bag he had stored in the closet and poured himself a straight double shot of 80 proof scotch.

"Hey, Al," Tony shouted across the room, "ya wanna drink?"

"No thanks. My ulcer's actin' up again," Al retorted, as he sat himself in an easy chair, picked up a remote to the television set housed in a large open armoire and turned on the picture.

"You baby yourself, Al. A little whiskey's what the good doc ordered." Tony swallowed a hefty gulp from the glass he filled with Johnnie Walker Red.

Reaching for the bottle, he poured himself another drink into the empty glass, filling it to the same level as before. "I wanna get out of this fuckin' place already." Jackelino drank the scotch like he was "Stella," gulping ice-cold lemonade on a hot summer day in New Orleans.

"Cool it, Tony." Pucci's annoyance at Tony was shown by his harsh tone. "We stay put until Vincent says we go."

"I don't like hangin' aroun'." Tony filled his empty glass again. The amount he already drank made him light-headed, providing a carefree attitude that also gave him the bravado to stand up to Al Pucci, who out-ranked him on the family's table of organization. Pucci was a "capo," a captain. Tony was a bottom-of-the-ladder driver, a soldier, and a low-level hit man. Johnnie Walker Red scotch now removed the difference.

"I got a bad feelin' Al. Let's get the fuck outta this town already." Pucci ignored him as he continued to watch a *Three Stooges* movie being shown on the comedy channel.

A moment later Tony repeated, "I got a bad feelin'. Let's get outta this mother-fuckin' town."

"You drink too goddamned much and you talk too goddamned much." Pucci was angry over his partner's repeated whining. After a pause, and thinking he was coming down too hard on Tony, a more solicitous Pucci did a complete one-eighty. "Come on, ya big ape; let's get somethin' ta eat. Ya gotta mix some food with all that booze." Puccci picked up the phone and dialed the operator, who connected him with room service. He called in their food order.

Forty minutes later the trays were delivered. The two men ate, as Moe, Larry, and Curly carried on with their typical hijinks on the TV screen.

After calling Scarpizzi on his cell phone as he had been instructed to do, Pucci turned to Jackelino. "We're stayin' here tonight. I'm gonna speak ta Vincent again in the morning and find out what the next move is. I'm tired. I'm gonna get some shut eye."

Pucci walked into the adjacent bedroom and closed the door. The capo and the soldier spent the second night at the Claridge Hotel, their assigned job successfully performed and a very active day's work now behind them.

The "Do Not Disturb" sign was still on the door at 10:00 a.m. when the loud ringing of the telephone awakened Al Pucci.

"There's a 3:15 to La Guardia. Take it."

"Gotcha, Vincent."

Showering quickly, Pucci put on the clothes he had left draped over a chair the night before and walked into the adjoining bedroom where Tony Jackelino was still in a deep stupor from all the scotch he had consumed.

"Wake up, big guy," Pucci commanded in a loud voice, shaking Tony's shoulder. He barely opened his squinting eyes, still half asleep. "Get up. C'mon. I just spoke ta the boss. We're takin' the 3:15 outta here. So get ya fat ass outta bed and I'll order us some breakfast."

Two hours later, they checked out, exited the lobby, and started to walk toward the rental Tony had parked in the guest lot the day before. As they reached the car, Al Pucci spoke.

"Pop up the hood, Tony."

"Don't you have your remote starter?" Tony asked.

"I got it. But this ain't my car, you moron. It's a rental, remember?"

The remote referred to Al Pucci's remote control engine starter he always carried and used to start up his car at a safe distance as a precaution, ensuring that he, and more specifically his boss, Vincent Scarpizzi, would be clear of the explosion zone should a bomb be wired to the car's ignition.

Pucci raised the hood of the car. Observing nothing suspicious after inspecting what was under it, he slammed it shut. The two entered the car as Tony Jackelino sat behind the wheel. Al Pucci got into the passenger seat. Tony turned the ignition on, positioning the gear shift in reverse in order to back out of the parking space. Once out, he moved the gear to a drive position then turned the wheel to the right. The vehicle started to move slowly toward the exit onto a road leading to the airport. Entering state highway 114, the rental picked up speed as it reached 55 mph, the posted speed limit on the road. To make sure the vehicle would not exceed the legal limit, and to avoid the radar gun of a state trooper, Tony turned the cruise control switch to the "on" position, maintaining a steady 55 mph speed. After cruising at that rate for ten minutes, a sign appeared at the side of the road. It read "Airport," an arrow pointing in the direction the Ford rental was proceeding.

Suddenly, as if a thunderous bolt of lightening had struck, there was a violent explosion. The volcanic magnitude of the force ripped the car apart shattering it into shards of scattered metal. A huge fireball engulfed the remains that instantly blew the wreckage skyward as it incinerated the two, now *late* loyalists of the DiPienza crime family.

Neither capo nor soldier had ever suspected that Louis Varga, Hector Santiago's Colombian boss, having failed to hear from either Santiago or Mendoza for more than 24 hours despite Vargas' many attempts to reach him, would dispatch his own Colombian hood to check out the situation.

An inquiry by one of Vargas' operatives at the airport's car rental desk disclosed that Al Pucci was the renter who had given the Claridge Hotel in Syracuse as his address. This, combined with a thorough search for Santiago and Mendoza coming up empty, left the answer to their missing status unmistakably clear. It was evident that the warning passed along from Santiago to Varga—that there would be a war following Santiago's last meeting with Vincent Scarpizzi — was now very real indeed. With the disappearance of Hector Santiago and Willy Mendoza, Louis Varga was convinced that the battle had just begun—except that it was now round two, and payback time!

Miguel Gomez was the loyal Varga soldier who traced the rental car to the Claridge Hotel, locating it in the guest parking lot. Receiving direct orders from Colombia to take out Scarpizzi's hoods, acting with the precision of a highly trained assassin, Gomez inserted two sticks of high explosives together with four blasting caps, placing them deep into the exhaust pipe of their car. Gomez knew the intense heat generated within the exhaust system as the vehicle moved at a steady speed would flare up the blasting caps, triggering them to a flash-point of ignition. This would cause the explosives and gas tank to blow up violently. It was as if four .380 caliber bullets had been fired from a semi-automatic weapon directly at two sticks of dynamite strapped to a loaded tank of gasoline at point-blank range, but with far more accuracy and greater devastating impact. This calculated method of execution had been employed by Miguel Gomez against the enemies of Louis Varga many times before, and always with one-hundred percent success. And with the explosive demise of Al "Fatso" Pucci and Tony "the Jackel" Jackelino, the unblemished string would continue.

CHAPTER
TWENTY-FIVE

Matt rose from the couch, careful not to awaken Jenny, still asleep. He slipped into the bathroom, washed his face quickly, straightened his clothes, and left, shutting the door quietly behind him. He had orchestrated the order of business for United States marshals for that day, feeling satisfied about his role in directing the arrests soon to be made.

Federal indictments had quickly been handed down by a sequestered grand jury.

The first target on the list of arrests to be made—*the vice president of the United States!*

Matt received a call from one of his assistants, who reported that two black SUVs drove to the gate of Hasting's Washington home that morning. It was reported that the vice president fled from the White House after being confronted by a cold-eyed President Harrington.

Approaching a secret service man at the entrance, a U.S. marshal accompanied by two Justice Department agents, said with authority, "I have a criminal arrest warrant in the name of the United States of America against Jarrett Lee Hastings." Several minutes later, the two vehicles proceeded to the entrance ramp. Four agents exited the car, and walked at a fast pace toward the house. Its front door was already open. The vice president was waiting outside. Handcuffs were placed on him immediately.

"You have the right to remain silent. You have the right to..." the pro forma Constitutional words were passed along. There was no hint of southern hospitality in the icy-official process as Mississippi's "favorite son" was pushed into the back seat of an unmarked black van. He was unceremoniously driven off, where the vice president, the second highest ranking public official in the United States, would soon be arraigned before a federal magistrate, ironically the lowest ranking judicial officer in the federal court system.

At precisely the same moment, two hundred sixty-five miles north of Washington, six FBI agents stormed the building of the Arista Construction Company in College Point, New York. Vincent Scarpizzi was sitting behind his desk, puffing nervously away on a thirty-five-dollar imported Cohiba. Cuffing him, the lead agent announced coldly, "Vincent Scarpizzi, you're under arrest." Constitutional rights which Scarpizzi could repeat *verbatim* were read, as the Havana cigar was gruffly yanked from his mouth, and crushed down hard into a large ashtray where it was snuffed out in an undignified fashion. "Where you are going, Mr. Scarpizzi, you won't find Cuban cigars on the menu. *But have a nice day!"*

Scarpizzi had forgotten that his closest ally, *Omerta*, the unwritten mobster "law of silence," held no significance to someone not of his own kind. And it was quite clear that George Fowler was no Sicilian *gumba* of the mafia boss Scarpizzi. But he was undeniably the squealing "rat" who handed the head of the DiPienza crime family over to the feds while carving out a very sweet deal for himself.

When Governor Niles Martin stepped out of the executive mansion to get into the rear seat of his limousine to be chauffeured to a political breakfast meeting, four federal agents ambushed him. "Governor Niles Martin, we have a warrant for your arrest."

"You must be kidding."

"I'm afraid not, sir," a U.S. Marshal said, as handcuffs were snapped quickly around Martin's wrists.

With the powerful arms of federal agents gripping each elbow, the Governor was briskly escorted to the rear seat of a black unmarked vehicle. It was not the executive limousine he had been accustomed to, and the breakfast served would be tossed at him on a tin plate. It was a far cry from *The Chateau Imperiale*—Albany's five-star restaurant—the free-spending tobacco lobbyists, and their Mitzi Browns.

Not far away, Martin's confidante and "bagman" Pat Hughes had maintained his silence despite intense federal heat and pressure. He could have cut a very nice deal for himself by becoming a government witness against the governor, but refused. Such loyalty would perhaps gain him a reward in some higher place, but at "fed-land" he would have to pay the ultimate price for sticking to the role of loyal soldier to *his* boss. As Hughes always said,"Living on the edge is just part of my job. It goes with the territory." Hughes could lay odds that his being caught one day was just a matter of time. But for him, it was a great trip while all the goodies lasted.

Pierre Treausance, unlike Pat Hughes, sang like a sparrow as he was burying his pal and mentor, Vice President Hastings. Provided with around-the-clock protection after he gave the feds a full account of both his own, and Hastings' role in the issuance of the gambling license to the Pecontics, he was confined to his home in Washington under the watchful eyes of federal agents.

The night before he was to testify in front of a grand jury, Treausance got up from a chair in the living room of his suburban Washington house. He walked over to one of the federal officers assigned to protect him."I have to take my dog for his nine o'clock walk. I see that Sam here is getting pretty restless. He'll start wailing in a minute if I don't take him out. Okay to leave?"

"Sure, but I'll be right behind you."

Treausance stood on the sidewalk in front of his house holding the leash of his schnauzer. Suddenly he was startled by the loud roar of a truck's engine. Bearing down hard and moving at high speed, a massive tractor-trailer mounted the curb. It struck Treausance squarely, flinging him twenty feet high into the air, crashing him down with a thud. The truck raced away as the agent, unable to push Treausance out of its path in time, jumped backwards into the bushes to protect himself from the twenty-ton rig. The agent let go eight quick rounds from his 9 mm automatic at the massive vehicle, but it continued its high breakaway speed, disappearing into the night. His pet was spared. Treausance was not so lucky. He was killed instantly. And with his death, the lips of the federal commissioner of Indian affairs were forever sealed.

Louis Varga was safe back home in his Colombian fortress and sanctuary. With Hector Santiago, his New York chief and under-boss, Willie Mendoza, dead, the elaborate plan for a network of Indian gambling casinos hatched at Luigi's, a remote restaurant in Queens, New York, had now become a ghost of all those who had dreamed of unlimited wealth and power...except for one man still at large.

CHAPTER
TWENTY-SIX

The Syracuse-to-Washington flight arrived on time. Earlier that morning, Joe Roundtree had called Jenny at her apartment where she was staying temporarily to avoid the media. "I have ta see ya. It's real important."

Joe's son Harry was with him when they boarded a taxi at Washington's National Airport. A suitcase retrieved from the baggage carousel was carried in Joe's hand.

"Dorchester Towers. Grant near Bryant," Joe instructed as he and Harry sat in the back of the yellow, metered cab. "Do ya know where it is?"

"Got it," the cabbie answered.

The taxi moved towards the airport exit. It exhibited an overhanging sign, displaying an arrow pointing to downtown Washington.

The older man seated in the rear of the cab looked like a different "Joe Roundtree." A few weeks earlier, not only was he the chief of the Pecontic tribe, but the king of the hill as well. He was a full partner in the biggest money deal anyone could ever dream of. And that was only the beginning. As chief of the tribe, he would have the unrestricted power to say "yes" to casino gambling on the Pecontic reservation. His signature alone was his open passport to unimaginable riches and the glory that followed it. He was also a partner in the scheme to bring full casino gambling on Indian reservations in Rochester, Niagara Falls, the Catskills, and New York City.

But the plan of expanding the gambling enterprise into a widespread network of Indian casinos throughout the country was the ultimate prize Vincent Scarpizzi promised Joe Roundtree he would be part of. It was an idea born of genius! The grand opening of the casino in Syracuse would prove they had the formula, the power, the track record, and the right people in the highest levels of influence primed, ready to guarantee the success of an empire to make Chief Joe Roundtree a multi-millionaire, and more.

It all could have been, except for two people. One was already dead, removed permanently because of his meddling. No longer could he do harm to Joe Roundtree. Another was a justice department agent who single-handedly had destroyed Joe's euphoric dreams of limitless riches and power beyond his wildest expectations.

At any moment Joe knew the iron jaws of the United States Department of Justice, and the Federal Bureau of Investigation, would clamp down and destroy everyone connected with the casino license, including Joe Roundtree. There was one man singularly responsible for the sudden destruction and overwhelming shame that consumed Joe. This person had to be dealt with.

Anger and hatred darkened Joe's ability to be rational. As if possessed by an uncontrollable evil force, his mission was clear: *I must destroy the one man who has destroyed me — that son-of-a-bitch Matt Connors. If I, Joe Roundtree go down, I'll take my mortal enemy down with me.*

Overtaken with blood lust and guided by a family code passed along by his persecuted forebears, vengeance now remained Joe Roundtree's only reward.

The taxi stopped in front of a green, canopied building. The door was opened by a uniformed doorman wearing a tag. The name "Dorchester Towers" was embroidered in gold thread on his blue and gray jacket.

As Joe and Harry stepped out of the taxi, the doorman asked courteously, "Who are you here to see, gentlemen?"

"Miss Jenny Roundtree," Joe answered.

"And who shall I say is here?"

"You can tell her it's her father."

The doorman entered the lobby. Joe and Harry waited in the vestibule area secured by a large glass door. The initials "DT," surrounded with a gold crest were carved on the surface of the glass. The door self-locked as the doorman walked to a neatly dressed male seated behind the high desk. Several telephones and twelve small security closed-circuit monitors were visible only to the man seated in the chair. A brass sign sitting on top of the desk read, *Concierge.*

Within minutes, the doorman returned, held the glass-etched door open and directed Joe and Harry to enter. "Take the elevator to the 18th floor. The apartment number is 18B. Miss Roundtree is expecting you."

Inside the elevator Joe opened the small suitcase. He removed two pistols wrapped in a newspaper. Handing one over to Harry, who put it in his jacket pocket, Joe took out the other and tucked it into his waistband, concealing it under his jacket.

Jenny was near hysteria as she opened the door to let Joe and Harry into the apartment.

"Pop, it's all over the news—Governor Martin, some mobster Scarpizzi, the vice president, others... They've all been arrested, charged with bribes and payoffs. They're talking about our tribe. *Our tribe...and the casino.* The police are out looking for *you.* They even flashed *my* picture. And the news people are saying that Chuck was murdered because he discovered a corrupt plot that involved the casino."

Jenny's face was sheet-white, strained with disillusionment. She stared hard at her father. Tears were forming in her eyes. She began to cry bitterly. "How could you? You lied to me. I trusted you and you lied!"

"Jenny, please. Jenny, please..." Joe was anguished at his daughter's highly emotional state, misguidedly blaming it on the man he had come to avenge.

Tearfully Jenny lashed out at her father. "And you, Pop, right in the middle of this whole thing. I can't believe it. I just can't believe it. How stupid and blind I've been all this time."

"You're wrong, Jenny. You're wrong."

"I can't believe anything you say anymore. Just go. They're all looking for you. *Go now.* You and Harry. I don't want them to find you here. Please." Tears continued to roll down her cheeks.

"If ya can't believe me then maybe you'll believe your good pal Connors. Go ahead, Jenny, get him here. He'll prove to ya what I'm sayin.' He'll tell ya that I was never a part of any a' this. Go ahead. Just get him here. You'll see that I'm tellin' ya the truth."

Jenny's disbelief was reflected in her blank look. She moved toward the telephone.

"What are you gonna do, Jenny?"

"I'm getting Matt on the phone. I'm going to ask him flat-out how you figure in any of this."

"He'll never tell ya the truth on the phone. Call him and tell him ya want to see him here. Now. Tell him it's very important. Get him here, Jenny. You'll see I'm right. Just get him here."

Jenny reached for the telephone. She dialed Matt's number.

"Matt, I must see you right away. It's terribly urgent."

Matt sensed panic in Jenny's voice.

"What's going on, Jenny?"

"Please, Matt. Please. Just come over right away. Now. Please, Matt." Jenny hung up the telephone. She turned her back stiffly to her father as she sat heavily in a chair, not uttering another word.

Thirty minutes later, Harry opened the door at the sounding of the chimes. Matt entered Jenny's apartment. He was surprised to see that it was Harry, not Jenny, who opened the door for him. Matt was equally puzzled to see Jenny's father there as well. Joe was standing in the small entrance hallway that led to the livingroom.

Jenny rushed to Matt.

In a lightning move, Harry pulled out the gun from his jacket pocket. In the same quick motion, he fired off one round at Matt. It slammed into Matt's left shoulder, throwing him violently around as he fell backward between the livingroom and foyer. Before Harry could get off another shot, and with blood spreading out on Matt's shirt, Matt grabbed his glock 9mm automatic strapped to his shoulder holster, and fired off two rapid shots. Each struck Harry—one in the neck, the other in the chest. Harry fell back, slamming hard against the wall. He slid down to the floor, blood pouring out from the entry points of Matt's bullets. Harry was dead.

Jenny screamed. She made a dash toward her brother's limp body. Shocked at seeing his lifeless son, Joe let go two quick rounds at Matt. The first one crashed into his right shoulder. The other grazed his left arm. Matt scrambled away, frantically trying to get out of Joe's line of fire. Through the madness he could hear Jenny crying out hysterically. "Stop it. Stop it. Stop it."

Matt slumped to the floor in front of the living room couch. He searched wildly for a shield, already light-headed, weak from loss of blood and the crushing pain in his wounded shoulder. He lay on the floor, his back arched tightly against the couch. Everything around him was getting darker, more blurred. The bullet that struck his right shoulder had caused an instant traumatic paralysis. He was unable to use the gun in his right hand. Attempting to switch it to his left, Matt sat helplessly on the floor, his back against the sofa, too weak even to raise the automatic weapon in his own defense.

Distracted for the instant by Jenny's screaming, Joe slowly raised his gun and aimed it pointedly at Matt. He was about to pull the trigger, when suddenly, Jenny threw herself onto Matt. She screamed, "Pop, don't. Pop...." Her shrill voice was cut short as two bullets fired from Joe's gun, struck her. The lead slugs struck Jenny in the back as she was still attempting to shield Matt from her father's onslaught.

Jenny crumpled into Matt's arms. Blood began to gush from her wounds. Her eyes rolled back as she let out a moaning gasp, then stopped breathing. The bullets fired from Joe's gun had pierced his daughter's heart.

"My God. My God. My little girl. Jenny. What have I done?" Joe began to wail uncontrollably as blood was spreading throughout Jenny's blouse. It enlarged into circles of bright red. Joe shook violently. He ranted wildly. Words became indecipherable. Hysteria filled the room.

Matt held Jenny close to him, his wounded arms trying to encircle her lifeless body. He continued to hold Jenny, cradling her as he rocked her back and forth. Tears were streaming down his face.

In uncontrollable shock, Joe Roundtree groaned, cursed himself loudly, repeated over and over, "My God! My God! What have I done to my Jenny? I killed my Jenny!" Suddenly he became silent. With complete calm he thrust the muzzle of the gun against the right side of his head, and pulled the trigger. He jerked back as he let out a loud sigh. Chief Joe Roundtree was dead before he hit the floor.

Unable to raise his arms, Matt screamed wildly. "Help! Anybody, help! Help!"

Within minutes, federal agents who had been directed to remain in the lobby of the building while Matt had gone to Jenny's apartment, broke the door down. The apocalyptic scene they came upon made even the toughest of veterans sick.

Joe and Harry Roundtree were dead. And a black-haired, beautiful Native American woman lay limp in the grasp of a wounded federal agent whose cataclysmic moans were tethered to a name he tearfully cried out. "Jenny. Jenny. Jenny…"

Drenched with horror, Matt Connors continued to cradle and rock Jenny in his blood-soaked arms.

CHAPTER
TWENTY-SEVEN

The remains of Joe and Harry Roundtree were returned to Syracuse, there to be interred in the sacred burial grounds of the Pecontic reservation. A shattered Charlie Roundtree, Joe's younger son, accompanied the coffins on the journey from Washington to upstate New York.

The ancient tribal rituals were carried out with customary honors given to a chief. Joe Roundtree who lived most of his life at its outer edge had now arrived home at the final page of his mortal existence. Charlie wished to return Jenny's body to the reservation as well. But when Matt asked President Harrington that Jenny be buried at Arlington National Cemetery, the wish was granted.

The president and several Cabinet members joined by members of the House and Senate attended the service at the Washington National Cathedral. Chuck's mother, Mrs. Elizabeth Llewelyn Bradford, also attended. The service, although simple and purposefully brief, was filled with an ever-present sadness.

At Matt's direction, the service at the grave site was attended by only a few invited mourners. Included in the small assemblage was Mrs. Bradford who stood up stoically as the casket was lowered into the ground. Surprisingly, a tear rolled down her cheek. It was an odd display for a woman who only months before showed no signs of emotion, even at the burial of her only son.

Still weak from the gunshot wounds and wearing a sling to support his right shoulder, Matt approached Mrs. Bradford after Jenny's casket had been fully covered with dirt.

Matt spoke in a whisper. "Jenny would have been pleased to have known you were here."

"I loved my son and I lost him. You may not believe what I am about to say. But Matt, I also loved Jenny. I know I didn't show it, but I did.

That's what makes this whole tragic affair so much more difficult for me." To Matt, Mrs. Bradford seemed to be expressing emotions she may have felt but had never exhibited before.

Matt touched her arm gently. She spoke quietly. "We all loved Chuck. And we all loved Jenny. But Jenny never knew how I really felt toward her. If only I had time. If only I could have expressed the things I had regrettably put off for tomorrow. Always tomorrow. And now I've lost my chance forever. If only..." She started to sob softly.

"Mrs. Bradford, you just cannot pile hurt upon hurt." Matt found it strange that he was now trying to console the woman he had always found to be so distant.

"But I do hurt, Matt and I just cannot deal with the pain or guilt of having behaved so badly in the past. I was even cold to Little Joe, my own grandson. How could I have been so indifferent? So unfeeling?" Tears began to run down her cheeks. She wiped her eyes, paused, then spoke again. "Matt, I have made many mistakes in my life. I admit that openly. But there is one mistake I have made in the past that I must correct now." She paused again. She took on a firm look. "I want Little Joe. I want to give him a home. Matt, I want my grandson."

"What?" Matt fired back, his eyebrows suddenly rising. Shocked, he continued, "You want to take Little Joe, now? After all that's happened? What are you saying?"

"What I am saying, Matt, is that Little Joe is Chuck's adopted son. I am his grandmother. *That now makes me his legal guardian.* And I want to give him the best chance in life I can. I want to do it, Matt. Lord only knows I want to do it. . ." She paused, and continued slowly, " *and I will.*"

"Don't do this to Little Joe." Matt was angry that he had to plead with a woman he disliked so much. "In Jenny's memory, I beg of you, don't do this to Little Joe."

"I have every right in the world to take him, and neither you nor anyone else will get in my way." The hard manner so familiar to Matt now returned.

"I will fight you on this, Mrs. Bradford. Do you hear me? Are you listening? You can't come into the store at this late hour even with all your money and walk out with what's not for sale. You may be the guardian officially, but in the real world a judge will make *that* decision. And how you have treated Little Joe in the past may be a pretty good indicator of what a court could decide in the future. So I'll say goodbye to you for now, Mrs. Bradford. Have yourself a good life in Oklahoma. And oh yes, I'll see you in court."

Defiantly Matt turned and started to walk away. Mrs. Bradford tugged at Matt' s left arm. He continued to walk briskly past her.

"Matt," Mrs. Bradford called out in a commanding voice as he kept up his stride, "I am not leaving Washington without Little Joe. *I am not.* And you can reach me at the Bartlett Hotel!"

Matt stopped and quickly spun around. Angry eyes continued to follow her as she entered a black limousine that started up and moved toward Arlington's exit. Matt watched as it turned the corner, finally disappearing.

Fifteen minutes later, Matt stood pensive, alone, next to the fresh mound that bore a temporary marker. It read, "Jenny Roundtree Bradford."

Deep in thought, his eyes tightly shut, Matt was not able to accept Jenny's death, nor could he face the harsh reality that he would never see nor hear her voice again. How could life have been so cruel to Jenny, so good and caring? Where was the real justice in a world that would sit by and allow a truly wonderful human being to become a victim of such tragedy? Matt was beginning to question his own faith that would permit the destruction of a life of such a beautiful and loving young woman. *Why?* he asked himself over and over. *It's not fair. It just isn't fair,* he repeated again and again.

Suddenly he felt an overwhelming guilt mixed with a depression he could not shake.

Whispering "good-bye" to Jenny, Matt returned to his car and headed straight to the Travers Academy to pick up Little Joe.

Back at his apartment, Matt and Little Joe shared the evening together. Although emotionally crushed, Matt displayed a cheerful facade to the seven-year-old boy he had grown to love, fully mindful that Little Joe was suffering a torment that only childhood could fully understand.

Darkness finally yielded to daylight as a sleepless Matt Connors glanced at the small clock sitting on his night table. It was 5:50 a.m., a new day for much of the world. But for him, it was the continuation of a horror that began with Chuck's death, and now with Jenny's.

The day's brightness did little to fill the emptiness that remained Matt's steady companion. He rose slowly from his bed, heavy with fatigue, the product of his mental and physical exhaustion. Walking into the hallway, Matt entered an area where a lighted floor lamp continued to throw a small ray of light that illuminated the darkened room where Little Joe had fallen asleep hours before.

Matt turned the switch off as sunlight began to enter the room. Upon seeing Little Joe still asleep, Matt closed the door partially behind him and quietly stepped out.

He returned to his bedroom. There he removed his clothes, walked into the bathroom, and got into the shower. With his eyes closed, Matt stood under the cool stream of water that cascaded over his face, tilting his head upward, inches from the shower's nozzle. He remained standing motionless as the spray continued its splash upon his body. His mind raced wildly. It was as if he were driving a car at high speed around sharp and dangerous curves without the ability to come to a stop.

Chuck, Jenny, Little Joe, he kept thinking, as they remained the central figures in the tragic drama he was painfully reliving.

After a while ,Matt reached for the shower knob and turned it off. Without the splashing sound of water hitting him, silence returned, and with it, the depression that doggedly refused to leave.

He dressed slowly and walked down the single flight of steps and into the kitchen. An hour had already passed since he first got out of bed. After boiling a small pot of water, he poured it into a cup, its bottom covered with instant coffee. Matt sat down in a chair next to the kitchen table, covering his eyes with his right hand as he supported his head, face down. As if controlled by some hypnotic power, he stared blankly at the coffee cup in front of him.

He was startled by the voice of Little Joe standing at the kitchen entrance. Upon seeing him, Matt sat up quickly and threw a big smile over to him. It was his way of sending the special message, even in the face of such distress, that "everything will be alright."

"Hey Buddy," Matt sang out cheerfully, trying to mask his true feelings.

"Wash up and come down. I'm going to cook you a super breakfast."

Matt was already preparing breakfast when Little Joe returned to the kitchen. There was orange juice, hot oatmeal, scrambled eggs, hash brown potatoes, crisp bacon, and toast Little Joe removed from the toaster when it popped.

Talk of baseball, school, and television, filled the conversation during breakfast. When matt finished, he brought his chair closer to the seven-year-old. Matt had been struggling all morning to muster the courage to say what he dreaded but knew had to be said.

"I have to tell you something that is very difficult for me." Matt hesitated as he dug deep within himself, trying desperately to gain the inner strength he needed. "Your grandmother wants to take you back to her house. She wants to take care of you."

Before Matt could continue, Little Joe broke in.

"No! I don't want to go with her! I don't want to go with her! I want to stay here with you!"

"That's what I want also. But I have to do what is best for you."

"No. I want to stay here with you." Tears began to fill his eyes.

"Listen to me," Matt said. He held Little Joe tightly. "Your grandmother loves you. She really does. And she wants to do everything she can for you. Little Joe, it's the best thing, it's—"

"—No it's not. No it's not. It's not the best thing." Little Joe's sobs became louder as he continued to resist Matt's efforts to convince him.

"Little Joe. Please listen to me. It's the best thing. It's the best thing for you."

Little Joe broke loose from Matt's hold. He ran up the stairs. "No it's not. No it's not." His cries were heard as he rushed into the bedroom, slamming the door shut behind him.

Matt knew he had no legal right to the custody of Little Joe. All he could do would be to attempt to block Mrs. Bradford's court action. But at the end of the day, he knew he would fail. The opportunities Mrs. Bradford could offer Little Joe, would be far greater than what he could ever provide, he rationalized.

There was no other choice, as difficult as it was, than to accept bitterly that Mrs. Bradford was Little Joe's grandmother. Nothing he could say, or do, could change that she was Little Joe's rightful guardian under the law.

Guilt-ridden, Matt's hand trembled as he picked up the telephone. A voice at the other end answered. "Bartlett Hotel, how may I direct your call?"

"Mrs. Elizabeth Bradford's room please."
"Hello, Mrs. Bradford, this is Matt Connors…"

A black Lincoln limousine came to a stop in front of Matt's townhouse. Although a government vehicle and driver had been offered to Mrs. Bradford while she remained in Washington, she declined, preferring to use the hotel's guest services and the independence that accompanied that choice.

Mrs. Elizabeth Llewelyn Bradford was in the rear seat accompanied by her confidential assistant. The driver opened the rear door, assisting Mrs. Bradford as she exited. Her assistant remained in the Lincoln.

Matt opened the front door, holding it in position as he watched Mrs. Bradford ascend the few steps to the entrance of his landing.

"Good afternoon, Matt."

"Hello, Mrs. Bradford."

As Mrs. Bradford entered the townhouse, nothing further was said. Matt closed the front door, escorting her into the livingroom. There, seated in a leather chair, Little Joe looked sad, frightened. Mrs. Bradford approached the boy, gently taking his hand.

"Little Joe. I know just how you feel. That you want to stay here with Matt."

"Why can't I?" Tears ran down his face.

"Because Matt and I believe it would be best if you lived with me." Her voice was soft.

"Isn't that right Matt?" She turned toward him, hoping for his support .

"Yes," Matt answered quietly.

Little Joe got up from his chair. Sobbing openly, he threw his arms around Matt's waist. "I want to stay here with you. I want to stay here with you," he repeated.

Matt kneeled. With both knees on the floor, he hugged Little Joe.

"Look, little buddy, we'll never be apart. You'll be living somewhere else, but we'll always really be together. I promise you that. " Matt stopped. His voice was beginning to crack. "You must go with your grandmother. Mrs. Bradford, please take Little Joe now. Just take him now." Matt was losing control of his emotions.

Taking Little Joe's hand, Mrs. Bradford started toward the door. Suddenly, he broke loose, running back to Matt, three steps behind. He threw his arms around Matt's waist and held him tightly. Matt and Little Joe remained that way. No words were spoken. The embrace was slowly released. Without looking back, Little Joe walked out the front door, down the steps.

"I'll call you everyday. I promise," Matt shouted out as the driver opened the rear door of the Lincoln. With Mrs. Bradford at his side, Little Joe tearfully entered the car.

Matt remained standing outside the front door of his townhouse watching in a trance as the black Lincoln pulled away from the curb. As the car moved further away from him, it became smaller and smaller, as the distance between Matt and Little Joe became greater and greater. And then the car was gone completely.

Matt remained still. He felt as if he were in the grips of a surrealistic experience as his eyes were fixed upon the spot, where just moments before, a black livery automobile carried away his Little Joe —and with it, another irreplaceable piece of his shattered life.

CHAPTER TWENTY-EIGHT

Matt remained in bed when the next morning arrived. The clothes he wore the day before had not been removed. The telephone rang five times, each call being switched to the recorded message on his answering machine when Matt did not pick up. The phone rang again. It was one of his deputies calling from the Department of Justice. "Matt, Tim Watkins here. Please call me. Thanks."

To Matt Connors, the Justice Department seemed so distant and removed. His thoughts were not of his job but of Jenny's death and how he had sent Little Joe away. Guilt was his bitter enemy—his arch antagonist as he fought without success to remove the dark shadows that consumed him.

As he lay there in his wrinkled shirt and trousers, a line from Act II of Shakespeare's *Romeo and Juliet* repeated itself in his head. *It is too rash, too unadvised, too sudden.*

Was I too rash? Was my action too unadvised? Was my giving up of Little Joe too sudden? Those questions plagued him.

The thought of handing Little Joe over to Mrs. Bradford continued to feed his agonizing guilt. Was it the right thing to do to this little boy for whom he had so much love and now felt so much pain? *It is too rash, too unadvised, too sudden*, kept repeating itself in a head throbbing with unconsolable images of the nightmare he had been through and the aftershock it was producing.

The troubled day continued its journey. The telephone rang repeatedly, each call left unanswered except for the recorded response, "Just leave a message at the tone. Thanks."

Matt felt neither time nor space. Remorse and anguish blanketed him as he returned to his bed hoping that sleep would relieve him even temporarily from his torment.

For days Matt remained at home, a prisoner of an overwhelming power he had no strength to fight against. Unshaven, unkempt, and with deep, pronounced circles under his eyes, Matt felt he was falling into an abyss, sinking deeper, deeper into a bottomless pit with neither beginning, middle nor end.

The telephone rang again. He let it go unanswered.

"Matt, this is John Harrington. We're all worried about you. If you are there, please pick up. I know what you are going through Matt, so—"

Matt picked up the telephone. He finally broke in.

"Hello, Mr. President." His voice sounded low and distant.

"Matt, we're all worried sick about you. I was going to call the D.C. police and have them look through your house but I wanted to try once more to reach you before I did that. Are you sure you're alright?"

"Really, Mr. President, I'm okay."

"Enough of that bravado stuff, Matt. Look, I'm coming right over to see you. I'll be there in a half hour."

"I appreciate that, Mr. President. But, let me call you tomorrow."

"No way," Harrington said firmly. "I'll be there in thirty minutes." He hung up the telephone before Matt could protest further.

Matt had eaten little in four days. His face looked gaunt even through the growth of beard left unshaven. With effort, Matt went to his closet, selected a pair of blue slacks and a long-sleeved pullover. He placed them on a chair, too fatigued to even change his clothes.

He sat down. He was dazed. Unsure. Wondering whether his conversation with the president was real or imagined.

Thirty minutes passed quickly. The front bell sounded. Matt opened the door. President Harrington rushed inside.

"Matt, thank God you're alright."

"As you can see, Mr. President, except for the sling on my arm, I'm fine. Believe me, I'm fine."

They walked into the livingroom.

The president sat in a large chair next to the fireplace. Matt sat on the couch facing him.

"Matt, you've been through hell and back. What can I say? Chuck. Jenny. And I know how much Little Joe means to you."

"It hasn't been easy; that's for sure. But I'm doing my best to get through it all."

"And you will, Matt. I know you will."

"I'm trying hard. Real hard. But there's just so much hurt I can handle at one time. I may have reached my limit. And there's nothing I can do to relieve the emptiness and guilt I feel."

"Matt, it's all very natural considering what you've been through, but you'll get beyond this. You'll see." Harrington's tone was firm, yet consoling.

"I wish I could Mr. President. But right now all the music has gone out of my life and I can't forget what I've lost. I just can't seem to stop the bleeding."

"You're feeling this way now. And it's understandable." Harrington paused, then continued slowly. "But you must pull yourself out of this. Come on. Be fair to yourself. You have to look at the other side of this terrible tragedy to see what you really have done for your country... Matt, it deserves the highest honors. "

Matt sat in silence, struggling for the right words. "I did what anyone in my place would have done. No more, no less."

"That's exactly what makes you so special. And why you have earned our nation's highest gratitude."

"But Mr. President, I seek no gratitude for doing my job. Nor did Chuck for doing his."

"I know that, Matt. I also know that right now you're in a depression. But that too will pass.

"I suppose."

"Trust me, it will!"

Matt had suppressed his feelings for so many days, feelings trapped inside. They had to be released. It was now time to challenge the painful isolation he was suffering, and attempt an escape from the darkness of his emotional prison.

Suddenly, Matt found himself wanting to talk.

"I keep on thinking of the first time I met Chuck. He had asked me to help an Indian tribe because their lands were being plundered by big oil companies. We fought them together—Chuck and I— *and we won*. The reservations were saved, but for whom? Years later we pass a law giving them the right to earn a decent living on their own land, to provide financial security and self-respect. So what do we do? We turn our backs and leave the door wide open for the worst elements of our society to come in and fill their pockets. And because of *our* failures, a mob boss like Scarpizzi is able to walk right in. That's why

Chuck is dead, Jenny is gone, her family also—and why Little Joe will grow up an orphan. It isn't right, Mr. President. It just isn't right."

As it kept pouring out, Matt could see the faces of Chuck, Jenny, and Little Joe. It was his catharsis.

"Matt, you can still make it right."

Matt pursed his lips. He remained deep in thought. His brow creased as he sat back silently. Minutes passed without a word spoken. Finally, a soft smile began to emerge. He started quietly, "I am truly grateful for your visit, Mr. President." Matt seemed to be at peace with himself. Nothing further was said.

Moments later, the president and Matt walked toward the door. Matt opened it as he escorted President Harrington down the brick steps of his townhouse and walked with him to a black sedan parked in front. The special agent holding the car door for the president was the chief of the Secret Service. Another agent was behind the wheel of the car. A third was on the street side of the vehicle, his eyes scouting the area vigilantly.

Before entering the sedan, President Harrington turned, pivoting sharply. He looked straight into Matt's eyes. "Oh yes, there's one more thing." He hesitated, then spoke as if giving an executive order.

"Matt, I want to appoint you attorney general of the United States."

Caught by complete surprise, Matt was in shock as he faced the president, staring at him in blank silence.

"Call me tomorrow morning at nine. You'll give me your answer then."

Matt remained stunned, motionless. His eyes, as if drawn by a magnetic field, were transfixed upon the black sedan pulling away toward the White House with the chief of the Secret Service, two Secret Service Agents, and the president of the United States inside.

Out of sight, Matt knew the long, restless night he faced, would be his unwelcome soul-mate.

As attorney general, he could try to correct the abuses suffered by Native Americans by trying to bring fairness to all tribal members —a mission Chuck and Jenny would have approved of. But if he accepted the role, he knew he would be filling the job of his best friend whose widow he had fallen in love with. It was a dilemma he knew would cause him unbearable pain.

Perhaps I should quit the service all together. That way I could get some relief from the every day reminders of tragedy that my job would produce. And if

I did leave the service I could even move to Oklahoma City where I could be close to Little Joe, and be there for him. Damn it. What should I do? he kept asking himself.

Making the right decision when Matt was so emotionally and physically spent would be the Mt. Everest he would soon have to climb.

Daylight was beginning to break when Matt, still unkempt and unshaven, left his apartment. He stopped at the small garden of flowers bunched against the red bricks that were part of the facing of his townhouse, snipped the longest stemmed red rose he could find, and gently wrapped it in white tissue. Making his way slowly into the garage, he saddled his tired frame behind the steering wheel of his car. It had not been moved in four days.

The short trip to Arlington National Cemetery was a lonely one. He parked his vehicle in the section reserved for government officials as he started the ten-minute walk toward Jenny's grave site.

Tranquility surrounded Matt as he gazed around at the uniformed gravestones lined up in perfect symmetry, creating geometrical lines that ran off silently into the quiet horizon. The single long-stemmed rose he carried in his hand seemed to blend harmoniously with the peacefulness that overtook the historic ground.

Matt stopped in front of a marker. It read, "Jenny Roundtree Bradford." There, he placed the rose gently on the fresh mound as he stood motionless, his head slightly bowed, eyes tightly closed. A serene stillness enveloped him as he started to speak. It was as if Jenny was there, physically present in all her beauty, hearing and reacting to every word he was whispering to her.

"Jenny, Little Joe is safe. He will live with Mrs. Bradford, but I will be watching him as if he were my own son. I promise he will never be alone. I will be close by always. I love you Jenny. Rest in peace, forever."

Matt drove away from Arlington surrounded by darkness, overcome with a despair beyond all human definition.

Upon returning to his townhouse, Matt was filled with the painful thought that yet another night was to remain his only comrade. And still, he had to deliver a decision to the president of the United States by morning—a decision he had still not reached.

Cornered by grief, and with the ability to reason severely clouded, he could not think clearly. To Matt, his fatigued brain seemed as if it were detached from his overwhelmingly exhausted body.

Attorney general? he asked himself. *How can I say "Yes, I accept," or "No, I cannot," when I am so physically spent, and torn?*

It was an agonizing evening. Matt paced the floor of his livingroom, thinking...thinking. He walked back and forth into the kitchen. He drank cup after cup of instant coffee, repeating the ritual throughout a night that refused to end.

Matt's mind raced without respite. He considered all the reasons for accepting such a high honor, but relived all the anguish that got in its way. His best friend Chuck was dead. Jenny, the woman he had fallen in love with, was also gone.

How could I accept a position made empty by such tragedy? he kept thinking to himself, as he continued to see the vivid and horrifying picture of Jenny lying lifeless in his arms. And then there was Little Joe...

By 3:15 a.m., he was still awake, *still searching for that answer.* Sleep would have brought him relief, but it did not come. Physically weary, he undressed, set the alarm for 8:00 a.m., and collapsed into bed.

I desperately need a few hours sleep, he repeated to himself.

As his head hit the pillow, his thoughts continued at a reckless speed. Extreme tiredness finally brought a disturbed sleep; the clothes he had worn for four days, remaining his only bed-mate.

Matt woke up at 7:30 a.m., groggy, as if in the peak of a sickening hangover. He undressed and stepped into a cold shower. Standing with his head raised for what appeared an endless time, the sharp, prickly streams of hot water struck hard on his face.

Slowly, his mind began to un-bury itself from its dark and secret place of hiding. As Matt shut off the spigots, a light began to shine... *he had finally reached a decision!* A sudden angelic peace began its upward journey as the troubling uncertainties he struggled with earlier, were now becoming removed.

He shaved away the fifth day of beard from his face. Removing a dark blue suit and grey striped tie from his closet, Matt picked out a starched white shirt and placed the clothes on the chair next to his bed. He dressed quickly, walked downstairs to the kitchen, and poured himself a cup of instant coffee.

At 9 a.m. he dialed the president's direct line.

"Good morning, Mr. President. This is Matt Connors. I have made my decision and with your permission sir, I would like to come to the White House to discuss it with you personally."

"That's great, Matt. But in ten minutes I'm holding a press conference. Turn on one of the networks and come down as soon as it's over."

"Thank you, Mr. President. I'll come by then."

Matt fell into a chair in the livingroom, facing the television screen as he clicked on the power to CBS. He waited a few minutes, then saw the president of the United States stand quietly in front of a podium about to address the nation. President Harrington spoke:

"My fellow Americans. Despite what you have seen on television, heard on radio, or read in the newspapers, our country is *not*, I repeat, *not* in crisis. Our nation is sound, secure, and is actively dealing with what has brought shame and dishonor to some of our most trusted federal and state officials. I will not dwell upon the reprehensible acts committed other than to say that we will deal swiftly to the fullest extent of the law with those who have betrayed and sold their public trust for self-gain. They are but a handful who by deceit and corruption dishonor and defile the integrity of our democratic institutions. And while their acts have dealt us a serious blow that has caused much pain and anguish, they have at the same time brought us closer as a nation. And we will emerge stronger for it.

Our esteemed public servant, the late Attorney General Chuck Bradford, gave his life—an innocent victim of those bent upon evil, corruption, and murder.

The vice presidency now sits vacant through a despicable course of conduct.

The New York governor's office is empty and awaits a successor—all because of greed and an egregious violation of decency.

While the acts committed are so repugnant to a civilized people, our democracy is not weakened. We survive because we are a government of law and it is the rule of law that makes our nation the greatest bastion of freedom in the world. For there is no force on earth that can remove the power of our citizens who join together as *ONE*, to combat those few who seek to corrupt, weaken, and destroy us. OUR PEOPLE ARE *ONE*. OUR WILL IS *ONE*. OUR FIGHT IS *ONE*.

AND WITH YOUR UNDYING SUPPORT, OUR NATION WILL FOREVER BE *ONE!* Thank you."

Following his address, and looking out into a sea of reporters, Harrington said, "I'll take only one question." He pointed to Bill Townsend of *The Washington Standard.*

"Mr. President. The attorney general spot has been vacant since Chuck Bradford's death. Will you be filling it, and if so, when?"

"Yes, Bill. I expect to be submitting my choice to the Senate within twenty-four hours, if not sooner. That's it. Thank you all." Harrington stepped off quickly and walked toward the door. His entourage followed.

Matt had been seated in the livingroom of his home, almost within arm's reach of the White House. He was struck with awe that in less than thirty minutes, he would be delivering his decision personally to the president of the United States, who was just seen and heard by millions of people around the nation and the world.

He got up from his chair slowly and shuffled upstairs into the bedroom. There, he made up the bed, pulling on the under-sheet, fluffing up the pillows, and stretching the light blanket tightly that served also as a bedcover.

Looking at himself in the full length mirror attached to the outside of a closet door, he adjusted the collar of his shirt and tie. He then put on his jacket.

When dressed, Matt walked downstairs, opened the front door, and locked it behind him.

Once out of his brownstone, he picked up *The Washington Post* tossed earlier that morning on top of the landing. After tucking the newspaper under his left arm, he started to descend the brick steps leading to the sidewalk and driveway. He retraced the decision he had reached earlier, reinforcing within his own mind that it was the right one to have made...the decision he would soon deliver personally to the president of the United States.

But unbeknown to Matt, Charlie Roundtree, Jenny's surviving brother, had been hiding behind a row of tall bushes across the street from the town house. Charlie had kept a vigil on Matt's entry door throughout the early morning hours.

As Matt walked slowly down the front steps, Charlie raised a high-powered hunting rifle he had concealed under his raincoat. Its telescopic sights were focused directly on Matt.

With tears streaming uncontrollably down his face, Charlie kept repeating almost incoherently, "You son-of-a-bitch, you killed my family. You son-of-a-bitch, you killed my family. You son-of-a-bitch—"

At that instant, Charlie fired off three rounds in rapid succession.

The first bullet struck Matt in the left side of his head, causing it to jerk back instantly. The second struck his left shoulder, spinning him halfway around. The third bullet crashed into his chest, its explosive impact propelling him back, hard, against the red brick steps.

The newspaper Matt carried scattered high in the air as it cascaded and drifted down in almost slow motion.

Matt continued to roll down the steps until his body came to rest on the concrete pavement below. John Matthew Connors was dead... *Arrowhead had claimed its final victim.*

The End

Petite Epilogue

ISMAEL RUIZ... was cleared by a grand jury, quit the Syracuse P.D., moved his family to Philadelphia, and vowed never to hold a gun in his hand again.

GEORGE FOWLER and his wife AGNES... live somewhere in the southwest with a new identity and are still in the Federal Witness Protection Program.

JOHN HARRINGTON... limited to two presidential terms by constitutional amendment, heads The International Commission Against World Hunger.

PETER CARLUCCI... continues as medical examiner of Onandagua County and reports daily to an office where his desk remains cluttered with autopsy reports, medical articles, and x-rays.

JOHN SCANLON... lost his re-election bid for D.A. and never forgave M.E. Carlucci for having gotten between him and his path of glory to political stardom.

ELIZABETH LLEWELYN BRADFORD... lives quietly in Bradford Manor and continues to raise her grandson.

CHARLIE ROUNDTREE.... stopped and arrested at the airport, was declared incompetent to stand trial, confined to a federal mental institution, and will be tried for the murder of a federal officer, should he ever be declared legally sane.

HAROLD HESHY GORDON.... forcibly retired from the practice of law, suns himself on a beach in the Carribean when he's not selling timeshare apartments.

And, VINCENT SCARPIZZI, JARRETT LEE HASTINGS, NILES MARTIN...are all serving long sentences in different federal prisons.

GRAND EPILOGUE

Thirty-seven years after the death of Matt Connors, the first Native American Indian to become attorney general of the United States of America takes the Constitutional oath of office in the historic rotunda of the nation's Capitol.

He is *JOSEPH ROUNDTREE BRADFORD.*

But to all who know and love him, he will always be *"LITTLE JOE."*

Printed in the United States
31937LVS00002B/78